ECUMENSUS

ECUMENSUS

The Next Vision

A Novel

CLIFFORD LANE MARK

iUniverse Star

New York   Bloomington

Ecumensus
The Next Vision

Copyright © 2008, 2009 by Clifford Lane Mark

iUniverse Star
an iUniverse, Inc. Imprint

iUniverse books may be ordered through booksellers or by contacting:

iUniverse
1663 Liberty Drive
Bloomington, IN 47403
www.iuniverse.com
1-800-Authors (1-800-288-4677)

Because of the dynamic nature of the Internet, any Web addresses or links contained in this book may have changed since publication and may no longer be valid.

This is a work of fiction. All of the characters, names, incidents, organizations, and dialogue in this novel are either the products of the author's imagination or are used fictitiously. The author respects and honors the people of Acoma Pueblo and this novel does not represent any actual person or event associated with Acoma Pueblo or its people.

ISBN: 978-1-935278-45-0 (pbk)
ISBN: 978-1-935278-46-7 (ebk)

Library of Congress Control Number: 2009924843

Printed in the United States of America

iUniverse rev. date: 2/27/2009

In 1931, Oliver Wendell Holmes said, "Man has destinies he does not yet understand."

On the horizon of our future, I sometimes get a glimpse of what those destinies might be. I first imagined them when I was only twelve years old and have seen them on and off since then. At times, the glimpses are in shadow. They seem fleeting and far away, but I have become convinced that they are larger than they appear. All that is required of me is to find a better pair of glasses and look for our destinies with imagination.

This vision story is a combination of perspectives, questions, intuitions, and imaginings. The people in my life who have encouraged my visions are present in the characters and thoughts of this novel. Ultimately, this story belongs to them, and though my name is on it, I cannot call it mine. Hundreds have influenced it. To all of them, and to all who read it, I dedicate this dream of unity.

Clifford Mark
Austin, Texas

Contents

Prologue: AD 1000 Acoma Pueblo, New Mexico   *ix*

Section I: Gathering the People   *1*

1	November 2009	3
2	The Fifth One	7
3	The Seven File	13
4	The Sixth One	19
5	Lunch with Xuan	24
6	The Meeting Place	29
7	The Council Meeting	35
8	Learning the Purpose	41
9	More to Learn	49
10	Moving In	60
11	The Blind Boy	65
12	Sunrise at Sandia Crest	69
13	The Pace Quickens	74
14	The Blind Boy's Dream	83
15	Thomas and Xuan	86
16	The Jemez Woman	100
17	The Bridge	107

Section II: Collecting the Energy   *117*

1	January 2010	119
2	Anna and the Priest	124
3	Sha'wanna	130
4	Settling In	134

5	Katzimo	139
6	Arrangements	147
7	Perspective	151
8	Well Planted	161
9	Questions	171
10	Illuminations	177
11	Whispering Spirals	181
12	Developments	189
13	Jemez Pueblo	198
14	Thunder Voice	203
15	The Equals Sign	207
16	Kahwehstimah	214

Section III: Envisioning the Ecumensus ... 221

1	June 2010	223
2	It Begins	227
3	Two More	235
4	The Rest of the Teachers	243
5	The Second Morning at Acoma	249
6	One or Two	254
7	Before the Dawn	260
8	Symbols	266
9	The Fourth Morning at Acoma	272
10	Teaching the Teachers	276
11	On Top of the World	282
12	A New Mesa	289
13	Laying Out the Prisms	296
14	The Sixth Day	307
15	The Sixth Evening	313
16	The Seventh Day	317
17	Ecumensus	323

Epilogue ... 331

Prologue:
AD 1000 Acoma Pueblo, New Mexico

She clutched her child to her breast and walked to the edge of the mesa that was her home. She trembled as she peered down to the farmland four hundred feet below. The men resumed their work in the cornfields but suddenly, a gust of wind spun her around, and she fell to her knees. The child screamed and clung to her as the last of the storm thundered away to the east. She searched for the piñon pine that marked the trailhead but it had been blown down in the storm; all traces of it were gone.

This trail was her only connection to survival. It snaked down the face of the bluff from her home atop the plateau and wound through the crevasses and ledges along the sheer face of this solitary mesa. It used to lead to the flat lands below but it was no more. Without this thread of life, she and her infant would starve. There was no way down to the rest of her people, and there was no way for them to rescue her and her child. She edged closer to where the trail had once begun and saw the precipitous drop. Overwhelmed by the feelings of isolation, she knew that she and her child would die. She swallowed hard and rewrapped the baby in its horsehair blanket as the horror of their inevitable fate shuddered through her. She looked at her child one last time as the primal scream began to build in her throat. It shattered the silence as she leapt to her death.

She was the last to live on this mesa—the last to die there, too. None would ever marvel at the panorama or see the majesty of its vista again. None would feel the power and the energy of this place again. None would dip their thirsty hands into its natural water cistern again. The mesa died with her and her child.

To the south, at the mesa they call Acoma, they learned what had happened by sundown. The council was assembled, and they chose not to rebuild the trail. They decreed that the dead woman's mesa would not have death again, and they made sure it would not have life again, either. The village on the mesa was abandoned, and it has been empty for a thousand years.

The forsaken mesa has known many names, but it is now just known as Enchanted. No one is sure what it was called when she lived there. No one knows what is left of its ruins. There are no written records of its life and only the stories of its death remain. Like a haunted house, the mystery of the mesa has grown through the years. A thousand summers have passed since that day. Ten thousand storms have pummeled the deserted rock. Twelve thousand moons have lit up the capstone mesa top and been reflected back to the infinite sky in the rainwater that fills the cistern.

For the people of Acoma, the stories sustain the fear of this mesa. Every child knows the tragic tale. Every young male is warned of the danger. Every mother feels the desperation of the woman who leapt with her child, and every man ekes out a living in the shadow of this mystery. They walk around this rock in silence, raise their corn in the fields at its base, and cool themselves in its afternoon shade. They do not look at it, and they do not disturb its slumber. They believe the stories.

Protected by distance and shielded by the passage of time, the stories are retold each year at the mesa that did not die. Like all oral traditions in the history of humankind, this story has changed through the years. Every teller learns what he thinks he hears, remembers what he wants to remember, and tells what he thinks is important. Facts are forgotten or lost. The stories are embellished by the actors who dream of more drama. The words are changed to fit each teller's rhythm and rhyme. The truth remains, but truth in the memory of a people is a thing that does not stand still. It wavers in the winter wind and shimmers in the light of the moon, until even memory itself is hard-pressed to be sure of the truth. Steeped like sun-brewed tea in the collective memory of Acoma Pueblo, Enchanted Mesa is covered in fear, shrouded in death, and enveloped in mystery.

The prohibition against scaling its heights has been kept; none will climb it, and only a few will gaze upon it. The stories and rumors swirl around it like dust devils on a dry summer day, so the Indians of Acoma Valley live only on Acoma Mesa, and they stay apart from the enchanted one. Their fear of it is always with them; their truce with it is no easy truce.

In the thousand years since she changed everything, Acoma Pueblo fought off the Spanish treasure hunters who came and went. It prevailed over the diseases, wars, and famines that were visited upon it. It resisted the raiders on their horses who burned them out and took what they did not burn. It missed the manifest destiny that streamed by to the north of them and did not stop. Somehow, it survived. No village in the United States has been alive as long. It is older than the newfound land of the Vikings, and it was a Pueblo for six hundred years before the Pilgrims first arrived. The name means *the place that always was*; Acoma.

But Acoma has a shadow. Enchanted Mesa stands like a sentinel over the survivors at Acoma and the fear they know each day. The mesa is quiet and alone and foreboding. The winds and the rains dance around it. The sun beats down on it all summer long, and for a thousand years, the mesa has remained the same.

Until now.

Section I:

Gathering the People

Chapter 1

November 2009

Thomas Walls accelerated through the yellow light and glanced both ways to see if he had been seen. He braked hard to make the turn into the drive and searched for a parking space. The three-story glass building in Albuquerque that housed his first-floor office reflected the morning sun as he hit the tire bump a little too hard. He felt the car settle back onto the asphalt, then cut the engine and loosed the seat belt buckle. He threw open his door, grabbed his overcoat as he got out, and slammed the door behind him. As he wrapped the coat around him and walked briskly to the entrance, he focused on the beginning of another week.

Thomas hurried through the lobby past the directory sign that read "Project 4000—Suite 101." Anna, his secretary, and Digger, the project archaeologist, were already there, so the office door—the first on the left—was open. He nodded wordless greetings to them both as he threw his overcoat on a hall tree hook and headed for his office. He glanced out the window as he circled around the desk and, finally, sat down behind it. He opened up his laptop, hit the power button, and then looked at his watch. He was forty-five minutes late.

His almost-bare office could have been nicer, but he had only been in it a few weeks and had not yet gotten settled. Though Anna would have helped him, he hadn't asked her to order him plants or wall hangings or more furniture. Besides the standard wooden desk, it contained just two chairs for guests, a credenza, a fancy nameplate on the desktop from his fourteen-year tenure at the Water Commission of New Mexico, a calendar, and an inbox. A small, framed picture of his two preteen sons in soccer gear sat on the credenza behind him.

Soon, Digger appeared at his door, and Thomas looked up at the lanky, young archaeologist in his hiking boots and blond hair.

"Good morning, Digger. What did the Acoma Indians say about using their Pueblo for the meeting in June?"

"G'morning, Thomas," Digger answered. "They're warming up to the idea, I think. They still want a lot of control over rituals and opening ceremonies and that kind of stuff, but they're coming around."

"Will they let us use one of their sacred kivas?"

"Yes, well maybe, but they have a longstanding tradition that only Pueblo people are allowed in their kivas. They think the kivas are special."

"Well, from what I can tell so far, the people who will be at our meeting are pretty special, too. Did you explain that to them?" Thomas asked.

"Yeah, I'm working on getting that point across, but they're really bound up by their traditions. It won't be easy," Digger finished.

"Look, man, everybody feels bound up by traditions," Thomas said. "That doesn't mean their traditions are right. The meeting isn't until June, so you've got seven months. Keep working on them, will ya, and turn up the heat a little bit while you're at it. This meeting has to be at Acoma Pueblo, and you're the one who can get it arranged."

"It'll get done," Digger assured him as he left his office.

Anna came in with Thomas's first cup of morning coffee and a notepad. Perky, young and innocent, Anna Maria Izturias usually had a softening effect on Thomas, but not today. He barely acknowledged her greeting as she sat down in front of his desk.

"What about the transcription exams?" he asked her as he looked up from his computer screen. "Any progress on that?"

"We'll get another update today or tomorrow on the group they tested last Saturday," Anna reported. "I think they're also testing ten more later in the week. Wouldn't it be better—I mean, you know, easier—if we could just use video or audio equipment to record this whole thing? Trying to find someone who can write fast and accurately is darned hard. It's a lost art," she concluded.

"Anna, we've been through this before, and the instructions from Mr. Layne are specific. He's convinced that electronic devices won't work during a meeting like this. Besides, there's no electricity up on top of Acoma Mesa, and that's where all of the meetings will likely take place."

"I know that, Boss," Anna responded, "but those people have been living on top of that mesa for a thousand years without electricity. Maybe we can use some of Mr. Layne's wealth to bring them electrical power. That would solve the problem, huh?"

"Apparently, it won't solve the problem," Thomas shot back. "They don't seem to want electricity up there. They've survived this long without it, so maybe they like it that way. Besides, electronic devices might introduce an artificial element into the proceedings." He looked back at his computer screen. "Just let me know when you get the next update."

Anna stood up to leave when Thomas added, "Oh, and will you bring me the Seven File, too?"

"Sure," Anna answered, and she left.

Thomas sat back and looked at the Albuquerque skyline in the distance. The so-called Seven File wasn't much of a file, just seven simple statements on one sheet of paper. Each statement was a clue about one of the seven master teachers who would be at the meeting. To Thomas, all the clues seemed vague and puzzling. He liked things more straightforward. When Anna returned with the one tattered sheet of paper with the seven scribbled clues, he swiveled around to face her but did not say a word.

"Boss," she began slowly, "you seem more agitated today than usual."

"Yeah, I know," he answered as he tried to calm himself a little.

He liked Anna well enough and even appreciated her honesty regarding his generally disagreeable moods. She was just twenty-two years old and kind of pretty. Her black, waist-length hair was tied up in a bun, and she wore a mid-calf skirt, a peasant blouse, and a turquoise necklace with a small silver cross hanging from it. Her girlish, western boots were round-toed and low-heeled, and she wore what Thomas took to be a look of concern on her angular, brown face.

"This whole project," he said, "is so wracked with uncertainty. In fact, my whole life is beset with uncertainty. My kids have moved to Mississippi with their mother. I'm single all of a sudden. I'm supposed to plan a meeting, and I don't even know who's coming to it or what they're going to do or how I'm supposed to facilitate it. I don't know the topics for discussion or how to make an agenda for it. That's why I look and sound agitated."

Anna sat down and listened as he vented. "Don't you think the details around this meeting will eventually become clearer?" she asked.

"Based on what?" he asked. "Seven sayings on a sheet of paper? That's not a lot to go on if you're looking for clarity." He took the sheet of paper and flipped it back onto his desk in disgust. It spun on the slick, wooden top and came to a stop facing him again.

"Well, my workload's kind of light today. Maybe I can help you with these clues, too," Anna offered. "Besides, I should take these scribbles and type them up so we can copy them easily for everyone."

Thomas stared off into space and said nothing for a minute. He wondered again how he had allowed himself to get drawn into this curious project. He consoled himself with the idea that it was a paycheck, but sometimes that consolation wasn't enough. *When this is over,* he thought, *I'll just go back to Mississippi and try to find a job near the kids. Until then, this will have to do.*

"Yes, you get those clues typed up," Thomas said as he reset his resolve. "I appreciate your offer to help figure them out, but I think I'll try it alone today. If I don't make any progress, I'll get you and Digger to help me tomorrow."

Chapter 2

The Fifth One

Xuan Lee, testing professional for a local employment agency, looked in the restroom mirror of the Albuquerque office building she had rented for the day's round of exams. She ran her hand through her short-cropped hair and still didn't like the way she looked. She moved a small, decorative hair clip back a bit further, straightened her black slacks, and buttoned one more button on her cream-colored blouse. After looking in the mirror, she unbuttoned it again. Gold hoop earrings dangled from her ears—ears she always thought too small—and she admired how well her eyeliner accentuated her dark eyes. With one glance in the mirror at her backside as she turned to walk toward the bathroom exit, she decided she looked fine and stepped into the hallway. Two doors down, she entered the rented testing room to proctor another set of tests on behalf of Project 4000.

Xuan was beginning to doubt if she would ever find a transcriptionist for her client's meeting in June. She had already tested some 130 aspirants. A few had graded out above 90 percent, but she felt sure none of them was suitable. It was her understanding that the meeting would last seven consecutive days—no breaks—and would be quite demanding on the person charged with taking all the notes. She briefly surveyed this group of ten and wondered which of them, if any, could handle the task. She cleared her throat and placed her # 2 pencil behind her ear.

"Hello, everyone," she said. "Welcome to the writing exams for Project 4000. My name is Xuan Lee, and I'll be proctoring the tests this morning. It is easiest to just pronounce my name as 'Swan,' and I'll be most comfortable if that is how you address me."

She looked around the room as she fidgeted with the top button on her blouse again and then pushed her glasses back onto the bridge of her nose. She went on to explain the format of the testing; there were six articles to be read aloud by her two readers as the candidates tried to write down what they heard as accurately as they could. Paper and pens were in place on the small tables, information cards were all collected, and she was about to have the readers begin when she spotted the seeing-eye dog lying next to the wall at the back of the room.

Xuan was surprised. She looked at her readers quizzically and asked, "Could the person to whom that dog belongs please raise your hand?"

A young man at one of the testing tables signaled that the dog belonged to him, but Xuan didn't see him at first. Rachael, one of the readers, pointed him out.

Xuan continued, "Oh, there you are. Will you need help with the information card?" she asked him.

He was chubby, dressed in baggy clothes and a hoodie, and gave no indication that he had heard her. The boy looked to be of Middle Eastern descent and about twenty years old, but all Xuan could see was his dark hair and a thin, indefinite beard. When he gave no answer, she turned to Rachael and said, "Will you see if he needs help, please?"

Though Xuan had requested two adjacent rooms in which to conduct her tests, she had instead been assigned only one very large room. It was spacious enough that she had divided the small writing tables into two groups of five. Her readers would work in the two opposite corners of the room, with a space of about twenty feet between the two groups. The setup was not ideal, and she asked Rachael and the other reader, Sylvia, to read quietly so as to avoid confusion or duplication. She glanced again at the blind candidate as Rachael approached her.

"He doesn't answer my questions," Rachael reported. "He seems to be very shy."

Just then, a woman entered the room and took a seat by the dog, away from the groups about to be tested. Xuan wondered who she was but went on with her announcements.

"Okay, everyone, please," she called to both groups. "You have everything you need for the first hour of dictation. Your readers will begin when I give the signal. When they have completed the first reading, you will have approximately twenty minutes to review your transcriptions and make any necessary corrections before the second reading begins. We'll do three articles this morning and three more this afternoon. Accuracy and efficiency are both important, and your test rating will be a combination of both. Our evaluations and your papers will be forwarded to the people who have hired us, and they will let my employment agency know if they want to interview any of you." With that out of the way, Xuan glanced up at the clock, jotted down the time, and then said, "Readers, please begin."

At this point in her routine, Xuan usually reviewed the information cards and completed other paperwork, but the blind boy and the woman now sitting in the back of the room had piqued her interest. She suspected they were somehow connected, and she went toward the woman to find out more.

"Hi, I'm Xuan Lee," she whispered as the readers began, sticking out her hand as she approached.

"Hello," the dowdy woman whispered as she took Xuan's hand and stood up. Xuan guessed her to be in her mid-fifties and somewhat overweight. She struck Xuan as a motherly type. "I'm a social worker and a teacher at the National Institute for the Blind, and my name is Susan Brundage. That's my client, Malik Mohammed."

"This is the first time we've tested a blind person in a writing test like this. Are you sure he can handle six hours of dictation testing?"

"Oh, I don't know," Susan answered. "He just became a client of ours three or four months ago, and I've never seen him in such a circumstance before. We're charged with helping him adjust to being blind. As far as I know, I think he'll be fine." Susan smiled. "According to his file, he's quite a writer. His mother was a court reporter, and he wrote us a few weeks ago telling us he could probably find work because he writes quickly and accurately."

"So that is why you're getting him tested," Xuan asked as they both sat down in the chairs that lined the back walls of the rather large room, "to see if he's any good?" She glanced at the group in which he was busy writing his exam.

"At first, that's what we were thinking," Susan whispered back, "but then a few of us were watching television in the group TV room at the institute the other night, and right after the show ended, he put five sheets of paper in front of me." Susan's faced brightened, and she leaned closer to Xuan as her voice rose a little. "He had written the entire dialogue of the show on those sheets of paper. He even wrote the commercials down, too. We were pretty impressed!"

"Really?" Xuan asked.

"Yes, that entire half-hour was written down perfectly, as near as any of us could remember. And he writes beautifully," Susan added. "It's really distinctive— almost like a girl's, if you know what I mean. Ever since we signed him up for this test, he's been doing little else but practicing for it."

"How do you think he learned these writing skills, considering his blindness?" Xuan asked.

"Oh, he's only been blind for about two years. It happened in the car accident that killed both his parents. That's how he eventually ended up at the Institute for the Blind. We help people like him learn how to cope with adult-onset blindness. He's quite a handful, because he's more independent than most."

"But isn't independence your ultimate goal there at the institute?" Xuan asked.

"Well, yes," Susan replied, "but it's a huge adjustment for him."

"I imagine that he's dealing with an awful lot," Xuan said. "Is there any other family?"

"I don't think so. His father was Lebanese, and his mom was from Kansas. No one has stepped forward to offer any other information on him, and he won't write us anything about it. Believe me, we've looked everywhere we could, and we've asked him repeatedly."

"How will he check his papers when he's done?" Xuan asked as she stood up to return to her temporary desk across the room.

"I don't think he has to—or he just has a lot of confidence in himself when it comes to writing."

"One of my readers mentioned that he might be too shy to speak," Xuan said.

"No, he's not shy. He's mute," Susan replied. "His hospital records indicate that he's been mute since birth because his vocal chords didn't develop properly."

"Mute? So he can only communicate through writing?" Xuan asked.

"Well, I can tell he knows sign language, but he's quit using it since he can no longer see what's being signed to him. We only have two-way communication when he writes a note or nods his head."

"Okay, thanks, Susan," Xuan said as she turned to leave. *That might cause some difficulty with an employer*, she thought. She wondered how this young man would do on the tests and wondered, too, what it would be like to work with a blind person during a seven-day meeting like the one being planned at Project 4000. She couldn't imagine he'd do very well. Besides, he looked awfully young.

~   ~   ~

When the morning round of three tests was completed, Rachael and Sylvia brought all of the exams to Xuan's makeshift desk. Fascinated by the information from Susan, Xuan asked her assistants to go through their sets of papers and put aside any with especially pretty handwriting. Not far into her stack of writings, Xuan found one with no name, but she recognized the tailored penmanship of someone who had obviously mastered the art of writing. The style was decidedly feminine so she put it to the side just as Rachael and Sylvia both found ones like it, too. The writing was beautiful, and when they compared all three of them to the texts from which the readers had read, they found that they were accurately written, as well. Xuan was impressed.

Then Rachael gasped and pulled out a second paper in her stack with the exact same writing style—the lettering, the clarity, the apparent accuracy. The only difference was that this one had a name at the top of it. It read, "Malik M.

Mohammed" in an even more stylized handwriting than the rest of the paper, with sweeping capital letters and flares and tails and loops. All of the letters were joined by a single line that underscored them and tied the words together into one grand name. Rachael showed it to Xuan and Sylvia. Had they guessed wrong? Did the first papers they had found belong to someone else?

All three of them searched through the rest of the exam papers and found two more with Malik's name. They compared the papers with the names to those papers without names. Except for the name, they were obviously identical: same letters, same writing style, same writer. It didn't require a handwriting expert to see that the unsigned papers were also written by Malik Mohammed.

"Sylvia, take a moment and check yours for accuracy, will you?" Xuan requested. "You too, Rachael."

Xuan did the same with hers. Per the instructions she had received from Thomas Walls, both groups of candidates were to be read completely different passages for the three morning papers. In the afternoon session, the six readings would be reversed, and the readers would be switched. At the end of the day, Xuan would have the same six papers from each aspirant. As a further control against any variances of the readers, each of the six texts would have been read to each candidate by the same reader. This was the plan.

"These two are perfect," Rachael announced after a few moments of checking.

"So are these," Sylvia said.

"You mean we've got all six papers from Malik already?" Xuan asked. "That's unreal! They're almost too good."

"Yes, we've got all six," Rachael confirmed.

Malik had somehow listened to both readers simultaneously, even though they had spoken quietly and were twenty feet apart, and he had managed to write down everything both of them had read. His writings were flawless. Both sets of three, all six, were perfect!

"I've read about this kind of thing," Xuan told her colleagues, "where people can listen to, and duplicate, simultaneous auditory inputs."

Rachael and Sylvia looked at her as she spoke.

"But this is the first time I've ever seen it for myself," Xuan went on. She looked at her watch and saw that the lunch break was halfway over. "Let's go get a quick lunch and discuss what we should do next."

When they returned, Rachael and Sylvia prepared for the afternoon round of testing as the candidates filed back in. Xuan watched as Malik Mohammed was the last one to return. She saw him in a wholly different light than before and knew that any further testing would be pointless, but the three women had decided to continue for the sake of the others. She took her cell phone out into the hall to call Thomas.

He didn't answer his cell, so she left a simple "call me" text message and returned to the exam room. Excited that the testing was all but over, she smiled to herself and she knew that her good news would be welcomed by Thomas, as well.

Chapter 3

The Seven File

When Thomas came into the Project 4000 offices the next morning, he found Anna at her desk in the reception area. Anna's area was more inviting than his office. There were plants in three corners and a single black file cabinet near the desk, on which she had placed a framed family portrait. There were two wall-hangings on each wall, offset from each other, and a large throw rug that covered the slate-colored tile floor.

Thomas passed Digger's open door and saw him on the phone, with his hiking boots propped on his desk. Digger quickly put his feet back on the floor and sat up straighter as he saw Thomas pass. Thomas smiled to himself and flipped open his cell phone as he entered his office, across the hall from Digger's. That's when he saw Xuan's text message and thought he might return her call immediately.

Before he could act, he moved in behind his desk and once again saw the paper with the seven clues Anna had brought him the day before. Right next to it was a freshly typed copy of the same information. In his mind, these mysteries were his to figure out. Doing so had become a matter of pride for him, and, besides, he liked clear job descriptions in the workplace. Anna was in charge of getting the office up and running, and Digger was in charge of arranging the meeting place at Acoma Pueblo. In addition to supervising the two of them, Thomas was supposed to plan the meeting, figure out who was coming, and let them know the plan. As he had told Anna the previous day, he did not yet want any help on this so-called "file" of clues.

"Mr. Layne on line one, Boss," Anna shouted from the next room.

"Thank you, Anna," Thomas shouted back. "Can we get the intercom repaired soon?"

"I'm working on it."

Thomas respected Mr. Layne and could tell he was an experienced executive. He had researched Layne on the Internet and discovered that he had been in his family's publishing business since his graduation from Harvard in the late '60s. Based on the info Thomas could find—and there was a lot of it—Layne had risen to the position of CEO, taken the company public, and then led a move to sell the business to a larger publishing house. As a result, he had retired at an early age, with almost twenty million dollars in his pocket and not enough to keep him busy.

"How's it going this week, Thomas?"

"It's going fine here, Mr. Layne," Thomas replied as he leaned back in his office chair and spun it around so he could look out the window while he talked. "The negotiations for the use of Acoma Pueblo are progressing, and we'll get updates on some more testing from Xuan Lee sometime today."

"Good," Layne answered. "Any progress on the Seven File?"

"No, not a bit," Thomas responded as he fiddled with a paper clip. "That file is a real mystery to me. The clues are pretty vague, and I have no idea where to find the people they're trying to lead me to." Thomas paused a moment as he looked at the sheet of clues on his desk. He quickly and silently read the first one again, remembered his earlier frustrations, and then continued. "In fact, I'm not sure the clues are really even talking about people. It's pretty crazy, actually."

"I thought the same thing, Thomas," Layne began, "but I think you can figure it out. Of all the people I interviewed for your position, you came more highly recommended than any of them, so I know you're a talented and effective planner. That part will be easy for you. The only difference is that you don't know who to plan for. When you figure that out, you'll be fine."

"I'm pretty frustrated," Thomas replied. "Do you want me to call in the fortune tellers and crystal ball readers to make some sense out of these clues?" Thomas was a little surprised at the irritation in his own voice.

"Well, no," Layne said with a smile in his voice. "I'd use some mediums with a little more credibility, like hypnotists or past-life regressionists. Are there tarot card readers in Albuquerque? Maybe the Oracle at Delphi is still around."

"Yeah, right," Thomas laughed. He was relieved that Mr. Layne hadn't returned his irritated tone.

"You know," Layne said, "the clue I like is number five; at least I think it's number five. 'Even the rocks are alive when cold runs deep on sacred mountain.' How many sacred mountains can there be in New Mexico? I think that'll be pretty easy to sort out, Thomas."

"Yeah, well maybe."

"In fact, I know you can figure out all these clues," Layne continued. "Just treat it like a quest. Take that piece of paper with you everywhere you go. Take it home. Sleep with it. Get obsessed with it. Go to every church or synagogue or mosque in Albuquerque. Talk to the priests and rabbis and imams and elders and preachers. Give them a copy of the clues if you want to. Heck, talk to all the little old ladies, too. Sometimes they know more than the others, anyway. Get out there in the so-called religious communities and Indian communities and mix it up a little. In fact, Thomas, why don't you go out to Acoma Pueblo and go through their visitor center and museum? Maybe you'll run into someone interesting."

"Okay, I will, but I just don't know what I'm looking for," Thomas said.

"That's the million-dollar question, for sure," Layne answered. "There is one thing of which I'm certain, however. This meeting is about finding a new direction for all of humankind, a direction that will cause a shift in the way we think of each other, the way we relate to each other, and the way we live with each other. That's how important it is, Thomas. It may even be that this meeting will produce a person like Jesus or Buddha or Krishna or Mohammed."

"No way! You think so, really?" Thomas asked.

"Yes, it's quite likely, and for some reason, I've been drawn to lead the planning for this meeting and you've been selected to do most of it. The seven people that you are trying to find in those clues may already know about the meeting, at least on some level, but our job is to handle the logistics, make the arrangements, let them know the details and facilitate it as best we can."

"Well, I'm just glad we've got some time to figure it out," Thomas said.

"I'm glad for that time, too," Layne agreed. "Even so, seven months will go by pretty quickly, and I'm not sure we'll figure out some things until the last minute. I do know this much, however, every effort we can muster will make a difference—if not for those who are coming, then maybe for us. At least it'll keep us busy."

Thomas finally felt the calming effects of Layne's voice sink in. He felt himself relax and noticed some confidence returning to his uncertain psyche.

"I'll tell you what," Layne continued, "I'll make arrangements to be in Albuquerque next week, and I'll bring some information that might give you more to go on. We'll spend the day together, and maybe we'll get Anna and Digger more involved. I'll let you know later in the morning when I'm coming. In the meantime, Thomas, do as I suggest. Live with that file. The mysteries will start solving themselves soon enough, and when they do, our workload will increase dramatically. Seven months may seem like a long time, and yet it seems awfully short sometimes, too. Unlocking the secrets in those clues will be the start of something huge. I think we can count on that."

On that note, the conversation ended.

~   ~   ~

Thomas picked up his cell phone again to return Xuan's call from the day before. He recalled being impressed with Xuan but had only met her once. He guessed her to be about thirty-five years old and of Chinese descent. He knew from her résumé that she had a degree in psychology, and he remembered her as energetic, intelligent, and friendly. She looked fit; he guessed that she probably worked out at a gym a few times a week. Thomas also got the idea that she was intrigued with Project 4000, though they hadn't talked about it directly. He placed the call and got the response that her message box was full, so he hung up and wondered why she had texted him to call her.

He pushed the intercom button and called Anna, then, remembering it was broken, he decided to get up and speak to her face to face.

"Anna, before I talk to Xuan, can you tell me if we ever got the testing update from her on Friday afternoon?"

"Yes, we did." Anna reached over and pulled the update from her inbox.

"Is there anything good in it?" Thomas inquired. "She's been testing for ten weeks and hasn't given her recommendation to anyone. We need some progress on this." He sat down in one of the reception area chairs and leaned forward. "Maybe it just doesn't get any better than those few who scored 90 percent."

"Maybe she's a perfectionist," Anna said as she retied her long pony tail and brushed some lint off her pants leg.

"I suppose that could be right, but perhaps she just needs a practical perspective on it. Perfection is too much to ask for." He stood to return to his office and then looked at Anna once more. "When I talk to her, I'll see what I can do to move things along."

Before he could leave, Anna asked him, "Have you read any of those test articles that are usually attached to her reports?"

"No, I haven't. They're just a collection of articles that Mr. Layne wanted to use for the exams. Why do you ask?"

"Well, I took a few of them home for the weekend and read them myself. I haven't been to the bookstore lately, so I needed something new to read. They're pretty darned complicated, if you ask me."

Thomas looked at her and smiled. "What's so complicated about them?"

"Well, maybe I just didn't understand them," she answered. "One is titled 'Radiogenesis Cosmology,' and I don't have an idea in the world what that is. Do you?"

"Radio what?"

"Radiogenesis Cosmology, or something like that," she replied as she stood up and grabbed her coffee cup for a refill. She paused to await his answer.

"I don't know what it is, either," Thomas answered. "I'm still trying to figure out what the clues in the Seven File mean. I don't think I could handle any more mysteries at this point."

"Did you make any progress on those clues yet?" Anna asked.

"Not really," he admitted, "but thanks for typing them up. Maybe I should take some of these articles home to read and see if anything in them might help me with the clues."

"Do you think the meeting we're planning has something to do with the cosmos, is that it?" she asked.

"No, I don't think so," Thomas laughed. "Mr. Layne thinks it has to do with the planet we live on, but he hasn't mentioned the entire universe or the cosmos, yet. He may be saving that information as a surprise for later."

"Okay," she said. "Do you want any help with the clues this afternoon?"

"No, not yet. First, I'm going to try to reach Xuan again."

Before he left her office, Thomas looked at Xuan's last report and made a mental note to take some of the articles home with him to read. He was about to call Xuan when Anna answered the phone and told him, "Mr. Layne on line one."

Thomas went back to his office to take the call.

"Hi again, Thomas," Layne said. "I just wanted to let you know that I've got a flight to Albuquerque Sunday, and I'll be in New Mexico through Thursday. Let's have a meeting on Wednesday at ten a.m. Does that work with your schedule?"

Layne was usually businesslike in these kinds of conversations, and today he was no different. However, Thomas also knew him to be especially enamored of this project and knew he was giving it a high priority. He had told Thomas in their interview weeks before that he had spent a lifetime studying the humanities, but when Thomas mentioned his own divorce, Layne had revealed his real motivation for Project 4000: something his wife had said to him on her deathbed. She had challenged him to do something truly important with their money. A project that promised to redefine the focus of humankind resonated with her final request.

Thomas confirmed the meeting and then placed the call to Xuan again. This time, she answered. He identified himself and asked how she was.

"I'm just fine, Thomas. No, actually, I'm great!" she replied. "You won't believe what happened in the most recent round of tests yesterday. I think we've found your transcriber. This guy is truly amazing!"

"That's good timing, Xuan. I was getting concerned that we might have to light some fires in this process or lower our standards to get it moving again. But you sound fired up already. You didn't lower your standards, did you?"

"No, Thomas, that'll never happen, and I can't tell you about this over the phone. I've got to show you this guy's work. Can we meet for lunch somewhere?"

"Sure. Where do you wanna meet?"

"Why don't we meet at Tres Amigo's about 11:45? They've got good salads. Does that work for you?"

"That's fine," he agreed. "I'll even buy your lunch."

"That's good, because you're going to really like this news, Thomas."

He hung up the phone and checked his watch. It was 10:30, and he decided he had time for a quick haircut before lunch. He grabbed one of the articles from his desk, told Anna he'd be back after lunch, and headed for his car.

Thomas got in and looked in the rearview mirror at his closely cropped hair and neatly trimmed beard. An African American with dark brown skin, he felt he looked pretty good for a man now forty and only a few pounds overweight. He had always been pretty muscular, and even though he had a stocky build, he believed others found him attractive. He wondered if Xuan might think the same but then quickly dismissed the thought as unsuitable for a business lunch meeting.

He arrived at the strip mall barber shop, sat down in the waiting area, and began to read the article titled "The Six Percent Rule." Once he was in the barber chair, the trim didn't take long, and he soon left, admiring the sporty look of his car as he approached it from behind. He was soon on his way to lunch, feeling excited about the good news Xuan had promised him.

Chapter 4

The Sixth One

Acoma Pueblo is some fifty miles west of Albuquerque, and its sacred, main kiva is not unlike most kivas. One must enter through the roof and descend a ladder into the windowless ceremonial room. There is a hole in the center of the floor from which the Pueblo people believe all life comes. Near this hole is a pit in which fires are sometimes lit, and there is a small stone dais at one side of the circular room. Four wall niches that represent the four directions of the compass hold crude wick lights or candles. Corn fetishes are positioned around the kiva to signify the Pueblo's longtime economic dependence on corn and to symbolize the nourishment that is crucial to their survival.

Jack Eaglefeather was the last to speak at the Monday morning council meeting in the Acoma Pueblo kiva. As it had been for more than eleven years, his status as town chief commanded the respect and attention of all six tribal councilmen huddled with him in the sacred space. Jack's father and grandfather had both been Pueblo town chiefs, and, though it was not an inherited position, Jack had chosen to follow in their footsteps. He was the first town chief from Acoma to be college educated and had been the only schoolteacher at the Pueblo for the past thirty years, as well. His thin frame sported a pair of ironed Levis, a long-sleeved white shirt, and snakeskin cowboy boots that were made and given to him by his uncle, now deceased. His silver and turquoise watchband fit snugly on his left wrist. He stood at the dais as he continued their discussion.

"I was unsure at first what to make of this request to use our sacred buildings for a meeting that will last for seven days and seven nights," Jack said. "I have long been opposed to letting anyone use our kivas but us. After all, this is our land, and the kiva is our most sacred space."

The others nodded in agreement.

"But, when I heard of this Project 4000, something inside of me spoke and said it would be okay. Yes, I know that this sacred place belongs to the Pueblo, and we are the caretakers of it, but I think the meeting they speak of in June may be a sacred meeting, too. I am told that it will determine many things—things that will impact many people in many places all over the world."

"Let the white men have their meeting somewhere else," Cha'amo insisted. He had hurried to the meeting and was still wearing his dark business suit from his job at the casino in Sky City. "We should continue to keep this place for our people and only for our people."

"He's right," Lezaun added as he re-tied the thin leather strap he used to contain his lengthy, unkempt hair. "The Spaniards, the Mexicanos, and the white man have all had their way with us for too long. Their diseases and alcohol and guns were a curse. Not once did things turn out well, and we have been weakened by their presence on our lands and in our lives."

Jack took a deep breath and continued. "I know. It has not turned out well in the past, and part of me wants to keep us apart from the ways of their world and the ways of all other men. But there's also a part of me that knows we cannot remain apart forever." Jack put his hands out in front of him as if holding a soccer ball and began to slowly bring them together until there were no more than three or four inches between them. "The world is getting smaller and more crowded," he reminded them and he clasped his hands all the way together for emphasis and raised his voice. "We're getting squeezed together whether we like it or not."

Cha'amo said, "The reservation system helps us stay apart. They can't ever get any closer than our fence lines. That has its benefits, you know." He smoothed out and admired his tie, a rare article of clothing in rural New Mexico.

"The reservation system was designed to keep us apart, Cha'amo, but I don't think it has worked very well," said Jack as he glanced at this watch. "I will always hate that system for what it did to the Pueblos. Now, I wonder if we're playing right into their hands by staying apart. We are poorer, we have a lower standard of living, we're less educated, and our young people are leaving and never coming back. That is far worse for us than what the others have done to us through the years."

Paytiamo was the next to chime in. The former army sergeant wore his hair closely cropped and covered it with an old, dirty baseball cap. His tan-colored work boots and faded, oily jeans were the uniform of a man who now drove a road grader for the highway department. "Do you think this meeting will change that?"

"We can't change what has happened in the past," Jack argued. "We can only hope to change what will happen in the future. Staying apart will not change the future. That's how they've defeated us for the last 200 years."

"But aren't these lands and this kiva ours to protect and keep sacred?" Cha'amo asked as he got up from the floor to stretch his legs.

"Maybe not," Jack answered. "These places are not sacred because they are ours. They are sacred because they belong to the Great Spirit. No matter what happens to us or to them, the Great Spirit will not let these places be destroyed. On the other hand," Jack softened his voice and leaned into his next comment, "if we share our sacred spaces, especially for a sacred cause, we will be in keeping with the energy of the Great Spirit. Perhaps this will bring us a better future."

Tesuque, his stringy hair falling into his eyes as he spoke through the gap in his front teeth, said, "We already know our past, and it has led us to where we are now. From this current place, our future is still bleak unless we change how we do some things. I am tired of our conditions, and I am ready to risk what Jack is asking us to do."

"It seems like the right thing to do," Jack said, sitting down again in the circle. No one rose to speak, and silence descended upon them.

"Okay, I say yes to them," announced Paytiamo, finally breaking the silence. "They cannot hurt us, these so-called masters. There are only seven of them. Perhaps, as Jack says, they will prove to be a good thing for Acoma."

Jack Eaglefeather searched the room, man by man, looking intently into each of his brother's eyes. He looked at Cha'amo and Lezaun and Tesuque and the others who had not spoken. They gave their assent with an almost imperceptible nod of their heads in response to Jack's inquiring eyes. Finally, Jack stood up and declared, "It is done, then. We all agree."

With that, they rose and locked arms with each other in a show of solidarity. Then, at Jack's signal, they pronounced the Acoma word for consensus in their council, "*Katzimo.*"

~   ~   ~

Shortly after Thomas had departed the office for his lunch meeting with Xuan, Anna answered a phone call from Jack Eaglefeather at Acoma Pueblo. Digger, the only one working on the negotiations with Acoma, had spoken of him and the Pueblo. She put the call through to Digger, who took it immediately.

"Hello, Digger. Our council met earlier today and decided we would allow your meeting to take place here at Acoma. I've been asked to meet with you again and tell you our final conditions."

"That's great, Jack! Tremendous! Your council's decision makes me very happy. I'll be honored to meet with you; just tell me when."

"We will have a special meeting next Tuesday night at seven o'clock at the Pueblo. Can you be at the Visitor's Center below the mesa at six thirty? One of the council members will meet you there and will bring you up to the main kiva."

"I'll be there," Digger replied. "Anything else?"

"We would also like your boss, Thomas Walls, to come," Jack added. "Is that possible?"

Digger hesitated. "I don't usually speak for the boss, Jack, but I know this is important to him and to what we're doing in concert with you and Acoma. I'll do everything I can to get him there, and I think he'll be glad to come. If he can't make it, I'll let you know."

"I understand, Digger. I'll see you Tuesday unless I hear different."

With that, the conversation ended, and Digger sat back in his chair. He hadn't noticed until now that his heart was pounding, his palms sweating. In a flash, he recalled his seven years in college, when all he wanted was to immerse himself in the history of Southwestern Indians—their ways, their traditions, and their history. He didn't know why exactly, but the subject had always fascinated him. Attending a real, live, present-day council meeting with Pueblo Indians in their most sacred meeting place was the chance of a lifetime for him. He felt as though he might now be participating in history rather than simply reading about it. It thrilled him no end.

"Anna! Anna! We got it!" Digger hollered as he leapt out of his chair and ran toward the reception area. "The Indians have agreed to let us meet at Acoma! Where's Thomas? He's going to want to hear this news as soon as possible."

"Did you try his cell phone?" she asked.

"Oh yeah," he said, and picked up his cell phone. As the phone rang he told Anna more and then got Thomas's voice mail but decided not to leave a message.

"Congratulations, Digger," Anna said. "That'll sure take some uncertainty out of this endeavor for Thomas. He'll be pumped up about it."

Digger felt her watching him as he paced back and forth in the reception room. His robust, tanned face set off his medium-length blond hair and red and green flannel shirt. Off-white cargo pants, a plain black belt, and black-trimmed hiking boots made him look every bit an archaeologist or, at least, an outdoorsy kind of guy. He also sported a small, leather carrying case on his belt that held a four-inch pocket knife.

"You know," he started, "I didn't expect this news so quickly, that's for sure. At our last meeting, I said something that made them all laugh, and they started speaking in Keresan, so I couldn't understand what they were saying."

"Maybe they were laughing because they liked you," Anna said with a smile. "You're awfully intense in my opinion, but it's endearing in a way." She picked up the family portrait on her desk and pointed to one of her seven brothers. "My brother Hector is a lot like you. You come across as honest, that's for sure."

"Well, I do get impatient sometimes," Digger admitted. "I was worried after that meeting that maybe I had broken some unspoken protocol or offended them. It's so hard to keep track of all their customs."

"Whatever it was, it must have worked," Anna conjectured. "Maybe they were just laughing to break up the tension."

"Well, Jack told me later that they liked my enthusiasm but found me kind of funny," Digger volunteered. "One guy, Tesuque, said that I seemed to speak from the heart, but then he added that maybe I drink too much. I think that is what really got them laughing."

"I can understand that, Digger," Anna said as she laughed herself.

Digger heard the sweetness in her laughter and saw the smile on her face. Maybe she was right. Maybe they just liked him. The main thing was that his negotiations had reached a successful conclusion, and the feeling of accomplishment washed over him as he smiled from ear to ear.

"Let the meetings begin," he half shouted to no one in particular. "We're on the way to Acoma!"

"Should we maybe put this meeting on Thomas's calendar?" Anna reminded him.

"Oh, yeah. Good idea. It's Tuesday at seven o'clock in the kiva at Acoma Pueblo, but we have to meet them at the Visitor Center at six thirty. That means we'll have to leave here no later than five o'clock to beat some of the rush hour traffic going west out of town."

"Got it," said Anna as she finished entering it into both their calendars on the computer. "You should probably tell him about it when he comes in from his lunch meeting with Xuan."

"Oh, I will," Digger assured her. "It'll be the best news he's had this week."

Chapter 5

Lunch with Xuan

Meanwhile, Thomas drove over the trickling upper reaches of the Rio Grande and past the small haciendas that marked this older area of Albuquerque. It had been developed in the '50s and '60s but was now surrounded by a mix of old and new residential development. His lunch spot with Xuan was in the midst of these tree-lined, curbless, two-lane streets; a location that offered a nice break from the concrete and asphalt that dominated the newest parts of the city. His Mustang GT was a concession to his version of a midlife crisis, a crisis that had been pretty tame if the examples of his friends were any kind of yardstick. He had bought the muscle car and changed from frumpy executive suits to more casual business clothing with a touch of masculine jewelry. He had grown the closely cropped beard, bought some western boots, and added a diamond stud earring in his left earlobe. He had also noticed an increasing interest in younger women but had not yet acted on it. The divorce had had less to do with this crisis than the decade of dysfunction that he had experienced with his ex-wife, Kelley.

Thomas had known for some time that they really weren't well matched, and their attempts to cultivate a less abrasive relationship just didn't take on any permanence. Their breakup came mostly as a result of exhaustion and discouragement. Thomas knew divorce would be a hard thing to do, but the marriage had gotten so difficult it didn't really seem to matter to either of them. He decided it was worth it to make a change, even if it meant jumping out of the frying pan and into the fire. His wife had decided to do the same, and the divorce was a mutual decision.

He didn't really miss her all that much. He had simply become numb. Outbursts of anger were minimal. There had been no affairs, no ugly scenes at the grocery store or office, no screaming matches in front of the kids. Simple fatigue carried the day. Even so, her decision to move back to Mississippi with the boys came as a surprise to him, and now that she was back there with them and all the grandparents, Thomas was trying to go forward with the rest of his life.

He did miss his sons, though. He called them almost every night and was glad this new job would last only a few more months so he could return to his home state to be closer to them. The current break, he reasoned, would probably do him some good.

Mr. Layne had been the one who found Xuan's testing company and recommended her for the testing contract. Thomas had no better suggestions, so he went along. He had only met Xuan the one time, and he had felt a fleeting attraction to her then. He liked her small, Asian frame, rounded face, and dark eyes. Her glasses were a nice touch, too, accentuating her smooth skin, delicate nose, and short hair.

Despite his newfound interest in younger women, Thomas had yet to find one who seemed interested in him. Besides, he reasoned, what twenty-five-year-old would be interested in a forty-year-old like him? He figured his infatuation was just conceptual insanity and not to be taken too seriously. In addition, he was sure he didn't have enough money to hold the interest of some young bombshell for very long. Someone in her middle thirties like Xuan, he thought as he drove to lunch, could be a wholly different matter. He wondered if someone like her might be better suited to meet the desires of companionship that he was only now allowing himself to admit.

He pulled into the restaurant parking lot and got out of his car. As he locked the car and turned to go toward the front door, a little Honda whisked by between the rows of cars. He glanced at the driver and was pretty sure it was Xuan, so he waited on the restaurant veranda and watched as she wound her way through the parked cars toward him.

It was a typical November day in Albuquerque—clear and crisp, with a cool breeze blowing from the west. The Sandia Mountains loomed dusty blue and pink on the horizon to the east. Thomas had been up to those mountains only once and had found the scenic drive outstanding. He relaxed with a deep breath as Xuan came up the three steps to the large railed porch. She was even prettier than he remembered, and her sunglasses gave her an added air of mystery. Her forest green business suit allowed her high-heeled calf muscles their maximum definition, and her briefcase gave her an air of seriousness.

"Hi, Xuan, I'm Thomas Walls." He extended his hand in greeting.

"Hello, Thomas," she smiled as she removed her sunglasses and fumbled for a place to put them in her purse. She shook his hand firmly but warmly. "I remember you."

"You look dapper today," Thomas offered. He immediately regretted how awkward he sounded.

"Oh, thanks," she responded sincerely, her eyes meeting his for the first time. "I think I'm about to move out of the suit-wearing thing. It feels outdated, if you know what I mean."

"It actually becomes you," Thomas said. Ladies dressed for business always attracted him. For that matter, so did ladies in uniform. He wasn't quite sure why this was, but he suspected it had to do with some sort of deflowering impulse that came sideways out of his libido. Or maybe it was the imagination-is-better-than-reality thing. Whatever it was, Thomas's death from years of numbness was beginning to reverse itself as he opened the heavy wooden door of the cantina-like Mexican restaurant. He allowed himself to drink in the unsuspecting sensuality of Xuan's hips as she walked in front of him through the foyer, and he nurtured his reawakened longings in the memory of her warm greeting glances.

As Thomas watched her sit down in the booth by the window and dig into her satchel, he sensed her excitement. She retrieved all six of Malik Mohammed's exam papers, put them face down on the table, then straightened them up a little. She looked at him with a big grin on her face.

"Thomas," she began, "you've got to see these! This guy is about twenty years old. He's blind, he's mute, and he's better at making a written record than a dictation machine. All six papers he wrote are perfect! They're readable, they're accurate, and they're exactly like the original texts we read to the candidates."

Thomas lifted up the stack and turned it over. He was instantly struck by the artistic writing style and studied the papers closely as Xuan described them. He recognized the titles he and Anna had discussed and even saw one they hadn't talked about, "The Tower of Babel, Revisited."

Mostly, he found himself listening to the sound of Xuan's voice and not her words. He loved the excitement in it. It had an uneven pace, and he felt her enthusiasm drawing him in. He was instantly captivated. He was also impressed by the measured strokes of the writer and the almost feminine quality of his penmanship. He looked more closely at the calligraphic signature on some of the papers and read the name out loud, as if he was announcing the young man to the whole room. "Malik M. Mohammed. His handwriting is certainly beautiful!"

"That's nothing!" Xuan blurted out. "What's really amazing is that he wrote all six of those papers in the first three hours."

"That's pretty good speed, isn't it?" Thomas asked.

"No, Thomas, you don't understand," Xuan replied. "He listened to both readers simultaneously and wrote down everything that both of them read at the same time."

"No way!" Thomas exclaimed.

"Yes!" Xuan replied. "I had all six of these papers by lunchtime! It's incredible!" She paused for effect and sat back. "I think we've found your transcriptionist."

"Amazing!" Thomas exclaimed. "This guy has taken listening to the next level."

"And writing, too," added Xuan. "It's as if he's meant for your project. I can find no flaws."

"Now, hold on a minute, Xuan," Thomas interrupted. "Did you say he's blind?"

"Yes, from an auto accident two years ago. He thinks being blind makes him a better listener."

"I'd be hard-pressed to argue with him," Thomas replied. "It really is incredible."

"Do you see why I couldn't explain this over the phone?" Xuan asked.

"Yes, I do now. Wow! I think you're right. This is just the person we're looking for. Congratulations!" Thomas looked again at the papers and then back at Xuan. "How does he take care of himself? Where does he live? How will he get to work every day?"

"Well, when someone goes blind after being sighted for most of their life, the Blind Institute gets involved to help with the adjustment. Malik is old enough to be on his own, but losing his parents and his sight at the same time made him eligible for some assistance. It looks like they are just watching out for him—providing some housing, helping him get around town when he needs it, and guiding him a little. I'll see if there's more, but I think that pretty much sums up their role." Xuan took a sip of her water.

"Okay. So how do we proceed from here?" Thomas inquired. He put down the file and looked right at her. "Do you want to conduct a preliminary interview with him and then bring me into the process, or should we just go straight to an interview with him and me?"

"No, let me screen him first," Xuan answered thoughtfully. "I need to decide how we should include his teacher at the institute and see if there's any special paperwork we need to consider. I also want to prep him on the project parameters and what to expect in his interview with you."

"Okay," Thomas said. "Can you do it this week and let me hear from you by Friday?"

"I'll try," Xuan offered. "I'll get it taken care of as soon as he and his teacher are available."

They soon ordered their food and talked about the weather, her employer, his boys, her family, and other matters. Thomas's interest in her was growing, and he felt the nervousness of that realization. His palms began to sweat a little under the table, and he wiped them on his pants. He checked to see if there was a ring on her finger and wondered if she would go out with him. She seemed to be flirting with him just a little and even touched his hand as he returned the stack of exam papers to her.

When their food arrived, Thomas was already getting up the nerve to ask her out. He knew one thing for sure: he would be thinking about that for the rest of the day.

Chapter 6

The Meeting Place

When Thomas returned to the office, Anna and Digger pounced on him before he even had a chance to remove his coat.

"We got it! We got it!" they both announced together.

Thomas took a step back in the face of their enthusiastic outburst. "We got what?" he asked.

"Jack Eaglefeather called and said the Acoma Pueblo is ours from June 15th to June 21st," Digger explained.

"Whoa!" Thomas smiled at both of them and at their obvious satisfaction. "Slow down a little. What are the terms of the deal? Did you have to make any concessions that will be impossible to live with, Digger?" he asked.

"The terms still have to be hammered out, but they're committed. I love it!" he exclaimed. "Here's the deal. We—I mean you and I—have to meet the entire council at the Pueblo next Tuesday night and agree to their terms. Anna already marked it on your calendar."

"Okay," Thomas said. "What do we need to prepare so that we get the best deal possible?"

"Nothing. They haven't asked for any money or rent or anything, so I guess we just have to show up and talk."

"Well, we can certainly do that, I suppose," Thomas said. "But guess what? I've got some good news, too. Xuan finally found someone to write it all down—and I do mean all of it. You won't believe this guy. He wrote six perfect papers and, get this, he's blind." Thomas enjoyed the looks of amazement on Digger and Anna's faces and added, "This ain't a bad day for a Tuesday, huh?"

"He's blind?" Anna asked.

"He's blind," Thomas said. "And he doesn't talk either, according to Xuan. But his writing is beautiful and accurate and fast and—what can I say? It's perfect."

"When will we hire him?" Anna asked.

"Well, as soon as it can be arranged. In the meantime, next week is getting busy. Mr. Layne will be here for our first group staff meeting on Wednesday at ten. Digger and I will be going to Acoma Tuesday night, and we'll all get to meet the transcriptionist sometime next week, too." Thomas started for his office and then stopped at his door and turned to face them.

"We've still got one major problem, however," he said. "We don't know who is coming to this meeting in June. Digger, let's spend some time with that clue file this afternoon, and, Anna, get that sheet of paper and make a copy for Digger. In fact, make two copies. I've decided to take you up on your offer to help, so we might as well get both of you involved. I'll see you in my office in ten minutes."

Thomas entered his office and closed the door. It had been a great day so far, but he wanted to relive the feeling of being alive again that he had experienced with Xuan. He loved her voice. He loved the way she looked. He loved the excitement in her face while she told him about Malik's transcriptions. He wondered the best way to ask her out. She seemed comfortable around him, but, heck, she was probably one of those people who were comfortable around everyone. She had greeted him warmly but, then again, he was the client, and people in her position were supposed to greet clients warmly or, at least, enthusiastically. Could he be confusing enthusiasm with warmth? *Yes, that's it*, he decided. He was just confusing the two.

On top of this confusion, his memories of dating weren't very good, and the prospect of dating again didn't feel all that promising, either. He didn't have Xuan figured for high-maintenance, but he suspected her tastes were refined, and he imagined she would require a certain savoir faire from him or any suitor. Though he was starting to come alive again, he didn't think he was all the way up to savoir faire just yet. He finally decided to let these thoughts rest a while as Digger and Anna entered his office.

With the meeting place now confirmed and the transcriptionist all but hired, Thomas knew the clues were the next major task to be completed. He was buoyed by these recent successes and decided he needed to attack these clues with renewed vigor, knowing that success might be just around the corner. He watched as Anna and Digger made themselves comfortable in the two guest chairs in front of his desk. He took a deep breath, relaxed, and began to read the first of the seven clues out loud.

"'Shankara, Arjuna, and Dvaraka—'" Thomas broke off reading and muttered, "Heck, I can't even pronounce these names. Does anyone recognize them?"

Digger responded and sat up in his chair. It was the first time he had seen these clues, and his fascination was apparent. "I recognize Arjuna. He's a figure in Indian mythology."

"As in Apache or Sioux?" Thomas asked.

"Neither," answered Digger. "As in the Indian subcontinent. They have some ancient writings called the Upanishads and the Vedas. Arjuna is a character in a work called *The Bhagavad-Gita*, so this clue probably comes from India." Digger then took over reading the clue's cryptic message: "'He came to the West in the 1920s and was no maker of religion.'"

"Okay," reasoned Thomas, "some Indian guy came to the West early in the last century and didn't make a religion. That's not much to go on."

Digger explained. "The main religion of India is Hinduism, although the population now includes a lot of Muslims, too. I think you should say, 'Some Hindu came to the West about eighty-five years ago and didn't make a religion.'" Digger looked up from the sheet of clues at Thomas and laughed at the look on Thomas's face.

Thomas realized his face was contorted into a frown and tried to relax again.

"He's a Hindu," Digger said, "and he's probably over a hundred years old. How many of those can there be, Thomas?"

"Yeah, right," Thomas conceded. "He should be pretty easy to find. I tell you what, Digger. You're in charge of this clue for now. Find this Hindu man."

"Okay, I'll take it," Digger responded.

"Good. I like agreeable employees," Thomas smiled. He was glad to get on with another seemingly unsolvable mystery and spoke the next clue aloud, as well. "'Abraham came from her tribe in Chaldea after the tower was destroyed.'" Thomas let out an exasperated grunt and continued, "What is this, *Jeopardy*? Okay, who is Moses?"

Anna and Digger both laughed, and this time Anna came to Thomas's rescue.

"Boss," she started, "there are several books and movies out lately about women in the church who may have been more prominent than the man-written histories have revealed. My priest is a church history scholar. Maybe he knows the name of a woman from Abraham's tribe."

"That's good, Anna, but she's not likely to be alive now, is she?" Thomas asked.

"Well, no," Anna answered, "but maybe her name will lead us to someone who is alive today and can come to the meeting in June."

"I suppose so," Thomas admitted. "Okay, this clue now belongs to you. By the way, see if your priest has time to pay me a visit. I'd like to talk with him."

Anna nodded as Digger spoke again.

"You know what, Thomas?" Digger said. "I may also be able to find something out about a tower in Chaldea. I've got several reference books from college on towers and bridges and ancient engineering feats. Maybe there's something about this tower in one of them."

Thomas got up and walked over to the corner window. He thrust his hands deep into the pockets of his tan slacks and furrowed his brow as he ignored the Albuquerque skyline in front of him. He hated that he was so frustrated, but he was glad that he had gotten Anna and Digger involved. He could finally admit to himself that it would take all of them to figure out these cryptic clues. Though he had looked at the clues several times, he had gotten absolutely nowhere. He tried to relax some more as Digger read the third clue out loud.

"'The mysteries of Mohammed are not known but by the few who dance with him.'" Digger read it again and then asked, "Who dances with Mohammed?"

Thomas, a little more relaxed and still standing at the window, answered softly before he could think, "Sufis."

"Sufis?" asked Digger. "Oh, yeah, whirling dervishes, you mean?"

Thomas spun away from the corner and strode back to his desk. "Yes, Mohammed's dance troupe. I learned of them when I was in college. Back then, we blacks were encouraged to embrace the Nation of Islam movement in this country as part of our liberation. I looked into it for a while but didn't find it particularly liberating. I'll take this clue and do some checking around."

"Listen to clue number four," Anna said. "'What is well planted cannot be uprooted. What is well embraced cannot slip away.' That sounds Native American, doesn't it?"

Thomas shrugged. He looked at Digger, whose blank expression indicated he didn't know, either.

"If it is," Digger finally spoke up, "Jack Eaglefeather might know. We can ask him next week at the Acoma council meeting."

"Read it again, Anna," Thomas asked.

"'What is well planted cannot be uprooted. What is well embraced cannot slip away.'"

Thomas was lost in thought. After a moment, he spoke. "It doesn't quite sound like an American Indian saying to me. It might be something else. It sounds Chinese or maybe Asian." He thought about Digger's suggestion and reiterated it. "Well, ask Jack, and I'll keep thinking about it, too."

"Okay," Digger agreed. "Now, listen to the fifth clue. 'Even the rocks are alive when cold runs deep on sacred mountain.' Now that sounds American Indian to me," he concluded. "Number four must be from somewhere else."

"Couldn't they both be American Indian?" Anna asked.

"I don't think so," Thomas answered, "but I think Digger is right. The more I think about number four, the more it sounds Asian. Number five sounds Native

American to me, and Mr. Layne thought it might even be a mountain here in New Mexico. Read the next clue, please."

"The sixth one is, 'Everyone who is seriously involved in the pursuit of scientific truth eventually becomes convinced that a spirit is manifest in the laws of the universe.'" Digger read it again and then repeated, "'Pursuit of scientific truth.' Is science a religion?" he asked.

"It is for some," Thomas observed.

"There are also churches based on science," Anna reminded them. "As much as I hate science, that clue sounds strangely familiar to me."

Thomas watched as she pursed her lips around her pen and cast her eyes on the ceiling of his office. He wondered if the answer she was looking for was inscribed thereon.

"Oh, I know," she said, "I did a paper in high school on Einstein. Does that sound like something Einstein would say?"

"Yes, or Bertrand Russell," Digger suggested.

"Heck, it could be any number of people," Thomas said. "Darwin, Descartes, Newton, Copernicus. Anna, you've got a head start on this one, so you take it, too. It appears to be a direct quote, and I think there are sources that list famous quotes. Why don't you get on the Internet or visit a library and see if you can track something down?"

"So, what if it is Einstein?" Digger inquired. "He's dead, so it's unlikely he'll be able to attend the meeting."

"True," Thomas said, "but we've got to start somewhere. Three of the people we've identified are already dead, so I'm beginning to think that these initial discoveries are just scratching the surface of these clues. We're just knocking on the door."

"Yes," Digger agreed, "but it feels like we're making some progress, because we seem to have found the doors to knock on."

Then Anna read the seventh clue: "'The teacher opens the door, but the students must pass through it themselves.'"

No one spoke. The words of the clue seemed to echo what Thomas and Digger had just said. Then Anna continued, "I get it. I mean, I think I understand. What you both said is right. These clues are just a beginning. They compel all of us to look beyond the simple phrases and uncover what makes them significant to our purpose and what we're doing. These little clues are, in effect, doors to something else."

Thomas could tell the thought was gaining clarity in Anna's mind as she went on.

"They require that we research and think about the clues, the people, and the observations they make," she said. "Now I see the reason behind them. By looking further, we're also being challenged to become more involved ourselves."

Digger said, "Anna, you've either read too many mystery novels, or maybe, just maybe, you're right." He picked up on the thought she had started. "What you describe is exactly how I felt at my first archaeological dig. We uncovered a small shard of pottery that was markedly different from any we had seen at that site. It turned out to be the location of an entirely new and distinct culture that no one knew existed. It was a tiny clue, but it drew me into the emotion of discovery—an emotion of caring about what that little shard was trying to tell me about a people long dead and gone. It was exciting, and I became hooked. It made me really feel alive in archaeology and the study of it became a passion from that day forward."

Thomas sat pensively and listened to Anna and Digger. His remark about scratching the surface, which had triggered their insights, was a purely rational reaction from him, an offhand comment, really. Now he realized he had unwittingly given them a clue beyond the clues, and he hadn't recognized it until they had reflected it back to him. He was humbled by this give-and-take dynamic. In that moment of discovery, he, too, was drawn in a little bit more.

"Anna," he started, "you're right. You've made me see this simple list of clues in a wholly different light. This simple little paper with seven cryptic statements now has an infinite set of possibilities for me. Some of my frustration is lifted."

"I know. Now it feels like we've just barely begun," Anna answered, "and there's a lot more to uncover. I can't wait to dig deeper and see what we find."

Chapter 7

The Council Meeting

Digger surveyed the handmade ladder as he readied himself to climb down into the main kiva at Acoma Pueblo. Leather straps held forearm-sized rungs into notches on two parallel poles some twelve feet long. Unsanded and unvarnished, each cross piece was smoothed by the regular tread of feet, each pole worn glossy by hands that had gripped them through time. He reflected on this moment of discovery as he began the descent and wondered how many had descended before he came to this moment in time and how many would do so after he was gone.

Inside, he saw the expected markers—the smoky wick lights in the niches, the smoldering embers in the fire pit where embers had smoldered for hundreds of years. He saw the half-wall dais of rock behind which Jack now stood in silence, and he saw the small hole in the floor through which these Native Americans believed all life had come to this place.

Thomas followed Digger into the kiva, and they were led to the other side of the circular stone room some fifteen feet across. The seven councilmen were there, and two others, as well. Digger and Thomas sat down on the sandstone floor near the fire as Jack cleared his throat and spoke.

"My Indian name is Iyatiku, from the Pueblo corn god. Iyatiku is the spirit guide for all town chiefs like me. In all other Pueblos, Iyatiku is a goddess, but when we first came to Acoma, after our time at El Moro Rock, our men became town chiefs. It is said that when the woman threw herself off the other mesa, our men could no longer follow the goddesses. It has been so for Acoma ever since. Our corn god is male. Our power comes from Iyatiku, who tells us how to walk the straight path of peace and harmony. He hears all that we ask and knows all that we need from his home below the earth. My father and his father and his father before him were also known as Iyatiku. When I was a boy, my mother called me Jack. Since my father became one with the clouds, I am Iyatiku for Acoma. Katzimo!"

Digger already knew the story, except that he had never heard the word "Katzimo." As he looked around the kiva, he wondered what significance the word held. The crude wick lights burned at four points in the circular structure. He knew these represented the four cardinal directions in the world of men: the rising energy of the east, the waning energy of the setting sun, the warmth and bounty of the southern sun, and the sacred clarity of the sunless north. He watched as Tesuque placed the fetishes—bundles of corn and feathers that were taken from a small storage alcove in the eastern wall. Digger knew these to be *irrarikos*, and he knew them to represent the corn god, Iyatiku.

He looked at Jack and was again reminded of his commanding presence. Despite his education at the white man's college in Las Cruces, Jack still spoke and acted in a way that Digger thought was unique to the Pueblo Indians.

In previous encounters, Digger had met all but two who were present. He acknowledged them with a nod but said nothing. The councilmen all sat together in a semicircle with Jack in the middle. Digger and Thomas sat to their right. The two whom Digger had not yet met also sat together, but they were apart from the circle, and soon they began to smooth the dirt floor near the sacred hole of creation.

From around their waists they pulled out several small pouches tucked in their belts and poured the contents into small piles in front of them. Digger counted ten piles of different-colored sands. The two men, alternating with each other, started taking small amounts of sand from the piles and sprinkling them on the smoothed-out floor. The younger man grabbed a handful of yellow sand and created a vertical line as the older one sprinkled watermelon-colored sand on either side of it. The first one then mixed in a dusky blue sprinkling on top of the red, while the second one spread sky blue sand at the uppermost end of the yellow line. Then the older man swept a handful of tan-colored sand perpendicular to the other end of the yellow line. At first, there seemed to be no discernible design into which they cast their sands. Neither the color nor the amount followed any observable plan, but, after a while, Digger saw they had made the borders of what appeared to be a picture.

The men worked with total concentration as they reached over and around each other to either pinch some sand or sprinkle it on the floor of the kiva. After about twenty minutes of this, the picture began to emerge more clearly, or so Digger imagined. He could make out earth and sky and clouds. The yellow sand seemed to form a column in the middle of the picture that went from the earth through the clouds to the top of the sky.

He looked at Thomas and saw the look of concentration on his face. He was watching every move. Digger marveled at the incredible focus and lack of hesitation on the part of the two men. They had established an unspoken rhythm with each other. As he watched, the sky immediately above the earth in the picture started turning purple, like mountains, perhaps, and he thought he saw some buildings near the bottom of the picture like the buildings of a Pueblo town. The yellow column got wider over time, now touching the buildings. The column blocked out the view of the mountains as it extended from the top of the sky to the buildings at the bottom of the picture. Digger wondered if it was an ear of corn that symbolized the life-giving connection between all Pueblos and the corn crops on which they depend. Or was it something else?

He was transfixed by the proceedings. Not a word was uttered nor a glance exchanged between the two artists. They went on pinching and sprinkling without pause. Like two experienced ballroom dancers, they never missed a beat and always seemed to know what the other was going to do a split second before it was done.

Finally, they both stopped. Just as there appeared to be no leader and no follower, neither of them stopped first, or last; they just stopped and sat back. The piles of sands from their pouches were all used up. They looked to the Iyatiku as Thomas and Digger continued to study the depiction in front of them.

Only when Thomas and Digger finally took their eyes off their creation and looked at the Iyatiku, too, did he speak to them all.

"For one week," Jack said, "since I told Digger of our meeting tonight, these two have been collecting the sands for your special sand picture. They have not spoken to each other about it and knew nothing of each other's sands—not colors or amounts. This has been created for you, our guests, and it will be up to you to decide the import and meaning of their picture." Jack looked directly at Thomas and Digger and then finished. "You must not speak of it to anyone else until its meaning is known. In time, we may all know what it means."

Jack signaled the two men, who leaned forward, pushed the sand into one pile, scooped it into their hands, and ceremoniously threw the sand down the life-giving hole in the kiva floor. Digger felt an involuntary tug in his stomach as the picture was destroyed. He wanted more time to study it, but it was no longer visible except in his memory. He searched the spot where the creation had been and tried to recreate it in his mind's eye. He watched as the two creators smoothed out the dirt on the kiva floor again, sat back, and closed their eyes.

After another long silence, Jack spoke once more.

"Digger, you are the first white man allowed in the main kiva of Acoma. Thomas, you are the first black man. Once before, a hundred years ago or more, a Spanish man entered this kiva. He did so without the permission of our fathers. It was wrong that he did so. He could not be killed in this place, because it is sacred to us, and he was not killed when we made him leave. It is said that he died five days later near Laguna Pueblo. His death was a mystery to some but we believe that Sus'sistinnako, she who created all things on earth, had him punished for breaking with the patterns of life. This will not be so for both of you. You are our guests."

Then Jack went on, "You see, the kiva is a powerful place, and we believe it will be a good place for the meetings you plan to have. Your masters will be welcome, but we must insist that we have one person from our council in the kiva whenever your people, or the masters, are in here."

Thomas and Digger both nodded that they understood the stipulation.

Jack continued, "We must also perform a cleansing ritual for the kiva every afternoon at two o'clock. This is so that purity is maintained in the kiva."

Digger watched as Thomas hesitated for a moment, and then concurred with a nod.

"The masters themselves may sleep here if they wish, but no one else," Jack added. "I will show you the other sleeping quarters later." He then fell silent.

Digger wanted to add his voice to these proceedings but Jack still seemed to hold the floor in an unobtrusive yet unmistakable way. Digger felt he should respect the silence, and he did.

Ten minutes sped by as Digger became lost in the moment again. Tesuque stood and gathered up the corn fetishes and laid them in a row by the base of the ladder. Then he returned to his place in the circle and sat down.

Digger looked again at Jack as Jack finally spoke a simple pronouncement, "Sus'sistinnako katzimo—this is in agreement with the pattern of life at Acoma."

This seemed to signify the formal conclusion of the meeting. Cha'amo and Juan Lezaun stood up and began talking to each other about the sand picture. Tesuque looked at Digger and smiled a toothy grin. The others seemed to relax, and Jack stood up and walked over to Thomas and Digger. He motioned for them to stand, too.

"Will you have planning meetings about this meeting of the master teachers?" Jack asked.

"Yes, at least once a month, probably more," Thomas answered.

"May I come to your meetings?" Jack asked.

To Digger, this simple request carried more weight than first met the ear. He wondered if Thomas heard it as a demand. After all, he and Thomas had been admitted into their council meeting—in their sacred kiva, no less. Digger felt Thomas should handle the request like a diplomat and return the respect with an invitation to their meetings.

"May I have time to think about it?" Thomas finally answered.

"Yes," Jack responded. "I might be of help in discovering who your guests will be. After all," he added, "they will be our guests, too." With that, he smiled the knowing smile that Digger recognized so well.

"We are honored that you wish to join us," Thomas began, "but I would still like some time to think about it, if I may."

Jack nodded, and then Digger remembered that he wanted to ask Jack about one of the clues they had discussed the day before.

"Jack," he asked, "have you ever heard the saying, 'Even the rocks are alive when cold runs deep on sacred mountain?'"

"Yes, I have. The Navajo like to say it," Jack replied. "The sacred mountain it refers to is just north of here. We call it Kahwehstimah, but the mapmakers call it Mt. Taylor."

"Do you know what the saying means?" Digger inquired.

"Yes. Most Indians think that everything is alive within the Great Spirit, but rocks only show their spirit when it is so cold that they crack and split apart. Your people call this thinking pantheism—the belief that our gods are alive in everything around us," Jack explained. "Most people like me have no separate religion, as you know it, and we have no religion that is apart from our living, either."

"What about the Spanish influence and Catholicism in your past?" Digger asked.

"The Spanish from Mexico tried to give us their religion, and there seemed to be no harm in adding it to our lives. It made them happy to think they had converted us." Jack chuckled and then added, "It was not our life, however. It seemed to be someone else's life, and we could not live it at Acoma."

"We were right, Thomas," Digger said. "It is a Native American saying."

"Yeah, we may have finally figured out one of the clues," Thomas acknowledged.

"It's time to leave the kiva," Jack announced.

Looking around, Digger realized that everyone else had already slipped away unnoticed. Thomas climbed up the ladder to the outside again. Digger followed, and Jack Eaglefeather was the last to leave.

As the three of them emerged from the warmth of the kiva, they encountered a few snow flurries on the mesa top. Digger noted that Jack led them off the mesa and took them back to their car along the exact same path Tesuque had brought them in. Like Tesuque, Jack led them in silence. Only their footsteps could be heard as it started to snow a little harder. The north wind picked up as they walked toward the west.

At their car, Thomas turned to shake Jack's hand. Digger did the same. The snowfall in the quiet valley was magical, and they all seemed to sense it. Words of peace and gratitude were on their lips, but Digger knew this momentous agreement between them needed no more words. There would be plenty of words as they worked together to create the meeting in June. Tonight, he knew that snowfall, handshakes, and the looks in their eyes said it better than words.

Chapter 8

Learning the Purpose

Russell Layne walked into the Project 4000 offices on Wednesday morning, December 15, 2009, at ten o'clock. He had driven in that morning from Santa Fe, some seventy-five miles to the north, and encountered the remnants of an Albuquerque snowstorm that had powdered the city the night before and changed his mood as he drove through it. It finally felt like winter in this Spanish enclave at the headwaters of the Rio Grande.

Layne liked winter. Yes, it had its inconveniences, but winter always felt like the time to rest and build up the energy for spring. Layne saw it as a time to think and plan and prepare so that when conditions allowed it, he could burst into spring all ready to go. This winter, his focus would be on Project 4000, because he was certain it would need a good running start if they were to be ready for the meeting in June. He had put all his other projects on hold or delegated them to others. He wanted a singular focus and, now, he was walking right into the midst of it. Soon, the New Year would be upon them and, like every New Year, he knew this one would be full of promise, hope, and resolution.

Layne was a large, rugged-looking man with big hands and a calm demeanor. Once everyone was gathered in the conference room, he moved confidently to one end of the eight-person conference table. He stood for just a moment as all eyes turned to him. First, he looked out the window and took in the new snow's lacy creations on the Ponderosa pine tree just outside the glass. He smiled.

One by one, he looked into the eyes of all who were there: Thomas, Digger, Anna, and Xuan. He noted that Thomas met his gaze, and he nodded to him. Layne's oversized hands, palms down, rested on the red-oak table. He said nothing for a moment as he gathered his thoughts. He had no notes.

Finally, like the experienced speaker that he was, he began to talk in a voice he knew to be resonant and calming to those who came under its spell.

"It is nice to see each of you again. I've thought of you often over the last few weeks, and I understand from Thomas that progress is being made on several fronts. I hope you will forgive me for being so slow in revealing the exact nature of our endeavor. I plan to reveal as much as I know about it to you today."

Layne noticed the nervous laughter when he acknowledged their feelings of uncertainty—especially from Thomas. He hoped his tone of voice, his quick and ready smile, and his leadership would alleviate that nervousness. He was not surprised to see Xuan, a non-staff member, in their midst. Thomas had told him of her interest and her success in finding the transcriptionist. They had decided her inclusion in this meeting could do no harm.

Layne continued, "This meeting is the first of what I hope will be one meeting every two weeks from now until June 15th of next year. As you may have heard from Anna, I'll be moving into these offices after the New Year, so, who knows, maybe we'll meet more than that."

The possibility of more frequent meetings evoked another round of nervous laughter.

"Okay, I get the point," Layne said. "You don't like meetings any more than I do. In any case, it is time you all knew a little more about what we're doing." With that, Layne took off his suit coat, loosened his tie, and plowed right ahead.

"I suspect that all of you except Xuan are thinking you're crazy for taking a job that is guaranteed to end in about seven months. Well, the truth is, you are. But, I think you'll be able to say when it's over that this upcoming seven months was an experience you'll never forget. I also feel confident in saying this: it will be an experience that will change your entire life from this day forward."

Layne reached for a water glass, took a sip, and paced a few times back and forth. He knew he had everyone's attention, and the pacing was just one of the many speakers' tricks he liked to employ. He watched as Thomas poured himself a glass of water and took a sip, too. He could feel Xuan's eyes upon him and saw that Digger was doodling on the writing tablet Anna had provided to all of them. He noticed that Anna was fingering her necklace, from which dangled a silver cross, as she stared straight ahead.

Layne cleared his throat and went on. "The publishing business gave me lots of excuses to read. My favorite subjects have always been philosophy, history, and religion. They have been woven together in countless ways throughout time, and they have provided frameworks of thinking upon which the progress of human-kind has been charted, measured, and inspired. In our meeting in June, history and religion will collide as never before. The result of the collision, an event like none have ever seen, will be that the worldview of everyone on this planet will expand and change forever. If humankind does not respond to what is heard and seen at this meeting, I think everyone, including all of us, will soon perish. It is, to my way of thinking, a dire set of circumstances in which we find ourselves."

Everyone in the room shifted nervously in their chairs. Thomas loosened his tie and poured himself another glass of water. Xuan uncrossed and recrossed her legs. Digger, the archaeologist, leaned forward in anticipation of more, and Anna changed her position so she could face Russell Layne directly.

"In my readings of everyone from Joseph Campbell to Ram Dass, Alan Watts to Jesus of Nazareth, Lao Tzu to Rashad Fields, Augustine to Aquinas, Aristotle to Socrates, Levi to Locke, Homer to Hume, and dozens of others, I have come to believe certain things about the path of humankind. In my studies of Buddhism and Hinduism and Islam and Christianity and Judaism and Confucianism and other belief systems, I have seen what I think are unmistakable trends on the roads of religion and history. From what I've read about Mayans and Aborigines and Native Americans and Africans and Greeks and Chinese, I have detected certain truths that live just below the surfaces of all cultures. These foundations reveal those deeper truths that surpass all understanding and tell of constants that never seem to completely disappear."

Anna asked, "Do the dire circumstances you mentioned include the end of the world like so many have predicted?"

No one said a word as Layne thought about the question.

"Yes and no," he finally responded. "It all depends on what happens. There's little doubt that resources are dwindling. There's no doubt that populations are increasing exponentially, and there's no doubt that competition over resources spurs wars and consumption of more resources. Water is becoming increasingly precious. Air is fouled, and food is thrown away despite an increase in hunger. Yes, it all depends on what happens," he concluded.

"So how do religion, history, and philosophy solve problems like food, air, and water?" Digger asked.

Layne took another sip of water. "That is a challenge, Digger, but first let me explain why a man like me is standing in front of you now. Two events in my life over the past few years have made me sit up and take notice of the impending need for paradigm change. The first of these events, while I was in India a few years ago, was an encounter with one whom the locals refer to as guru. In a meeting with this guru that included some forty other people, he singled me out for a message. In part, he said that I should use my resources to convene a meeting of great minds and wise men in the Western United States. He added that he would be there if he could, and his assistant handed me a scrap of paper which I stuffed in my pocket. Frankly," Layne chuckled at the recollection, "I wasn't very impressed with this fellow, and it felt like I had opened up a fortune cookie from a Chinese restaurant. I didn't give it too much thought.

"Three or four years went by," Layne continued, "and last year, I was here in New Mexico visiting the Pueblo at Santa Fe. I was just a regular tourist accompanied by friends, when an elderly priest invited me into his office under some pretense or another. Once we were inside, he asked me if I'd been to confession lately, and I admitted I was a nonpracticing Jew but not a Catholic. It had been years since I had seen the inside of a synagogue. Then, he asked me if I had forsaken my rabbi to follow some guru or something. I laughed and told him the only guru I had ever met had not impressed me much but had left me with a fortune-cookie message. He perked right up and immediately asked me if he could see the message. I didn't have it with me, so I told him it was some sort of instruction to convene a meeting of wise men in the West. The priest immediately grew silent and fingered the turquoise cross that hung on a silver chain around his neck.

"'Now I understand,' he muttered. 'You understand what?' I asked him. He answered me slowly. 'For many months I've had a recurring dream about many powerful people meeting at the Acoma Pueblo west of here, but you weren't among them. Even so, when I saw you milling around here today, something told me you were powerful, so I decided to talk to you. Now, I must find out how you relate to my dreams about this meeting.'

"My friends were impatient to leave, so I gave him my business card and went on my way. When I got home to Syracuse two weeks later, he had sent me an e-mail in which he explained what he knew and invited me to spend three days with him in the mountains north of here. I decided to accept his invitation, and while we were together, he gave me the seven clues that Thomas has been working on these last few weeks."

"Where did he get those clues?" Thomas interrupted.

"They came to him in discussions with his mentor and in dreams he had about this meeting. He told me the dates of the meeting and wished me luck. He also gave me this." Layne pulled from his pocket a simple, clear, crystalline prism worn smooth from years of handling. "When he gave it to me, he laughed and said, 'My guru would want you to have this.'"

Russell Layne paused at this point in his story and looked for reactions and responses from the others. Thomas was the first to speak.

"Mr. Layne," he began, "given that most of us are downright cynical about meetings and any good that can come from them, why should any of us hold out hope that this meeting will be any different?"

"Good question, Thomas," he answered. "It may even seem a bit flaky at this juncture, but according to some things I've read here and there, each two thousand years in the history of humankind is called an age. It designates a cycle of time or the completion of certain events or markers of progress. I think we're near the end of the sixth age of humankind right now and about to transition into the seventh age. According to others that I've read, each age has a so-called master soul whose actions and thoughts form a keynote mentality or guiding philosophy that colors and impacts the entire two thousand years. The most well-known master soul, the one who has so greatly influenced these last two thousand years, is Jesus of Nazareth. The names of master souls from the five previous ages have been lost to the collective memory of humankind."

Layne looked around at his small audience, rested his hands on his hips a moment, and went on. "In addition, each age enjoys the wisdom of master minds or sages who support, explain, promote, and even serve as guides in the ways of that master soul. Their influence is often limited to where they live or with whom they associate. Some are better known than others—like a pope or an ayatollah or a Dalai Lama. Others are less well known, but throughout any given age, there are lots of these master minds and sages to support and assist the master soul." He once again rested his hands on his hips, smiled at everyone, and finally sat down in his chair.

"I'm fascinated by this," Digger admitted, "but it takes a lot of explaining. What does this background have to do with us and our meeting in June?"

"Yes, it does take some explaining," Layne agreed, "and there is one more tidbit I must give you before I can answer your question about the meeting." He looked at Anna and could tell she was following closely. Xuan and Thomas still seemed to be on board, as well, so he began to tell them more.

"Apparently, at the beginning of each age, some of these sages gather together with the master soul for seven days of contemplation and meditation. There, they analyze the spiritual progress of humankind and devise the spiritual plan for the upcoming two thousand years. When they have come to an agreement on how to proceed, they give their blessing to that master soul and pledge their support to his age-long endeavors to carry out their agreed-upon plan."

Layne sat back in his chair, prepared to field questions. He felt tension in his shoulders and neck as he rolled up his sleeves. He felt that he had laid it out pretty plainly, but as is often the case with new information, he knew his audience might not absorb everything on the first pass. From what he had learned while hiring all of them, he knew Thomas would be the skeptic and Xuan the rational disbeliever. Anna might be shocked, he thought, and Digger would likely be fascinated and entranced.

When no questions were immediately forthcoming, Layne spoke again. "We, ladies and gentlemen, are the organizers of the meeting at which the wise men and sages will gather to determine the spiritual path of humankind for the next two thousand years. The next two thousand years will take us to somewhere around AD 4000. That's why I selected the name Project 4000. Our job is to help this meeting take place. We know the dates for this meeting. We know the place where the masters of this upcoming age will assemble. We have some admittedly vague clues as to who these sages and wise people might be. We have a few instructions to go on and, frankly, the rest is up to us."

"Who is the master soul for the upcoming age?" Anna asked with a look of concern.

"It's not yet been revealed to me or to anyone I know," Layne answered. "The last master soul, Jesus of Nazareth, said he would be with his people until the end of the age. That tells me it will probably not be him, so the next master soul may be a Buddhist or a Muslim or an African or, who knows, maybe not any of these. It probably won't be a Jew, like last time, and the next master soul may come from a heritage with which we are not familiar or comfortable. They may even be a woman. I don't know."

"Or maybe they will come from a more cosmopolitan background," Digger added under his breath.

"Maybe so," Layne smiled. "We are charged with figuring out the rest of the details, and we only have six or seven months in which to do it. I will add this, however, something the priest told me in the mountains: the agreed-upon focus for this age that is now almost over has gone astray of its original intent. I think this is to be expected, and it doesn't surprise any of those who have known that focus. Thomas's cynicism about meetings is only exceeded by my certainty that no plan, no model, can retain its vitality for two thousand years. No plan of man is that good."

"How would you describe the plan for the last two thousand years?" asked Digger.

"The plan of the last age," Layne replied, "was to develop a pattern or model that would serve to collect, conserve, and disseminate spiritual truths in a way that humankind could grasp them. In the West, that model is now called 'church' or some reasonable facsimile. Accordingly, churches of all kinds, in all lands, in most cultures, and in most religions have developed in a basically similar manner. Whether they are called mosques or temples or shrines or more Western versions of the concept called church, they all have common elements—a meeting place, some kind of leader who is generally conceived of as a pipeline to a god, a bunch of followers with varying degrees of dedication, a fervent belief in some hero, regularly scheduled meetings, and lessons of various depths and understanding. Most of them also have a few poorly developed techniques and rituals. On the whole, this has worked pretty well to keep the faith alive, such as it is, and even to advance it, in some cases."

"So will this meeting try to abolish churches or religions?" Anna asked. She fingered her turquoise rosary as she searched Layne's face for an answer.

"I don't think so, Anna," Layne answered. "I don't think there will be any need for abolishing. Things that no longer work usually just fall into disuse by themselves if given half a chance."

"Or they undergo a major renovation," Thomas said.

"Yes, that is a possibility, too," Layne continued. "Two things, however, have crept into the picture to make the model no longer viable and, to my way of thinking, downright dangerous. The first of these is that these pattern churches and, on a bigger scale, pattern religions, have taken on a life of their own and have become purveyors of their own institutional truths and traditions. These complex and ofttimes convoluted dogmas and systems are a far cry from the simple truths with which the age began. Many of them are now simply preserving the large and frozen structures of their own making and are propped up by habits more than truth."

Xuan asked, "That pretty much describes all religions, doesn't it?"

"I think so, at least on some levels," Layne responded. "The second thing that has fouled the model is that these churches and religions have become so bound up in the cultural milieu in which they have developed that they are more cultural institutions than keepers of spiritual truths."

"That means they've now got cultural baggage," Digger interjected. "My anthropology studies convinced me that churches become the cultural carriers of tradition, and eventually their so-called sacred business is relegated to a secondary position of importance."

"I think that pretty well sums it up," Layne agreed.

"So has the church become its own worst enemy?" Digger asked.

"Maybe so, Digger," Layne said, "or at least an impediment to further learning and development."

Layne look around the table for more questions. There were none, so he finished with this: "I've got a story from one of my readings that says it better than I can. I will tell it to you, and then we'll break for lunch. It's an old teaching story from the Zen Buddhist tradition, I think. It seems there was a certain Zen monastery in China around the fourth century. They kept a cat on the grounds to keep the mice population at bay, but this cat had the annoying habit of wandering through the meditation hall during evening prayers. The constant disturbance became a preventative to meaningful meditation, so the wise, old leader of the monastery gave the instruction for the cat to be tied up for one hour every day during the evening prayers. This solved the problem, but sometime later the leader of the monastery died, and, soon after, the cat died as well."

Layne took another sip of water and sat forward in his seat. He cleared his throat before continuing. "A new leader was selected and a new cat obtained, and the leader again instructed that the cat be tied up during evening services, as this had been the habit under the previous and well-respected leader. This so-called habit of tying up cats every evening for an hour eventually took on a certain importance of its own and became a ritual. It was dutifully passed on and on for hundreds of years in that monastery. It became a time-honored tradition that none dared to break. After all, a well-respected and learned man of their monastery had decreed it hundreds of years before, so it must be the right and only way. Certain knots were developed that became the preferred knots for tying up cats. Certain handling techniques were developed. A cat bed was built and then upholstered and then gilded. Paintings of cats and tributes to cats and songs about cats soon dotted the monastery walls. Cat lineages were tracked and charted. Eventually, papers and treatises were presented at monastic conferences on the importance of this tradition and the necessity of tying up cats in order to create proper prayer. In that order of monks, cats are now considered sacred."

Layne stopped and then smiled broadly at the conclusion of his story. Everyone smiled and slowly began to laugh at the idea of sacred cats tied up with sacred knots. Soon they were all laughing out loud, and Layne seemed to enjoy the delayed reaction.

"So our job," he raised his voice over the laughter, "is to untie some cats—and, from what I can tell, all the religious models around the world have lots of cats to untie."

He stood up and stretched. "We'll talk some more at lunch"

Chapter 9

More to Learn

Xuan offered Thomas a ride to lunch. As they left the office and walked to the parking lot together, she was bursting to talk with him about all they had just heard from Russell Layne. They had barely reached her car when she opened the discussion.

"Mr. Layne is convincing, isn't he? I mean, the little Baptist College I went to in Texas didn't offer much religion except Protestantism, so I can't really say what I think yet, but I'm definitely intrigued with his premise."

"I never guessed you for a Baptist," Thomas replied with a chuckle. Then he thought better of his comment and quickly added, "Hell, I don't even know what I believe anymore, so why am I laughing? At least you know your beliefs."

"Oh no, I'm not Baptist any longer. I guess I relate more to Zen Buddhists than the Baptists. The Baptist stuff seemed to be about guilt and inadequacy more than anything else. All the role models were men; God was father, Jesus was son, ministers were men, and elders were men. The older I got, the less comfortable I felt about the whole setup. It was like women weren't good enough to be anything but background. I just couldn't figure out a way to relate to that and still feel good about being a woman."

"Yeah, I think I know what you mean," Thomas replied. "Even the Mississippi Black Baptist Caucus seemed more like black guys trying to be white guys." Then he added, "But I'll tell you what, the gospel music was awfully good."

"So you're a Baptist?" Xuan asked.

"Oh, no," Thomas answered. "That affiliation didn't last much past childhood. In college I tried the Nation of Islam thing, but now I'm just floating and wandering more than anything else. What's the Zen thing about, anyway?"

"I'm not really sure about that, either," Xuan explained. "It seems more personal somehow, not like a big organization or an institutional system. You know, I can meditate in my own way, in my own time, and make it more or less what I need it to be. The Tao is more like a river of life of which we are all a part, rather then a God figure or an Allah figure from which we are all separated. But, I picked it up because of a guy I was married to, so I'm not real sure, either. Maybe I'm a wanderer like you, Thomas."

"You were married?" Thomas asked.

"Oh, yes," Xuan replied. "That didn't turn out too good for me." She looked away from Thomas and reflected on her feelings from that experience, feelings that sometimes still caught her off guard. She slowly continued, "I spent a lot of time getting over that. It still causes me pain sometimes." She worried that she might be revealing too much but then plowed ahead with rare abandon for her and added, "I really haven't let anyone close since then." She smiled sheepishly as she paused to search for her car keys and then unlocked her car door and got in. She felt Thomas's eyes on her and looked away again. When he finally lowered his stocky frame into her small, sporty car, their eyes met once more for just a moment.

Thomas spoke up. "I'm just a few months into a divorce after fourteen years of marriage, myself," he volunteered. "Do you still feel the need to hold yourself back from another relationship?"

"Yes, but I've finally come to realize that living with the anxiety about being hurt again is really no way to live," she said. "It's made me quit too easily."

"I get that," Thomas responded. "My wife and I had gotten pretty numb about everything in our relationship, and that's no way to live, either. Even though we were married, we were both pretty disconnected. I felt kind of dead for the last five years in that marriage."

"That's a good description," Xuan said, "disconnected."

"Yes. But this Project 4000 experience is slowly changing all that." He faced her as he spoke. "Every once in a while I feel like I'm alive again. In fact, Xuan"— he looked down just for a moment and then back up. Their eyes met again while she fumbled for the ignition, inserted the key and turned on the engine—"I felt it at our lunch the other day. I tried to dismiss it as a, well, you know—maybe it was your perfume or the way you looked or a little loneliness. Heck, I don't know. But I felt something, that's for sure."

Xuan sensed his vulnerability and was instantly attracted to it. "Well, Thomas," she smiled at him, "I do believe you've managed to embarrass yourself, but I can't tell for sure. I don't see any red in your face."

"Cute. Could I see any red in your face if you were embarrassed?"

Xuan was relieved that she could tease him. His quick and easy reaction relieved any tension surrounding their surprisingly personal revelations.

He continued, "No, you won't catch any red in this face, but my stammering usually gives me away. I've got to work on that, I think."

Xuan laughed and was enjoying the almost instant intimacy and comfort she felt with this man. She wondered again if she might enjoy spending more time with him.

"Hey, this is a nice car," he offered as he ran his hand across the leather upholstery, appeared to study the dashboard, and tried to change the subject.

"Whoa, mister," she interrupted. "I don't want to talk about my car—not now, anyway. Maybe I can embarrass myself, too. Let's see. I liked your cologne and, uh, you looked—what was that word you used—oh yeah, 'dapper,' too. Of course, I could never admit to even being the slightest bit lonely. No, that wouldn't do for a woman in my position." She laughed as she turned the corner.

The restaurant was up ahead on the right, and she signaled her turn as she stole a glance at Thomas. She liked his well-kept look and the rich brown tone of his skin. His hairline was beginning to recede just a little, but it suited his age and gave him a mature image she found appealing. She liked his broad mouth and full lips, too.

He rubbed his hands together in a manner that made her think he was still nervous and then spoke once again. "Would you consider, uh … well …" and he quit in midsentence.

Xuan parked the car in the restaurant parking lot and shut off the engine. She looked at him for a moment and decided she would just wait for him to finish.

He looked out the window and then down at the door for the handle as she put the keys in her purse. "Would you consider," he began again, "going on a date with me?"

She smiled in a half-flirting, half-teasing kind of way and then answered, "Yes, I'll consider it. How much time do I have before I have to answer?"

"I'll give you half an hour," he laughed. "Okay, one hour, tops. But then the offer goes away, and I'll never make myself so vulnerable again." He opened his door to get out.

"Fine," she smiled. She already knew she'd say yes but was enjoying the suspense of the flirtation too much to give it up just yet. With that, she got out, and they went into the restaurant to join the others for lunch.

Digger, Anna, and Russell Layne were already in the waiting area when Thomas and Xuan came in. Chinese food in Albuquerque wasn't something the tourist bureau bragged about, and the Rice Bowl was one of just a few Chinese restaurants. They were seated shortly, ordered their drinks, and watched as the usual teapot and cups were delivered along with the chopsticks and water glasses.

"Does anybody know what's good here?" Layne asked of no one in particular as he scanned the menu.

"The kung pao chicken is good, and so is the chow mein," Digger answered.

"All right, thanks. Can I interest anyone in an appetizer?" Layne looked for an answer, but everyone was studying the menu.

The offer went unanswered, and Xuan glanced at Layne as he returned to his menu.

In a few minutes, the waiter returned with their drinks and Layne asked them all a question. "Does anyone feel more clarity about what we're doing at Project 4000?"

Xuan was the first to speak. "Why do you think everyone is at risk of perishing if there is no new model? That's a pretty bleak picture, don't you think?"

"Yes, it is, Xuan," Layne replied. "The only answer I have for you is that when patterns and models are paraded as the actual truth they are supposed to represent, something, usually the truth itself, gets lost in the shuffle. Over time, the model itself becomes the new 'truth,' or a kind of shadow truth, really. Some even think it a lie. In defense of the model, terrible wrongs are likely to be perpetrated and then defended as 'right' and then as 'holy' and then as the only 'truth.' The religion is just the model. It has lost its direct connection with the truth itself."

Digger interrupted as quickly as he could get in a word. "So you're saying the religion is incorrectly viewed as the truth when it's really just a model or facsimile of the truth?"

"Exactly," Layne answered. "Many people, too many people, are fighting throughout the world for their models and facsimiles and religions. They're fighting for the right to tie up the cat in a certain way and have lost the real purpose of the evening prayers."

"And what? If this continues, everyone will perish?" Thomas asked. "That's a pretty big leap, don't you think?"

"Maybe so, but maybe not," Layne answered. "The priest in Santa Fe who has served as my guide here in New Mexico thinks the wars over religious supremacy will continue to escalate worldwide. Oddly, the so-called peacemakers are becoming the war mongers in the name of their religions. He thinks it's approaching critical mass, and I'm inclined to agree."

"So what used to be viewed as a solution for peace is actually the problem?" Thomas asked.

"I think so," Layne responded. "Maybe it's unavoidable. After all, the plan is two thousand years old, and the world has changed immensely in that time. As a possible proof, the people at the last meeting like this one alluded to a previous meeting like this one—a meeting two thousand years before theirs. More pertinent to our endeavor, they also hinted at a future meeting just like the one we are planning. Maybe it's just a natural plan adjustment that is required every two thousand years."

"Do you know for a fact that this previous meeting actually took place?" Digger asked.

Xuan remembered that Digger was an archaeologist, and she figured he was just looking for an old tablet or an ancient coin or the ruins of some building—some kind of material proof that would satisfy his tactile urge to hold or see or read.

"No, Digger. There's no proof of it," Layne replied. "The meeting took place in Alexandria, Egypt, but as you probably know, the library there was destroyed within fifty or sixty years of that meeting, and any notes contained there were thought to be lost. Then, the people who took part in the Crusades, a classic example of religion gone awry, took it upon themselves to finish the destruction and obscure the historical records forever. Any record of the meeting there is certainly lost to us now."

"Are we working on a hunch, then?" Digger interjected.

"I suppose we are," Layne said, "although I prefer to call it intuition or a priestly dream or a guru's prediction. I don't really know what to call it. In addition to the paper that holds the seven clues, there's a scrap of paper that vaguely describes all of you. Digger, you were described simply as a searcher. In our interview, you kept talking about your archaeological digs and explorations, and it felt like you fit the bill."

Digger smiled at the description.

Layne turned his attention to Thomas. "Thomas, you were described as a skeptic and an organizer, that's all. It wasn't until we had that talk about your divorce that I knew your skepticism was heartfelt doubt that had not yet turned into cynicism. I could see your heart, and it became apparent that you had the right mindset to organize this group and this meeting, so I gambled on you a little."

The waiter brought their food, and everyone was busy for a moment. Russell Layne finished his descriptions of the people on the slip of paper he had committed to memory. "Xuan, you were just described as a seeker and a tester. When I knew we would need a uniquely special person to make a record of the meeting, I thought you were the best one to find him or her. And Anna, the paper described you as innocent as Mary in the Bible. When I saw your fresh face and bright smile and heard that you were a practicing Catholic, I knew you were the one for us. Besides, I noticed that your middle name is Maria, a simple variation of Mary, which was my wife's name, too. That sealed the deal for me. I have no doubt that you are perfect for this venture."

Thomas asked, "Where did these bits of information come from, anyway?"

"The priest in Santa Fe, Father Garces, saw them in dreams he had last summer," Layne answered. "He gave them to me along with the clues when we met in the fall." He finished arranging the food on his plate and began to eat. Then he remembered Digger's question. "Actually, Digger, the descriptive piece of paper—finding you folks just as you were described—and those clues is what gives me the confidence to think this is more than a hunch. I hope I am right."

After a few minutes, Anna asked Layne, "Will the master soul of the upcoming age be at the meeting in June?"

"I don't know for sure, Anna, but I think so," he replied. "When Jesus of Nazareth presented himself at the last such meeting, he knew it would be easiest to establish his model within the traditions he knew best. Jewish temples and synagogues were not too far from the model of church that he and the sages had all envisioned."

"But it didn't turn out to be easy," Anna answered.

"No, the Jewish community didn't see him as a master soul, just as a prophet," Layne agreed. "But the church eventually got built, once Paul and Peter took over the effort." He paused to look at Anna directly before continuing. "As for the master soul of the upcoming age, I don't know who it is, as I told you this morning. I think he or she will be there if this meeting follows the pattern of the last one."

"It'll certainly be more of a meeting if he or she is there, that's for sure," Thomas interjected.

Xuan poured herself some more tea and asked, "Are any of the master teachers coming to this meeting people who have lived on earth before?"

"I don't know," Layne answered. "I find it curious to talk about reincarnation, Xuan. Two-thirds of the world believes it accurately describes the reality of the soul's journey. Western Christendom says they don't believe in reincarnation, and yet their most fervent hope is that Jesus of Nazareth will reincarnate or come again and take them to some place called heaven."

"Well, what do you think of it?" Thomas asked.

"I think reincarnation is quite likely," Layne began, "especially for those who have mastered the spiritual truths. I think learning how to die and how to return to an earthly existence is a technique that can be learned and mastered. In any case, I suspect all the masters at our meeting will be highly evolved souls who have been here on earth many times before." He stopped and looked at all of them and asked, "Do you believe in some form of reincarnation or not?"

Xuan answered quickly, "Yes, I think so, but I have no proof of it."

"Ah," Layne said, "proof is a hard thing to come by." He was silent as he continued to eat. He appeared to be waiting for another question.

After a few minutes, Thomas cleared his throat as if to speak. Everyone looked expectantly in his direction as he wiped his mouth with his napkin and placed it back in his lap.

"Mr. Layne," he began. "What if no one shows up for this meeting?"

"Well, Thomas, you truly are a skeptic, huh?" Layne chuckled to himself. "I suppose I should have guessed it based on your name. If no one shows up, I guess we'll just chalk it up to experience, close down the office, and go our merry ways." He laughed again.

"Actually," he continued, "I thought Xuan would be the one who would be testing me, but doubters and testers are all cut from the same cloth, I suppose. There's room for both of you. I think it was Alfred, Lord Tennyson who said 'There is more faith in honest doubt than all the creeds combined,' or something like that. None of you have to buy into this adventure just yet, but I do insist that you remain open to the possibilities and reserve final judgment until you see how it all develops. As I told you this morning, I've been exposed to all kinds of spiritual philosophy for thirty years or more. All those years of seed-sowing are finally growing into something inside of me, and it's all coming together in this adventure. At sixty years old, perhaps I've got a head start on all of you, but I am finally committed to acting on that which I've read and wondered about through the years. Every step I take seems to increase and strengthen my determination to complete Project 4000."

Xuan was impressed with Layne's resolve, but Digger spoke up before she could offer a comment.

"I really got excited at the Pueblo Council meeting the other night," Digger said. "It was an archaeologist's dream come true for me. Will we also be allowed to attend this meeting?"

"I don't know, Digger. Are you a sage or a master teacher?" Layne answered with a smile.

"No, not at all." he answered.

Layne finished his answer by saying, "I don't think anyone will attend the actual deliberations except the transcriptionist and the seven masters." He turned toward Xuan and asked, "By the way, how is that coming? Thomas tells me you may have found our transcriptionist."

Xuan stole a glance at Thomas and was glad when he signaled her to answer the question. "Yes, I think we've finally found our person," she said, "just a few days ago, and he is amazing. He wrote six perfect papers, and we're going to interview him next week."

Digger added, "We've also secured the main kiva at Acoma for the meeting place."

"That's great!" Layne reacted. "You know, those are important accomplishments that just reinforce what I'm saying. Thomas, have some faith. You guys are better than you know. There's energy around this endeavor that is almost palpable. Every day I'm pleasantly surprised at some new piece of information, some discovery or realization that comes to one of us, as if we were intended to find it out. In and of itself, it might not even be particularly significant, but taken as a whole, the cumulative effect is undeniable. We can no longer ignore any of it. It gives me chills to think of it!"

Xuan watched as Layne seemed to savor their successes. She felt reassured by this and liked that his logic was so full of just-plain common sense. She didn't feel like he was beating them over the head or that he was particularly insistent. His manner seemed fatherly to her, his presentations comfortable. His stories and explanations kept her riveted to what he was saying. *Maybe,* she thought, *maybe what he said was full of truth, too.*

Then he looked at her and said, "Xuan, let me put you on the spot for a moment. If you're done with our contract for the testing, and it sounds like you're pretty close, would you consider taking a leave of absence from the agency and going on our payroll until the end of June?"

"Oh, gosh," Xuan answered. She was surprised by his offer of a job. Then she remembered that Thomas had also asked her on a date. She felt her entire life beginning to change all in one day. "That's the second time today that someone's asked me a question regarding my future," Xuan answered. "How long do I have to answer you?"

"How long did they give you?" Layne queried back.

"I think it was half an hour," Xuan answered, "but that was an hour ago."

"And what was your answer to that first proposal?"

Xuan squirmed in her seat just a little and made sure not to look at Thomas. "Well," she said, "I think I'll answer yes to that one."

"So, it took about an hour to get a tentative 'yes' out of you, huh? Well then, I'll give you a week, but your answer cannot be tentative. If you decide to do it, just let Thomas know, and he'll work out the details and get you on our payroll."

She liked that he was smiling at her.

"I hope you say yes," he added.

With that, Russell Layne pushed back his plate and asked if anyone wanted dessert. There were no takers, so he announced, "I've got a little shopping to do, and then I need to look for a place to live in this fair city. My flight back to Syracuse tomorrow isn't until early afternoon, so, Thomas, can we meet at the office around nine?"

"Yes, that's good for me," Thomas responded.

"Good! Anna, you brought the company credit card, right? Please put this lunch tab on it, will you? I'll see all of you in the morning."

He started to leave when Digger suddenly asked, "Don't you want your fortune cookie, Mr. Layne?"

Layne stopped, turned around, and smiled. "Actually, I'm still a little busy with the last one I got, Digger. You open mine and let me know if it's anything I should be worried about."

He winked at Digger, turned toward the foyer, and walked out of the restaurant.

"I like him," Anna said once she was sure he was gone. "And I'm starting to like this project, too. What do you think, Xuan? Are you going to come to work with us?"

"I like him, too, Anna," Xuan replied, "and I'll consider the offer—that's for sure. It might just be the right thing for me, if my boss will grant me a leave of absence."

The fortune cookies and check came to the table shortly. While Anna busied herself with the check and the tip, Digger opened and read his fortune aloud.

"'You will marry your current lover, and you will be happy,'" he read, and his face went glum. "Great!" he said. "I don't even have a girlfriend. So much for that prediction."

"'Prosperity will come to you late in life,'" quoted Thomas from his slip of paper.

Xuan watched with interest as he tossed it on the table and threw his arms in the air in mock dismay.

"I guess I'll just have to muddle through on a bureaucrats salary till then," Thomas said.

Xuan smiled when she read hers, but she tucked it into her coat pocket and didn't offer to read it aloud.

Anna was done figuring the bill when she picked up the next to last cookie. "Let's see. 'Patience, hard work, and virtue will serve you well,'" she read. "That's pretty true for me," she added with a giggle. "I'm patient, I work hard, and I'm virtuous. I guess that makes me kind of boring, too."

Digger picked up the last cookie, presumably Mr. Layne's. He broke it open, only to find it empty. "Well, I guess Mr. Layne doesn't have anything to worry about."

As they all readied themselves to depart, Xuan looked forward to another ride with Thomas. She smiled at him as he helped her with her coat and they walked to her car together.

She clicked open the door locks, and he slid up alongside the car and got in. She wanted to talk about Layne's job offer but figured he'd want to respond to her acceptance of his proposal, too. She started her car, maneuvered it away from the curb, and stole a glance at him.

"Did I understand you correctly, Xuan?" Thomas opened.

"About a date, you mean?" she asked, still preferring to talk about something Layne had said at lunch.

"Well, yes," Thomas stammered. Nervousness returned to his voice as he continued. "We could take in a movie and then maybe have a few drinks or even dinner if you want."

She thought about his ideas for a minute and eventually countered with a plan of her own.

"You know what I'd really like to do, Thomas? I'd like to get up early Sunday morning and meet you for sunrise up there on the top of Sandia Crest." She pointed to the east. "Then, after sunrise, we could go to a little church I know up there and maybe sit in meditation or go to services if you want. How does that sound?"

"I'm not too good at the early-morning thing. What time would we have to get up to make sunrise at Sandia Crest?" he asked.

"I'm not sure," she replied, "probably about four thirty or five o'clock. Maybe you can go to bed early on Saturday night." She looked him right in the eyes, which seemed a little glazed over as he thought about her proposal. "Come on, Thomas. What do you say? Sunrises are really spectacular up there, and it's so peaceful and quiet that time of day."

"Oh, I've been up there, but never that early in the day," Thomas finally responded. "I'll have to drink about a gallon of coffee just to keep my eyes open between four thirty and five o'clock."

"Okay, you bring a gallon of coffee, and I'll bring some juice and muffins," Xuan replied.

"I must be crazy."

Xuan started in on a new topic. "Thomas, do you think I should accept Layne's job offer? I mean, if I say yes and I'm granted the leave of absence, it would mean we'd be working together."

"That sounds good to me," Thomas assured her. "We could be in charge of the doubt department, and, besides, I think I'd enjoy seeing you every day."

"No, it's not that," Xuan countered. "If I'm working for you, then it's not advisable to be dating you, too. That never works."

"I don't know, Xuan, I might not like sunrises," he smiled, "and you might not like me that early in the morning. I'll probably just sit there like moss on a log, so we won't have to worry about dating after a few hours of that."

She looked at him and laughed back. "Maybe so. But if you talk too much, you'll just spoil the sunrise, anyway." Xuan reflected some more and then, her mind made up, she said, "Mr. Layne gave me a week to decide, so let's just go out Sunday, and we'll see if there are any sparks between you and me. Then I'll decide on the job offer next week. Does that sound okay to you?"

Thomas nodded his head in the affirmative.

Xuan smiled and admitted to herself that the sparks were already flying—at least they were for her.

Chapter 10

Moving In

Thomas had just arrived at the office Thursday when he heard Layne come in for their nine o'clock conversation. Anna already had the coffee percolating, and Digger was in his office researching the ancient tower clue on the Internet.

"Good morning, everyone!" Thomas heard Layne exclaim in the outer office. "Where do I find the coffee around here?"

Anna pointed down the hall and said, "In the coffee room—last door on the right, Mr. Layne." She started to get up from her chair and asked, "Do you want me to get it for you?"

"No, but thanks just the same. My lovely departed wife taught me how to make and get my own coffee, so I don't mind one bit." He headed down the hall and offered a "good morning" to Digger as he passed his office door.

"Hi, Mr. Layne. Did you find a place to rent?" Digger inquired.

"Well, I've narrowed it down to two possibilities, and I'm supposed to meet someone at eleven to make the choice and finalize the arrangements," Layne answered. "Both places are managed by the same real estate company, so it's just a matter of deciding which unit."

Thomas looked at his watch and noted it was almost nine, so he retrieved the clue file and jotted down the conditions requested by the council at Acoma Pueblo a few evenings before. He briefly remembered the creation of sand art he and Digger had witnessed and wondered again what it might portend. The memory of being in the sacred kiva brought back many good feelings, and he knew somehow that Acoma Pueblo was the right place for this meeting in June. He sensed that Jack and his people felt the rightness of it, too.

Russell Layne came back down the hall with his cup of hot coffee and signaled Anna and Digger to join him as he entered Thomas's office. Digger stopped halfway in the door and went back to his office to get the fourth chair they would need. In a minute, all of them were present, and Thomas looked at Layne expectantly.

"Oh, did I call this meeting?" Layne joked.

Everyone laughed, and Layne proceeded.

"I just want to have a more specific discussion on the clues to understand the progress you're making on them. But first, I want to say that I'm ecstatic about finding the transcriber and getting the Acoma Pueblo council to allow the meeting on their sacred land. Those are essential accomplishments for us. So, Thomas, tell me where we stand on those pesky clues, will you?"

"We don't have any specific names, yet, if that's what you're wondering, but I think we've figured out a few things."

"Like what?" Layne asked.

"We've decided that researching the clues is really a good way to get all of us more involved. In fact, Anna and Digger and I have all been working on them together for the last few days. I've come to think that it's more about our involvement than it is about just exactly who the clues are meant to describe."

Anna said, "Or it might be that we need to become more deeply involved before we can figure out the names or be open to the revelation of who they are."

"Yes," Thomas concurred, "we've decided that's the main purpose of the clues, at least right now. We've figured out that the first clue has to do with a Hindu person, and the second clue seems to involve a Jewish person and a tower of some kind, like the Tower of Babel. The third clue is about Sufis or Muslims, and we think the fourth clue has Asian or Buddhist roots." Thomas paused for a moment and then continued. "The fifth clue is Native American."

"That's right," Digger said as he looked at Layne. "Jack confirmed that the clue about rocks on Sacred Mountain is Navajo and may even date back a thousand years or more. By the way, Jack also suggested that these clues may be insights about worldviews rather than clues about specific people."

Thomas watched as Layne digested this information and saw him lean back in his chair. He stroked his chin a few times as he seemed to reflect on what he was hearing from the three of them.

"Okay," Thomas went on. "The sixth clue is about science. We think science has become a bit of a religion, too, and that's why it's in here with the others."

"Or it might just represent the scientific point of view," Digger added.

"But the seventh clue really got us thinking," Anna broke in. She switched her notepad over to her other knee as she jotted a few notes about what was being said. "It's about teachers who open the door to understanding, but once the door is opened, it further suggests that each student must walk through the door themselves."

Thomas said, "Bottom line, we understood it to mean that we have to get more involved with the intent or spirit behind this meeting."

"Okay. So is it all about intent, then?" Layne asked. His smile got a little larger every time one of the others made a comment about becoming more involved and getting caught up in the mystery of what they were doing. He was growing more sure every day that he had assembled the right players for this endeavor that he was funding and directing.

"I think so," Anna responded. As she leaned forward, her notepad fell to the floor, and she bent to pick it up before she continued. "I feel like these clues are taking on a life of their own, and if we delve into them with all the energy we can muster, they will continue to reveal even more. It's like they will just take us along for the ride. I think there's a lot more to discover in each one of them."

"I think she's right" Digger said as he ran his fingers through his hair. "These clues are like an archaeology dig, except that our tools are words and concepts. It feels like we are unearthing wisdom, if that's even possible. Every clue or even each part of a clue has a dozen more insights and discoveries just waiting to be uncovered or brought out into the light."

"But we have to somehow be able to truly see them," Anna added. "We have to really open our eyes and maybe our minds."

Layne asked, "So, what if it requires more than open eyes and minds?"

"Like using our imagination, too?" Anna theorized. "Or our hearts, maybe."

"Seeing with imagination, huh? Now, that's bound to increase the possibilities," Layne said. "If we don't perceive with imagination, we're just looking at things in the same way we've always looked at them."

Thomas reentered the discussion by swiveling back around in his chair, where he had been absent mindedly gazing out the window as he listened to the discussion. "And looking at things the same way is repetitive," he said. "It's like continuing to wear the blinders of habit and tradition and even ignorance."

"And that blindness means that we'll never get to the bottom of these clues if we don't perceive them with imagination," Digger said.

Layne suggested, "We can just call it 'imagiception,' if you want."

"Or 'perceptgination,'" Digger countered.

"Are we trying to find a one-word mission statement or something?" Thomas asked.

"Well, a mission statement is not a bad idea," Layne said. "Every collective enterprise needs to adopt a mission statement just to help keep everyone on task."

"If we get to vote on it, I like imagiception," Digger added.

"Not me," Anna argued. "I like perceptgination."

"Either one works for me," Layne said.

"They're both pretty easy and uncomplicated," Thomas concluded. "If I can adjust my thinking on these clues to include some imagination, maybe they'll get less frustrating for me."

"I think it's more than that, Thomas," Layne said as he leaned forward in his chair. "I think imagiception or perceptgination—or whatever we decide to name it—is crucial to this entire endeavor. In fact, I think it's absolutely critical."

"Well, perhaps you're right," Thomas admitted. "Maybe we could discuss the clues again right now, the four of us, and see if we can apply some imaginception to the thought processes surrounding them. I mean, I feel a little better about them already, but we're a long ways from knowing who these people are and how we're going to get them to Acoma."

"True," Layne replied. "I see that, too, but let's focus on what we do know and not what we don't know. We have a Muslim, a Jew, a Hindu, a Pantheist, a Buddhist, a scientist, and, what, a teacher? Is that right?" He looked at Anna.

She nodded her head as she checked her notes. "That's right," Anna confirmed, "but it seems like we're missing a Catholic or a Christian."

"That's an interesting observation, Anna," Layne said. "The clue reads that the teacher opens the door, but the students must pass through themselves. Right? And did you guys come up with a specific worldview that could be associated with that clue?"

"No," Anna answered. "Do you think it could be Catholic or Christian?"

"I don't know," Layne answered. "The highest expression of most religions is spiritual practice. Simply believing is not enough though it suits a lot of people. First, it takes learning, then participation, then regular practice. A teacher shows the way, and the student must set out on the path. Believing is not enough."

Digger reminded them, "But the Bible says, 'Whoever believes in me shall have eternal life.'"

"He's right," Anna affirmed.

"But this clue doesn't talk about beliefs," Digger said. "I took it to mean the teacher opens a new door or another door. The major worldviews all seem to believe that their old doors, doors that seem more closed than open, are the only right beliefs available. This clue says to me that just believing in the old doors is not enough anymore. There are new doors to be walked through, too."

"Hmm," Layne said. "I see what you're saying. Maybe it's not a Christian or Catholic clue. I'll ask the old priest in Santa Fe to see if he can amplify what you guys have developed. He's the one who gave us these clues in the first place, and he may have a different take on them. Besides, he's Catholic."

"So what do we have, then?" Thomas asked suddenly. "We've decided that all the so-called major religions are sending someone to this meeting?"

"It sure looks that way, doesn't it?" Layne answered. "If so, what you guys have figured out from these clues so far has a lot of fascinating potential!"

"Where does that lead us?" Digger asked.

"What we may have is this," Layne answered. "If every religion is represented at the meeting, and out of this meeting there comes an agreed-upon understanding or set of guiding principles for the next two thousand years, it could be huge!"

"Yes," Anna chimed in. "Every religion would put the weight of their influence behind it, like an endorsement, and then it would eventually get spread around to the entire world."

"Right! And the followers of those major religions could perhaps be persuaded by leaders they already trust to consider and embrace an adjustment to their worldview," Digger imagined.

"No, wait! Slow down," Thomas reasoned. "Our job is to arrange the meeting. After that, we let nature take its course. Thinking about where it might lead after the meeting is just rank speculation, that's all."

"I disagree," Digger countered. "We are not speculating. We are imagining. There's a big difference, Thomas. At least there is for me. Our mission is imagiception, isn't it? Didn't we just agree on that?"

"Okay, okay," Thomas muttered, "but we shouldn't let ourselves get carried away. We still don't know who these people are, or who the master soul is, or what sort of insight they may provide the world. In my opinion, it's too early to even imagine it." Thomas took a deep breath, calmed himself a little, and looked at Layne. Even though he felt himself opening up a bit to this exercise, he knew changes in his way of perceiving would not take place all at once.

"You know what? This kind of discussion is great!" Layne remarked. "Maybe we should get carried away. I love the intensity that I feel in these discussions with you guys. Working here is certainly going to be fun for me!"

With that, he glanced at his watch. He had to sign a rental agreement before the flight back to New York, so he stood up to leave. "Thomas," he said, "let me know if you need any help with the details on hiring Malik or Xuan. I think they're both going to be joining us for the stretch run to June."

He turned to Anna. "Do we have enough offices for them and for me?"

"Yessir," she smiled at the question. "We've got three open offices right now."

"Okay," he said. "Save one for me, and I'll see all of you in a week or two—that is, if I can wait that long. This is really gonna be great!"

Chapter 11

The Blind Boy

Xuan tossed and turned all night in her bed the night before the interview with Malik M. Mohammed. She couldn't switch off her thoughts about him, Thomas, Project 4000, and Russell Layne.

Ultimately, she understood that her restlessness wasn't just about any of these things, not really. Her restlessness was about her. She sensed that her life was about to change in ways that could not be reversed. She couldn't put her finger on it yet, but that was the sense she got. She didn't feel anxious, per se, or nervous, but she was agitated and edgy. Maybe it was excitement, or something akin to that, but her usual diversions around the house weren't taking her mind off all of this other stuff. Her favorite television shows weren't holding her attention for very long. The plants packed into every nook and cranny of the kitchen area and its south-facing bay window were wilted and in need of trimming. She was feeding her cats and tropical fish, but then ignoring them. She realized she was probably a little nervous about interviewing a blind person; especially one who didn't talk, but she also knew it was more than that—much more than that.

Once she arrived at her office the next morning, she went over Malik's application again and reviewed the information card from his teacher at the institute. Xuan figured Susan would be at the interview, too, so she jotted down a few questions for her and called Thomas to see if he had any others. He wasn't much help, but his flirtatious comments about their sunrise date coming up on Sunday relaxed her a little as Susan and Malik were shown into her office.

Susan led the blind boy to one of the chairs directly in front of Xuan's desk, a neat and well-kept white melamine office desk. All her active papers were on the credenza behind her along with her personal computer, so all Xuan had on the desk was a small framed picture of her parents, a bigger picture of her three cats, and the single sheet of paper that held the list of questions she planned to ask.

"Hi, Susan. Hi, Malik." She looked at Malik and was reminded how young he really was. Absent his hoodie, she could more easily see his rounded face, unkempt hair, and sketchy attempt at a beard. She was still concerned that his youthfulness might prove to be a problem when things got tough, but she dismissed the concern for a moment and addressed him directly.

"You wrote the best papers of anyone who has taken our tests, Malik. That includes about 140 people, so congratulations! My client was quite impressed and wants to hire you for some work if you are still interested."

Malik just nodded his head and smiled.

"Okay. Good. My client is also willing to provide you with any resources you might need in your office in consideration of your blindness, but first I should tell you a little of what will be expected of you." Xuan looked at Susan and continued, "Please interrupt me if you have any questions."

Xuan then watched as Malik reached into his shirt pocket and pulled out a small notepad and pencil. She watched him feel around with his hands in front of where he sat until he found the edge of Xuan's desk. When he did, he laid his pencil and paper where he could reach them and sat back again in his chair. Xuan watched with interest as she kept speaking.

"Your primary job will be to make a record of a seven-day meeting that will be held in late June of next year. There will be seven or eight people in the meeting, and their discussions may go on all day and most of the night for the entire seven days. There will be no other recording devices of any kind at the meeting, so your written records will be the one and only record of the meeting when it is over."

She paused and asked Malik, "Are there any questions so far?"

Malik shook his head, so Xuan continued.

"You'll also be expected to help on other assignments during the next six months leading up to the meeting, and you'll have to be at the Project 4000 offices at least four days a week. You may be doing some research and taking notes at the meetings in the office and other things like that. It's quite possible that your records will eventually be published, and, if that turns out to be the case, you will be paid additional monies to edit and clarify your notes for as long as that may take you after the meeting is concluded."

As soon as Xuan finished her last comment, Susan asked, "Xuan, will there be time to eat or sleep during those seven days of meetings?"

"Yes, all of that will be taken care of, though I don't yet know the details," Xuan replied. "The meeting will take place at Acoma Pueblo—about fifty miles west of here—and the people at Project 4000 have not yet finalized all the details with their hosts, the Pueblo Indians of Acoma."

Just then, Malik began to scribble something on his notepad and handed it in Susan's direction.

Susan read the note and then asked him, "You've been there?"

He nodded and then scribbled a second note and handed it to her, as well.

"Malik writes that he was there with his dad a few months before the accident," Susan said.

"How well do you remember it?" Xuan asked him.

He quickly scribbled a note that said, "Pretty well," and handed it in Susan's direction again. Once Susan took it and held it up for Xuan to see, he began a second short note and extended it in Xuan's direction.

She noted this with interest as she took it and then held it up for Susan to see as well.

"Have you been there?" Susan asked Xuan.

"No, I've not been there yet," Xuan admitted, "but I hear it is pretty spectacular."

Malik smiled and nodded.

Xuan continued, "The next matter concerns logistics, like getting to work on time and arranging transportation. The Project 4000 offices are in Northwest Albuquerque off Coors Road."

"Getting people to where they need to be is one of our functions at the institute," Susan explained. "If the folks at Project 4000 will tell us when to have him there, we'll get him there on time every day. Coors Road is only a few miles from the institute."

"That's good," Xuan said. She had never worked with the seeing impaired and was relieved to know of the support available in this case. "When can you start, Malik?"

Malik wrote something quickly and handed it toward Xuan again.

It was just one word, "Now," and she read it from a distance before it was even in her hand.

"Okay," said Xuan, smiling at his eagerness. "Is this your first job?"

Malik nodded, but Xuan noticed the even more revealing ear-to-ear grin on his face. She liked his smile and was glad to see the enthusiasm it conveyed.

"I'll try to get your interview with Thomas Walls as soon as possible. How would next Tuesday work?"

"Tuesday afternoon at four o'clock would be fine," Susan answered.

"Okay. Good. I'll call Mr. Walls and make the arrangements. Unless you hear otherwise from me, I'll see you both at their office on Tuesday at four o'clock." They got up to leave, and Xuan stood up and handed Susan directions to the Project 4000 offices.

She shook Susan's hand and then noticed that Malik had extended his hand in the direction of her voice. Xuan smiled, took his hand, and shook it warmly. "Thank you both. I'll see you Tuesday."

"Thank you, Xuan," Susan replied, "from both of us."

As they left, Xuan returned to her chair. When she heard the door close behind them, she sat down and breathed a big sigh of relief. She hadn't realized until now how tired and tense she was from a long week and too many sleepless nights. She rubbed the back of her neck with her right hand and tried to relax it. She looked out her window and watched as Susan and Malik slowly made their way through the parking lot. She knew she would sleep well tonight, if only from fatigue, and she took just a moment to entertain a dream about sunrise with Thomas on Sunday.

Chapter 12

Sunrise at Sandia Crest

Thomas and Xuan huddled against the predawn cold atop Sandia Crest, some 8,500 feet above sea level in the mountains east of Albuquerque. The wind was calm as they sat on a wooden bench, with views in every direction.

"Thomas, how do we open people up to the possibility that their religion may have some of the answers but not all of the answers? A closed mind seems to go hand in hand with religious beliefs." Xuan's words broke a ten-minute silence.

Thomas sat quietly and sipped on his fifth cup of coffee. He was just trying to wake himself up into something that resembled social interaction. *Never mind friendly*, he thought, *conversant would suffice*. The sun was still partly hidden behind thin clouds on the eastern edge of the world. The sketchy shadows were shortening just a little, and it was almost full light—but this sunrise sky was less about light and more about red and pink and orange.

"I don't know," Thomas started. "I think my mind is closed from being up too early, but opening up a mind isn't a very easy thing to do, even when it's fully awake. In my case, not even five cups of coffee is working very well." He stirred his coffee a little, recrossed his stiffened legs, and continued. "Maybe no one knows how to open up a closed mind, but one of the testing exams was about how human beings, all human beings, perceive the world. It's titled 'The Six Percent Rule,' I think. Did you read it?"

"I read it, but I don't remember it being about open-mindedness. Besides, I read it from the viewpoint of accuracy in writing, not in terms of content," Xuan admitted.

"Well, it's not really about open-mindedness, per se, but I read it last weekend, and it made a lot of sense to me," Thomas said.

"Tell me about it." She requested as she moved closer to him.

He felt her wiggle around for a moment, trying to get comfortable on the hard wooden bench. He looked toward the sunrise. The light played on the craggy peaks to the south of them, and he noticed the piñon pines moving gently in the morning breeze. Some of the clouds were still crimson and pink near the horizon, but now that the sun was freed of their cover, it danced and sparkled in the snow at their feet. Thomas placed his arm around Xuan's shoulder and drew her close. It felt natural to him as she leaned into his embrace.

"It's really pretty simple, I guess," he began. "First, the author talks about the five senses—you know, sight, smell, hearing, touch, and taste. He writes that we don't see very well—certainly not everything that is out there. Our distance vision is limited, and darkness inhibits our sight, too. He asserts that we don't smell all the smells, either. We're not as tuned into that sense as dogs or cats or almost any of the rest of the animals. We don't hear sounds in the lower and higher registers, so we're missing quite a bit of sound input. He claims that our touch is not very well developed, and neither is our sense of taste. So, of all the possible data we could be picking up through our sensory perception, he says we're maybe picking up about 40 or 50 percent of it, maybe less." Thomas stole a glance at Xuan to make sure she was still listening. It looked like she was.

"Okay," she said. "I'm following you so far. We only take in about half the data we could."

"Right," Thomas replied, "and after we take in this data, or about half of it anyway, we are then charged with processing it and understanding it in our minds. It is pretty much commonly accepted that we only use about 10 to 15 percent of our minds."

"That's on a good day," Xuan interrupted with a laugh, "at least for me."

"Yeah, I read somewhere that Einstein might have used as much as twenty percent of his brain," Thomas admitted. "In any case," he continued, "if we receive about 40 percent of the data and then process it on a brain that only works at about 15 percent maximum, then most human beings are only able to fully process about 6 percent of our world."

Xuan sat up. "Wait a minute, you lost me," she interjected. "Where did you get the 6 percent?"

"Well, 40 percent of the data times 15 percent of the brain utilization, and you get 6 percent," Thomas explained.

"So what is this writer saying," Xuan asked again, "that we're able to understand just 6 percent of what is to be understood and missing 94 percent?"

"Yes, I think so," Thomas responded. "We don't see it all, hear it all, smell it all, touch it all, or taste it all. Based on that, how do people then make the claim that they know it all, understand it all, perceive the whole truth, or think they are more right than anyone else? Either we don't receive most of the information

because our senses are limited, or we don't process the information very completely because our brains aren't utilized to their full capacity."

"So, we're missing more than 90 percent of reality?" Xuan asked one more
time.

"Sounds like it to me," Thomas affirmed. "We're a long ways from knowing all
of it, that's for certain."

Xuan straightened up from her seat on the bench with a look of disbelief.
From the edge of the bench she continued, "Thomas, that's incredible! If we truly
understand only 6 or 7 or even 8 percent of our world, then we're virtually blind
to what is really going on and what is really true. We're not just missing some of
it. We're missing almost all of it."

"Yeah, and it makes me wonder how much I've been missing for the forty years
I've been alive," Thomas added.

"It makes me wonder how much of what I think I know is really true."

"And maybe that's where open-mindedness comes in. A humble mind is usually fertile ground for an open mind—a teachable mind," Thomas said. "How can
anyone think they have all the answers if they don't have even half the data?"

Xuan stood up and walked a few steps out into the snow and then turned to
face Thomas again. The look of stunned disbelief was still on her face. Though she
appeared to want to talk and started to speak, nothing came out of her mouth.

Thomas watched for a minute or longer and stayed quiet himself. Then he
could wait no longer.

"What, Xuan?" Thomas looked at her and could see her still searching for the
right words. "Just say what it is you want to say." He sat up straight and waited
for more.

"Thomas," she hesitated. "You don't know me very well yet, but I am really
into my intellect. I'm one of those people who are absolutely convinced that I can
reason my way through anything. I think I can sort out the mysteries of life right
here in my mind. I've always been confident that if I think about it long enough,
the answers will come to me. This writer, however, is saying that my intellect cannot be the only basis of my understanding. When I think about it, that assertion
is scary to me."

"Yes, it's a humbling realization, isn't it?" Thomas agreed. "Maybe that explains
why I'm such a wanderer. I can't figure it out with my limited-use brain, so I just
muddle through in a state of abject ignorance."

"Or simple apathy, I suppose," Xuan added. Then she thought some more and
said with exasperation, "But it's more than that, too, a lot more. This realization is
an indictment of all those people who think they have all the religious answers—

that they have it all figured out beyond any doubt. Just think of all those people you've met or read who act as if they know the only truth."

"Okay, I've got them pictured in my mind. It's everyone with a religion or a belief system to defend or promote," Thomas chimed in.

"That's them," Xuan said. "Then these people take their limited understanding and call it a universal truth or parade it around as the 'only truth,' or the 'real truth.' They try to foist it on others and put it on television and dismiss those who see it differently or disagree. Then they fight wars over their little truth or shun people or sever family ties and quit speaking to each other. They even kill for it. My goodness, Thomas, we human beings actually fight over our collective blindness, as if pretending we're not blind will somehow cover it up or hide it from everyone else."

Xuan's agitation had turned into pacing back and forth in the snow in front of their bench. Thomas watched her trample the snow and heard it crunch beneath her boots as she walked over it dozens and dozens of times. Her face continued to have a look of dismay on it, and Thomas guessed that she was beginning to realize the depth of the collective misunderstanding and the millions of ill-conceived actions that had been taken in the name of right or truth.

"You know, Thomas, this is approaching worldwide madness!" she exclaimed. "Mr. Layne and that priest could well be right. It's dangerous! The Irish Catholics are ready to kill for it. The Christians are ready to kill for it. The Muslims are ready to die for it. The Jews are ready, too. The whole world is ready to kill for their little portion of the truth."

"Yes, and it's a pretty darned little portion," Thomas added.

"At the very least," Xuan continued, "they attack the others with words and then weapons because they think their truth is better, or correct, or even universal, for crying out loud!"

The tension that Xuan had generated over this was too much for Thomas this early in the morning. He poured a sixth cup of coffee, took a sip, and joked, "Well, look at it this way, Xuan, maybe one of those enlightened religious groups can get a hold of some nuclear weaponry, and then the fun can really begin."

"That's not the least bit funny, Thomas," she retorted.

He felt another rise in her intensity

She kept talking in that agitated tone of voice. "There is no tyrant worse than a tyrant who has convinced himself and his people that he has the power of God or truth or Allah or the universe behind him. The history books are littered with stories of these tyrants, and the modern religious landscape has no shortage of them, either."

"You're right. It's not funny," Thomas admitted. "It's not that these people don't have a portion of the truth, perhaps, it's just that no one has the whole truth. Layne is right—it has gone seriously astray, and everyone needs to get realigned before it gets worse."

Xuan was still pacing in the snow. "Thomas, I want to accept Mr. Layne's offer of a job. The prospect of this adventure has obviously touched a nerve in me. I haven't been this worked up over something in a long, long time." She looked at him as she asked, "Is that okay with you?"

Thomas thought about the question. He now knew for certain that he wanted a personal relationship with this excitable woman. He liked everything about her. He also knew that office romances were usually ill advised. He wasn't sure how to answer.

"Thomas?" Xuan sat down next to him again.

He felt her searching his face for an answer. He knew she must like him, at least a little bit, and he felt a twinge of regret that their peaceful sunrise experience had turned into such an intense discussion on the follies of religious chauvinism.

"Thomas?"

"I don't know, Xuan," he finally answered. "You'd be a tremendous asset to the project, but, selfishly, I want to explore something personal with you, too. I'm not sure how to do that if we're co-workers."

Xuan, her hands still thrust in her coat pockets, leaned against the back of the bench and looked away from Thomas toward the vista below. Thomas caught her eye as she stole a glance back in his direction. She turned to look at him directly.

"I know the rule about office dating, too," she said, "and yet, suddenly, everything I know or think no longer carries much weight. Maybe it's time we didn't pay so much attention to what we think about dating on the job and just allow things to happen. Besides, the job is over in six or seven months. It's not like we're jeopardizing long-term careers. What's Layne going to do, fire us?"

Finally, Thomas turned to face her directly, too, and reached for her hand. "I'll try it if you will. It's going to be an intense six months, but I've been numb for so long that a big shot of intensity and adrenaline may be just what the doctor ordered. If nothing else, it may be what I need."

Xuan looked back at Thomas, and he felt from her an intensity that seemed to match his own.

"Good," she said. "It's probably what I need, too. More than that, Thomas, it's what I want."

He looked into her eyes and stood as he pulled her up by the hand. "If you're ready, then so am I."

Chapter 13

The Pace Quickens

Thursday, December 21st dawned cold and dry in the city of Albuquerque. Digger was in his office when Jack Eaglefeather reached him on his cell phone. It was their first conversation since the meeting at the sacred kiva the week before, but every time Digger thought of the experience, it brought a smile to his face and he reveled in the memory of it.

"Hello, Jack, how are you?" he asked.

"Just fine," Jack responded. "I've come up with another source for you on the clue you asked me about last week at the kiva."

"Wonderful!" Digger said. "I can look it up on the Web. What is it?"

"Well, no. It's not that kind of source. I'm not sure why the thought of her came to me, but I think you may want to meet this woman from the Jemez Pueblo. She is a keeper woman, and her medicine is very strong," Jack explained.

"Can you arrange a meeting for me or introduce her?" Digger asked. "I'll drive over to Jemez if you think it'd be okay."

"I don't think we can set it up that way, either," Jack answered. "She doesn't work by appointment. These keepers just kind of show up when they feel it is right to do so. I'm told she is coming to Acoma Pueblo on Thursday or Friday. That's all I've heard."

Jack sounded a bit elusive, but Digger didn't think pushing him would do any good.

As Digger hesitated, Jack broke in with a question. "Will I be allowed to attend your meetings?"

"Oh, right. I'm glad you asked," Digger responded. "Yes, we will be honored to have you participate in our meetings as often as you can. Right now, they are planned for once every two weeks, but it is my guess they'll eventually be once a week and maybe even more frequent than that."

"Good," Jack replied. "Just let me know the schedule, or leave a message for me at the Visitor Center and an e-mail on my computer. I'll attend as many as I can."

"Okay, and you'll let me know more about talking to the keeper woman from Jemez Pueblo?" Digger reminded him.

"Yes, I'll call you when and if I find out exactly when she is coming," Jack promised.

After he hung up the phone, Digger mulled the conversation over in his mind and wondered if he should just go to Acoma on Thursday morning and be there to meet this woman, no matter when she showed up. From what Jack had said, he knew that these uniquely gifted people usually traveled on impulse rather than schedule. If he wasn't there when she chose to be there, he might miss her. He didn't want that to happen.

~   ~   ~

In his office nearby, Thomas checked his calendar and was reminded of his four o'clock interview with Xuan, Malik, and Susan. Xuan had mentioned her concern about working with Malik when there was no one to help him, so Thomas promised himself that he would, at some point, make sure he and Malik could communicate well enough to serve the purposes of the Project.

He also thought about the best way to conduct an interview with Xuan for the job Layne had already offered her. It was just a formality, really, so he began to think of ways he could make it fun for both of them. He wondered if a dinner interview would be suitable. The idea appealed to him—and would allow him to put it on the company expense account, too.

As he sat at his desk thinking these things over, Anna entered his office.

"I really don't know where to begin to solve the science clue," she blurted out. "Do you have any suggestions for me?" She sat down in front of Thomas's desk.

"Well, let's see, Anna," Thomas began. "Why don't you try these three ideas: first, try a search engine with some keywords that include science and/or spirit and see what you find. Second, select a few of them and e-mail them with a concise explanation of what we're looking for. I'll help you draft the e-mail if you want me to, and you can copy it to all of them. Third, check with some of the scientists who are exploring the cutting-edge stuff, like the mind-body connection stuff or the spirit-psychology stuff. See if there is someone in that group of people that we might want to talk to." Thomas paused and then asked Anna, "Does that help, at least a little?"

"Yes, I think so. However, I want you to know how much I dislike science," she reminded him.

"Your dislike is noted, but this isn't chemistry- or biology-type science, Anna. This is more universal mysteries—type science. Maybe you can just treat it like one of those detective stories you like so much. It's just a different kind of mystery, that's all. In fact, we've been getting kind of lucky lately; maybe you'll figure something out quickly and it won't be painful at all."

"We can always hope," she answered as she rose from her chair.

Just then, the phone rang, so Anna went out to get it and then stuck her head back in the office door. "It's Xuan on line one."

Thomas picked up the phone. "Hi, Xuan, are we still on for four o'clock?"

"Yes, as far as I know," she replied. "There's something else, too. My boss e-mailed and let me know that I have been granted a leave of absence from my job at the agency. I have to be back on July first, but for the next six months, you are paying my salary."

"Well, Mr. Layne is," Thomas corrected her. "When can you start?"

"Effective January first, I'm all yours," she said. "Of course, that still depends on the compensation package you're offering."

Thomas couldn't see her smile through the phone but sensed she was teasing, so he teased her back. "We all make minimum wage around here, Xuan. Will that be enough?"

"Forget it, mister," she laughed. "I'll stay right where I am now, thank you just the same."

Thomas joined in her laughter. "Actually," he suggested, "I had this devilishly good idea to interview you over dinner tonight at that French restaurant on Thirty-Third Street. We can talk job details then, if you want."

"Oh, okay. I'll need to change clothes before I can go anywhere ritzy like that, but it does sound like a good idea," she agreed. "You want me to bring my résumé?"

"That would be appropriate," Thomas said and, without missing a beat, "and bring three letters of reference, will you?"

"In your dreams, big guy," Xuan laughed. "Listen, my next appointment is here, so I'll see you at four."

"Okay, see you then." Thomas hung up the phone. He clenched his fists and raised them over his head in celebration. He pushed away from the desk and spun around in his chair just for fun. He couldn't contain his excitement but calmed himself a little as Anna walked past his door, got a quizzical look on her face, retraced her steps, and looked again. He tried to look normal, but his cheeks puffed out and he couldn't stifle a laugh.

When Anna had gone on down the hallway, Thomas wondered if she guessed something was up. He smiled to himself and thought, *Well, that's okay. Something is up.*

~   ~   ~

As three o'clock approached, Thomas decided to close his office door and ruminate on clue number three: "The mysteries of Mohammed are not known but by a few who dance with him." He surmised, of course, that this was a reference to Sufis—often better known as Whirling Dervishes. Most people thought of them as the mystical branch of Islam. Over the previous weekend, Thomas had searched the boxes of books at his nearly vacant house and found two books from college: one a book on Sufi wisdom and the other an anthology of Sufi teaching stories and parables. He had read the second one, or most of it, on Sunday night and had brought it with him to work. He picked it up again while sitting in his office and began leafing though it, hoping to find some inspiration on how to proceed with his clue.

He figured that Sufis were still around, but he didn't know of any. Historically, he knew there were numerous orders of them in the Near and Middle East, but he was also fascinated to discover that there were several teaching stories about Jesus or Issa in the Sufi oral traditions that had not yet made it into the popular literature.

Anna came into his office while he was reading, and he engaged her in conversation about what he was learning.

"Do you know anything about Sufism or Islam, Anna?"

"No, not really," she admitted. "I heard once that their stories formed the basis for a lot of the Grimm brothers' fairy tales, but that's about all I know."

"Well, I didn't know that," Thomas replied, "but reading these teaching stories again has made me realize some of the major contributions Sufis have made to the world as we know it today. They were chemists and poets and philosophers and teachers and storytellers."

"Oh, I guess I've heard of Rumi. Was Kahlil Gibran a Sufi, too?" she inquired.

"This book I brought from home has teachings stories from Jalaludin and Ibrahim Khawwas and Mulla Nasrudin, but no Gibran." He held it up for her to see. "You know," he muttered, "maybe my clue is like your Einstein clue. Maybe these ancient Sufis will lead us to some modern person who's coming to the meeting."

"If it's Jesus, then I'm interested," Anna said. "I'm not too interested in scientists, poets, or people I've never heard of before."

"Yeah, it's a lot easier if we can stay in our comfort zone, isn't it?"

"Is it a comfort zone thing?" Anna asked, "Or is it that we're so convinced that what we already know is right that other stuff holds no interest for us?"

"I don't know, really, but as the world changes, it seems that what we know has to change with it. If we don't open our mind and grow in understanding, there is no way we can keep up. Opening up to new understandings may be the only way to keep up." Thomas finished.

"I suppose I shouldn't be so opposed to change, then. Is that what you're saying, Boss?" She got up to leave.

But Thomas had one more thing to say. "Maybe so, Anna. I think all of us will be forced to change a lot over the next six months."

Thomas went back to his musings, and it was ten till four when Xuan knocked lightly on his office door and Thomas looked up. Seeing her brought a smile to his face. All at once, he remembered their meeting with Malik, looked at his watch, and heard Anna pick up the ringing telephone in her office. He signaled to Xuan to come in while he rose from his desk chair to greet her. When she was inside his office, he quietly closed his door behind her so they could have a moment of privacy.

"So you think you want a job here, do you?" he opened.

She had wandered over to the window and now turned back and began walking toward him. She looked right into his eyes. She answered his lighthearted question with a hint of a smile on her face. "I do," she started, "but truthfully, I think I'm a little more interested in you than I am in the job." She was standing right in front of him now and almost touching him—but not quite.

He smelled her perfume and almost reached for her but stopped himself. She kept her eyes riveted on his, and he felt himself reach to loosen his tie. There was no tie to loosen. He began to perspire just a little. His mouth was suddenly dry, and he tried to swallow and wished for some water.

She inched a little closer, and now she took both her hands and pretended to straighten the lapels on his coat. She picked at an imaginary loose thread as Thomas lightly put his hands on her waist. The look in her eye softened as he bent forward to kiss her upturned face. He drew her into his arms as she let her hands continue up his lapels and around his neck. Their lips touched softly, and her weight fell against him. Their kiss was brief; their embrace was warm and long.

Her hair smelled good to him, and she fit so well within the circle of his arms. They remained that way for a moment, saying nothing as he savored their closeness. Finally, she pulled away gently, and he loosed his embrace. She turned and straightened her dress and flipped her hair back with a brush of her hand as he cleared his throat and walked around to the other side of his desk.

Xuan retrieved her briefcase from under the window and placed it beside one of the chairs. She looked at him one more time and then sat down for business as Anna's voice announced the arrival of Malik and Susan.

Thomas asked Anna to bring in an extra chair when she led them down the hall to his office. He stole one more glance at Xuan and saw her looking back. She winked ever so slightly, and then the door was opened for the interview.

Thomas stood back up to greet Malik and his teacher with a warm smile. Xuan stood and introduced them as Anna brought in the other chair. When everyone was seated, Thomas began the interview.

"First, Malik, let me say that you are an impressive writer. You are to be congratulated on your achievement during the testing." He looked at Susan as Malik smiled at his praise, and then he looked back at Malik. "I know Xuan has told you some of what we're doing here at Project 4000. We think this seven-day meeting that you will record for us is an important meeting—perhaps the most important meeting that has been convened in a long, long time."

Seeing he still had their attention, Thomas continued. "However, the meeting isn't until June, and there is a lot of other work to be completed before then. You will be instrumental in that work, too." Thomas looked at both of them as he spoke and then said, "Susan, your role is important, too, because we need Malik to be here almost every day. Is that a reasonable expectation for us to hold?"

Susan nodded as Malik got out his pad and pen. "We'll have him here at eight o'clock every morning if we can pick him up at 4:30 every afternoon. Will that work?"

"That'll be perfect," Thomas answered. "Malik, you'll also be the only notetaker at our meetings. At the end of every day, I want you to turn your notes over to Anna, and she'll take care of getting them filed. You two will work closely together."

Malik nodded to indicate he understood.

"Good," Thomas continued. "In addition to taking notes at all our meetings, Malik, we may have you do some research, too. How will you accomplish that?" Thomas was curious to see Malik's ability to solve logistical problems.

Malik began immediately to write things down on his pad and soon handed the note to Susan.

"He can research using audio or videotapes or discs from the library or online," Susan verbalized from his note.

"Do you read Braille, Malik?" Thomas asked.

Malik shook his head.

"Are you willing to learn it?" Thomas inquired.

Malik nodded.

"Okay," Thomas answered. "What special equipment do you want or need in your office?"

Malik quickly scribbled some words and this time handed the note in Thomas's direction.

Thomas leaned forward across his oak desk to get it and read the words "television, DVD player, CD player, audio cassette, PC, and Braille machine." He was glad Malik handed the list to him and not his teacher and liked the fact that Malik reinforced his willingness to learn Braille by including the device on his list.

"Let's see. We better add a VCR, too, for use with older video formats." He glanced at his own notes and then posed a question to Susan and Xuan. "Are there any wage figures I need to factor in with respect to the institute, or can I feel free to offer what is in the budget Mr. Layne gave us?"

Susan and Xuan glanced at each other, and Susan said, "Federal minimum wage standards are the only applicable rules I know of," she answered. "Our expenses are covered by a government grant."

"The budget calls for ten dollars an hour, but there's no health insurance, and the job will only last six months or so. Will that be agreeable Malik?"

Malik smiled and nodded yes.

"Fine," Thomas said. "I like agreeable employees. When we get to the meeting in June, we'll pay overtime for your work after forty hours per week, and we'll pay double time over sixty hours a week. Does that sound fair to everyone?" He looked at Susan as he finished this question, because he figured her to be the one who might object.

Malik nodded yes, and so did she.

"Lastly," Thomas said as he prepared to end the interview, "there is a good chance your records will be published in some form or another, and you may be needed for a few months after the meeting wraps up in late June. If that happens, your job may be extended, and you'll be compensated for that time period, as well. Now, do you have any questions of me?"

Malik nodded and began writing his questions on the small pad he always carried with him. When he finished, there were four questions. He handed them toward Thomas, who read them all before answering.

"No, I haven't worked with a blind person before, Malik, but I look forward to it. I have great confidence in your abilities, so I'm not too concerned about it."

He reread the next question. "No we're not a big company. There are just four of us right now, but we'll likely have a total of six or seven once we roll into January. I think you'll end up with an office of your own, too."

He continued down the list. "Let's see, do we have a kitchen? Yes, we do, and it has a microwave, refrigerator, and coffeemaker." He then read the last question aloud, "'When do I start?'" Thomas thought about it for a minute and flipped his calendar over to January. "Let's start right after the new year, so that would be January fourth at eight o'clock. Is that okay with everyone?"

Malik turned in the direction of his teacher from the institute, as if to make sure he hadn't forgotten anything.

"Mr. Walls," she shifted in her chair as she spoke, "one of my jobs is to protect Malik, and I am concerned about that week of the meeting. It sounds like a rather grueling schedule, don't you think?"

"Yes, it does, Susan," Thomas answered. "I'm concerned a little bit, too, and frankly, we don't yet know as many details as we'd like. As it gets closer and more defined, however, I will personally keep both of you informed of everything we learn about the schedule. That's about all I can promise at this time to assuage your fears." He turned to Xuan and asked her, "Do you have anything you'd like to add?"

"No, I don't," Xuan replied, "except to say that I give you my word, too, Susan, that this looks like it will be an incredible event. By the time it gets here, I don't think anyone will be able to pull themselves away from it long enough to sleep even if they want to."

That seemed to satisfy Susan, at least for the moment.

Thomas got Anna on the intercom and asked her if she had the packet of employment forms for Susan and Malik. She affirmed that she had them ready.

Thomas spoke to his new employee. "Just pick those up as you leave, fill 'em out, and bring them with you on the fourth."

With that, everyone stood up, and Thomas extended his hand to Susan. "Is there anything the institute will need in order to complete this hire?" he asked her.

"No," she answered. "I've already gotten all I need from Xuan."

"Okay. Thank you," he said. "It was nice to meet you."

As he had done with Xuan before, Malik stuck his hand out in Thomas's direction.

As he took it, Thomas said, "Malik, it is a pleasure to meet you, too, and I look forward to having you with us in January."

Malik nodded and smiled, and Thomas noticed his handshake was firm. Susan and Malik left the office, got the necessary papers from Anna and went on their way.

When they had departed, Thomas looked at Xuan. "I wasn't too hard on him, was I?" he asked her.

"Pretty easy, actually," she smiled back. "I'll expect you to be a lot tougher in my interview, because I want a lot more money than you gave him."

"Well, can you take notes better than he can?" he answered.

"I've got my own set of skills," Xuan replied, "but they don't include taking notes or transcribing multiple verbal inputs for pay."

"It's a good thing you found someone to do that for us then," Thomas said. "As for your compensation, I never talk money on an empty stomach. Do you want me to pick you up tonight for dinner or take separate cars to the restaurant?"

"I think, Mr. Walls, sir, that I wish to be picked up," she said. "How about seven?" She was standing up now, too, with her briefcase in her hand, and quickly looked at her watch. "I'd better hurry. See you at seven." She exaggerated the swish in her hips as she walked to the door, looked over her shoulder at Thomas, and smiled ever so slightly.

He grinned as she left and began looking forward again to their dinner date just a few hours away.

Chapter 14

The Blind Boy's Dream

After the interview, Susan drove Malik back to the dormitory at the Institute for the Blind. Malik felt the movement of the car and heard the noise of the road. He could tell it was dark as no light was visible to him at all. His blindness didn't allow him to see details or even shapes but he could make out light and dark. He had even figured out how to guess the approximate time of day, at least on sunny days, by first getting someone to point him to the north and then by looking for the brightest spot in his limited field of vision and relating it to north or what he considered to be noon. He was almost always within an hour of the correct time, occasionally closer, and he took pride in this newly developed skill. He hoped to one day have a compass that would allow him to find north without anyone's assistance.

For his twentieth birthday a few weeks earlier, Susan had gotten him a watch that verbally told him the time but he didn't use it much and, when he did use it, it was only after he first tried to figure out the time by himself. He then used the watch to see how closely he had guessed. Doing this exercise was giving him confidence that eventually his blindness would not hold him back from doing anything he wanted. Getting his first job was having the same effect on him. He was determined to never let his blindness become an excuse.

"You know, Malik," Susan started, "there's something mysterious about this new job of yours. I like Xuan and I like Mr. Walls well enough, but there's still something I can't figure out about the whole thing."

Malik thought about what she said but didn't immediately respond. Instead, he chose to reflect on the interview and the independence that would certainly come to him just by having his own money and a job. He didn't really care, at least on some levels, what the job was. He just liked having it, having an income, having a schedule to follow, and having a life away from the dormitory.

He ran his hand through his thick, wavy hair now hanging a few inches beyond the collar of his shirt. He thought maybe he should get it trimmed. He wondered if maybe he needed some new clothes, too.

"*Mysterious?*" he thought to himself as he replayed Susan's word in his mind. Since the first time Xuan had told him about the meeting for which he would be the only witness, something about it had seemed strangely familiar. He couldn't explain why it was familiar but it was.

Then, when Thomas had mentioned it again just a few minutes before, Malik had gotten the same feeling only stronger. He liked the feeling. It seemed to connect to his insatiable yet unexplained drive to write down the words he heard. Maybe it was the way his mom rehearsed his Lebanese dad every night when she was helping him learn English. Maybe writing had finally become his compensation for not being able to speak. Whatever the reason, he knew that this new job and the person he had become were matched like no other thing he had ever known. How unusual, he thought, that a blind boy had been chosen to be a witness to what Thomas called the most important meeting in a long, long time. He pulled out his pad to finally respond to Susan.

"It is all so ironic," he wrote.

She read it and smiled. "Yes it is. I suppose that's a better word than mysterious."

He felt her looking at him and observed a small change in light as they passed under a well-lit freeway bridge. He was feeling contented and was sure that it showed. He felt her touch him lightly on the arm and he returned the gesture in her direction. She took his hand and squeezed it for a moment and they rode the rest of the way home in silence.

When they got back to the dorm, Malik immediately retreated to his room. Susan checked her office for her e-mail and phone messages and nothing needed attention with her eleven other clients. The smell of dinner permeated the small dormitory and she saw Malik come in on the far side of the dining hall as she entered at the opposite side. The television blared at one end of the room as she went toward Malik. She let him know she was near and escorted him into the waiting line. He thrust a handwritten note toward her and she hurriedly tried to read it while they waited to get their dinner. It was a two-page note and written in his usual flawless writing style.

"Susan, I know you're worried," the note began, "but since my interview with Xuan, the dreams I wrote to you about before the writing tests have come back almost every single night. I see myself in a room with six or seven people who are talking in serious and quiet ways. I see myself at a table with a candle or oil lamp and a bowl of ink. There are also several brushes. My head is down and I am painting or writing things on a roll of stiff paper. Sometimes, they quit talking and just sit quietly for a while but I am still writing or painting. I think they are giving me time to catch up because I can't write fast enough."

Susan looked at Malik, the dinner line moved slowly forward and she went back to reading his note. "The people at this meeting are all different. One looks Chinese, another is black. One of them has a turban around his head and another just has a cloth draped over his head and tucked in the collar of his robe. They all wear sandals but the sandals are different. Their languages sound different as well, but they all seem to understand each other and I can understand them, too. They look at me once in a while but I don't know they are smiling except in my dream because my head is down as I write what they say."

Susan neared the end of the note from Malik. "Maybe this meeting, my new job, will be like my dreams. If it is, I already know it will be alright. I like this dream. It doesn't scare me like the nightmares I had after the car wreck. Besides, I like dreaming because I can see again. When I dream, I am no longer blind."

Susan wiped a tear from the corner of her eye and looked at Malik as he stood beside her. She spoke to him quietly. "I like your dreaming, too, Malik. I like it a lot. Maybe this is a special meeting and, who knows, maybe it is connected in some way to your dreams. I don't know. But I do know this, young man, special meeting or not, you are a very courageous and determined person. I am proud to be your teacher. Thank you."

She reached out and squeezed his arm. He thought she was going to hug him and wished that she would. He wished he could see the pride she spoke of in her eyes. He thought of his mom and how she used to hug him and run her fingers through his hair. A new job doesn't replace a mom, he thought to himself, but a new job was the best news he had received in almost two years and he didn't know if he could wait for January fourth or not.

He heard Susan get his cafeteria tray off the stack and place it under his hands. "You know," she said, "whatever your dream turns out to be, we're going to have to take you shopping for clothes. A new job requires new clothes; at least that's what my mom always said."

"*Yes,*" he thought to himself, "*finding out where my dreams will take me requires new clothes and a haircut, too.*" That thought made him smile again.

Chapter 15

Thomas and Xuan

Thomas picked up a newspaper at the corner store near his home and took it inside with him when he arrived at his home. The "For Sale" sign in the yard wasn't attracting much traffic, and most of his belongings were now in Mississippi with the ex-wife and the boys. Thomas was a bachelor in an almost-vacant house. He was pretty sure he wouldn't be showing this place to Xuan. It wasn't very impressive anymore.

A bed and television were still in the spare bedroom he was using. There was one set of towels in the guest bathroom, and there was his recliner; the only piece of furniture now parked in the middle of the otherwise empty living room. The sole remaining indicator of his home ownership was the display of family pictures that ran along the twelve-foot entry wall. He threw the folded paper on the recliner and paused to look at the pictures.

The most numerous pictures, in all shapes and sizes, were the ones of his boys, from infancy to last year's soccer shots. Derreck was the oldest. He was tall and rangy like his mom and more athletic than his younger brother, Jesse, who was stocky and stout like his dad. Thomas wanted to call them, as he did almost every night, but looked at his watch and realized he didn't have enough time to call and still get ready for his date with Xuan. He figured he would wait until tomorrow to call them.

He was about to sit a few minutes in the recliner and relax with the paper when the picture of his father in his full-dress U.S. Army uniform caught his eye. They had lost him in the 1991 Gulf War, and even though he had been dead some eighteen years, Thomas still wished he were around. There was an uncle and two cousins on his mother's side who had also been lost in that war; two more relatives who were lost in the next war, and no less than three relatives in the current war as well. Thomas muttered a silent prayer for all of them and for his boys back home in Mississippi and sat down with the paper.

His attention was drawn to a front-page story about another day in the apparently endless wars in the Middle East. It seemed to him that the front pages were always filled with news of conflict. Maybe it was his newfound perspective on these matters, but all of it seemed to have religious ramifications. There were reports of conflicts between Jews and Muslims, conflicts between Shiites and Sunnis, conflicts between Protestants and Catholics, and conflicts between Christians and Muslims. He couldn't turn a page without seeing the conflict between those who believed a certain way and those who believed another. The world was full of religious strife, and the compromise so desperately necessary for resolution seemed to get further away with each passing day. Unless people were able to imagine that compromise, Thomas knew it would just keep getting harder to find.

He distracted himself with the Sports Page for a moment, then folded and tossed the paper on the floor next to the recliner. He leaned his head back, and his mind wandered to something Layne had said a few weeks before—that the religions and their leaders who pretended to be about peace were actually heading for war. Thomas knew that religious wars for peace always ended up being wars without winners. There was typically no acquisition of land or resources, and there was only an uneasy peace at their conclusion. Even worse, they seemed to demonstrate again that military might does not equate to right.

From Thomas's perspective, wars never could make things right. *The only real winners of a war*, he thought, *are the ones who figure out how to stop it before it starts.* After any war starts, everyone loses. His wall of pictures served as a reminder that his family had certainly lost a lot in every war. He knew it was true for the rest of the world, as well. In fact, when Thomas added it all up and looked at the history of humankind, he surmised that those celebrated as warriors were too many— those lauded for peace too few. The question that arose was how to reverse the ratio. War was the insanity that kept repeating itself. Peace was the sanity that never lasted long enough.

Then Thomas went to the bathroom, turned on the shower, undressed, and got in. At first, he just stood under the gentle stream of water and felt its warmth cascade over his head and face and shoulders. The shampooing provided a vigorous sensation of massage, but the relaxation didn't last long.

His mind turned to thoughts of his Bible-toting aunt from his Mississippi youth who could talk forever about the Book of Revelations. She was fond of quoting the ominous phrase, "He who appears to be the Prince of Peace is truly the antichrist." Thomas wondered if Layne might be alluding to the same thing. After all, the plan for the church some two thousand years ago had started out well enough. Peace was elusive then, too, he supposed, but it seemed that religious conflict had never been more widespread than now. *Religious loyalties are now more likely to spark wars than stop them*, he thought. He remembered how his brothers and his cousins used to laugh at this unmarried aunt behind her back and snicker whenever she got started on her crazy talk. Now it was he who laughed, as he realized maybe she was not so crazy after all.

He wondered, too, as Layne had suggested, if collective religious organizations like churches, mosques, temples, synagogues, shrines, and all the rest of it, truly believed the so-called revelations they were parading as the final and universal truth. *If they do*, he thought, *and if these so-called truths turn out to be incomplete or misleading, then these unintentional lies are rendering church models invalid in every religion. That's probably why they are no longer achieving the intended results.*

Thomas was suddenly flooded with all sorts of questions and wondered aloud, "Has the beacon of peace, the church model in every religion, become the bastion of war?" Weren't many of them largely ineffectual, controlling, and futile? Weren't many of them more often the cause of war than peace? Was the age-old plan teetering on the brink of collapse? Was the peace less secure than before? Were the church-led war machines finally demonstrating their ultimate futility? Was the church now the antichurch?

Putting that last idea into words—even as just a question—shocked Thomas for a moment. He was uncomfortable about even having thought it. Still, he now understood more completely why Layne was saying that without a new model or altered worldview or adjusted paradigm, the world was moving closer to the edge and was increasingly at risk. He shuddered to think of it. Thomas turned off the shower, dried, and got dressed for his date with Xuan.

Her apartment wasn't too far away, and Thomas arrived there a little after seven. He wore his best blue suit and the long-sleeved white shirt with the cufflinks his boys gave him for his fortieth birthday. He felt that he looked quite classy. He adjusted his red tie and rang the doorbell. There was no answer, so after a few moments, he pressed the button again and then finally rapped loudly on the door.

Xuan appeared eventually, opened the door just a crack, and said, "Five more minutes, Thomas, okay?"

Thomas smiled and nodded as the door closed in front of him. "Take your time," he laughed through the door. "I'm in no hurry."

When she appeared at the door again and opened it fully for him to enter, he was stopped in his tracks. Right in front of him, in a black evening gown and two strands of pearls, stood the most gorgeous woman he had ever seen. Xuan looked stunning, and Thomas was stunned.

"Well, are you just going to stand there, or are you coming in?" she asked while she tilted her head to the left and put on her second pearl earring.

"My goodness!" he finally managed to stammer. "You look a whole lot better than dapper, Miss Lee. You are positively riveting!"

"Oh, I know," she said without a hint of ego and a dismissive flip of her hand. "I always try to look my best for job interviews." She reached up and kissed him lightly on the cheek. "Ooh, you gorgeous man! Let me find my purse, and well go."

Thomas was still entranced. With her short hair slicked back and absent her glasses, Xuan looked like a different woman. She was even more beautiful than he remembered, and the double strand of pearls perfectly accentuated her elegant neck and modestly cut gown. He still couldn't make himself move from the porch.

Finally, Xuan said, "So you really are just going to stand there, huh? Well, okay, I'll be right back." She smiled and disappeared.

She came back with a shiny blue satin wrap and matching purse. She locked the deadbolt behind her, slipped her single key into her evening purse, then turned and looked at Thomas still standing there. She gently placed her arm in the crook of his elbow.

"You know, Thomas," she began, "I think I'd rather interview for the job on company time next week. This is my first real date in years, and a date sounds a lot better to me right now than a job."

Thomas looked at her, still mesmerized, and responded, "Layne already offered you the job, Xuan, so I agree. Let's just have fun this evening." With that, he opened the car door, offered his hand to help her in, and closed the door behind her. When he reached the trunk on the way around to the driver's side, he pumped his fist into the air in silence and wished he could let out a scream to tell the world how excited he was about this lady named Xuan.

When they arrived at the expensive French restaurant, he gave his keys to the valet, and Xuan was escorted around the car to meet him. He held out his arm. She took it and smiled up at him.

Thomas wanted so badly to just sweep her up into his arms and wrap himself completely around her, but he knew that would spoil the true purpose of formal dates at formal places—the tantalizingly sweet anticipation built on the restraint of impeccable manners and private imaginings. He knew the unspoken fantasies were supposed to build and build into an almost unbearable tension. He knew the tension and anticipation would only grow as the night went on and that, soon enough, they would resolve in some as-yet-unknown way. For him, the details of that resolution were not as important right now as the buildup, and he was savoring every minute of it. He wondered if Xuan felt the same.

He felt her leaning on him just a little as they walked arm in arm through the foyer of the restaurant to the podium of the maître d'. He noticed how their legs brushed together with every alternate stride. He felt her arm lightly but firmly pulling on his and he caught her looking up at him as he glanced down at her. She giggled and squeezed his arm as he recognized the promise in the moment. He pulled her arm against his coat and felt her give in to the gesture. *Yes*, he thought, *she feels it, too.*

Not a word was spoken. He reveled in the knowledge that he was quickly getting comfortable with her. She seemed to be getting comfortable with him, too. He wondered what kind of lover she would be and worried that it had been more than a year for him. He felt her shudder involuntarily the moment he thought it, which made him wonder if she was thinking of it, as well.

"Good evening. Two for dinner?" asked the maître d'.

"Yes, two," Thomas answered. "We'd like a private room, please, if there are any available."

Xuan looked up at him, and he wondered what this spontaneous request for privacy was going to cost him when he got the final tab for the evening.

"This way, please."

The maître d' led them through a corner of the plush main dining room to a row of curtained rooms along the back wall of the restaurant. He parted the deep red velvet curtain and showed them their private dining room, complete with a burgundy leather booth, a black walnut table with matching chairs to the side, and red-framed wall hangings all around.

Xuan gasped when she saw it. She let loose Thomas's arm and took a moment to look at every picture—classical copies of Monet, Gauguin, and Van Gogh. She finally sat down but still seemed entranced by the setting as she looked around at every other feature in the room: curtains, moldings, carvings, and fresh-cut flowers.

Thomas watched her a moment, looked around briefly himself, and then sat down, too.

The maître d' gave Thomas the wine list and left them alone.

Thomas felt Xuan's gaze on his face in the candlelight as he browsed through the assortment of wines. He looked up and asked, "How's your knowledge of wines, Xuan?"

"Not very extensive, I'm afraid. In this setting, I think anything would probably taste great. What do you like?"

"A cabernet sounds good," Thomas said. "Does that sound okay with you?"

When she didn't answer him right away, Thomas looked up from the list and found her looking at him tenderly. He felt himself blush as he returned her look.

He offered his hand on the table between them, and she reached for it and softly slipped one little finger under his smallest finger. He smiled and held her gaze for a long, long moment.

"Is that a yes?" he whispered. He knew it was before he asked. She simply nodded her head slightly and continued to get lost in his brown eyes.

"Thomas, this is our first time together where there isn't some sort of business purpose hanging over us. That's nice, huh?"

"It's been hard for me to concentrate on anything else since we decided to have this date," Thomas admitted.

"Me, too," she said, "and what has been interesting to me is that I've been torn between thinking of you and what attracts me to you and, conversely, thinking of me and what sort of person you might be seeing in me. Does that make any sense?"

"No, not really," Thomas replied. "Can you explain it with different words?"

"Well, let me see," she answered. "I'm understandably very curious about you and what kind of person you are. I've seen your humor and your insights, and I've also seen your frustration and vulnerability."

"Okay," Thomas nodded his head. "What's the other half of the debate in your mind?"

"The other half has to do with who I've become since the last time I was involved with someone. Have I gotten set in my ways, or selfish? Would I even want to be around someone else on a regular basis? My life with my three cats, two tropical fish tanks, and about a hundred potted plants is pretty full and, yet, uncomplicated. As you get to know me and learn who I am, I'm not sure that I will even like the person you find in me."

Thomas saw her discomfort and felt her vulnerability, too.

"Even so," she continued, "I guess it will be worth it no matter what happens to us. I need to find out who I am again, anyway. Does that make more sense?"

"Yes, in a way it does," Thomas answered, "but your public persona is so upbeat and energetic and rational. I've never seen an uncertain side to you at all."

"That's exactly what I mean," she said. "New relationships are all about revealing more of who you are to each other every day. It's much easier to hide behind public pleasantries. That's probably why new relationships scare me." She looked around at their private dining room again and then back at him. "Of course, I'll try to overcome my fears if you'll promise to bring me here for dinner once a week."

"So, it's my money you're after," he smiled at her banter. "I should warn you, almost all of that goes to the boys and their mom in Mississippi."

"That's okay," she answered. "Spending time with you is bound to be more fun than spending what little money both of us have. Time is about all I can offer, too."

Just then, the curtain parted, and the waiter asked if they wished to order some wine. Without taking his eyes off Xuan for even a moment, Thomas answered, "Yes, we'll have that 1999 Ecco Domani cabernet sauvignon, please."

"Yes sir," the waiter responded, "and how about an appetizer? We have the finest caviar."

Thomas, still looking right at Xuan, raised his eyebrows inquiringly in her direction. Ever so subtly, she shook her head. "Just the wine, please," Thomas said. Then he finally took his eyes off Xuan and looked at the waiter and said, "We're in no hurry tonight, so take your time, okay?"

"Yes, sir," the waiter responded. He retrieved the wine list and left.

Xuan leaned forward and whispered, "Will the waiters think us unfriendly if we don't even look at them all night long?"

Thomas laughed. "They probably will, but I can't help it, Xuan. I can't take my eyes off of you. You've gotten a hold of me in a way that no one ever has before. Everything I know about you and feel about you and find out about you is captivating and uplifting. I've been walking on air for days. I don't want to be my normal, cautious self, and I sure can't figure out what's happened to my skepticism. I can't even explain it to myself."

"Oh, Thomas, that's so sweet," Xuan replied, "but I don't know what it is, either. I feel like a teenager with a crush, and I've kicked myself a few times for not wanting to slow down or think about what I'm doing or what I'm saying. While I was watching you study that wine list, it occurred to me that going slow must not be what I want. I've done that before, and it didn't work any better than rushing in headfirst."

Her eyes went down to the table for a moment and then back up to Thomas as she went on. "In fact, I'm done trying to explain me to myself. This new job, this meeting in June, and my attraction to you, Thomas—none of it makes much sense. It's really illogical. On the other hand, it all feels really good, so I'm just going to run with it for a while—and logic be damned."

Thomas momentarily diverted his eyes from hers. He was slightly uncomfortable with the intensity of their conversation, but like the moth inexorably drawn to the flame, he let his eyes meet hers again.

"I know what you mean about being scared and having to look closely at yourself while you're caught up in someone else," he said. "Part of my hesitation is that I don't know what went wrong in my marriage. I don't know where I went wrong and why I became so hard to live with. You've got me wondering about who I've become, too. That ought to give both of us pause."

"Maybe." Xuan thought for a moment. "And maybe not. It goes back to what I was saying at sunrise the other morning. I am pretty reliant on my intellect, and I think I miss out on a lot of other perspectives and feelings with that rather singular approach. There's nothing very rational about what I've all of a sudden decided to do with my life for the next six months, so I don't want to think about it too much. I'm choosing to just feel my way through and trusting that it will be okay. It's like some great adventure—the meeting, the thinking about what it means, the attraction to you—and 'okay' isn't the right word, either. I feel like it's actually going to be exciting and challenging and new and wonderful all at the same time."

"Yeah, me too." He stroked his closely trimmed beard and shifted in his seat. He fiddled with his wedding ring and realized with a start that he was still wearing it. It suddenly looked so out of place. He ignored it as he was drawn to look again at her. He smelled her perfume across the table. He watched her bright eyes as she seemed to search in his for some kind of connection between them. "You've already done so much, Xuan, to lift me out of the funk I've been in for years. You've provided a different perspective on this Project 4000 business. Truthfully, you are a very welcome new wind in my life, because I find myself just wanting to let go of everything I've always known and to be pulled along and fly through life again."

"If that's true, then maybe you can let go of your old wedding ring someday, too," Xuan said. She smiled as she said it.

He realized it was a suggestion, not a demand.

She also confirmed to him what he already knew: first, that she had noticed the ring, even if he had become unaware of it himself, and second, that leaving it on even one more day was incongruous with all he was feeling and thinking about this new woman in his life. He looked at her even as he reached for the ring with his right hand and began to work it off the third finger of his left hand. It wasn't easy, but the more it resisted his attempts, the more he wanted it off. Soon enough, the mission was accomplished, and he stuck the ring in his coat pocket.

"You're right," he said softly. "Now I'm completely ready for something new, too."

They hardly noticed when the waiter came in with the wine and then waited for an okay from Thomas. He tasted it without a word, nodded his head to signal his approval, and watched as the two glasses filled with wine.

Thomas offered a toast with the simple words, "To a great awakening."

Xuan lightly clinked her glass with his and then gasped as she realized what he'd said. She put her glass down and fumbled for her purse as she tried to explain herself. "Thomas, do you remember the Chinese restaurant lunch with Mr. Layne last week?"

"Well, yes."

"Remember, I opened my fortune cookie but didn't read it aloud, even though Digger asked me to."

"I think I remember that," Thomas replied as he shifted in his seat.

She finally found the slip of paper in her purse and she placed it in Thomas's hand.

He read it out loud. "'You will soon have a great awakening.'" Thomas looked at Xuan. "I'll be darned," he exclaimed softly. "What made you keep this?"

"I don't usually put much stock in these sorts of things, but with Layne's job offer and your offer of a date, I thought it might somehow prove relevant. The more I carried it around and the more I thought about it, the more I came to realize that it represents the exact opposite of everything I've always stood for. It makes me doubt my totally rational approach to life and makes me want to awaken to something else."

Xuan leaned forward and once again placed her hand on Thomas's.

The intensity in her voice and the tightness of her grip were not lost on Thomas as he awaited her next observation.

"When you asked me out," she said, "I knew right away that I would say yes. Layne's offer was a wholly different thing, and this silly slip of paper matched his hypothesis about the meeting almost perfectly. Even more, it matched my previously subconscious desire to awaken again, myself. Now, you make a toast, and the words of awakening are almost identical. That's pretty incredible, don't you think?"

Thomas leaned back away from the table and collected his thoughts for a moment before he leaned toward her again and responded. "Maybe that's exactly what this is all about. I mean, I've been numb for so long I thought it was normal. The New Year is coming up again, and those bothersome New Year's resolutions to improve and change and energize my life may actually have a chance to succeed this time. Maybe this theme of awakening will catch on in lots of lives, not just ours, and maybe our meeting in June is meant to focus the energy for that awakening." Thomas paused and took a sip of wine and then continued.

"Mr. Layne may not quite have the whole picture, either. This isn't just about religion gone awry; it may also be about people creating a new collective energy of awakening and changing. If so, they are currently doing so without much knowledge of the other efforts around the world that are going in the same direction.

Ultimately, it seems to me, all these efforts are amassing into this larger, single energy. Right now, each individual person may be feeling it in their own little sphere, but they aren't yet aware that all the little spheres may be joining together to create a potentially great big sphere of awakening."

Thomas seemed to run out of words for a moment, and Xuan picked up the thread of his thoughts.

"Yes, you're right, and so is Layne," she theorized. "On one level, it is about religion, because religion is the collectivization and institutionalization of one man's experience in answering every man's ultimate question. What is also happening, I think, is that the turn of the millennium ten years ago caused millions of people ask the ultimate question with increasing intensity and a feeling of urgency. More people want to know their relationship to the universe in which they live. Millions want to know their relationship to the force or the God or the Tao or Krishna or Buddha or Allah or whatever name they've given it."

"Right," Thomas continued, "and all that these universal questions really need in order to find a suitable answer is a focusing event that will bring it all together in one time and one place. Perhaps that is what we are creating in June—the focusing event."

Xuan took a sip of wine and went on. "On another level, however, when millions are asking the questions and, in some cases, leaving their religions in frustration, it must mean that the religions are no longer providing a satisfactory answer. It could be that millions are now claiming the right to search for themselves without the protection or obfuscation of a religion."

"Exactly!" Thomas agreed. "It's like Layne said about the pattern building of the last two thousand years. Humankind needed a pattern to follow. Humans weren't sufficiently evolved two thousand years ago to directly seek or nurture or trust the messages within themselves. The pattern builders made churches and religions of all kinds to help them, but they knew it wasn't the final step in mankind's journey. Two thousand years ago, humankind needed the priest and the minister and the mullah and the shaman and the rabbi and the community surrounding the church. Layne is saying now that the pattern can be changed and moved forward again."

"Okay," Xuan said. "If there is more movement toward true awakening, and if the world condition now requires an awakened population more than ever before, there must be fertile ground for this meeting in June?"

"Yes. And for the messages that come out of it, too," Thomas added.

"That's the same energy that is drawing us into it, as well," Xuan concluded. "Need is a vacuum, and just like any other vacuum, the need for awakening must somehow be met and filled."

Xuan fell silent and looked at Thomas. He looked back at her. It was as if their minds had been tied together in one stream of consciousness. They had developed and experienced, together, a new understanding of what was going on for them, as well as what might be happening in the world around them. Their minds had worked in concert to push and pull each other to another plateau of knowing. She looked again at him. He looked again at her. He exhaled and sat back in the booth.

"Wow!" he exclaimed in disbelief. "Did you feel the energy we created together just now?" He only had to study the look on her face for a moment to get his answer. They both reached for another sip of wine. Thomas proposed another toast, "To a great adventure."

They raised their glasses together again, and the waiter entered with the menus. They smiled to themselves as they searched the entrées.

Thomas quickly decided to order a small steak, then put the menu down and watched Xuan as she perused her options.

She finally set her menu down, looked at him, and asked, "So what's on your mind now, Thomas?"

"You. Dinner. Lots of things," he said. "At home tonight I remembered all the men my family had lost to wars over the years. They're all on a big picture wall in my living room, and looking at them got me thinking about all the religious wars, which then got me thinking about my crazy aunt—the one who never married and went to church four or five times a week."

"I've got one of those," Xuan said. "What's an unmarried old lady to do?"

"Yeah, right," Thomas answered. "Well, one of her fixations in life was the Book of Revelations, you know, the last book in the Bible. She seemed really concerned as to whether her so-called prince of peace was the real thing or the antichrist. She was always unsure, for some reason."

"What did you think of her prince of peace?" Xuan asked.

"What I most remember at her church were the songs about soldiering and mighty fortresses and things like that. It didn't seem very peaceful, so when Layne posited the theory that the peace mongers have become the warmongers, it wasn't a very big leap for me to agree with his contention."

"Right, me too, but it does seem a little blasphemous to wonder if the church has become a backward force in the development of humankind, doesn't it?" Xuan frowned at her own conclusion and offered it tentatively.

"Yes, it does," Thomas agreed and leaned forward. He lowered his voice as he finished the thought. "I've always looked at churches as keepers of the undivided truth, but it seems that they are so divided that they no longer know what the undivided truth even looks like. That often means they are causing more conflict and harm than good."

"Maybe they are all just too far removed from their original inspirations," Xuan suggested.

"I don't think there's any doubt that the inspirations of Jesus or Buddha or Mohammed have been diluted with each and every passing generation since those original inspirations became known to others. There have been fifty to a hundred generations since those people walked the earth. I'm sure all of their teachings have been distorted and diluted," Thomas agreed. "Plus, those inspirations have been tailored and altered and customized to fit hundreds of cultural settings, thousands of overbearing governments, and millions of believers and practitioners."

"Right," Xuan added, "and alongside all of that, there have been hundreds of inventions, thousands of discoveries, untold new insights, and millions of new words, concepts, and understandings."

"Yes, so it really isn't too far-fetched to conclude that the religions of the world are at cross purposes to their original intent and are way behind the learning curve," Thomas said.

"And at cross-purposes to the goal of spiritual development," Xuan admitted. "It's like they're preserving the dead structures, leaders, and models of the past understandings. There is no longer any focus on growth or development of their understandings. They are just trying to hold on to the comfortable and the familiar. That's why there has to be a new plan, and that's why there has to be a meeting that can focus this development of a new plan on a fairly grand scale. I think Layne is right; I think this meeting we're helping to organize is essential. The trend of contentious religious models has no viable future, and it must be reversed or replaced."

"If you read the newspaper or listen to the news, the urgency seems more apparent every day," Thomas interjected.

"Oh, I know," Xuan concurred. "We've got an awesome responsibility here with the planning of this meeting. We can no longer spend our time and resources on religious conflicts, conflicts about which partial view of the world is more right than some other partial view—especially when all of them are partially wrong, at the very least."

"Yes, and many of them seem more wrong than right to begin with," Thomas agreed. "It's like we're arguing over who gets to have the right to be the most wrong. That's just plain crazy. It's collective insanity."

"Yes, and it makes me hungry. What are you going to order?" Xuan asked him.

"Steak. I'll need my strength for the next six months if I'm going to work hard all day and romance you all night. That's bound to require a high-protein diet." He welcomed the change of pace in the conversation and was glad to get back to flirting with this woman. He liked the way she flirted with him.

"What are you having?" he asked.

"I don't know," she smiled, "maybe some salmon or trout, and if you're planning to romance me during the week, by the way, my bedtime is ten o'clock. I need my rest or we'll both be sorry; trust me on this." She laughed again and looked at him with a rueful grin.

"Well, Xuan, what is your bedtime on the weekends?" he inquired.

"Now, sir, that just depends. Lately, it's been a rather boring nine o'clock, but I think it might change under certain circumstances."

"What circumstances might that include?" he prodded.

"Well, French restaurants usually give me the energy to stay up as late as ten thirty or eleven."

Thomas laughed. "Heck, Xuan, I could stay up into the wee small hours just listening to you talk and watching you laugh."

Thomas looked on as she seemed to hesitate for a moment. He thought she might respond flirtatiously, and he felt his anticipation building again.

Finally, she said, "If I'm still talking at midnight, it will be in my dreams while you're talking to yourself in your car on the drive back to your house."

Thomas laughed nervously. He hoped his disappointment didn't show. He looked down at his almost-empty wine glass and wondered what to make of her seemingly distancing remark.

They ordered their food and conversed and ate and finished the wine, but didn't order any more. They shared a dessert and laughed and flirted some more. They ordered coffee and held hands while they explored each other's eyes. Finally, they left the restaurant sometime after eleven, and Thomas drove Xuan home.

At the door to her apartment, she turned to face him. He knew the moment had come to either resolve the wonderful tension they had built together or let it hang over them for another day and see if it could be coaxed into an even sweeter torture tomorrow.

"Thomas," she started as she took his hands in hers. "I can honestly say that I've never been more tempted to invite someone into my house as I am right now. Never! It's been such an exquisite evening."

"Yeah, it has," Thomas agreed. "And I accept your invitation. Do I need to watch out for any cats that might be lying in wait for an intruder like me?"

She laughed and took him in her arms and kissed him full and long on the mouth.

They embraced each other tightly, and he noticed once more how nicely their bodies fit together, and they kissed again. The passion of the moment was palpable; he felt it from his head to his toes.

But then they stopped—both of them.

Thomas spoke first and said, "Actually, I heard what you said, and I know you are tempted to invite me in, but, the truth is, you haven't. I can respect that, even though I don't want to."

Xuan smiled, and he thought he saw a glimmer of disappointment in her eyes.

"Will you consider going out with me again?" he asked. "This time, you only have five seconds to answer." He laughed, his arms still wrapped casually around her waist, and wondered what she might be thinking.

She didn't answer except to kiss him again and pull him tightly into her once more. "Call me in the morning," she whispered, "and thank you, Thomas." She pulled away, unlocked and opened her door, and then turned back for one more kiss. "Good night, sweet man."

He watched her start inside and gently said, "Good night, Xuan."

She smiled over her shoulder and went through the door.

He heard the deadbolt lock click behind her and just stood there for a moment before he turned and walked toward his car. He wanted to turn around, go back, and bang on her door—to change her mind if he could. Something inside of him resisted that urge, however, and he knew he could survive without her for at least another day. After that, he was not so sure.

Chapter 16

The Jemez Woman

Digger was convinced that meeting the Jemez keeper woman was important and that he should not take a chance on missing her when she came to Acoma. He decided he would get there first thing Thursday morning and stay through Friday, if needed. He let Thomas know his plans, left a message for Jack Eaglefeather, and departed directly from his Westside apartment around six Thursday morning.

Digger still saw himself as a student of archaeology and anthropology rather than someone who had mastered either field of study. When he accepted Layne's offer to join Project 4000, he did so thinking it was not much more than a temporary job. He didn't think it would be much different than an internship, except he would get a paycheck every other Friday. Jobs in other parts of the country didn't seem to fit him as well as this one, so he took it and looked forward to learning even more about the Indians of the American Southwest.

Because he might be spending the night at Acoma or a nearby campground, he brought along some provisions. He packed two jugs of water, some dried fruits and nuts, and a copy of the Bhagavad-Gita in his old International Jeep. In addition, he brought along his newest acquisition, a compendium of Indian healing arts that discussed shamans, medicine women, and those who are called "keepers." Jack had described the Jemez Pueblo woman as a keeper, and Digger wanted to know more about them.

Jack met Digger at the visitor center shortly after eight o'clock. As usual, he was direct and to the point.

"Digger, I think the old woman is coming today sometime before noon. Since you're already here, we can take a moment to look over the sleeping areas for the meeting in June."

As they ascended the main trail to the top of the mesa from the west, the mesa blocked the early-morning sun, but as soon as they crested the top of the plateau, the sunlight struck them full on, as if to herald their arrival. The temperature was below freezing on this late December day, but there was no wind, and many people were already stirring. Smoke rose from almost every chimney, and fifteen or twenty people were already outside going about their morning routines. Those they encountered paused to size up Digger and offer a brief greeting to Jack. Some of them just uttered the one word, "Iyatiku," and Jack responded in various ways and smiled.

It was not Jack's custom to stop and make small talk, nor did he introduce Digger to anyone. One woman, however, was carrying a small child in her arms that would not stop crying, and Jack stopped to see if he could be of help. He reached out his arms as he made little clicking sounds with his tongue, and the child, reluctantly at first, consented to be held by someone other than his mother. Jack smiled at him, spun him around, and danced for a moment with him, tickled his ribs, tossed him up in the air, and finally got him to laugh through his tears. Jack was laughing, too, and soon gave him back to his mother. He reached out and tousled the child's dark hair as he departed with Digger, and they headed once more for the abandoned monk's quarters, now in shadow on the west side of the old church.

Digger knew that the Iyatiku served many roles: teacher, counselor, and diplomat. He had also seen Jack in the role of mayor, judge, and mediator. Digger could tell Jack was revered for who he was and how he conducted himself, more than just for the roles he played. He was beyond reproach, and his standing in the community gave him more influence than anyone else. Digger suspected it was Jack who had decided that the June meeting at Acoma would be a good thing, and he knew it was Jack who had convinced the others on the council to allow it. Digger felt honored to walk through his town with him this morning.

The 320-year-old church on the eastern edge of the mesa was the most imposing structure on the Acoma lands—lands not well known for significant architecture. With two bell towers, eight-foot-thick walls, and some forty feet of height, it was positioned near the even older cemetery. As they got near the church, Jack directed Digger through a low-arched opening and into a courtyard adjacent to the church. Digger could see the sky above him and the tall western walls of the church that made up one side of the enclosure. In the middle of the smooth dirt courtyard was an old statue and one dilapidated wooden bench that appeared to be held up by cobwebs and habit.

Besides the tall church wall on one side, the rest of the courtyard was surrounded by ten or twelve small rooms with even smaller doors that formed the other three sides and completed the perimeter. These abandoned monks quarters were made for the smaller people of a bygone era. Digger peeked inside one of them and decided their six-foot-high ceilings and five-foot-high doorways made them unusable. Only the door from the courtyard into the church was large enough to be of any use, and, at first glance, Digger could not readily see how this area could be utilized for the meeting.

Now that Jack assessed the abandoned courtyard more closely, he seemed to come to the same realization. "I might have been wrong about this area being suitable for sleeping. It's dirty and pretty rough and I don't know of anywhere else that's suitable, either."

Like a good archaeologist, Digger began to explore the courtyard even more closely. He wondered if the dirt floor was hiding older floors below it or artifacts of history from a few hundred years before. Before he could think about it much, he wondered it aloud.

"Jack, do you think there's anything buried below this courtyard where the monks used to live and cook and congregate?"

"Actually, there are rumors of a stone floor a few inches below us." Jack answered. "I've never seen it myself. In fact, there are also stories that this court-yard used to have a roof, too, but if it did, it fell down before my time and I never saw that, either."

"I'd say the roof story is accurate," Digger responded. "Look at those notches in the tops of the walls every few feet. They might have been used to support and solidify roof beams of some kind. See how they are evenly spaced?" Digger reached up and ran his fingers along the old notches and surveyed the tops of all three courtyard walls more closely. "Yep. There was some kind of a roof here. Cool!" Digger kept studying the tops of the walls and then turned to Jack and asked, "Are there any pictures or paintings of this area that show this part of the church?"

"I've never seen any," Jack answered. "Why do you ask?"

"Well, I was just thinking that none of those small doorways or the rooms behind them looks very inviting for sleeping, but if this courtyard had a roof and a clean floor, it might make a good place to sleep fifteen or twenty people. Of course," he hurried to continue, "if you were to build it back again, you would probably want the roof and structure to look like it did before. A picture would help make the renovation authentic and restore the original look."

Jack looked around, again and nodded in Digger's direction. "Katzimo, my friend. I'll check with the historian at the Visitor Center to see if she knows where we can get our hands on a picture. I like your idea." He continued to look around and size up the place as he spoke.

"Before I forget," Jack continued, "the Acoma Pueblo has agreed to feed the masters while they are here. Do they like curry on their Indian food?" Jack smiled and waited for Digger's response.

"You use curry on your food here, Jack?"

"No. Never. It was a joke, Digger."

"Well, anyway, Layne thinks there might be a lot of fasting—at least by the master teachers. On the other hand, the food around here has sustained this Pueblo for a thousand years and I think whatever your cooks decide will be perfect, don't you?"

"Yes," Jack answered. "I've eaten Pueblo food all my life, and I like it pretty good."

When they were back outside the abandoned courtyard, Digger felt the peace of Acoma surround him again. The views allowed him to see the full dimension of this sacred locale. The Enchanted Mesa to the north drew his attention for a moment, but he focused instead on the view to the east, where the rock-topped bluffs were interspersed with the arroyos and canyons that defined the Acoma Valley. The mesa on which he stood felt like a hub in the center of some distant and larger wheel. The bluffs that alternated with the canyons in every direction formed the spokes of this imagined wheel; a wheel whose far-off outer rim could not be seen from where he stood. But Digger could imagine it quite easily. He felt it in his bones from his place atop the mesa. He knew it must be there, and, soon enough, the giant wheel could be seen in the eye of his imagiception.

He also understood why the Pueblo people chose this mesa on which to build their community. It took them out of harm's way. They could not be easily attacked from the flatlands 360 feet below. Digger knew that those who dwelt on this high plateau saw all who came to visit long before they arrived. This meant they could prepare for them, friend or foe, and their defense was staunch. The flat land extending from this hub to the mesa spokes and canyons beyond was irrigated and farmed. It fed them most of the year. At night, they slept securely atop the mesa and told their stories while cradled in the center of their universe.

As Digger imagined what it had been like a thousand years ago, he also realized that nothing much had changed on Acoma Mesa. It had never been much different than what he saw today. Routines were the same. Methods had not changed. Hopes and fears were as they had always been. This sameness made him feel connected to this place like no other place he had ever been. The simplicity, even the harshness, made him appreciate the resilience of these people. His admiration for Jack grew as he surveyed all that he could see and all that he could imagine. He felt honored to be witness to such a lengthy and continuous survival story.

Momentarily lost in this private reverie, Digger was startled when he heard the excited calls of a young boy as he came running up to Jack.

"Iyatiku!" the boy shouted. "Iyatiku!"

Jack knelt down in front of the boy, who explained what he had heard and seen. He spoke in Keresan, which Digger did not understand. Jack stood as the boy departed and looked to the west.

"The boy says someone is coming up the trail to find me," Jack explained. "It's probably the keeper woman from Jemez. Our traditions throughout the nineteen Pueblos require that all people announce themselves to the Iyatiku when they first arrive at another Pueblo." Jack looked at Digger and continued. "Do you speak Spanish? Sometimes this one speaks English and sometimes Spanish and sometimes Keresan. I never know with her."

"I speak a little Spanish," Digger answered. "I hope I can keep up."

Jack motioned to a flat rock nearby, and they both sat down facing west.

"She wouldn't like it if we made a fuss over her," Jack said as he tugged on his sleeves and dusted off his Levi's. "She is old but very independent, and we should act as if it is nothing special to see her."

Digger mulled these words over as he finally saw her come into view around a nearby dwelling and head in their direction. She didn't look anywhere near the eighty years old that Jack reported her to be. Though her face was weathered and wrinkled, her eyes were bright, and her stride was strong. She did not smile with her mouth, but Digger saw in her a woman at home with herself—no airs, no pretense, and no one to please.

"Men should not be Iyatiku," she started. "It is not right. Only women are Iyatiku." She said this to Jack but was studying Digger as she spoke. When she finally looked up at Jack, she did not smile. "I told your father the same thing, and I told his father the same thing, too. Men should not be Iyatiku." She looked again at Digger and asked, "Who is this one? Maybe he wants to be Iyatiku?"

Digger watched as Jack finally gave up a smile for this woman and stated in an unaffected tone, "He wants to meet you and see if you know anything about the longest day or the meeting at Acoma."

"Our people have known how to predict the longest day since our years at Pueblo Bonita," she answered. "Why does this one want to know?"

"He only wants to know of the meeting at Acoma that will end on that day next summer," Jack replied.

She exhaled through puckered lips and waved her hand at Digger in a dismissive manner. Digger held his silence, and, after a few moments, she looked him over again and then slowly lowered herself to her haunches. She stared at the ground between her sandaled feet, and when she looked up again to the east, her eyes became transfixed on a point far away, a point that only she could see. She took both her hands and idly fingered the strands of silver and turquoise around her leathery neck. A sudden gust of wind fluttered the old cloth headband that tied back her whitened hair. Slowly, deliberately, she drew some lines on the ground in front of her and then studied what she had drawn. She remained still for a minute or more. Finally, she spoke.

"There will be seven and then seven more. One is blind. Many will come to this meeting. The ones who don't understand will leave. The ones who understand will disappear. There will be a big wind, and the Iyatiku will be left behind. The other one will be blown afar like the seed of the dandelion."

She became silent again and gradually drew in her gaze from the distant point on which it had been placed. She looked again at what she had drawn at her feet. "I wish I could be there," she finished.

She then looked at Digger with her bright, piercing eyes. "You have a question?"

Digger hesitated and then blurted out, "Is one of the seven a Navajo?"

"She used to be a Navajo, but she lived at Chaco Canyon with the Anazasi before that. She likes being Navajo, so perhaps she will be a Navajo for this meeting," she answered quietly. "Or maybe she will be an African."

Digger looked quizzically at Jack, who didn't return his look.

Jack had a question, too. "Will our fathers be there?" he inquired.

"Yes," she responded, "and many other fathers. And many mothers, too." She looked again at the drawing in the dirt and then added, "Many sisters. Many brothers."

Jack nodded and looked at Digger as if to prod him to ask another question.

Digger asked, "Who is the blind one you spoke of?"

"He will write the words and live at the Pueblo," she answered. "Many will seek him, but only the Iyatiku knows where he goes."

Now it was Jack's turn again. "What is the big wind?"

"Yellow. And taller than the clouds at sunset," she whispered. As she did, she abruptly waved her hand in a broad movement horizontal to the ground, as if to say "no more." She lowered her head into her hands and, still on her haunches, sat silently for several more minutes.

Digger didn't dare to move and, at first, neither did Jack.

Finally, Jack got up, and, with his hands thrust deep into the pockets of his Levis, he walked slowly around the rock.

Digger watched as Jack looked to the southwest and seemed lost in thought. Digger saw the keeper woman rise to her feet and look at him closely. He averted his eyes and looked back at the crude drawing on the ground. She watched him for a moment and then spoke to Jack.

"Iyatiku, train your daughter to be Iyatiku. A thousand years have passed. It is time, again. Katzimo." She turned and began walking back the way she had come.

Jack called after her. "Keeper? Iyatiku cannot be a woman at Acoma until the fear of the Enchanted Mesa is gone." He watched as she slowed down. "And you know that as well as I do."

She whirled around and faced him. "The fear is almost gone, Jack. She is among us again, and you must find her." With that, she turned west once more.

Digger watched her as she strode away from Jack and him.

"Do you need to go with her?" Digger asked after a short silence.

"No. She'll be here tomorrow," Jack answered. He looked shaken as he looked at Digger once more. "What do you make of her words?"

"I don't know yet," Digger answered. "I was hoping you understood better than I. Did you notice her drawing was very similar to the sand painting the other night in the kiva?"

"Yes, I saw that. Did you and Thomas have time to figure that one out yet? If not, maybe this drawing will provide an insight to that one. I didn't understand her yellow wind answer, but I'll think about it over the next few days."

Digger didn't understand the seeds of the dandelion answer, either, and was about to ask Jack, but Jack seemed flustered and impatient to get back to the Visitor Center. He started walking that way when Digger asked him, "Did you know they hired someone to take notes at the meeting?"

"No. Is he blind?" Jack asked over his shoulder as he walked.

"Yes, he is," Digger answered. "Should I tell him of this woman's words?"

"No," Jack quickly responded as he turned around.

Digger noted again the worried look on his face.

"Don't tell anyone about this until you and I can talk some more." Once again, Jack turned to walk away.

The young archaeologist found Jack's walking away from him atypical and a bit disconcerting. He shouted after him. "Jack," he started, "either her drawing has upset you or it's something that she said. Can you tell me which one it is?"

Jack whirled around. "Yes, I can. I don't have a daughter, but this woman acts like I do. That confuses me, and I hate any confusion in my life. Now, I must find out more."

Chapter 17

The Bridge

Russell Layne and Anna decided right before Christmas to throw a small New Year's Eve party for the planners of Project 4000. Anna was in charge of the arrangements and arrived at the renovated Excelsior Hotel and went up to the twelfth floor a little before eight on December 31, 2009. She was quickly shown around by a hotel employee, and she checked out the city lights that twinkled in every direction through the plate glass windows that formed two of the walls of their room. She noted the intricately engraved double doors leading to the grand ballroom next door and thought it all looked perfect.

As she caught a glimpse of herself in the glass, she stopped to straighten her silky blue party dress and fussed with the jet black hair that streamed down to her waist. Malik came in with his teacher Susan and Anna greeted them both while she wondered what might be required to make Malik feel comfortable. She also looked forward to finally meeting Jack Eaglefeather.

A few minutes later, Russell Layne came into the room wearing a dark sports coat, dark slacks and a red sweater. He was pushing a wheelchair. In it, dressed in black pants and black shirt with the small white collar of a priest, was an old man of the cloth. She walked toward them both, smiling.

"Hi, Mr. Layne."

"Good evening, Anna. You look lovely tonight." He took a moment to look around at the room and commented, "You've found the perfect place to spend the last evening of the first decade of the twenty-first century. Well done!"

"Yes, soon it will be 2010." Anna's eyes then met the steely blue eyes of the priest. She immediately crossed herself, as did he, and then extended her hand.

"Anna," Russell Layne continued, "meet Father Pedro Garces. Father, this is Anna Maria Izturias."

Father Garces looked warmly at Anna and took her hand lightly. "Bless you, child," he said in a low and soothing voice. "You are involved in a great adventure here. Did you know that?"

Without averting her eyes for even a moment, Anna nodded in response and said, "Yes I know, Father. I also know that you convinced Mr. Layne to get this adventure started. I am very pleased to finally meet you."

The old priest laughed and winked at her and then whispered, "I'm always thrilled to meet sweet Catholic girls myself."

Layne toured the room, peeked through the double doors, and glanced at the views to the east and south.

Anna felt her usual anxiety at being around priests melt away in the warmth of Father Garces's laughter. She liked him immediately and introduced him to Malik and Susan.

Anna saw the priest take Malik's hand and heard him speak to the blind boy quietly.

"Son, you have a very special role in this project, and I hear you are well equipped for it. Like John the Baptist and his voice in the wilderness, I think your writings from the meetings will be a voice to the world like no other. It will be strong and accurate."

Malik nodded his head, and the priest continued. "Though certain sayings through time have been attributed to people like Buddha and Jesus and Mohammed, they spoke their words when there was no one to write them as they spoke. I have always wondered if they were quoted accurately. There will be no doubt about the words of the masters that are coming to this meeting, because you will be there to accurately tell their stories. I think that will make a great difference and will give these stories long-lasting influence. You are blessed, Malik, and the entire world will be blessed as well."

Malik extracted his hand from the priestly grip, pulled out his pad and pen, and hastily scribbled the words "Thank you." He tore off the page and pushed it in the direction of Father Garces's voice.

The priest read it quickly and smiled. "You're welcome, my son."

Jack Eaglefeather arrived at the party wearing a western shirt, bolo tie, tan slacks, and his usual snakeskin boots.

Though she had never seen him before, Anna knew right away who he was. She went up to him and offered her hand in greeting. "Mr. Eaglefeather? Hi, I'm Anna Izturias. Welcome. It's nice to finally meet you."

"Thank you. You are the one who answers the phone," he said as he gently took her hand.

"Yes, I am, and I'm so glad you could come tonight. Let me introduce you to everyone." She steered him toward Father Garces and Malik.

Jack said hello to the priest and instantly confirmed that the old keeper woman had been right about Malik.

Before too long, Digger, Thomas, and Xuan all arrived at the same time, having ridden up in the elevator together. Anna made sure everyone was properly introduced. Layne offered to get drinks for all of them, and when he and Susan returned with something for each of them, Anna sensed it was time to begin.

Layne looked at his watch and announced, "It's almost time for dinner. Let's take our seats and find out what is in store for us this evening."

Anna liked it that theirs was a circular table, and when all of them were seated, she watched and listened as Russell Layne stood up to speak a few words.

"Welcome to the last few hours of the tenth year of the twenty-first century. As we gather here together, we are also ten years into the seventh known age of humankind." He paused to sip his drink before he continued. "The world has changed markedly over the last two thousand years, the sixth known age of humankind, and we can safely assume that it will change dramatically during the next two thousand years as well. The transition from one age to the other doesn't happen in a day, and I'm told it takes twenty years, one entire generation, to initialize and turn the corner, if you will. We are halfway through that twenty-year period tonight, and the pace of that transition is about to accelerate. This passage will not be fully known or understood for many more years, but I am sure that Project 4000 will constitute a critical step in seeing and turning the corner. Its import will become increasingly obvious as the years unfold."

Layne looked at each one of them as he considered his next words. "I have good reason to believe that there are millions more throughout the world upon whom this passage is also well impressed. For most, it is not much more than a subconscious and unexplained feeling. They are restless and searching, but for what they do not yet know. My friends," Layne paused for dramatic effect, "what they are searching for will be revealed at Acoma Pueblo in a few short months.

"As in other ages before this one, what is found there may or may not meet the expectations of some people. That is not our concern. Our job is to set the table. Sages, wise men, and master souls will bring the nourishment and understanding. With that in mind, I offer a toast to each one of you, and I wish for all of us the kind of successful event we have begun to envision. Even more, I wish for a vision grand enough to serve mankind well for the next two thousand years."

Russell Layne raised his glass and lifted it toward the center of the table.

Everyone else did likewise, except for Malik, but Anna watched as Father Garces took Malik's hand and raised it along with his own to complete the toast. She thought it sweet of Father Garces to include him again.

Layne continued to hold the floor and said, "I promised my friend Father Pedro Garces that I would allow a smattering of religion to grace these proceedings, and he has kindly volunteered to offer a prayer before we eat."

Layne sat down, and Father Garces, unable to stand up easily, remained in his wheelchair and reached to his right for Susan's hand and to his left for Malik's. He lowered his head and closed his eyes as the circle of hands was completed.

He started his prayer slowly, allowing each utterance to float through the silence before it sank into the hearts and minds of those present.

"Mother ... Father ... God ... Allah ... Buddha ... Krishna ... Jesus ... Great Spirit ... Tao. We offer our prayer to all the names and faces of the one universal spirit and to all the saints and visionaries of the true and only light. We bow to all of you and ask this simple prayer: Open our hearts each day so that we can know our highest task. Strengthen our minds so that we can persist in this that we have chosen to begin. Unify us in our endeavor so that we can show the world the power of unity in the universe. Bless this food, these people, and this night. Peace. Aum. Amen."

Anna crossed herself, opened her eyes, and raised her head. She had never heard such a prayer from a Catholic priest—or anyone else, for that matter. She looked around the table as everyone returned to the moment in front of them and to the unified cause that would lead them into the New Year. She picked up and sipped from her glass of wine and observed the room in silence. As it had been earlier in the evening for her, everything felt perfect once more.

Then, Father Garces spoke to them all. "Russell Layne and I have talked about the seventh clue some more. For those who may not know it yet, it tells of teachers who open doors for all of us—different teachers, same doors. Then the clue tells us of the requirement that no teacher can fulfill for us, the requirement for each of us to walk through that opened door on our own." He paused a moment and looked at Anna.

She felt his fatherly look all the way to her heart.

"Russell also told me of Anna's interpretation of that clue, and she is right. It does speak to all of you on the need to be fully and completely involved in this developing, collective vision of the meeting in June."

The old priest rested for a moment, closed his eyes, and took a deep breath. "As you may know, I have had a vision of this meeting, too, and I must share it with you tonight, for this ninety-five-year-old body will not last much longer." He coughed and took a drink from his glass. "The meeting is also a door—a very large door. Many teachers will be there, and the door will be thrown open wide so that all who wish to walk through it may do so right away. Contrary to what my religion has come to represent, contrary to what all religions have come to stand for, there is no one to save you or me or any of us. There is no one to carry us on the back of their own illumination or enlightenment. There is no one to intercede on our behalf. That is the larger meaning of the seventh clue."

No one spoke for several minutes. The priest looked tired and old as he sat there in his wheelchair; his head was down, and his weathered hands were folded together in his lap. Finally, he lifted his eyes and looked around the table with a benevolent gaze and chuckled softly. He leaned forward slightly and said, "I know what my wise and knowing guru would say right now. I can guess what action he would deem appropriate for this very solemn moment. He would look at all of us very sternly, and with a twinkle in his eye, he would say, 'Eat your dinner.'"

Everyone laughed and began to do just that.

~ ~ ~

Anna had chosen the menu. After the shrimp cocktail came the Caesar salad and then baked salmon with croquets, green beans, and new potatoes with onions. There were two kinds of bread and the traditional apple pie for dessert.

She enjoyed the company of the priest and Jack and thought them both to be jovial dinner companions. Along with Russell Layne, they kept the conversation light and funny. Even Malik entered into the banter with notes that he would hand to the priest to be read aloud. Thomas and Xuan sat close to each other, and Anna wondered if they were holding hands under the table. They laughed a lot and seemed to enjoy the repartee. Digger was unusually quiet, and Susan seemed to enjoy herself, even though she was in a group of strangers.

At ten thirty, Thomas stood up and announced, "I've promised the lovely lady on my left a dance, and, if she'll join me, I think I'll go through those double doors and make good on that promise right now." He looked at Xuan.

She smiled, pushed back her chair, stood up, and took his arm. Together, they headed for the ballroom doors.

"I'd certainly be careful what doors you go through from here on out, Thomas," the priest said over his shoulder as they were leaving, "especially double doors." He winked at Anna, and she winked back.

"Warning received, Father," Thomas said over his shoulder, and Xuan smiled, too.

Anna saw Jack signal Digger. The two of them got up and headed toward the balcony on the east side of the room. She moved her chair closer to Father Garces, which put the cleric between her and Malik and Susan on the other side of Malik.

"Mr. Layne told us that you have dreams about this meeting," Anna said to the priest. "What are they like? What are they about?"

"They are difficult to describe," he began. "I don't always trust them. The characters go in and out of focus. Sometimes I am in the dreams myself, and sometimes I'm not. Once in a while the characters talk to me. One time there was someone—I don't know who exactly because I couldn't see his face—who was bent over and writing down what was being said. I could only see the top of his head."

Just then, from the priest's right, Malik thrust one of his hands forward, almost striking the old cleric in the face. In it was one of his scraps of paper.

The priest took his hand and then the paper and read the question that was scribbled there: "Did you notice the people's feet?"

Father Garces searched his memory pictures for a moment and found no recollection. "No, Malik, I don't remember seeing their feet. Why do you ask?"

Malik began writing quickly and intently on his pad. Anna and Father Garces waited for him to finish. When he did, he again pushed two small pages out in the direction from which their voices were coming and again almost struck Father Garces.

The priest pushed his wheelchair back a little and took the notes. Malik wrote, "I dream of a meeting, too. The people in my dream all look and talk differently, and I am busy writing what they say. They all wear sandals on their feet, but all the sandals are different, too."

Before the priest could respond to Malik, Anna piped in, "Father, do you recognize any of the people in your dreams?"

The priest laughed at having two comments at once from his young audience. "I don't recognize their faces, Anna, and I haven't noticed their sandals, Malik. I guess I'm going to have to remember more details the next time I have this dream." He then turned to Malik and asked him, "Do you think the meeting of which you dream is in the future or in the past?"

Malik scribbled one word and pushed the paper toward Father Garces. "Past," it said.

"That's fascinating," the priest mused. "I think my dream meeting is in the future. I think my dream is about the meeting all of you are planning, the meeting that Malik will be transcribing for the entire world to see."

Before the priest could go on, Anna broke in again and reflected on this last observation. "I think it is really interesting that Malik's blindness will allow the world to see more clearly. Isn't it ironic, Father?"

Father Garces looked at Malik with his best priestly smile as he affirmed her observation. "It really is ironic, I suppose, but one of my teachers in college many years ago used to say that sometimes one has to close one's eyes in order to truly see. Now I know what he meant, and I think he was right."

Malik quickly scribbled another note and handed it over. "I hear better, too, now that I can't see," it said.

The priest again smiled at Malik and said, "I imagine you do, my boy. I imagine you do."

~   ~   ~

Meanwhile, Jack and Digger were engaged in a discussion out on the balcony. Jack started it with an admission.

"I don't have much confusion in my life, Digger. It's always been that way for me. My grandfather and father were both strong and decisive men. I have usually been decisive, too, but the words of the Jemez keeper woman have confused me a great deal."

"Is it because you don't have a daughter, Jack?" Digger asked.

"I told you I don't have a daughter, but I may be wrong. I visited the women's council two days ago and asked them about the keeper woman from Jemez. I told them what she said, and all of them found it odd except one old woman. She knew my father better than the others and said she knew something that might help me figure it out. She reminded me that many years ago, while I was home from college for the summer, I knew a young woman from the Jemez Pueblo. She asked me if I had been with her and I told her I didn't remember." He looked at Digger and continued, "You must understand, Digger, I drank a lot in those days."

Embarrassed by the recollection, Jack turned away from Digger for a moment and looked at the lights and the mountains beyond. "This woman who knew my father said he came to her the next summer to ask if I could still become Iyatiku if I broke a sacred Pueblo law. My father didn't say which law, and she didn't ask, but she knew the young lady had given birth that spring at Jemez, and she wondered once or twice if maybe I was the father."

"No wonder you've been worried, Jack. Do you know what has become of the woman or the child?" Digger asked.

"No, but I must find out," Jack answered. "Perhaps the child is my daughter."

"Do you know what sacred law you might have broken?"

"Oh yes," Jack answered. "An Iyatiku is not allowed to have children out of wedlock. If I had known of it, I could not have allowed myself to become Iyatiku when my father became one with the clouds."

"Did your father cover it up, then?" Digger inquired.

This question troubled Jack the most. He thought a long time before answering it. "He might have done that if he thought it the best thing for the Pueblo. Many of our young people who could have become Iyatiku were already gone and never planned to come back. By the time I was ready to be Iyatiku, I had been living and teaching at the Pueblo for twenty years. It was widely accepted that I would be the next Iyatiku, and many respected me. Some even thought I would become wise one day. But if my father chose to overlook the sacred law in this instance, it would be the only time I ever knew him to do it. It troubles me."

"Are your sons being trained to assume your position?" he asked Jack.

Jack answered slowly, "No, not really. Not yet, anyway. There is no law that it must be one of them, and no law that it can't be, either. They don't live at the Pueblo anymore, and, besides, there is still time before the training must begin."

"What if the Jemez woman is right? Will you train a woman to be Iyatiku at Acoma?" Digger persisted.

"The women's council agreed that the fear of Enchanted Mesa may soon be dissipated. If that is so, then anyone can approach me about it. The women's council may even insist that I seek a woman for the job. If a woman demonstrates strong medicine and is honest, it doesn't matter, really," Jack answered, "as long as they are kind and peaceful, too."

Digger looked to the east and leaned on the balcony rail. Finally, he spoke his mind. "Jack, I want to discuss other things the Jemez Woman said the other day. Thomas and the others should know of it, but you asked me to wait before I tell them. Can we talk about it now, you and me?"

"I like that you respect my wishes, Digger," Jack began, "and I can tell you have been troubled by all of this. I think the Jemez Woman is amazing, and she's probably right. There will be seven of us and seven of them."

"You mean seven masters, Jack?" Digger asked.

"Yes. Seven teachers or masters or sages, something like that," he answered. "And it makes sense that I will stay behind to shelter the blind one at Acoma Pueblo while he writes his final notes."

"Where do you think I will go?" Digger asked.

"I don't know."

"What do you think the yellow wind is?"

"I don't know that either," Jack responded. "Her picture in the dirt made me think of a tornado, but the sand painters' yellow column looked different, somehow. Did you and Thomas come up with anything on what that might mean?"

"No, not yet," Digger said. "I wanted to talk some more with you, first."

"After the Jemez Woman visited the other day, I remembered an old, abandoned stone house at the southwestern edge of the Pueblo lands," Jack said. "I went there yesterday. It's well hidden in one of the canyons, and there's a natural spring near by. The voice in me said to get it ready for Malik. That's where he will live after the meeting. I will take care of him there until he can finish the notes."

Digger listened intently to Jack. "Do you think I will live or die, Jack? Can you tell me that?"

"Living and dying are different from what she said, my boy. She just said you would leave," Jack reminded him. He reached out and gently touched him on the shoulder.

"Try not to worry, Digger," Jack went on. "I've seen nothing about this meeting that makes me worry, and I don't think you should worry, either. Everything will work out, I'm sure." Jack offered his hand to Digger and shook it with strength and confidence as he looked him straight in the eye.

It was a long moment between them, and it helped Digger calm his fears.

Then Jack finished, "Even my worries about these Iyatiku matters will resolve themselves. Perhaps I should take my own advice."

~   ~   ~

When Jack and Digger reentered the room, Anna met them and told them it was time to uncork the champagne. She asked Digger to get Thomas and Xuan from the dance floor. By the time they all returned, it was 11:45.

Russell Layne assumed the honor of opening the champagne and carefully poured everyone a glass. Soon, they were all in a circle, and they closed ranks until they were touching shoulders. Even the priest stood for this moment.

"I think we can all hold our glasses in our right hands while we place our left arm around the person next to us," Layne suggested. "Directly or indirectly, we are all connected to each other tonight and for the foreseeable future. Part of me is anxious, but it is the kind of anxiety that also contains exhilaration. It's like climbing a mountain or driving a fast car too fast. We can be scared, I suppose, but it will cause us to focus even better. If we keep our eyes open and try not to worry, there will be lots of fun, too."

He looked around at all of them and continued. "We will, I suspect, become like a family over the next six months, and, as I promised some of you at lunch the other day, this experience will no doubt change each of us forever. I also think we are committed to finish what we have begun."

With that, Layne raised his glass, and the others followed suit. He toasted the New Year with, "May we all embrace the winds of change about to blow through our lives with perseverance, dedication, and trust. May we do so with the innocence of little children and with all the love we can muster."

Glasses clinked, and Thomas muttered, "Hear! Hear!"

The priest whispered, "Amen."

Everyone smiled and drank the champagne. They heard the countdown from the ballroom next door, and the band played the first notes of "Auld Lang Syne." The second decade of the third millennium had begun.

Section II:

Collecting the Energy

Chapter 1

January 2010

The first working day at the Project 4000 offices in January 2010 was chaotic. Xuan Lee moved in, and with her came three boxes of stuff. Malik Mohammed arrived and, with Digger's assistance, set up the equipment that had been promised for his office. Anna Izturias oversaw all of it and made sure phones were hooked up, power cords and computers were supplied, new furniture was delivered, and everyone felt at home.

Thomas arrived late and seemed distracted. As soon as Digger saw him, he excused himself from helping Malik and headed across the hall to talk with his boss.

Digger barged into his office and blurted out, "Thomas, we've got to talk about the sand art we saw at the council meeting. Until we give it some sort of interpretation, I can't continue a necessary discussion with Jack that, in turn, will lead to an important conversation with you that will then help me make some sense out of another meeting I had with the keeper woman from the Jemez Pueblo."

"Whoa, Digger, slow down a minute. You lost me," Thomas said as he removed his coat. "Now start over, please."

"Okay." Digger took a deep breath and began again. "When I met that Jemez Pueblo woman last week, she made a drawing in the dirt for Jack and me that we agree looked a lot like the sand art you and I witnessed in the kiva at Acoma."

"Gotcha," Thomas said. "Go on."

"Okay. She also said some things that revealed a lot about the meeting, but I promised Jack I wouldn't discuss what she said with anyone until you and I conversed about the sand art. Once that happens, then he and I can talk some more about what she said," Digger explained. "Only then can I understand it better so I can report it accurately back to you."

"Okay, now I understand," Thomas said as he sat down at his desk. "This is getting kind of complicated, isn't it? Let's see. Maybe the sand art is a depiction of the meeting in June. That's what it looks like, anyway. It could be the Acoma Pueblo set against a mountain backdrop and elevated on a plateau like Enchanted Mesa or Acoma Mesa, right?"

"Maybe so, but I think the most important question is, what does that yellow column in the middle of the sand art represent? I've thought about it a hundred times and have yet to come up with an answer I like."

"It could just be the symbol for an ear of corn," Thomas said, "or maybe the perfect ear of corn representing bounty and a thousand years of relying on the Corn God to supply what is required at Acoma. Does that sound like a plausible explanation to you?"

"Yes, I suppose," Digger said.

"Well, it's certainly logical to me. Isn't the Pueblo economy tied to corn?" Thomas asked. "They've got rituals centered around it and annual festivals and those irrarikos things in the kiva. Corn is essential to them, so I'm not surprised to see it show up as a major symbol for a sacred meeting like ours. In fact, it seems like a very reasonable presumption."

"So, you think it could be some sort of confirmation to their council that our meeting there would be good? The perfect corn affirms the perfect plan, or something like that?"

"Does that seem feasible to you?" Thomas asked.

"Well, perhaps," Digger replied, "But what if it's a shaft of light or a column of wind that signifies an even bigger event of some sort? Shafts of light have symbolized important transformations or changes for thousands of years in mythologies, tribal tales, children's stories, and sacred texts of all kinds. There are dozens of them, maybe hundreds."

"Well, Digger, you're the archaeologist in this conversation; do you think it could be something like that?"

"That's just it," Digger said. "I don't know for sure. The transforming event theory fits with what Russell Layne has been saying about this meeting. He calls it a new direction, but it could still be some sort of symbolic blessing of what we're doing, or it could just simply represent the perfect ear of corn and the abundance that is promised. It could be almost anything, Thomas."

Thomas leaned back in his chair and looked out the window as he listened to Digger's frustration. "Don't you just love symbolism, Digger? I mean, it's clear as mud to both of us. Now that I think about it even more, I suppose it could also be a shaft of sunlight, couldn't it? This meeting ends on the longest day of the year, the summer solstice, right?"

Digger nodded.

"Right," Thomas said, "so that adds to the possibilities, doesn't it?"

"Yes, it does." Digger ran his hand through his hair and down the back of his neck. "A lot of the older southwestern cultures have an astronomical basis—the Mayans, the Chaco Canyon people, and the Pueblo Bonita culture. There are probably others, too. Perhaps this is about astronomy or solar influences of some kind? That just adds even more to the mystery of it, I suppose."

"Well, yes, "Thomas agreed, "but astronomical influences are not very fashionable these days. Of course, Jesus was reportedly born under a star, and several sages and wise men saw the star and followed it to his birthplace."

"Oh, yeah, I forgot about that one," Digger admitted. "I should tell you, however, that the Jemez Woman described it as a 'yellow wind.'"

"Hmm! That's interesting. A yellow wind, huh?" Thomas sat back in his chair and stroked his thin beard. He reflected on the foregoing discussion and all the possibilities that had been raised. Finally, he told Digger, "You tell Jack whatever you want about our thoughts on this. It's got too many possibilities for us to select just one narrow interpretation. It could be a blessing or an affirmation or a symbol or a solar light or a transforming wind. Heck, it might even be all of those."

"Okay," Digger agreed. "I'll call him on his cell phone this morning. That will allow him and me to have some other discussions, too."

"Good," Thomas concurred. "On another front, I've scheduled a general staff meeting for Tuesday at ten o'clock. Let Jack know about it when you talk to him. If he wants to meet with us earlier Tuesday, say about nine o'clock, we can discuss this some more. Does that sound all right with you?"

"Yep, got it," Digger said. "I'll get on it right now."

"Good. By the way, you're doing a good job here, Digger. There's a lot of productive thinking on this project, and you've helped it along. I want you to know I appreciate it."

With that, Digger departed Thomas's office, and Anna came in before Thomas had time to collect himself. She plopped down in one of Thomas's chairs.

He looked up and said, "Good morning, Anna. Are you getting everyone settled in?" He had come to appreciate Anna's organizational abilities and liked her helpful attitude. "You know," he continued, "I want to thank you for the party the other night. I enjoyed myself."

"Oh, that's good. You're welcome," she answered. "I had fun, too, and I really like Father Garces. He's such a precious old man. He's sure not like any priest I've ever met."

"I know what you mean," Thomas agreed. "The minister at Ebenezer Baptist Church back home in Tupelo could learn a few things from the good father."

"We all could," Anna added.

Just then, Russell Layne walked into Thomas's office. "Sorry I'm late," he said, "but I had to take Father Garces to the hospital late last night, and I went to check on him this morning before I came in."

"Oh, no! Is he all right?" Anna asked.

"I think so," Layne answered. "The doctors think it's just fatigue, but they're going to run a few more tests today. He asked me if you'd come visit him this afternoon, Anna." He turned and looked at Thomas. "Is that okay with you?"

"Sure, no problem."

"Good," Russell said. "I see that Xuan and Malik are getting moved in. I guess I better go find a furniture store and get going, too." He looked at Anna and asked, "Which office did you assign me, by the way?"

"The best one, of course," she said as she got up. "Follow me. I'll show it to you."

Thomas took this opportunity to check in on Xuan and found her unloading her last box as he walked into her new office.

She had already hung her degrees and certificates and a few pictures on the walls. Now, she was bringing out the desk trinkets: phone file, paperweight, name plate, and a picture of her parents.

"Have you told them about this adventure yet, Xuan?" Thomas opened as he looked at the picture.

"Told who?" she asked, raising her eyes from the box and seeing the picture Thomas was studying. "Oh, my parents, you mean? No, not yet. I will eventually."

"Any idea how they will react to your new job?"

"It'll be okay with Daddy, I imagine," she said. "Mom will probably freak out a little. They're both pretty conservative."

"I've not thought much how my folks will respond, but I've come to believe that this is not such a radical thing that we're doing. In some ways, it's just a small paradigm shift, when you boil it all down. I mean, nothing is being thrown away so much as other things are being added."

"Oh, I disagree," Xuan replied. "Too many people, it seems to me, are really locked into their version of the truth, and there's no room for any other versions of the truth or any other visions. That will be hard to overcome."

"Well, maybe so. It's sure going to be interesting to watch it unfold." He looked at Xuan as she arranged things on her desk and then said, "By the way, do you have any plans for the weekend?"

Xuan stood up from what she was doing and looked at Thomas. She brushed her hair back from her face and straightened her blouse. "No, Mr. Walls, I don't have any plans, but I'd like some." She smiled at him and asked, "You know anybody?"

"Yes, I do, Ms. Lee," he teased her back, "but now that you work here, I'm worried that you might view my propositions as harassment."

"Oh, I already do," Xuan answered. "The question is what I plan to do about it, if anything." She smiled at Thomas as she reached behind him and softly closed the office door. She placed her hand on his shoulder and looked into his dark brown eyes. "I think I'd really like to get out of town for a few days this weekend. Does that sound good to you?"

Thomas drew her close and kissed her lightly on the forehead. "Yes, it does, actually. I just don't know if I can afford two hotel rooms."

Xuan looked at him for a long moment. "I think we can get by with just one room."

She tilted her head to one side, and Thomas saw the slightest smile playing on the corners of her mouth.

Then she added, "That is, if you don't mind sleeping in the car."

Thomas looked right back at her and said, "You're crazier than I thought if you think I'm going to sleep in that Mustang. No way, Xuan." He leaned down and kissed her fully on the lips. "No way."

Still holding him close, she asked. "Where should we go?"

"How about Pagosa Springs? It's in a gorgeous little valley high up in the mountains a few hours north of here, and there's skiing nearby."

"That sounds really nice," she answered. "I'll pack Thursday evening, and we can leave from the office after work on Friday."

"It's a deal," he smiled.

"It'll be fun," she agreed. "Now, Mr. Thomas Walls, have you got a job description for me to review, or are we just winging it here at this loosely run speculative venture?"

"We're winging it, but don't let that fool you for one minute, ma'am. See if Anna will get you a copy of the seven clues and update you on our progress. That's the next big mystery we have to solve," Thomas pointed out, "and we'll need everyone working on it."

"Got it," Xuan answered. "I like the big mysteries the best."

"Well if you like mysteries so much, you might be thinking of ways to keep me from sleeping in that car Friday night," Thomas suggested.

"No sir," she answered. "That's your mystery."

Chapter 2

Anna and the Priest

Anna arrived at the hospital to see Father Garces around 4:30 p.m. She thought about how he had said and done things she had never seen a priest say and do. He had a guru. He prayed to the saints of all religions, and he gave a crystal prism to Russell Layne. These were actions that set him apart from the priests she had known in El Paso and Albuquerque. She wondered if he was some kind of rebel cleric, but she was drawn to him anyway. She quietly entered his room and found him staring out the window.

"Hi, Father. How are you feeling?" she asked in her best hospital voice as she neared his bed.

He turned toward her and sat up just a little as he patted down his remaining gray hairs. "Hello, child, I'm glad you came. What is it like at the office today?"

"In a word, crazy," she reported. "Xuan and Malik are moving in, and I can tell it's going to get busier in a hurry. Plus, Mr. Layne is moving in soon, as well." Anna was never sure what to do or say in hospitals, and she felt her anxiety rising as she searched for things to talk about. She sensed the priest searching her face as she sat there in silence.

"Anna," he began, "you can ask me any question you like. I know I'm not your average, run-of-the-mill priest—probably not like any other you have known. So, come on, out with it. What do you want to know?"

Anna thought for a moment and felt her anxiety begin to subside. Finally, she asked him, "Mr. Layne showed us a crystal prism, I think, and he said it came from your guru. Is that true?"

"That the crystal came from my guru or that I have a guru?" The priest laughed quietly and easily.

"Well, both, I guess," Anna stammered. "I've never known a priest with a guru."

"Yes, most priests don't have them," the priest admitted. "He's really just a mentor, I suppose. I've had several mentors in seventy years as a priest. All of them have been Catholics, but about ten years ago, when I was eighty-five, I looked around, and there were none in the church to whom I could look up to any more. All of them had died or retired. As one of the oldest priests, it seems like the rest of them wanted me to be their mentor, and I had no one who could help me continue to grow."

He smiled at her. "It's not easy being so old, you know."

Anna laughed with him as he shared some more.

"About then, I was introduced to an old Hindu guru, and a trust soon developed between us. We shared our toughest questions with each other and derived some answers, but, more importantly, Anna, he showed me more questions." Father Garces rearranged the pillows behind his back and then continued. "Having more questions was pretty maddening at first, but I found myself growing again, so I opened myself up even further to what we were teaching each other. What was really interesting, though, was that most of what we were teaching each other was in line with the basic elements of our faiths and just served to expand them rather than refute them. Does that make sense?"

"I suppose so," she answered.

"I'm still a Catholic, in case you're worried, but now I think I am even more than that. It's like I'm no longer limited by the Catholic constructs, and my faith seems a lot bigger and much more universal. As a person, I see so much more dimension in my own being than when I was younger. I see that I am much more than a priest, too."

"But the Bible says Jesus is the only way. Do gurus believe that, too?" Anna inquired, still perplexed.

"Gurus believe in Jesus, yes, they do, but they believe in all men who have attained illumination like Jesus did. More importantly, they believe that illumination is available to all people without limits. If people were to think in the light, act in the light, feel in the light, and become one with the light, like Jesus did, they would become like Jesus in every way. In fact, Anna, many learned men and women think it is the destiny of all people to become illumined like him."

"So the Bible's wrong?" Anna asked with a worried look.

"No, child, the Bible's okay, but it's been through two thousand years of interpretation and translation, and it was written by men to begin with. So, for example, the phrase 'No man cometh unto the father but by me' has come to be interpreted narrowly by men of the church as if Jesus the Nazarene was the only conduit. I used to believe narrowly like that, too. Now I have come to believe that there is an expanded version. It goes something like this: 'No man becomes illumined except that he or she feel, think, and act as Jesus did; free of illusion, full of a very large faith and grounded in the belief that all of us are created to uncover the highest and best in ourselves.'

"I now believe that we are all programmed, like the mustard seed, to become our highest and best. Almost every religion has people like Jesus who can show us how to do it or point us in the right direction," he finished.

"But isn't the Bible the only book of God?" Anna continued as she remembered another one of the lessons she had learned in catechism.

The priest fell silent for a moment and looked out the window again. The sun was now completely gone, and the sky was darkening quickly on the short winter day.

"I used to think that, Anna, but I don't anymore. I still think it is inspired but nowhere near flawless. I think there are countless other inspired writings from before and after the Bible, too. It is sometimes comforting to think that our truths are the only truths, but they're not. If the Bible is the only source, that implies that an infinite God has finite favorites, like the Jews and Christians. That kind of thinking further suggests that God quit writing and quit inspiring other writers hundreds of years ago. I can't imagine either of those as true, can you?"

"I guess not," Anna replied in a voice filled with hesitation. "I think I even have inspired thoughts from time to time."

"Sure you do," the priest responded. "So do I, and so does everyone else. God has not quit inspiring the truth in all people just because one group of people wants to claim that he has. It is as if they take pride in the fact that their God is done writing or even dead in that way. Now that's a heck of a claim. I guess maybe they do all the writing for him these days." He looked at Anna and winked.

"That's interesting! I see what you're saying," Anna said. "What about the idea of Jesus being a sacrifice for us and our sins?"

"I'm afraid that may be the biggest misunderstanding of them all," the priest replied. "Do you remember the story when Jesus went into the temple and disrupted all the money changers and sellers of sacrificial animals? He got so angry! Do you remember that story?" he asked Anna.

"Yes, of course I do," she answered.

"Most biblical scholars interpret that event to mean that Jesus was mad at the loan sharks and similar types for desecrating the temple with issues of commerce, or that he was mad at those who were selling animals for sacrificial rituals that were pagan or cruel."

"That's how I remember it," Anna said.

"That's how it has been taught in most places and certainly in the Catholic churches I was a part of," he explained. "But I think there's another message in his

anger. He wanted the people to see that sacrificial animals and other sacrificial rituals were a waste of time and didn't do any appreciable good anyway. He thought
what was needed was for men and women to make the sacrifice of changing themselves and changing the ways they thought, the ways they acted, and the ways they
believed. He thought that any other sacrifices were, in a word, useless."

"You really think so?" Anna asked.

"Yes, I do, but despite that lesson, what did people immediately do when Jesus
was killed?"

"I don't know. They made him the sacrificial symbol?"

"Exactly!" the priest exclaimed. "Just like the priests before Jesus had their rules
for proper sacrifice, the church fathers after Jesus have taught and insisted that
Jesus was a sacrifice, too. They tried to make him exactly what he warned against,
and they have done exactly what his anger demonstrated he was concerned about.
The point was completely missed!"

"But he gave up his life," Anna argued.

"Only so he could show us what I think he really came to show us: that we
have the power to overcome death," the priest insisted.

"And he showed us this power through sacrificing himself and dying for us,
right?" she asked.

"Yes and no," Father Garces said. "If heaven is so great and being with God is
so great, then where is Jesus's sacrifice in dying? I mean, if you really believe life in
heaven is better than life on earth, where is the sacrifice in going to heaven?"

"Oh, gosh. I don't know."

"And, Anna, if one can overcome death, and I believe he did, what is the big
deal about dying? I mean, it looks like a terrible sacrifice for those who don't
believe, but to those who truly believe that they're going to be with God or truly
believe they can overcome death, there is no sacrifice at all."

Anna fidgeted in her hospital chair and fingered her cross. She looked at Father
Garces as he went even further.

"In overcoming death," he said, "Jesus proved to most people that it could be
done, and then, of his own free will, he voluntarily left the earth again after about
forty days. Nobody hung him on a cross the second time he departed or forced
him to wear a crown of thorns or buried him in a cave. He rejoined something
bigger than himself of his own volition. No sacrifice and no savior, but a great
example for everyone who could see it clearly and a great proof of the ability to
overcome death by anyone who was really paying attention. It is the second act of
ascension that deserves the attention, not the so-called sacrifice on the cross."

"Oh my, father," Anna muttered under her breath. "That's blasphemous." She stood up and turned away from the old priest. She wanted to get up and leave because his words had made her so uncomfortable.

Then he said one more thing.

"'All this and even more, you can do also.' Anna, these are his words, and I think they are the real message of Jesus—the most powerful words ever spoken—because they tell all of us of our true potential."

Anna turned back to face him. She reached for a tissue on his nightstand and wiped the tears from her eyes. The comfort she always gained from her religion was gone and had been thrown against the rocks of logic and reason. She remembered the revelations just a few years before, when the writings of Mother Teresa had told of her own crisis of faith that had lasted fifty years or longer. Anna wondered if that was now her fate, too, and she felt the tears well up inside her again. She suddenly felt lost and alone.

She looked at Father Garces through her tears and sensed that he knew what she was going through.

He spoke to her again. "Child, do not make the mistake of throwing out anything that you believe. I don't want you to do that, and there is no need to do that. What you believe is just fine as far as it goes, but now it must go much further. Build anew on what you know, and know that all the rest of us must build anew, too."

Anna felt him watching her as she calmed and collected herself little by little. She dared to look at him again and saw the smile of a saint, not a rebel. She knew that he was telling her his truth after a lifetime of service to her very own church. His sincerity was obvious.

"The trouble," he went on in a moment, "is that people like me have spent our entire lives telling people like you that our beliefs were the truth, the only, and the best. Now I see that there is a larger truth and my beliefs have been wrongly cast and poorly understood. Anna, if I could find a priest right now to whom I could give my confession, I would confess to living a priestly lie for seventy-five years and telling a story that I now know is incomplete and has been distorted for much longer than that."

His frail voice rose as he became frustrated and began again. "I have helped to promulgate several lies in the name of absolute truth. I regret that very much. The Catholic Church is not the universal church, and neither is any other church or religion."

His voice gained strength and rose even higher. "The Hindus don't have the whole truth, and neither do the Muslims, the Taoists, the Protestants, the Jews, or anybody else. All of our churches and synagogues and ashrams and temples and pagodas and mosques are shrines to partial truths!"

He was sitting all the way up in his bed now, and Anna was worried he might fall and hurt himself. She readied herself so that she could calm him down if needed.

"A shrine to partial truths, Anna, is also a shrine to partial lies. Neither of them deserves to be enshrined. Before I die, I'd like someone to understand that and to clear up that little entrenched set of lies—lies that have been repeated for hundreds of years and are being told all over the world by religions all over the world."

Anna saw the tears running down the old priest's cheeks even as she saw him try to smile compassionately at her. She held his silent gaze for several minutes, and she felt his courage and saw his fatigue. She knew he would not be with them much longer.

His eyes closed for a long moment, and, when he opened them again, the look in them was distant and far removed from his hospital room and from her.

He then whispered one more thing. "Never lose your faith, my child, but do not worry about the beliefs. Beliefs are of man and are awfully small. They will always be subject to misunderstanding. Faith, my child, is of an infinite life force that lives inside each of us. It is the real essence of who we are." He smiled again and said, "Whatever else you do, find that essence in you."

Anna whispered, "Yes, Father," and crossed herself as he closed his eyes again and seemed to rest. She watched the very last slivers of light disappear from the western sky and felt the dark invade the room. She looked once again at the guru's priest and saw the smile still etched on his wrinkled face.

Chapter 3

Sha'wanna

That same afternoon, Jack Eaglefeather traveled to Jemez Pueblo to investigate the rumors that had troubled him for several days. His anxiety rose as he drove the last few miles of dirt roads and past the cattle guard that marked the entrance to Jemez. He made himself known to the local Iyatiku and asked for help in finding the woman, now almost fifty years old, with whom he might have fathered a child. He had known her as Tuwabon. She still lived in Jemez, and the Jemez Iyatiku led him to her home.

The little girl who answered the door looked to be about seven years of age. Jack asked for Tuwabon by name, and the little girl turned back inside and asked, "Mommy, where's grandma?"

Soon, a woman who looked to be about thirty came to the door and asked Jack, "Who are you that you wish to see my mother?"

Jack removed his hat and said, "My name is Jack Eaglefeather. I come from Acoma Pueblo to speak with your mother of things long ago. Do you know where I can find her?"

"She is a powerful woman in Jemez Pueblo. Perhaps she is in council right now," the woman answered.

"I can look for her, or I can wait," Jack responded. "I have driven a hundred miles to see her."

"What is it you wish to speak with her about?" the woman inquired as the little girl peeked around her legs and looked curiously at Jack.

He didn't answer immediately and shuffled his hat from one hand to the other as he looked away from the woman's piercing eyes. "It is between me and her. That's all that needs to be said," he explained.

"She told me once of a man she knew at Acoma long ago. Is that you?" she asked.

"Perhaps she was talking of me," Jack said. "I don't know."

The young woman seemed intent on continuing her questions, and her interrogating manner made Jack feel like he was on trial. He tried to extract himself from this discomfiting exchange and offered to wait on the front porch bench. Then Jack noticed the lines in the woman's face soften a little. When she smiled, Jack was struck by how familiar she looked to him—*like looking in a mirror*, he thought to himself. He wondered if this woman was his daughter.

"Can I get you some water?" she asked.

"Yes," Jack replied. "Thank you."

She left for a moment, and when she returned with the glass of water she spoke. "My mother will be the next Iyatiku at Jemez, and I have begun to study for it myself. Is it true that the Iyatiku at Acoma is a male, not a female?"

"Yes, it is true," Jack replied. "It has been that way for a thousand years."

"That seems so odd to me," the woman said.

Jack did not respond and didn't reveal that he was the Iyatiku at Acoma. He saw her look past him at something over his shoulder and turned to look himself.

A woman walked briskly toward them, and the daughter called out to her mother. "Tuwabon, this man wants to talk with you. Do you know him?"

Jack, still holding his hat in his hand, waited for her to reach them. She showed no sign of recognition, but Jack nodded in greeting and opened their conversation respectfully.

"I am Jack Eaglefeather from Acoma Pueblo."

Tuwabon said nothing as she looked him over. Her face had no expression as she finally replied, "I am Tuwabon, and I will talk to you if you wish, but it must be in private."

"Yes, that is good," Jack agreed.

"Can you wait here for a moment?" She went past her daughter and into the house. Her daughter followed, taking one last look at Jack as she went inside.

When Tuwabon returned, she motioned for Jack to follow her, and they went around behind the home and headed down a path that led through a shallow arroyo. They quickly passed the perimeter of the Pueblo and walked out into the scrub brush and sage beyond. Neither of them spoke, until finally Tuwabon stopped on the path and looked at Jack again.

"I was told you would be coming," she said.

Jack saw her look away as she wiped her hands on her apron.

"Yes, Jack, she is your daughter, but she doesn't know it, and I don't plan to tell her, either—at least not yet."

Jack noted her even tone and economy of words.

"Too many years have passed, and she has asked about a father only once. When she was little, I told her she was my gift from Sus'sistinako, and she believes it. She derives much power from that belief, though I must admit she is inebriated with her power sometimes."

"Is she kind?" Jack asked.

"Have you become kind, Jack?" Tuwabon shot back at him. "Have you?"

Jack stared back at those eyes, remembering now what he had found so alluring thirty years before. "Yes, I have," he answered. "Did my father know she was my child?" he asked. He dreaded the answer to this question most of all.

Tuwabon's face tightened and her muscles tensed as she looked once more at Jack. "She never was your child, Jack Eaglefeather, but I think your father knew she was from you."

"I drank too much in those days, and I don't remember our time together. Did I force myself on you?" He searched her eyes for some kind of clue.

She blinked and then looked away. When she returned her gaze to him, he saw a tear forming in the corner of one eye.

She exhaled and composed herself. "No, Jack. I was young and foolish. There were no men at this Pueblo that I could stand, and I thought I was in love with you. The truth is, I knew you weren't in love with me." She looked away again and then back. "It makes me mad that you don't remember our two nights together."

"I never knew of your pain. I feel bad for you," Jack started.

"Don't waste your pity on me," she interrupted. "My life is good enough, and it is my life. I don't regret what's happened. When I was done being angry, I gave myself to my people here at Jemez, and, in return, they gave to me, as well. I think I will be Iyatiku one day, and overcoming my experience with you has helped make me strong enough for that to be possible."

Jack listened to her story and felt the urge to tell his own. "I eventually came back to Acoma to teach and grow more in the Pueblo ways. Now, I am Iyatiku for eleven years, but I know that I must give it up, because my father hid the truth and I did not know my role in creating your daughter."

"Perhaps there is a way to make it right," Tuwabon suggested as her anger subsided. "Did you ever marry?"

"Yes. We had two sons. My wife became one with the clouds ten years ago. Sadly, my sons are not involved in the Pueblo at all," Jack admitted. "Did you marry?"

"No. I told myself I did not want that life, and there was no one here I wanted. I don't think any of them wanted me, either." She laughed a little at the memory. "I was a handful, and my anger went on for many years. In addition to all of that, there was Sha'wanna, too." Tuwabon answered.

"Your daughter is called Sha'wanna?" Jack asked.

"Yes, it comes from the Zuni Pueblo stories. I liked the sound of it," she replied.

"I came to know of her only a few days ago from the old keeper woman," Jack admitted. "She came to Acoma on another matter last week and insisted that it was time to make Iyatiku a woman again at Acoma, like in olden times. She has always said that, even when I was a boy, but this time she said I should make my daughter the Iyatiku at Acoma."

Jack looked at Tuwabon for some sort of reaction, but her face remained stoic.

He continued, "That has mystified me since she said it, because I didn't know of this daughter. She wants to be Iyatiku someday, doesn't she?"

"Yes, and she will make a good one, but she is still too young," Tuwabon said.

"Is it allowed for her to be Iyatiku at another Pueblo?" Jack asked. He was unsure, because the rules at the female Pueblos were different than at Acoma.

"I don't know the answer to that question. You're not training anyone at Acoma?"

"None have approached me, and my sons aren't interested," Jack said.

"I will ask around here to see if anyone can guide us," Tuwabon offered, "but you must ask your council, too, to see if a female Iyatiku from another Pueblo would be advisable at this time. That's a lot of change for a Pueblo."

"Yes, I know," Jack agreed.

Darkness had descended quickly at Jemez, and Tuwabon suggested with a nod of her head that they return to her home. They walked in silence back up the path to the edge of the Pueblo and on to the house. Smoke curled up from the chimney as they neared the door, and Tuwabon stopped before they entered and looked at Jack with compassion. "I'm glad you came and we talked, Jack Eaglefeather. Would you like to stay for dinner?"

"Thank you, but I have a lot to think about and a long drive ahead of me," Jack answered.

Just then, the little girl burst outside and hugged her grandmother around the legs. She looked up at Jack, who smiled down at her but said nothing. She watched him a little longer and then looked up at Tuwabon again.

"Look, he smiles just like mommy," the child exclaimed.

Jack laughed as Tuwabon said, "Yes, a little, I guess." She picked up the child and smiled one more time at Jack as she went inside.

Jack turned away from Tuwabon, as he had done years before, and there was a tear in his eye as he placed his hat on his head and walked back to his truck.

Chapter 4

Settling In

Malik M. Mohammed was okay living in the dormitories at the Institute for the Blind. It wasn't far from the Project 4000 offices, and the drive with Susan to his new job didn't seem too long.

As they crept toward the signal light at Coors Road to head north for his second day, Malik reflected on the conversation they had started on their way home the night before. Though he had been writing all his life, he didn't find it convenient to write down his half of their conversations. Writing instead of talking was cumbersome, and being blind made it even harder. Even so, being unable to talk since birth had no doubt given rise to his penchant, and need, for writing. Sometimes there wasn't time or energy to write down everything he might have to say on a given topic. He had learned through the years to be concise, but he still felt shortchanged at not being able to vocalize and think out loud so he could hear how something sounded before he committed it to paper.

Susan had become somewhat adept at guessing his thoughts in the few months she had spent with him, so that he could sometimes just use facial expressions and body language to agree or modify or even negate something she might say. Usually this worked pretty well.

She reminded him of his mom in the way she could guess what he was thinking sometimes, even before he could write it or communicate it in some other way.

His first-generation, Lebanese father had not been so good at talking, and their communication had been less developed than his with his mom. His dad, however, had been able to reach Malik through his sight, and before the car wreck that changed everything, they had traveled around New Mexico a great deal. Malik had seen at least a dozen of the Pueblos, and together they had made quite a collection of souvenirs and artifacts. They had spent long summer weekends visiting lots of places with each other when Malik was between the ages of thirteen and seventeen. Usually his mom didn't go with them, but one time she did—and that's when the car drifted off the two-lane road near Santa Rosa and came to rest upside down at the bottom of a ravine alongside the roadway. Malik was asleep in the backseat and was the only survivor.

On a previous excursion, his dad had gotten it in his mind that Malik should have a dream catcher. Malik hadn't been very impressed by the rather large one his dad insisted they buy at the Navajo Reservation store near Gallup, but, since his parents' deaths, he never failed to touch it on the wall of his dorm room every night and think of his father before he went to sleep. The dream catcher was, he remembered now, quite beautiful and intricate. He could still visualize its large feathers, intricate weaving, and symbolic turquoise center.

His dad had been a dreamer, too. Malik felt he had inherited that quality from him, and rarely did he now pass a night of sleep without remembering at least one dream, and sometimes two. He pulled out his pad and hastily scribbled a question to Susan as they finally paused at the traffic signal. "Do you think my parents would have approved of this job?"

"I think so," she said. "From what I've learned of them, I think they would have loved it. It sounds like the kind of adventure your dad would've liked."

Malik nodded his head as Susan made the right turn onto Coors Road.

Malik remembered his trips with his Dad quite well, especially the one they had made to Acoma Pueblo. His dad thought it the most interesting of all the Pueblos. He was fascinated by the way it sat there in the middle of all those mesas. It looked unassailable, and he imagined the first time the Indians had seen it. They must have been ecstatic at finding a place that seemed so safe. His dad even wondered if maybe some boy like Malik had been the first to scale the rock face and find the things up top that were so essential to survival: the natural cisterns where the rainwater collected, and the long views in every direction that provided first warning of what was coming their way.

Malik reflected for a moment and wrote, "Have you been to Acoma?"

"No," she answered. "I'm not much interested in all that rocky mesa stuff."

Malik wished he could tell his teacher of his dad's fascination with historical sites. His dad would get so excited and animated whenever he was in the middle of something like Acoma. He often told Malik he could imagine anything. He had this ability to place himself into the moment of some battle that had taken place hundreds of years before. He could picture the men making the bricks and building a church or a courthouse. He could see them on the day they prepared for war or huddled together in an unexpected snowstorm as they readied for a hunt in early spring when the food stores had almost run out. This ability to imagine was something Malik thought his dad had passed along to him, too, and he realized that his father had given him a tool perhaps much better than the eyesight he no longer possessed. He had taught him imagination and vision not born of eyesight.

As he thought of his father now, he realized just how much he missed his boyhood moments with him. In fact, his dad had prepared him so well that Malik suddenly understood that his dad might have somehow known, perhaps just an intuition, that this adventure was in Malik's future. *Yes*, he thought, *his dad would approve*.

Malik then wrote Susan another note. "I saw my dad in a dream last night." He gave the note to her, and she read it at the next light.

"Really?" she asked him.

Malik nodded his head.

"Will you tell me about it tonight on our ride home?"

He nodded again.

Susan then steered the car into the parking lot of the office building that housed Project 4000. When she got in front of the door, she stopped and turned to Malik, "I'm running late. Can you make it in okay?"

He nodded as he fumbled in the backseat for his stick and backpack.

She said, "See ya this afternoon, Malik."

He closed the door and turned to feel for the curb and get his bearings. After a moment, he started toward the glass front of the building, and she headed back to the institute.

Malik entered the offices to find only Digger had arrived so far. He offered to make Malik a cup of coffee as he made his own. Malik refused the offer with a shake of his head and a smile and headed to his office.

Once Digger's cup was ready, he went down the hall to Malik's office holding a videotape in his other hand and asked, "Did Anna get the VCR hooked up to the television for you, yet?"

Malik fumbled for a pad and pen and wrote, "No, needs cable."

Digger read the note quickly and asked, "Is she bringing some cable this morning?"

Malik nodded.

"Good," Digger continued. "I brought this tape on ancient Egypt that I found at a used bookstore last night. I'd like to watch it today. Would you care to listen to it while I do that?"

Again Malik nodded his head.

"Okay," Digger responded. "Jack Eaglefeather is coming in for a meeting this morning around nine, and there's a meeting with everyone at ten. When Anna brings the cable, we'll hook it up and hopefully find time to watch it this afternoon."

~ ~ ~

Soon, the front door of the office opened again, and in came Anna, Thomas, and Xuan. Digger greeted Xuan as Thomas stopped to pick up his messages at Anna's desk. They all shed their coats and headed for their offices to start the day.

Xuan went into her office and closed the door behind her. For several days she had been feeling the urge to begin her meditation practice again. The urge hit her again this morning as she drove into work, and she decided to see if her office environment might be conducive. Her office window looked east, and she had already arranged her furniture so that there was a straight-backed chair facing that window. She put an ocean sounds recording in her computer CD player and turned down the volume to a barely audible level, just loud enough to cover the muffled sounds of office activity on the other side of her door.

She slowly began stretching her arms above her head and tried to work out a few kinks in her neck. She took a deep breath and let it out forcefully and then took in another. She bent at the waist and tried to loosen her back and upper legs. She twisted her torso both ways and then pulled one knee upwards to her chest for a moment, let it down, and raised the other. She took her shoes off one at a time, rotated each ankle, and loosened her lower legs by rubbing her calves. She felt herself beginning to relax and took another deep breath—this time more slowly. Her exhale was deliberate and measured. At the end of it, she remained still as she stood and held herself without breath for a few seconds. Then, she slowly inhaled again. She shivered as she felt a rush of energy coursing its way through her relaxed body. Her arms hung limp at her side. The hair on her arms tingled with energy.

She sat down on the chair and turned her gaze toward the sunlit window as she felt it begin to draw her out of herself and fill her with light. She imagined herself pulled into the beam of light and uttered a whispered word of gratitude and surrender. She took another breath and began to concentrate on establishing a rhythm to her breathing: in and out, in and out. She reminded herself to become nothing but the breathing itself. She recalled a day by the ocean when the steady roll of the waves connected her to the patterns from which all beings come. She closed her eyes and quieted her mind and fell into the silence.

~ ~ ~

On the other side of her door, Russell Layne arrived, Digger reminded Thomas of Jack's impending arrival for the nine o'clock meeting, and Anna reported that she had seen Father Garces. Layne let her know that his furniture would be delivered in the afternoon, and Digger asked her if she had remembered the cable for

Malik's VCR. She pulled it out of her purse, handed it to him, and asked if he had made the coffee.

"Yes," he answered with a grin. "But it's pretty bad. Maybe we could spill it down the drain and make some more."

Anna laughed.

Layne chimed in, "I'll have to show the boy how to make it good and strong. You leave that to me, Anna."

"It's all yours, Mr. Layne," she said. "I've got enough to do around here."

Thomas quietly eased himself into his office, and Layne, who had no furniture in his, went into Thomas's office, hoping to find a chair on which he could sit.

"So, Thomas, what is the discussion with Jack about, anyway?"

"Well," he started, "Digger and I saw a sand painting at the council meeting we attended, and their custom is for us to figure out its significance with no outside assistance. Then, at his visit to Acoma the other day, Digger was introduced to a woman from Jemez Pueblo, a keeper woman, who scratched out a similar scene in the dirt atop the mesa. Both of them noted some similarities to the sand painting in the kiva, but neither of them knew exactly what to make of it."

"What were the similarities?" Layne asked.

"I'm not sure, because I've only seen one of them. Digger thinks both can be discussed this morning with Jack, so that is what we've planned," Thomas said. "The Jemez keeper woman also said some other things that mystified Digger and Jack, so I hope we can talk about that, too."

"That's interesting," Layne mused. "I talked to Father Garces on the phone after his visit with Anna yesterday, and he mentioned our meeting at ten but not the one at nine. He can't come, of course—he's not strong enough right now—but he said we ought to devise some way to focus everyone's attention in a singular or unified direction at the beginning of each meeting."

"Hmm. I wonder what he had in mind," Thomas said.

"I don't know, but I'd like to be in on the discussion with Jack if you think it suitable," Layne said. "Maybe some unifying techniques can be discussed there as well, techniques we can use now and even later at the meeting in June."

"I think it'll be fine," Thomas said.

Just then, Anna announced Jack's arrival over the intercom in Thomas's office. He was right on time, and Thomas was eager to get started.

Chapter 5

Katzimo

Jack Eaglefeather's arrival produced the usual exchanges of pleasantries, and soon he joined Layne and Digger in Thomas's office. As was becoming his custom, Digger brought in the extra chair. They all sat down, and Thomas began.

"Digger tells me that there is more to discuss with respect to the sand painting we saw at the kiva. He and I are kind of baffled, really, but we think it has to do with the meeting in June. It could be a confirmation of the meeting, a symbolic acknowledgment of change, a representation of a transforming light or a wind of some kind that foretells a new pattern—but it feels like we're just guessing at this point in time. We'd like to discuss it this morning before the staff meeting at ten."

Digger spoke up next. "In addition to the sand art at the kiva and the drawing by the Jemez keeper woman, I'd like to discuss some things she said to Jack and me that are still running around in my head. I want to talk about that, too, if it's okay with Jack."

Jack cleared his throat and spoke in a quiet tone. He looked at Digger as he started and said, "Some of what she talked about is not for this meeting. Some of it is. She is a powerful woman, and she expressed a desire to be at the meeting in summer. That let me know that our decision to be involved in the meeting was good. I was glad for that."

Jack saw Layne nod his head, but he offered no voice to the discussion.

Jack continued. "I think the yellow column might be what you said, Thomas, a blessing of the meeting in June or a blessing that our people and your people are working together for something that will be good. Maybe the result of this meeting in June will be a wind, some new understanding, perhaps. That's what I think. The keeper woman said it was a yellow wind, but nothing in my experience matches that description."

"Yellow wind?" Layne repeated. "Do you think it's a light of some kind?"

"I don't know, and she wouldn't talk of it the next day, either," Jack replied. "I asked her as she left to go home, and she only looked away. She pointed to our mountain and said, 'Go to the sacred mountain of our people, Jack. Maybe it will talk to you of this wind.' That's all she said."

"You mean Mt. Taylor, right, Jack?" Digger interrupted.

"Yes, your people call it Mt. Taylor. We call it Kahwehstimah," Jack answered.

"Have you gone up there yet?"

"No, maybe later this month," Jack answered.

Thomas asked, "What else did she say about her drawing?"

"Not much, but she said there would be seven and then seven more at the meeting," Digger said. "And she said that one of the seven would be blind."

Layne exhaled quickly and whispered, "That's noteworthy. Amazing!"

Thomas looked at him and then, running both his hands along his temples and down under his chin as if to pray, uttered, almost under his breath, with both reverence and disbelief, "Damn. She knew that?"

"Yes," Digger said, "she knew that before we even officially hired Malik."

"I'm afraid to ask if there's more," Thomas finally said.

"There is more," Digger replied. "She said that after the big wind, many would disappear like dandelion seeds. She said Jack would stay but I would go with the wind."

"I still don't know what that means, exactly," Jack said. "When our people speak of death, they say it is 'to become one with the clouds,' and she said you would be like the dandelion. I don't think you will die at Acoma, Digger. You are too young and strong. But I don't know exactly what she means."

"She knew about the seven planners and the seven masters, too," Russell Layne reminded them. "Did she know who they were?"

"Just one," remembered Digger. "She said one was a Navajo, but she wasn't sure how she would appear at the meeting in June."

"Jack," asked Russell Layne, "I know the Navajos came down with other Apache groups from the Northern Plains and settled in the Southwest. Where did the Acoma Pueblo Indians come from?"

"The elders say that Acoma means 'the place that always was,' but I think we came from the Cliff Dwellers—the Anazasi," Jack answered. "Then we spread into this area and into Arizona. The Spanish called us 'Pueblos,' but our real name is 'Keres.' We have been invaded many times, and our blood is no longer pure. Our genes are muddy like yours. Some on the council at Acoma think the meeting on the longest day will give us new life, but no one can be sure."

Thomas looked at his watch. "It's a little past ten o'clock. We should include the others now, so let's talk some more after that."

Digger and Jack nodded, but Russell Layne suggested, "Maybe we should have time to absorb what we've learned. Let's meet with the others and then decide if another meeting is needed."

They all got up and stretched. Digger opened the door, and they went to join Xuan, Malik, and Anna.

~   ~   ~

They met in Russell Layne's office for what was really the first meeting that included all seven Planners. There was no furniture in it yet, and so it offered the most space for seven—even though that space was on the floor.

Thomas asked Anna to turn on the answering machine, and she went to do so as the others turned off their cell phones. Xuan led Malik to a place against the north wall and sat down next to him. He placed his pad and pencil on the floor. Layne sat down on the other side of Malik but around the corner and under the window that was cut in the west wall. Digger and Jack were together along the south wall, and then Thomas sat on the east side of the room in front of the door. Anna completed the circle with him when she returned.

No one spoke for a moment. All were cross-legged on the floor except Thomas, whose legs stretched out in front of him, and Anna, whose skirt forced her to sit with both her legs to one side. Digger removed his shoes, and Xuan hadn't put hers back on after her morning meditation.

She watched as Russell Layne took a moment to make eye contact with everyone in the room and then reached out to his left and lightly touched Malik on the knee. He seemed to choose his words carefully.

"I bring greetings from Father Garces," he began. "He told me last night that we should devise a special way to begin our meetings, something that would bring us all together into the here and now of what we have set out to accomplish. It has been said that whenever two or more minds, two or more hearts, are gathered in the name of a good thing, there arises from that collective focus a certain energy that is more pronounced or larger than just the sum of those minds and hearts." Layne hesitated. "I don't know the right words exactly, but I think that is what is meant. We must establish that collective, higher identity among ourselves at all of our meetings, and the question is how to do it."

He stopped speaking and looked around the room.

"Is prayer the way to do it?" Anna asked.

"Maybe chanting," Jack offered.

"Or silence," Xuan said.

Malik picked up his notepad and wrote one word.

Layne read it aloud: "Visualization."

"Meditation?" asked Thomas.

"Yoga?" Digger suggested.

"Or music," Layne added.

"Maybe all of the above," Thomas said.

Xuan knew from his laugh that he was nervous. She watched as everyone turned their heads in his direction and waited for him to say more.

"You know," he stammered, "we've just described, from our own individual perspectives, that with which each of us is most familiar. They would all work to achieve a common focus, wouldn't they?"

"Yes, I think they would all work, Boss," Anna answered, "but how can we do all of them at once? It would all be a big jumbled mess pretty quickly."

"I think maybe we can figure something out," Xuan answered.

"So do I," agreed Layne. "If not all at once, then maybe we can alternate how we set the focus each time and employ all those methods over time."

"I think we each need to also bring in something to the office that has significant personal value to each of us. That'll make it feel more like our space and will help us focus," Jack suggested.

"We can bring in pictures," Anna said, "or a favorite book."

Malik wrote again, and Xuan read it. "I have a large Navajo dream catcher," the paper said.

"I think we need a picture of Acoma Pueblo," Digger suggested.

"And a picture of a sunrise that symbolizes a new beginning," Xuan said.

"We should have a mountain, too," Thomas added, "or maybe a picture of the ocean."

"I need smells, too," Xuan said, "like incense or maybe fresh-cut flowers."

The images of things important to these seven were now whirling around the room as a part of each one of them. They held them in common for a moment and then began to expand on them in thought. Digger imagined himself at Acoma at sunrise. Jack found himself at Mt. Taylor looking south over the lands of his people as the north wind blew gently at his back. Xuan heard again the sounds of the ocean from her morning meditation and smelled the incense she imagined. Anna found herself beside a lake that she pictured near her childhood home in El Paso. Malik saw himself touching his father's dream catcher and then, quill in hand, writing the letters he did not recognize in the dream of long ago. Thomas remembered the morning at Sandia Crest with Xuan as the sunlight played on the snow in the pines, and he felt the stirrings of life within himself again. Russell thought of the time in India when he stood on the banks of the great Ganges River and was mesmerized by the infinity of its ceaseless flow.

Silence overtook them, and, at first, they all sat alone. Soon, however, the reverie that came from within each one of them grew large and embraced all of them. Encircled now by this reverie, enriched by it, and enhanced through it, they sat transfixed and yet unaware. For several minutes, no one uttered a sound. Eyes slowly closed as the silence deepened.

From his place in the room, barely audible at first, the Iyatiku began to speak in a low, low voice. It sounded like a chant of some kind. The words were soothing but unintelligible to the others. The sounds, the vowels he intoned, were the same as in every language. The rhythm was steady and sure. The tone was almost prayerful and, in a short time, hypnotic. Though foreign to all but Jack, it was familiar in the feelings it invoked.

Anna thought it could be Latin. Digger was reminded of a Hindu chant he had heard. To Xuan it sounded like a Tibetan monk. Thomas was taken back to his childhood church and the deep male voices of music sung there. Malik remembered the sound of his father's Muslim prayers, and Layne just let himself sink further into the moment that had been created and felt the power of their connection to each other. The seven were as one.

After a while, Jack stopped. He held the last note of his chant until his breath ran out. The silence returned and engulfed them all again.

It was not broken for several minutes.

Russell Layne was the first to open his eyes and change his position. The noise he made caused the others to begin stirring, too, and soon everyone was present again in the room, together and yet in a different way than before. They all soon placed their attention on Layne. Even Malik sensed it and turned his head toward their leader expectantly.

"Hi," he mumbled sheepishly, clearing his throat and shifting his legs again. "Where do I begin? I suppose I should tell you that in the meeting with Digger and Jack and Thomas, I learned some things that all of you should know. First, from sources who could not have known of our endeavor in any specific way, we have received what can only be another confirmation as to what we're doing. Digger and Thomas and Jack witnessed a depiction, a so-called sand painting, of the Acoma Pueblo set against a large, yellow column—most likely a column of light, a blessing perhaps.

"Weeks later, Jack and Digger watched as a different person, a keeper woman from another Pueblo, drew almost the same picture in the dirt at Acoma. She told about the seven of us, even knowing that one of us is blind, and she spoke of the seven masters that are coming to this meeting in June. She also said that she wished she could attend. Frankly, I am amazed again, though I ought to be used to this by now. If any of you are having doubts, this should put them to rest, and, if you can't do that, you should talk to Thomas or Digger or Jack."

Xuan asked, "How is it that these different people know of this?"

"I can only guess," answered Layne, "and it is pure conjecture. Maybe it is like other forces we know of now, forces that were in place and acting upon our lives even before we knew of their existence or knew how to explain them. For example, there was the force of gravity before Newton named it. There was electricity before Benjamin Franklin saw it on the kite string or before we knew it was in the water so we could dam it up and use it for power. There are so many forces out there that we don't yet know how to explain or describe or utilize. Perhaps we are building an unnamed force from our own collective efforts."

"Do you really think that building a force is possible?" Anna asked.

"It may be more accurate to say that the forces behind this event have been in existence since time began and we are simply tapping into those forces. These meetings have been taking place every two thousand years for maybe twelve thousand years. I think this is the seventh one, but maybe Digger will find out more about it in his research. As I've said before, I think the meeting in June is just another meeting in the series. Malik thinks he has seen such a meeting in a dream. There may be others like him who can dream of past events, too. Maybe those who did the sand painting did so without conscious awareness but created that depiction from some subconscious or super conscious place within them. The Jemez keeper woman may be attuned to things of which we have no idea. My thoughts are all conjecture, but the possibilities are infinite."

Xuan speculated, "Maybe we all know just a little portion of the truth, a bit of the big picture, and it requires a coming together like this, in a common quest, to begin to piece together a larger picture."

"It's like a jigsaw puzzle," Digger suggested. "Each of us has just one piece, but how our pieces come together is what makes a world."

"Maybe even a new world," Xuan said.

"Maybe that's right," said Layne. "Whatever the explanation, I think it is a force with which we will become increasingly intimate over the next several months. It will bind us together in a dozen ways. It will draw others to us. It will focus us like never before. It will be incredible to watch and to share, and the whole of it will be much bigger than whatever parts we manage to assemble."

Everyone nodded in agreement.

"Katzimo," Jack pronounced, just as he had done to end the Pueblo council meeting at Acoma in November. Then he smiled and looked at Digger.

Russell Layne stood up. They all stretched, again.

"Wait a minute," Thomas's voice stopped them. "I want to review the seven clues. Well, not review them so much as remind everyone which clue they are assigned. Let's see. Xuan, you've got the clue that seems to be Chinese, right?"

"Yes, sir," she answered in a playful tone as she drew her hand up to her temple and saluted.

"And Digger," Thomas continued, "you have the clue that seems to be Hindu. Right?"

"Yes, and the American Indian one, too," he added.

"No, I am going to ask Jack to work on that one." Thomas turned to the Iyatiku. "That is, if you are willing."

"I am willing," Jack replied, "but I don't know exactly what is expected. We are already sure from the keeper woman that it is a Navajo saying."

Russell Layne interjected, "Yes, but there is much more to these clues than simply figuring out their origin. We need to dig deeper."

Jack smiled and said, "All right, I'll dig deeper."

Thomas regained the floor. "Okay," he said, "Anna, you've got the clue that you thought might be Catholic, unless Russell, I mean Mr. Layne, wants it. The other one of you can take the science clue. You two work it out."

"Can we work on both of them together?" Anna asked, looking first at Thomas and then at Russell Layne.

"I like that idea," Russell said. "I also prefer it if you all would just call me Russell. Is that okay with you, Thomas?"

"Fine by me," Thomas answered. "That leaves me the Sufi clue, and the teacher clue becomes Malik's to work on," he concluded, casting a glance at Malik as he finished speaking.

Malik hastily wrote something and, once finished, stuck the note out in front of himself and waited for it to be taken and read.

Xuan, again, was his voice. "I don't know that clue," he had written.

"Oh, yeah," Thomas mumbled. "It's something like 'Teachers will open the door, but one must enter of one's own accord.' Anna will bring that file to you, and I'd like it if the two of you would figure out how that new Braille machine works and write all the clues in Braille for Malik's use. Okay with you, Anna?"

"Uh huh," she agreed. "We'll try to do it this afternoon—but didn't Father Garces explain that clue pretty well at the New Year's party?" Anna reminded them.

"Yes," Thomas said, "but there is probably more to be figured out. Let's make the next meeting a discussion of the clues."

"When is that meeting?" Digger asked.

"Next Tuesday, same time." Thomas informed them. "Once a month, unfortunately, will not be enough. There's too much to accomplish." With that, he looked around the room as if to solicit questions or comments. None were forthcoming at first.

Then Anna blurted out, "Can we really bring in a few things for our meeting room? It's so bare and boring!"

No one answered for a moment.

Then Russell Layne quietly answered by saying, "I think it is imperative after what we just experienced. Yes, bring in what is important to you."

As it ended, they were now all thinking of what to bring and how their contributions would impact the energy of the room and the energy of their meetings. The potential seemed unlimited. Unlike before, the idea of weekly meetings sounded promising to all of them.

Chapter 6

Arrangements

After lunch, Jack and Digger planned another trip to Acoma for Thursday. There was word that the Jemez woman would be there again.

Anna and Xuan heard part of their discussion and had a discussion of their own. Anna hooked up the cable to Malik's VCR, and he ended up listening to the documentary Digger had found as Russell Layne watched it and waited for his furniture to arrive. Thomas worked on the Sufi clue in his office.

About mid-afternoon, Anna and Xuan approached Thomas.

Xuan spoke first and said, "You know, Thomas, I think I need to see the Pueblo at Acoma so that I can get a feel for it. Anna agrees and wants to see it, too. Can we get Jack's permission to have our own little tour?"

"I see no problem with that," Thomas answered. "I'd like to see it again, too. I'll ask him this afternoon before he leaves. Maybe all of us can go together."

"Oh good," Xuan responded. "I love field trips!"

"But also," Anna interjected, "once Russell's furniture arrives this afternoon, we won't have a good place for all seven of us to meet. If each of us is bringing in some things for the meeting room that are important to us, where will we put them? Where's the new meeting room going to be?"

"I was thinking about that, too," Thomas replied. "What if we made the reception area into a conference room of sorts and put everyone's stuff there and made that the place where we meet each week? Do you guys think that will work? Is it big enough?"

"That's a possibility," Anna said and looked at Xuan. "Let's go look it over."

With that, she and Xuan left Thomas's office and studied the rather large and underutilized reception area. They agreed that it could be reworked into an excellent meeting place.

Thomas came in and looked around but did not say anything as they looked at him for approval. He, in turn, looked at each of them and saw that the wheels were already spinning.

He simply said, "Go for it."

No more was needed as Anna and Xuan began planning what they would do to change the room.

Russell Layne's furniture arrived later that afternoon. Before Jack left, it was decided that everyone would go to Acoma on Thursday. Anna made the arrangements to rent a van for the trip, and they planned to depart about 8:30 in the morning.

Digger and Malik messed with the Braille machine after the movie on Egypt, and then Russell and Anna worked on setting up his furniture while they discussed the clues they had agreed to work on together.

Xuan mused some more over her clue while sitting in her office, and Thomas did the same in his. Jack left for Acoma to make arrangements for the Thursday visit, and Digger went to the library at the university to follow up on something he had seen in the tape on ancient Egypt and the library at Alexandria.

Near the end of the day, Thomas wandered into Xuan's office and sat down in the chair facing the window. He said nothing for a moment.

Xuan looked up and smiled at him but didn't interrupt his thoughts as he gazed absentmindedly at the two leafless trees now cast in afternoon shade outside the glass. Finally, he turned so he was watching Xuan as she thumbed through a book of sayings from Lao Tzu, a Tibetan mystic.

"I made reservations at an old lodge in Pagosa Springs for Friday and Saturday night," he said. "Are you still able to go?"

"Yes, of course," she said. "I drug out my suitcase last night and started packing." She put down her book and looked at Thomas. "Were you able to get two rooms, or are you still sleeping in the car?"

"All they had was one room," he answered, "but it's got two beds. I thought maybe that would be okay."

"Hmm. I suppose so," she responded. "But that makes it a slumber party, and a proper slumber party requires proper pajamas. That means I'll have to go shopping."

He smiled at the thought. "You may not need them. There's a fireplace and everything necessary to stay warm, but it's been a while since I've gone to a slumber party, so I'm not up to date on the rules. Are you sure pajamas are required?"

"Oh, yes," she replied quickly with another smile. "There are rules and protocols. I think you even need a robe, too."

"Great!" he deadpanned. "Now I have to go shopping, too."

"What? You don't have a robe, Mr. Walls?"

"What" he responded? "You don't have pajamas?"

"Well, it's just that I might want some new ones, that's all," she said. "It'll be cold at the higher elevations, too. I might want the kind with feet in them that button all the way up to my chin."

Thomas finally laughed. "Do you favor the kind with the little trap door in the back?"

"Oh, no!" she exclaimed. "Those lack style for a woman of my position." She winked at him and said, "Haven't you got work to do?"

She got up and slowly went around her desk to where Thomas was sitting. He looked up at her as she got near, and their eyes met in a different way as a smile played at the corners of her mouth. She reached for his hand, and as he took it, she pulled him up from the chair. She put her hands on his waist and then buried her head in his chest.

"Well," he started slowly, "I do have work to do, but I'm really interested in a lady at my office, and I'm having trouble focusing on the work." He bent his head slightly and caught the scent of her hair and kissed her gently as his arms enfolded her and pulled her close.

She turned her head and kissed his neck and then turned in further as his lips moved down to find hers and brushed against her cheek. Finally, he was kissing her and she was kissing him. She held him tighter and kissed him harder, just for a moment, and then buried her head again in his chest.

She sighed. "I'm falling for you, Thomas, and it sure feels good."

"It's a little scary, too," he added.

"Yeah, I know," she said quietly. "Maybe if we keep the pajamas on, we'll be okay."

He laughed softly as he pulled away a little and lifted her chin up so he could look in her eyes. "Don't you worry, Xuan, we'll know just how to handle those pajamas."

"You promise?" she asked him with a plea in her voice.

"I promise," he whispered solemnly as he looked into her eyes. "I promise."

"Okay then," she said, pulling away. "Now, shouldn't we get back to work?"

"Oh yeah, work. Okay. Have fun shopping tonight."

"I will," she smiled as he turned to go.

He gave a slight wave of his hand as he left her office. She ducked her head while looking at him over the top of her glasses and then turned and started back around her desk. When he closed the door behind him, she stopped and leaned on it and felt her racing heart. She let out a deep breath, but it didn't help her settle the emotions that were running out of control inside of her. "Oh my goodness," she muttered under her breath. "What have I gone and done?"

She sat down and didn't move for a while. Finally, she looked at her watch and saw that it was past five o'clock. She left her book open on the desk, found her shoes, and slipped them on. She took one last look at her new place to meditate and reached over to touch her wooden Buddha on the windowsill. She closed her eyes in a silent remembrance of the morning and then walked toward the door and thought of new pajamas.

Chapter 7

Perspective

It is not widely known that Albuquerque, New Mexico, is a mile-high city, too. It sits in a valley near the upper reaches of the Rio Grande with mountains to the east, highland hills to the north, and flat-topped mesas to the west. Even farther west, Interstate 40 slowly rises to seven thousand feet in elevation until it reaches the grandest canyon of them all near Flagstaff, Arizona. This centuries-old westward route, which eventually turned into Route 66 and then Interstate 40, passes through beautiful, scenic country. But it is harsh country, too: mountainous deserts cut with canyons that ripple through the mesas and sandstone spires that stand as nameless testaments to the incessant power of water and wind.

The water forces that created these mesas are long gone, and the rainfall with them. Blue skies are deep and rich but hide no bounty, only wind. Puffy clouds hurry through, destinations unknown, and seldom stop to rain. Red and orange cliffs outline the sky, and the dark green scrub brush offers no respite from the cold wind of winter or the dry heat of summer. As with any rugged land, some people have made peace with it. It is, however, an uneasy peace, with no luxury afforded and little comfort gained. A precarious and ever-changing balance provides no more than a constant struggle to survive, and victory over the land is never won for long—even for those who call it home.

The planners took off through this land, as scheduled, on Thursday morning. It was a clear and cold January day. Acoma Pueblo was fifty miles west down the interstate highway and then twelve miles south of it. The drive took them an hour in the rented van; Digger did the driving, because he knew the way.

All but Russell Layne came along for what Xuan had termed a field trip, and their conversations—about Web sites, speculation about attendance in June, and strategies for how to spread the word—were thorough and spirited. They planned to meet Jack at the visitor center on the flats below the Pueblo some time close to ten o'clock.

151

"A Web site would be a huge asset," Xuan contended. "We could make it interactive, and we'd likely get a lot of help from people all around the world with respect to the clues, insights, ideas, and general information."

"Yeah," Digger agreed, "and we could link up with all kinds of other sites: libraries, historical organizations, and publications, too. That really does have a lot of potential. Thomas, what do you think?" he asked as he looked in the rearview mirror at his boss.

"Well, I think it's a good idea, but the timing will be critical," Thomas answered. "We don't want to go online too early, and right now, I think it's too early to solicit outside help or publicize anything that we are working on. When we do decide to go public, if we go public at all, we need to be sure we can handle the phone calls, the e-mails, and all the information we might receive in whatever form it comes to us. I think we ought to put it on the agenda for the Tuesday meeting next week and make a decision then."

Anna said, "That discussion should include consideration of the expense of doing it in terms of added computers, a bigger internal network, and additional staff, if any."

"Right," Thomas replied as he stretched his legs and shifted his body around in the middle seat of the van.

From her seat in the back row, Susan asked, "Besides you seven Planners and the seven master teachers, do you expect anyone else to come to the meeting?"

"I do," Thomas said, "but how many will come is a good question. I don't have any kind of guess in that regard."

"An interactive Web site might help us gauge that number, too," Xuan suggested.

"I hadn't even thought of that question," Digger said. "It won't take very many to stretch the resources of the Pueblo and to create a large expense for cleanup and food. I wonder if Jack has considered the logistical aspect of hosting this meeting and of all the other things we're planning."

"Publicity from a Web site, if it gets much attention at all, could attract hundreds or thousands of people," Anna said.

Xuan asked, "You think that many people could spend the entire seven days away from their normal lives?"

"Well, maybe Anna's right," Thomas agreed. "There could be thousands, but I don't want to worry about that today. For this trip, I'd just like to focus on seeing and feeling and understanding the environment of the meeting space here at Acoma."

By the time these words were spoken, they had already left the interstate, passed the signs directing them to Sky City, crossed the cattle guard, and were headed south on the paved, two-lane road through scrub brush no taller than the van. They drove across a meandering, wet-weather gulch as the road carried them toward the place they were scheduled to meet with Jack.

As they went through the valley, Enchanted Mesa soon loomed in front of them on the left. The distant mesas that formed this valley and surrounded them on all sides were now dwarfed in comparison to this towering edifice just a few hundred feet off the roadway. Everyone in the van but Malik craned to get a better look and to marvel at the abrupt and overpowering singularity of this rock. In an otherwise flat terrain for ten miles in every direction, this monolith dominated the view.

"I want to stop and get out so I can really see this mesa, Digger," Thomas said. "I think it is important for all of us to see it unobstructed."

"But Thomas," Digger argued as he glanced at his watch, "Jack is waiting for us, and the meeting takes place on the next mesa, not this one. This one is not that important."

"Yeah, I know," said Thomas, "but this mesa is really intriguing to me—even more than the other one—because it is empty and is supposed to be enchanted."

"Okay, Boss, but I hate to make Jack wait for us."

"I'll explain it to him," Thomas answered.

Digger shrugged his shoulders and found a wide spot in the road just past a bridge over the gulch. When he had stopped, everyone climbed out of the van to get a good look at the abandoned pinnacle. Malik got out but stayed close to the van as the others crossed over the road and were startled by a covey of quail that flew up just twenty feet past the far edge of the asphalt. Thomas was quiet and seemed content to absorb everything that he could see and feel and hear and smell and taste as he studied this immense, one-of-a-kind natural feature. A coyote slinked through the gulch below the road, and Susan pointed it out just as it scurried into the brush alerted by the voices of the Planners. The lengthy shadows of the morning sun played tricks on the faces of the four-hundred-foot-high rock. Crevasses, caves, and teetering slabs of stone provided an unending canvas for the steeply angled light as it painted every surface it could find and slowly rose to find even more.

"No one has been up top there for a thousand years," Digger explained to Xuan as he pointed to the mesa top high in front of them. "I bet there's some fascinating archaeology up there, and I'd love to explore it."

"You've not been up there, Digger?" Xuan asked.

He shook his head as he continued to gaze in that direction.

"Is there something to be afraid of?" she asked.

"I don't think so. The trail to the top was washed out in a storm, and it's no longer passable. Besides, no one is allowed up there anymore, by decree of the Iyatiku at Acoma," Digger replied. "Fear of death is probably part of the reason."

"It could be fear of life, too," Xuan said as she turned around slowly and looked once again at the panorama of the Acoma Valley. "It's really isolated out here. If more than twenty people end up coming for this meeting, there doesn't look to be any place to house them."

"It is pretty sparse," Digger agreed as he looked briefly back at Malik, who had rolled up his sleeves and seemed to be enjoying his moment of personal reverie in the crisp and chilly air.

Digger walked across the road and back toward the van as Thomas signaled to everyone and spoke quietly to Malik. Soon, they rolled on the last few miles and saw Jack as they arrived at the Visitor Center. Digger pulled up next to him as he spoke to one of the tour bus drivers. Jack got in the van and directed Digger to continue.

As they rose up the roadway to the Pueblo on top of the mesa, they soon found themselves in the midst of the humble, plain buildings of Acoma. Most were constructed from adobe, but cinder block and handmade brick were apparent at frequent intervals. Flat roofs, small doors, and minimal windows were the repeated features. The narrow dirt roads between the clusters of houses were unkempt and irregularly shaped. There were no curbs or gutters, no phone or power poles, and no street lights. A community building in the center of the collection of houses was set apart from the rest. A few crude benches lined the front of it. The two or three trees atop the mesa, the church at the southeastern corner, and a natural water cistern completed the notable features of the simple, old town. It didn't take long to see most of it, and finally, Digger pulled up in front of the old adobe church that had been built 320 years before.

~   ~   ~

It was not that Acoma Pueblo was ever particularly beautiful or modern. It wasn't. It had been built for survival and nothing else. It was not that it was ever quaint or endearing because of its architecture or design. It wasn't those things, either. Acoma Pueblo was, from the very beginning, functional and enduring. When the site was discovered, it was like no other place on the continent, and on the day the Planners arrived, Acoma wasn't much different than the day it had first been settled. In a time when small and scattered tribal settlements near creeks and rivers were the norm, Acoma Pueblo was a city on a mesa that thrust it up into the sky. Its distinctly male hierarchy made it unique among the Pueblos, but, through the years, it was known for little else. There was no time for fancy or quaint. There was no energy for advances in thought or tools or advances in the standard of living. Acoma Pueblo was only designed to survive. And it had.

Jack Eaglefeather, Iyatiku of Acoma Pueblo for eleven years, led the Planners from the van and over the last two hundred feet of dusty streets to the old, adobe church. A few townspeople had begun setting up their worn-out tables and were carefully displaying the pottery they hoped to sell to the bus-riding tourists who would come later in the morning.

The smell of a few small cooking fires reached the group as they walked along in silence. A dog barked in the distance, and Susan gingerly picked her way over some uneven ground. Thomas led Malik by the arm, and Xuan soon felt herself surrounded by an energy she couldn't explain. She wondered if it was the sacred energy of which Thomas had spoken to her once before.

The wind gusted up as they entered the break in the low adobe wall by the cemetery in front of the church, and Xuan pulled her coat closer as she felt a shiver down her spine. Digger and Jack stopped at the doors of the church. The doors were twelve feet tall and set deep into thick, tapered walls eight feet thick at their base and almost forty feet tall. Jack turned to face the rest of them and spoke.

"The Spanish priests from Mexico thought we should have a church here. This was the gathering place on this mesa even before the Spanish came, so building here made sense to us, too. There is an energy here that was here before there was a church. Something about it makes people choose to meet right here. It has always been so at Acoma. The church was first built in wood and burned down a few years later. Then it was built with mud and stone and only lasted fifty or sixty years. This time it has lasted over 320 years. For me and many others it holds a million memories."

Jack led them inside. The dirt floors were swept and the paint on the rock and stucco walls appeared fresh. The benches were scattered and in no order at all.

When he had been led to a bench on which he could sit, Malik began writing down what he heard.

"How old are these benches?" Xuan asked as she gazed at the dozen rough-hewn wooden pews in disarray on the packed dirt floor. They each appeared to be made from just one log. They were smaller than most church pews she had ever seen. The backs were short and looked uncomfortable. The bench portion was none too ample, either. "They look so little," she commented.

"They are," Jack answered. "The story is that logs were hauled here from twenty-five miles away in the 1680s. The priest in charge of construction wanted to use some exotic wood from Mexico, but the Acoma people insisted on wood from Kahwehstimah, our sacred mountain. There was a small revolt over it, and the priest was killed. It was several months before a new priest was assigned to this place, and when he arrived from Mexico City a year later, he allowed a group of my ancestors to trek to the sacred mountain to cut the right trees and haul them back. It took almost four months, and several Indians died along the way. The survivors insisted that the dead ones come back with them, and so they were strapped to the logs and carried home, too."

Digger counted the pews. "Were there always just twelve logs?"

"I don't think so. I think they planned to bring back eighteen or twenty," Jack continued. "When they lost six people, though, it took too much effort to carry the logs and the dead. They decided just to finish the trip with twelve logs. The six people who died along the way are buried here in the church floor, but before they were buried, their blood was drained and used to cure the wood."

"What was the purpose of that?" asked Digger.

"Our people believe that everything is made up of living energies. The pine cone or seed energy combined with the energy of water, and the energy of soil and the energy of sunlight is required to grow the trees on sacred mountain. As they grew, those energies became part of the tree. When those trees—the trees that you sit on now—were felled, that energy didn't leave them. It came here from the sacred mountain in the form of a log and is still here." Jack spoke reverently as he absentmindedly rubbed his hand on the bench nearest him. "Sitting in this church throughout my life, I have felt the energy in every one of these pews at one time or another."

"But why the blood?" Digger asked.

"Same reason," Jack responded. "The people who died bringing these logs here left their energy behind, too; the energy that came to them in the corn they ate and the water they drank and the sun in which they labored. They have the energy of their parents and their parents before them, the energy of their lives, the energy of the wind, the energy of their love, the energy of their words. That energy didn't leave when they died. Blood is a carrier of energy, much like sap in a tree. Their blood was rubbed into the wood so that their energy could combine with the energy of the trees to create the sacred sitting places in this church."

"So why are the dead ones buried in the floor?" Thomas asked.

"Because there is energy in sacrifice, too," Jack whispered. "I am mindful of what they did every time I walk on this floor or think of this place. Their energy is part of me, and, now, it is part of all of you, too. They are alive in you. And in me. They have not died at all."

~   ~   ~

Digger wanted to ask more questions. Jack's explanations just fueled the innate curiosity that had led him to become an archaeologist in the first place. Initially, the stories didn't seem too significant as such things go, and he didn't feel any special energy in the pews. He wondered why Jack had told the story.

But Jack had moved to a place near the front of the old church and, raising his outstretched hands above them all, began to intone unintelligible sounds that gradually became louder and stronger as he closed his eyes and settled into a rhythmic pace.

At first, everyone was simply quiet as they watched and listened to Jack, but eventually they all closed their eyes, too. Xuan adjusted her posture and took a deep breath. Malik sat and listened as only he could listen. In a few minutes, the outside world was far away, and each of them found themselves within the sounds of Jack's voice. Once there, each of them was transported to another time and place.

Digger imagined himself sitting under a tree on the side of a mountain and heard people behind him cutting down a nearby pine. He turned and saw it fall. He got up and helped them carry it to a wagon that held several other logs. In his imagination, he saw the horses, restless in their makeshift harnesses and eager to be freed from the wagon. He felt the dry wind on his face and wiped the sweat from his sun-drenched forehead with the back of a hand more brown than red. Then, he was behind the wagon as it made the slow and tedious trip down the rocky mountain slope, and he saw the small, dark-haired man slip and fall in front of the horses. They couldn't stop the wagon from trampling him, and two logs tumbled off the load as it finally lurched to a stop. The man didn't get up; Digger knew he was dead. He watched as they strapped the dead man to one of the fallen logs and put both of them back on the wagon. There was no time for remorse or misgiving or sorrow. They started on their way down the mountain again.

Digger imagined himself leading the horses as they approached the mesa they called Acoma. Many people ran to greet them. He embraced two young children, and a man in priestly garb came up with water for the loggers. Other men came from the fields around the mesa to take over the rest of the journey to the mesa top. They unstrapped those who had died and laid them at the door of the unfinished church. They removed the harnesses from the horses, and Digger saw several men talking to the priest. Their voices rose in discord, and he saw the priest throw up his hands and walk away. They had a celebration that evening and made plans to carve the logs in the morning. Finally, in Digger's imagination, they moved the bodies into the church and began to dig the burial holes.

Jack's chanting sounds ceased, and Digger's imaginings stopped. He remembered again where he was. Now he felt the energy from his pew as it ran through his body. He could feel the energy coming up from the floor under his feet and could sense the former events as if they had happened just yesterday or this morning—or even as he watched. He understood as never before that energy is timeless and bound up only by forgetfulness. And he knew, as Jack had said, that the energy of this place was in him now.

What was more, it felt as though it would be in him from now on.

The Planners got up, and Jack led them out of the church in silence. Once outside, he spoke again. "I must return to the Visitor Center. Digger can take you around by the natural water cistern on the north end of the mesa and then back to the van." Turning to Thomas, he inquired, "Will we meet in your offices on Tuesday, as usual?"

"Yes, around ten," said Thomas.

Jack said, "The meetings in June can now take place in the church instead of the main kiva. It will be a better place to meet, and our guests can stay in the old priests' quarters off to the side of the church." He smiled briefly, but his face immediately resumed a solemn look. "The church liked all of you, and that is good. Katzimo."

With that, he turned to the west, and Digger led the rest of them north, toward the water.

"What just happened to us?" Susan asked. "I think I just carried a bunch of logs from some mountain to this place right here!"

Malik stopped and scribbled a note, thrusting it out to no one in particular. Susan took it and read, "Malik writes that he carried logs, too."

"I was there, too," added Thomas, pensively, "and saw one of them die when he lost his balance and fell in the mountains."

"I saw another one die two days after being bitten by a snake," Xuan quietly revealed.

Anna said, "I felt that church—I mean really felt that church, in my body—like nothing I've ever felt before. What is that? How does that happen?"

The conversation hushed as they rounded a group of houses and saw two Pueblo women sitting against the wall behind their table of pottery.

"I don't know," Digger whispered as they passed. "Obviously, we all felt something. We all experienced some part of the story he told us before he began chanting. It sounds like we all had similar experiences but not the same experience. The guy who died in my experience was run over by the horses when they lost control of the wagon coming down a treacherous slope. Xuan, you saw a snake bite," he continued, looking at her for a moment as if to confirm his memory. "Thomas saw a man fall to his death. The energy for those specific details must have come from the specific people buried beneath the dirt floor of the church where each of us sat. Each of them has a story that each of us felt, but I have no idea how we felt it."

Thomas interjected, "I don't think it's that hard to figure out. I think Jack just wanted to help us to feel connected to the church, a sacred connection, so that we are fully prepared in June. Why else would he tell us that story?"

"That must be part of it," said Xuan, "but what about the chanting? Where does that fit in? Was it the same chant he used in the meeting a few days ago?"

Everyone shrugged because they did not know.

Xuan looked at Malik. "Malik, you're the expert listener in this group; was it the same chant?"

Everyone looked at Malik, and he shook his head as if to say "no."

"Did you understand it?" she asked.

Malik shook his head again from side to side.

"I'm sure none of us understood it," Digger offered, "not like we would if it had been in English, and yet it still had an impact on all of us. It touched us somehow at a place not dominated by our understanding. That's really fascinating to me."

By then they had reached the natural water cistern at the north edge of the mesa. It was a sandstone depression that had collected rainwater for thousands of years and helped to sustain its people for centuries. One lonely, gnarled mountain pine tree grew at its edge.

"I can imagine the memories this place has," Xuan remarked as she seemed to be looking past the water to the edge of the plateau.

Beyond it was Enchanted Mesa, and beyond that, in the distance, were the mountains.

"Is that snow-covered peak the sacred mountain from Jack's story?" Xuan inquired of no one in particular.

"Yep, that's Kahwehstimah," Digger answered.

He watched as everyone seemed to be entranced again. No one said a word.

"Well, I'm chilled to the bone in this cold," Susan said. "Can we go back to the van?"

She touched Malik's arm to let him know she was near, and Xuan looked for Thomas. Anna walked next to Digger and turned to look back to the north one more time. All were silent as they walked.

They all got into the van and descended from the mesa past the visitor center, heading west to the other entrance on a ridge a few miles away. They were all lost in thought as they traveled along.

Digger finally asked Anna to remind him the words of the fifth clue.

"Even the rocks are alive when cold runs deep on sacred mountain," she remembered aloud.

"Even the rocks are alive." Digger repeated the words slowly. "Even the rocks are alive. Hmm. Just as those pews are alive with some energy from long ago and the church building is alive, even the rocks are alive."

"Yes," said Xuan, "even the rocks are alive. Some geological energy formed them, uplifted them, put them on top of the mountain, eroded them, heated them, and cooled them. Eventually, cold weather can make them split open or crack. They look lifeless to most of us, but if one is in tune with some bigger picture, some longer timeframe, they have an energy, a life all their own."

Thomas added, "It takes an extreme event like severe cold or heat for anyone to see a geological life force for what it is."

"It also takes a different perspective," Digger said. "It takes a view of the world that we're not accustomed to using."

"That's it!" Anna exclaimed. "It's not the clues that are difficult. The difficult part is gaining the perspective that allows us to understand the clues. Jack just changed the perspectives of each one of us, and when he did, we were able to understand that clue from the inside out instead of the outside in. He didn't just connect us to that church building; he connected us to the perspective of the people who built it and energize it even today."

"I think you're right, Anna," Digger agreed. "It's like we were trying to understand the clue from a rational point of view, but until Jack could get us to understand it from an intuitive or experiential point of view, we were locked out."

"Even more," added Xuan, "it matters less that it may be a Navajo saying than the fact that it is a way of looking at life. My guess is that there will be someone at our meeting in June who understands this perspective very well."

Thomas asked, "So, how do we identify him? And where do we find him?"

"Or her," Susan interjected.

"Yes," Digger tossed out, "like the Jemez keeper woman Jack and I met here last month, who seemed to know so much about us and the meeting."

Xuan read one of Malik's notes aloud for everyone. "Can we go to the sacred mountain?" it asked.

"I think we have to," Digger answered.

Thomas agreed. "Yes, we need to do that soon."

At that moment, the van finished the climb up the ridge to the western rim of the Acoma Valley and turned north. The sacred mountain loomed ahead of them in the windshield some twenty-five miles away. Its energy awaited them, too, but it would not reveal its secrets until another day.

Chapter 8

Well Planted

As they left work Friday and set out for Pagosa Springs, Colorado, Xuan was glad to be getting out of town for a few days. Everything she was doing at Project 4000 was intense and required a great deal of personal investment. A relaxing weekend in the mountains of Southern Colorado was bound to do her good. She also looked forward to exploring her relationship with Thomas.

She was open to knowing him more intimately. She liked that he was a father and seemed so responsible in that regard. She liked that he seemed unafraid to be vulnerable and even that he seemed a little bit brokenhearted over the failure of his marriage. She was physically fascinated by his unusual combination of strength and gentleness and even found it tempting. She also wondered if she would know, or remember, how to handle herself in a romantic relationship should it develop.

He drove them along without a word, and Xuan lost herself in the early winter sunset as it finished painting the sky west of Albuquerque. She caught him looking at her and wondered just what he was thinking. She reached out and touched his arm as it rested on the stick shift while his Mustang rumbled along toward Pagosa Springs. She had never fallen in love with a man because of the car he drove, but she had to admit that the untamed power in this particular car was having its effect on her.

He accelerated suddenly to pass a truck, and she was thrown back in her seat. She involuntarily gripped the armrest on the door a little more tightly than before and felt her nails dig into his arm just a bit. He seemed pretty focused on his driving and she liked that, too—not that he might have a hotrod attitude somewhere inside of him but that he could be alone, even in her presence, and be so concentrated on his driving just for the fun of driving.

When the pass was complete and he eased off the gas and settled back into their lane of travel, he looked at her and she looked back.

"So, Mr. Walls, what kind of lodge have you found for this little slumber party of ours? Is it old and rustic or modern or what?"

"Actually, it's the original ski lodge just outside of town. It was built in 1930, but the pictures on their Web site look pretty neat—you know, a three-story log structure with old leather furniture, stuffed animals mounted on the walls, and throw rugs all around. We got the last available room for the weekend, but at least there's a fireplace in our room. We can ski, if you want to, and they have a four-star restaurant downstairs, so it should be pretty good."

"Oh, it sounds perfect, Thomas," Xuan responded. "I think I'm going to like living luxuriously for a day or two. Maybe we can have some champagne by the fireplace and a room service dinner, too."

She leaned across the console of the Mustang as he placed his arm around her and pulled her close. She closed her eyes as the transmission purred along just below her heart. He flipped on the sound system to a Van Morrison CD called *Avalon Sunset*. The sweet and haunting melodies accented her mood, and Xuan soon got lost in a pleasant reverie.

They motored along through the moonless New Mexico night and arrived in Pagosa Springs just after nine o'clock. When they checked in and opened the door to their room off the main lodge, Xuan was immediately impressed.

"This is so quaint," Xuan said as they entered the main part of the room. "I love it already!"

Thomas glanced briefly into the bathroom and then joined her in the bedroom area, which had two double beds and a small fireplace in the corner by the window. Perhaps as an afterthought, someone had managed to squeeze in a two-chair sitting area just past the same window. It was all very cozy, if not a little crowded.

"Well," said Thomas, "it's got all the promised elements, but I wouldn't recommend their interior decorator to anyone."

"Ah, come on, Thomas," Xuan said. "It'll be just fine. Besides, I'm tired of driving, and I'm hungry."

"Okay, let's check out the room service menu." He picked it up from the table in the sitting area and browsed through it quickly. "Soup and salad is enough for me. What sounds good to you?"

"Actually, that sounds good to me, too. What's the soup?"

She stood next to him now and tried to read over his shoulder. Thomas turned away so as to screen the menu from her curious eyes, and she laughed as she grabbed his shoulder to turn him back around. He let himself be turned back to her but then placed the menu behind her and prevented her from turning around to see it.

"It's bitter root soup, I think." He smiled at her and pretended to look over her shoulder at the menu.

"Bitter root?" she laughed. "I've never heard of that soup."

"They also have squash soup with sun-dried tomatoes and piñon nuts," he responded.

She still couldn't easily turn around to see for herself and, frankly, didn't want to very badly. She liked being in his arms. She began to slowly run her hands up his sweater vest until they were around his neck. Then, as she felt him relax a little and begin to look at her in that way she liked so much, she quickly ducked out of his grasp, tore the menu out of his hand, and fell on her back on the bed, laughing.

"Let me see these exotic soups!" She held the menu up in the air and tried to read it quickly.

Thomas grabbed her feet, lifted them up in the air, and rolled her over sideways and then landed knees first, on the end of the bed behind her.

"Let me read these soups, Thomas," she squealed in mock protest.

But he pulled her closer and wrestled the menu from her hands.

"They also have chicken noodle and vegetable beef," he admitted as he looked down on her in the bed.

Xuan turned to face him again and tried to stifle a giggle. Their eyes met and locked in on each other. She calmed herself and reached for him gently. Thomas lowered his head closer to hers until, finally, slowly, their lips met. Softly, they kissed. She rolled toward him even more as he stretched out beside her. She felt his hand in the small of her back, and they lay there kissing each other on the lips and the chin and the nose and the cheeks and then the lips again. There was passion, and yet there was restraint. She sensed the need to hold back, if only for a while, and felt his restraint, as well. It felt right to her, but not so right that she was ready to rush into something more. Not yet. It felt so good to be exactly where she was, and soon they were holding one another and losing themselves in each other's eyes. She felt his gentle touch as he caressed her shoulders and ran his hand tenderly along her spine. She touched his face and traced his cheekbones with her finger. She could not remember feeling this good in a long, long time.

Finally, he whispered, "I think we both know this isn't just a slumber party, don't we?"

His slight smile and penetrating look told her it was okay to answer him truthfully. Actually, she sensed that it was more than okay to be truthful. His question required all the truth she could manage.

She thought about her response, and when she spoke, her voice was just as certain as it was soft. "I hadn't dared to hope for anything more, but being alone with you makes me want so much more." She shifted her position on the bed. "Even so, I don't know for sure if I'm ready for more just yet." She searched his eyes for a reaction and studied his face while she awaited his response.

Finally, he spoke. "When you're ready, I think you'll know."

She sighed and looked away for a moment. Then she looked back and earnestly replied, "When I'm ready, I think we'll both know."

They lay there an hour or more after that. No words were spoken. He dozed a little, but she was too keyed up to sleep. She watched him as he rested his head in the crook of his left arm. His right arm was draped over her hip. He twitched involuntarily when she shifted her weight and moved her legs just a little. Finally, she woke him as she rose to change clothes for bed.

"Hey, hey, sweet man." She nudged him with a kiss on the forehead. "You think room service is still open?"

He rolled over and stretched. "Oh, man, I don't know. I'll call 'em."

She got up and left for the bathroom. He watched her for a moment and then reached for the phone by the bed. There was no answer at room service, but the front desk told him he could order a few food items from the bar, so Thomas knocked on the bathroom door.

"Xuan, the bar is the only option. Anything sound good to you?" he shouted through the closed door.

She cracked the door just a little, but all he could see was her face.

"I'll have what you're having," she said from behind the door, "and see if there's anything to eat, will ya?"

"Yeah, I will," he answered. "I can hardly wait to see those new pajamas when I come back."

~   ~   ~

When he returned in twenty minutes, Thomas saw that Xuan had started a fire in the fireplace and was sitting on the floor with a blanket around her shoulders. There were no lights—just a candle on the mantle and the yellow flame of her newly lit fire. Thomas came in with a tray and immediately stopped to adjust his eyes to the light.

"I'm over here by the fire," Xuan called out softly. "What did you bring us?"

"Not much, I'm afraid: a few Cokes, an imported beer from Holland, I think, a roast beef sandwich, and a bottle of water. The selection wasn't all that great. Any of those sound good to you?" he asked as he sat down on the floor in front of the fireplace.

"The Coke sounds good, and I'll split the sandwich with you."

"Do you have your pajamas on under that blanket?" he inquired as he moved the tray from between them.

"I sure do," she exclaimed proudly, and she spread her arms as the blanket fell from around her shoulders. The pajamas consisted of an off-white silk top held together with eyelet buttons that led all the way up to a lacy, brocade collar. There were matching silk bottoms with brocade trim that matched the collar. "Do you like them?"

Thomas looked them over for a moment and smiled. "So where are the teddy bears?"

She laughed and replied, "I changed my mind about those bears. I didn't want to scare you."

"That collar scares me. Those are the most formal pajamas I've ever seen. Shouldn't there be a bowtie or a hat?" He laughed at the thought of silly accessories.

"Oh, you don't like my pajamas," she said as if her feelings were hurt. "They were on sale, and I like the feel of them." She immediately drew her blanket back around her shoulders and scooted a little farther away from him. "Let's see yours, mister fashion guy."

"Oh, no," he laughed. "They're probably worse than those. Maybe we can just go without them altogether."

Thomas raised his eyebrows and smiled but was surprised at his own suggestion and didn't expect much response from Xuan. She gave him a taut little smile and quickly went back to her mock pout.

Thomas opened the beer, leaned back on his arms, and gazed into the fire for a long moment. Finally, he spoke.

"Remind me, again, what clue you are working on. Is it the one that goes, 'What is well planted cannot be uprooted, and what is well embraced cannot slip away?'"

Xuan was quiet for a minute and then answered, "Yes, that's it. It's from a Chinese poet philosopher named Lao Tzu. I've meditated on it a couple of times but haven't gotten very far yet."

She moved away from the window, turned sideways and lay down next to Thomas. She placed her head on his chest. Her leg crossed over one of his, and she looked intently into their fire.

"I like the way you embrace me, Thomas. Do you think this clue is about the loving embrace between two people?"

"Heck, I don't know. It could be, I guess," he mused. "But I think it's about something more. What do you think of when you hear the words 'well planted'?"

"Let's see, trees are well planted," she suggested.

"Yes, but they can blow over in a storm. I remember the giant oak in our yard that blew over on the family car when I was just a boy. It happened during a big spring storm, and it was pulled out by the roots."

"Okay," Xuan thought out loud. "Seeds are well planted. I used to help plant seeds in my mom's vegetable garden. The soil had to be mixed just right, and then we pushed them down in the dirt with our fingers. They always came up, but only if I planted them like she told me to."

"Seeds, huh," Thomas replied thoughtfully. "Seeds are well planted if they sprout and then grow, but is that all there is to it?"

"No. They need water. And sunlight. And good soil," Xuan answered. "Okay. What is well embraced?" she queried.

"Well embraced? So it doesn't slip away, huh?"

"What's that parable say about sowing seeds in rocky ground?"

"Rocky ground means they are not well received, and, of course, they can't be well embraced, either," Thomas replied.

"So nothing grows," Xuan concluded.

"Right, but it's not the seeds' fault," Thomas said. "Lack of good planting and lack of a good embrace is no reflection on the quality of the seeds. The seeds are still encoded to be what they are supposed to be."

"Encoded? As in genetically encoded?"

"Yes. Genetically designed to produce a certain set of features or outcomes. You know, an acorn makes an oak tree, and dandelion seeds make dandelions."

"Thomas, what if the seeds are thoughts and ideas? What if the seeds are truths of some kind?"

"Like natural truths? Truths about human nature, for example?" Thomas was still struggling for clarity. "If you're right, exactly what are the seeded truths about the nature of humankind?"

"That's a huge question, Thomas," Xuan laughed. "We're only up here for a few days."

"You're right, again," Thomas said. "If the seeded truths about the nature of humankind are not well planted or well embraced, the seeds don't grow, or don't grow right. They are uprooted or lost."

"Or they slip away into some forgotten recess of the human psyche. Maybe that's how they are obscured or cast aside in the pursuit of other things."

"Maybe so. Remember the Tower of Babel?" Thomas asked. "The people had one language or one understanding, a common tool that linked them all together. It was powerful. But they tried to build a tower up to their god, and it was eventually perceived as a waste of time. They misused the power, and so their common language was taken away from them."

"What do you mean, taken away?" asked Xuan. "Who took it away? I remember it as some vengeful god waving some sort of magic wand to create these multiple languages, so the project failed."

"I think that's how the story ended," Thomas answered.

"Well, isn't that vengeful image actually creating a god that is more like a person—I mean, revenge and anger are human traits. Do gods need to be praised, need to be worshipped, or need to have homage paid to them like some human king?" Xuan asked. "That may be something a king requires, but not a god. That's just personification, isn't it?"

"I suppose so. But that's how it was understood in those days. Gods were made in the image of men and ascribed human traits. All the old gods were personified. They were projections of man's strengths and weaknesses," Thomas said.

"Then that's likely how most religions were built," Xuan responded, "as projections of man's finite understanding."

"Okay, maybe so," Thomas agreed. "If that's the case, then, what is the real message of the Tower of Babel story?"

"It could be that the encoded truth, the highest common seeds in each one of those people, made them realize that the project was off point. The encoded pattern inside each of them, the highest good in each of them, saw the pointlessness of building a monument to some up-in-the-sky god. Maybe they realized that God was not outside of them, not up in the sky or in the clouds, but inside of them, instead."

Thomas could tell that Xuan was feeling her way along and wasn't entirely sure where she was going with this line of conjecture. She looked to him in the hope he could clarify her thoughts for both of them.

"So despite the temptation to build an incredible monument to their finite view of God," Thomas surmised, "the encoded truth inside of them overcame the misguided effort and killed the project."

"Yes, but it got reported as a vengeful god outside of them, not an encoded truth inside of them."

"That's an interesting position."

"Well, almost. Doesn't it still seem that the religions of the world are monuments to men's views of gods?" Xuan theorized. "All religions have evolved into towers of Babel, and they all speak a sort of different language of understanding. Now, those man-made religions need to be significantly altered or done away with. They are monuments to belief systems that are full of limits and half-truths and personifications, aren't they?"

"Or maybe they need to find the common language again," Thomas said.

"Wouldn't that be a fine thing to happen?"

"Well, the common thread wasn't taken away," Thomas continued. "Not really. The well-planted truths may have been obscured by the overriding complication of having to communicate in different languages, but the thread, the seed, the encoded design for human beings—whatever you want to call it—was not destroyed. It may have been obscured by religions or hidden by misunderstanding for a long time, but it is not lost forever."

Xuan turned suddenly and faced Thomas. "Yes, those seeds, those deeply rooted common threads that link all mankind together, are too well planted to have been completely lost or uprooted! Is that what you think?"

"Maybe so," Thomas answered, "and they need to come back into the light once more."

"Then that is a reason for optimism and hope, despite all the discord and religious wars that are going on today!"

"Possibly," Thomas cautioned. "But it feels like those seeds are still far from view and deeply hidden. While the religions of the world, the churches of the world, have helped in some ways to bring them into view, those same religions and churches are doing plenty of other things to keep them hidden."

"Yes," Xuan agreed, "and those religions and churches are very powerful."

"Sure they are, but we don't need more languages or more religions," Thomas said. "We need unifying phenomena, one language, commonly held truths, something we can agree on."

"Isn't that what Jack was showing us the other day?" Xuan exclaimed. "He tried to make it experientially obvious. He made us see that those benches and those long-buried bodies were still possessed of an energy that we could feel right then, right in that moment. Then he used a chant that none of us understood, per se, but all of us understood at some other level of understanding, some intuitively cognitive place that is common to all of us. He demonstrated the common seed that exists in all people in a way that none of us could ignore!"

"Yes, he seems to have proved what we're saying right here: that the encoded truth is still accessible deep inside of us. If those truths are deeply planted and well embraced, then they haven't slipped away. They are still with us and are not gone forever." Thomas looked at Xuan as he spoke. "The seeds of our true natures have been inside all of us since the human race was conceived."

"And they are not gone even now, thousands of years later," Xuan said.

"No, they are not gone," Thomas agreed. "Where would they go? They must be truly essential and basic and common to everyone." He paused and then went on. "And they are inspiring us to find them at the meeting in June."

"I wonder what those truths are," Xuan said as she yawned, "and I wonder if they can wait until tomorrow to be rediscovered."

The fire had gone out as they talked. The room was chilled. Xuan snuggled up to Thomas, and he whispered, "You know, I really like talking with you. We feed on each other's thoughts. We draw them out of each other and extend them in conversation, and we end up in realms of the mind I've never experienced before."

"Yeah, I know what you mean. We're also ending up in realms of the heart into which I've never ventured," Xuan admitted. "I like that, too."

She looked at Thomas, and he felt an urge to move even closer.

"But I can't go any further tonight," she continued. "I'm exhausted. Why don't you get ready for bed, and let's get some sleep."

"Yeah, that sounds good. Now you'll get to see my dreaded pajamas."

He smiled as he kissed her lightly and squeezed her tight for a moment. She extracted herself from him so he could rise from the floor, and he felt her watching him as he moved to his suitcase, grabbed his sleepwear and shaving kit, and headed for the bathroom.

When he had left the room, Xuan got up and returned the blanket to the bed nearest the fireplace. She turned back the sheets on both sides of the bed and arranged the two pillows. She retrieved the candle from the mantle and put it on the nightstand. She looked in the mirror and unbuttoned two buttons on her high-collared pajama top. She fussed with her hair, looked again, and unbuttoned one more button. Then she got in on one side, fluffed her pillow, and pulled the covers up to just above her waist. She changed her mind and refastened two buttons and rearranged his pillow beside hers. She smiled as she waited for him to return, lay her head on the pillow, and took a deep breath as her eyes slowly closed.

In the bathroom, Thomas looked in the mirror. He regretted his divorce, but he knew that he had stopped living and loving in that marriage. Studying himself in the reflection of the glass, he realized that he was finally willing to leave that regret behind. He was moving forward again in so many ways. He felt himself opening up with Xuan, and he knew he would sleep well.

When he came out of the bathroom and saw what Xuan had done with the bed, a tear came to his eye. He was stopped in his tracks for a moment by the realization that he would be sleeping with her and not in the other bed—or, worst of all, in his car. He was moved by her trust with him, and as he leaned over the bed, he was inspired to whisper, "Xuan, I trust you, too." He kissed her lightly on the cheek.

She seemed to be already asleep and didn't respond. He smiled at her innocence and vulnerability as she lay there unaware. He blew out the candle and quietly got under the blanket next to her. He felt her roll over close to him and place one leg over his. He slipped his arm under her head and stroked her hair. She mumbled something, but he didn't understand what she said. He felt warm and safe with her, and the hot tears of vulnerability rolled down his face and fell in her hair. He pulled her partway on top of him and lightly stroked her face with just one finger. Then he kissed her ever so softly.

Now fully conscious, she gently pushed away from him and locked into his eyes as she unbuttoned her pajama top the rest of the way. She lowered herself into his arms again, embraced him once more, and returned his kiss with a long one of her own. She ever so gently bit his lower lip as she cradled his head in her hand, rolled to one side, and pulled him toward her again.

"Now, Thomas," she whispered. "Please. Right now."

Chapter 9

Questions

Digger awoke on the Saturday morning after the group trip to Acoma with no specific plans. He thought he might go mountain biking, but he stepped outside to find a light rain falling. The thermometer on his apartment porch showed thirty-eight degrees, and snow was forecast for later in the day, so he came back inside, dropped an English muffin in the toaster, and poured himself a glass of orange juice.

He had not yet figured out much on the clue he had been assigned, so he walked over and switched on the computer in the dining room that doubled as his home office, clicked on the Internet icon, and entered his password. When the toaster popped, he retrieved his muffin, topped it with grape jelly, and returned to the table that served as his desk.

He quickly went to a search engine and entered a word from his clue: "Arjuna." After a few moments, the first ten entries appeared on his screen, with a thousand more behind them. He began scrolling through them to see if any caught his eye. A distinctly Hindu name appeared in one of the results on display. The name was Paramahansa Yogananda.

He clicked on it and found a biography that detailed the man's visits to the United States in 1920. The biographical sketch also described the yogi's founding of a movement called Self Realization Fellowship, located in the greater Los Angeles area, where there were still five SRF communities. Digger read that the fellowship focused on meditative practices but, despite its thousands of followers around the world, was not considered a religion by those who categorize such things.

He reread the scrap of paper on which he had written his clue: "Shankara, Arjuna, and Dvaraka. He came to the West in the 1920s and was no maker of religion." Digger seemed to have found what he was looking for. Even so, he knew there was more to uncover.

He read that Yogananda passed away in 1951, so it seemed obvious to Digger that he wouldn't be at Acoma in June. He also read a quote from this yogi to the effect that the religions of humankind were like the colors of the rainbow that are produced when one light shines through a prism. The yogi likened the one light to the one true source of all things. Digger thought to himself that this teacher would likely be welcome at Acoma if he could find a way to be there.

Digger also remembered what all the planners had been learning as they delved into their clues—that the clue was only a beginning, a point of departure. He knew he must tap into the energy that the clue invoked in him to explore it even further. So he began to research other references, names, book titles, and summaries he could find on the Internet, knowing he would want to confirm his findings in more traditional sources if he found anything pertinent.

Digger already knew from his collegiate studies that some of the oldest writings known to man came from India. As a group of writings, the Vedas, the Upanishads and the Bhagavad-Gita were some of the most revered of all the sacred texts. The Bhagavad-Gita was favorably compared to Homer's *Iliad*, the works of Shakespeare, and portions of the Koran, the Bible, and the teachings of Confucius. It was a series of dialogues between a warrior, Arjuna, and the presumed divine presence named Krishna.

What Digger couldn't immediately discern was the specific learning this clue held for him in the context of Project 4000. The obvious answer, that Hindu truths were part of a larger spiritual truth, was no great stretch for him. However, he was left to wonder, what else? This question would tug at him for the entire weekend.

The rain didn't let up all day so Digger read some more and mused over various things as he listened to music. He played with his new Siamese kitten, started a load of laundry, and, at lunchtime, fixed a bowl of soup and left it to cook on the stove. He loved soups—soups of all kinds. He was thin, by most standards, and he ate carefully, but he stayed busy with hiking, biking, and lots of other outdoor activities, so he was robust and healthy. He attributed his health to his love of soup.

One of his readings after lunch involved historical accounts that Aryan or Jewish tribes had invaded India around 1200–1500 BC. His general opinion regarding the advances of civilization, supported by his studies in anthropology, held that both the invaders and the invaded eventually evolved into a hybrid culture and usually ended up sharing tools, food, language, ideas, and, of course, genes. This sharing, he liked to think, was always a two-way street. The invaders were subjected to this merging influence as much as the invaded.

As he reflected on this Aryan/Hindu interface, he couldn't help but notice similar-sounding words and concepts that were now a part of both cultures. He wondered if the words *aum* and *amen* sprang from this cross-culturalization. They mean roughly the same thing and were used in approximately the same way. He wondered if a Brahman from India became the Abraham of the Aryan Old Testament. Was the flute-playing divinity, Krishna, the model for the Christ, sprung from the Aryan traditions? Were they all just word and sound confusions, or was it more than that? Did these common-sounding words spring from one culture, only to be borrowed by the other? Did they come to both cultures from some common, even older source? If so, he wondered, what was that source? Where did it come from? When did it originate, and what happened to it?

He reflected, as well, on the events at Acoma the previous Thursday and was fascinated by Jack Eaglefeather's simple chant that had no explicit meaning that Digger could discern, except that it produced a common, almost identical, experience for everyone present in the old adobe church that day. He wondered if Jack was tied in to some ancient tradition or teaching. Was there a secret language that had been passed down from the Anazasi to the Pueblo Indians and then from Iyatiku to Iyatiku and, finally, to Jack? He wondered if the language of Jack's chant was thousands of years old, even older than Jack's native tongue. Did the language of the chant, if it was a language, predate all the known language groups around the world? Was it the mother of all languages? What if it was no language at all, but rather some sort of prelingual collection of sounds without words—sounds that conveyed meanings at primal levels and fostered prime experiential knowing, too? Did this collection of sounds develop as a common strain in otherwise different language groups? Was there once a single language, as the story of Babel suggested? Had that language managed to somehow survive into modern times? Was it still alive today but only known to a few?

Digger was in his element now. This kind of internal dialogue and focused thinking got his juices flowing. He was fascinated by the possibilities his emerging questions raised. Part of him knew that the answers were sometimes less important than the questions, and so he loved the questions and the almost infinite possibilities they represented.

Too late, he smelled the burning pan in which his homemade soup had evaporated and rushed in to remove it from the flame. He placed the blackened pan under the faucet, and soon it steamed with cold water. He pounded the counter in frustration and searched for a new lunchtime soup, this one from a can.

Soon, however, he returned to his ruminations. He was becoming convinced that it was the questions that were the seeds of progress, and he imagined that throughout the history of man, it was the teachers who asked the questions, imparted the secrets, or taught how to look for the answers. He imagined that maybe some of them also taught a root language. Was it just his imagination, or did all of this actually happen? It was logical to presume that these teachers lived at different times in different tribes or cultures. Maybe some of them knew each other somehow. Maybe they knew that their knowledge was secret or sacred—but, equally possible, maybe they didn't know. Maybe they just passed on what they knew and let the knowledge take root wherever it could be understood. This might explain the uneven but generally forward march of civilization—not a straight line but more like the ragged path of a butterfly.

Or, he asked himself, did these teachers intentionally seek to advance the tribes of people they encountered by seeding ideas and truths and principles? Or maybe it was an accidental seeding and lacked any intent at all. Did the secret of the wheel and the making of fire come through these messengers? Was there an inherent development from a root knowledge that was passed on sporadically in a two-steps-forward, one-step-back sort of way? Was it possible, he wondered, that new levels of understanding developed, only to be surpassed by the next level of teaching from the root knowledge? Could it be that some civilizations embraced the teachings and used them well, while others quickly forgot them or missed the finer points or felt threatened by them and turned their back on them entirely? Or killed the messengers? Digger knew that all change, even positive change, was more often refused than embraced. Killing the teacher was part of that refusal.

Wasn't it even possible, he wondered, that some of those who were given the secret knowledge or inventive insights kept them for themselves and then set themselves up as priests or imams or mullahs or shamans or ministers and misused the power that their knowledge afforded them? Absent a rigorous or altruistic intent to advance, didn't some of the knowledge or insight lose its newness or vitality? Didn't some accepted insights soon turn into feedback loops that served only to reinforce themselves? Like the backwater of a flowing river, didn't those feedback loops serve to separate these insights and truths from the flowing river of progress until they became isolated and stagnated and dead with inactivity?

As he asked these questions during his day alone, he understood more clearly the haphazard advances and retreats of civilization, the ebb and flow of ideas and thoughts. Digger figured out why only some ideas and teachings eventually came to be accepted as truth. He understood, again, but with a new appreciation, the archeology of ideas. He felt the excitement of discovery and experienced the opening of his mind through the process of archeological exploration. He was reminded again why the questions one asked were more important than the answers. It was because the questions framed the outermost extent to which the answer could reach, and so a poorly asked question limited the answer. On the other hand, a well-framed question propelled the answer and uncovered the infinite possibilities so that newer and greater heights of understanding were reached.

Most of all on that day, however, Digger simply remembered why he loved being an archeologist—an explorer and a seeker of truth, ideas, and understanding.

As he checked on his soup and turned down the flame to simmer, Digger realized that Project 4000 would produce a moment in time that could also be a teaching, an imparting of secrets, or an insight for humankind. He came to understand how that might happen, and he wondered what the teaching would be and how it would be received. He wondered who would hear it and who would turn their back on it. He was reminded how small and close and connected the world had become because of telephone and television and Internet and high-speed travel and instant translation devices. Perhaps everyone would hear the teachings. Was it possible, he mused, that this event might have worldwide implications, just as Russell Layne had predicted?

In the very next breath, however, he thought of those who wouldn't believe or listen or be open to anything that might come out of their meeting. How would that be overcome if, indeed, it could be overcome? *For crying out loud*, he thought, *new ideas are always met with resistance.* People who were invested in the old and limited understandings would certainly be challenged by something new. That had been going on forever. Some would be scared. Others would feel ripped from their comfort zones and unable to question the very boundaries they had erected in order to feel safe. Even if old understandings were like stagnant backwater at times, it was still water nonetheless. Even if it was no longer flowing or vital, it was safe. These people might have to turn away and close their hearts in order to maintain some semblance of continuity for themselves and their closely held beliefs. Not all people would be open, Digger concluded.

In fact, he realized, it might be that most people would not be open. *Maybe*, he thought, *that's why an age of humankind takes two thousand years to complete. It might take that long to open enough minds to move the world forward.* He knew the product of the meeting in June would be embraced by some, but he had to devise a way by which he could accept the nonacceptance that was likely, as well. *The words from the meeting will fall on deaf ears*, he thought to himself.

But then he leaned back in his chair and smiled. He realized he was a part of this event, and his excitement was enough to spur him on. He didn't feel as though he was studying history or archaeology anymore. It was more as though he was, in some small way, making history or participating in archaeology. He could see his role, and seeing his role made it so that history was not apart from him—an object to be studied—but, rather, a part of him, and he was a part of it. That made it wholly different. That gave him a feeling that warmed him like soup and nourished his young heart. For today, soup and ideas were sufficient to sustain him and nourish him for another week. He poured his soup in a bowl, placed some crackers in front of him on the table, and reached for a spoon.

Chapter 10

Illuminations

At four o'clock that Saturday afternoon, Russell Layne was called to the hospital where Father Garces had been readmitted, suffering from fatigue and an irregular heartbeat. When he arrived, the elderly priest was sleeping peacefully, and Layne went out in the hall, placed a phone call to Anna, and asked her to join him there.

She was glad to wrap up her Saturday housecleaning chores and soon was at the priest's bedside with Russell Layne.

"He's very fond of you, Anna," Layne began. "I'm glad you were able to come."

"Oh, sure," Anna said softly. "I like him a lot."

She and Layne sat down near the window to talk while they waited to see if the padre would awaken soon.

"I know I've asked this question before," Anna started, "but do you know if someone like Jesus will be at our meeting? I mean, he was at the last one, so it would make sense for him to be at ours, too, wouldn't it?"

"I still don't know the answer to that one, Anna. What I've read about that meeting two thousand years ago describes Jesus as a Jewish mystic from Nazareth. Reportedly, there was also a Persian sage, a Hindu wise man, an Asian teacher, a Magi, an African healer, and two others at that meeting. They all deferred to him and pledged their support for his efforts when the meeting was over, and that's about all I've been able to find out. The information on the meeting is pretty scarce, but it seems that Jesus was possessed of foresight and wisdom uncommon for that place and time. As we might say today, he was illumined."

"The Jewish tradition doesn't consider him a messiah, but the Christians do. Why is that?" Anna asked.

"Jewish expectations were tribal and narrow, so they couldn't see the next progression of humanity. They expected a warrior to accomplish the Jewish agenda and not a peaceful man with a larger mission."

"So, now it's the Christians and Catholics who have a view of Jesus that may blind them to a larger mission, too."

"Hmm. That could be right," Layne said. "Followers of other religions are blinded, too. I think that through the centuries there have been dozens or even hundreds of messiahs, messengers, and enlightened ones in addition to Jesus. We only know of a handful. Buddha and Krishna and Mohammed were certainly enlightened. I think Elijah and Moses might have been christed, too"

"What do you mean, 'christed'?" Anna interrupted.

"Let's see, how should I explain it?" Layne thought out loud. "'Christed' comes from a Greek word that means anointed or enlightened or illumined." He laughed quietly and said, "Some people actually think it's a last name, as in Jesus Christ. Or they think it's a person. It's neither one. It actually refers to a state of mind or a state of being whereby one is so in tune with the universal purpose in their life, and the universal principles behind their existence, that they are able to recognize, understand, develop and utilize powers of which most of us are not even aware."

"You really think there's been more than one?" Anna asked.

"Oh, yes, I think so," Russell answered. "As I said, I also think we only know of just a few, but I'm guessing there have been dozens, or maybe even hundreds, that we don't know of yet. Sadly, we may never know of most of them."

"Oh, wow! That's so amazing!" Anna replied. "Where did they come from?"

"I think they have come from everywhere," Russell conjectured, "from all over the world and throughout all of human history. We have called them saints or mystics or kings or a hundred other names. What they've been called depends on a cultural point of view and the naming concepts available in a given culture or language. They have been accorded a name or title in keeping with the highest title a given culture can bestow."

"So, do you think there may be several at the meeting we are planning?"

"If the collective understanding of the world is going to accelerate, I'd say it's a very good possibility," Layne answered. "Ultimately, it's the naming concepts that have limited the historical understanding."

"So, some languages have limited the perception of illumined beings?"

"Maybe all languages," he said.

"Do you think there are so-called christed beings living among us today?"

"I certainly hope so," Layne answered, "or we won't have any at our meeting."

"So, I might actually get to meet an illumined being?" Anna asked.

"Yes; maybe several."

Just then, a movement in Father Garces's bed caught their attention, and they looked over to see the priest rolling over on his side to face them.

He managed a weak smile as he whispered, "I hoped I would be illumined enough for you, Anna."

She stood up and walked the few steps to the bed and took his hand. "You are, Father. You are definitely illumined enough for me." Then she quickly changed the subject and asked, "How are you feeling? Can I get you anything?"

"You could hand me that water," he suggested as he pointed to a glass on the stand by the bed. "Hi, Russell."

"Hi, Father. Have you been listening to our conversation?" he inquired.

"Yes," he said, still in a whisper. "You and I agree, for the most part. The world would be in even worse shape than it currently is if there had been only one christed person for the last ten thousand years. Remember, Jesus said he would be with us to the end of the age. Generally speaking, that is two thousand years. Lots of folks took Jesus to mean that the world would end at the end of the age. Or they interpreted that comment to mean that he would be back at the end of the age. Instead, I think it means there will be a new christed being, or maybe several, as you suggest, and the next age, the next two thousand years, will be different, because the understanding will be accelerated in the least explored frontier of all."

"What do you mean by least explored frontier of all?" Anna asked.

"I mean the heart-mind-spirit connection of the human experience," the priest answered. "What we know of these connections is woefully inadequate, and our survival as a species may well depend on an accelerated rate of learning that is not burdened with outdated understandings, rigid thinking, or the arrogance of religious chauvinism."

"Maybe the world will end, at least the world as we know it, and a new world will begin," Russell Layne posited.

"Yes, and I think the key is how we know it, how we perceive it and how we understand it. The world won't change until we change how we view the world," Father Garces said. "That new-world understanding must be seeded soon. As I find myself nearer and nearer to my own death, I think of it as an imperative. I think the book you publish of the accounts of the meeting in June will speed things along."

He then looked at Anna and said, "I have dreamed that you will help Malik and Jack get it published."

"Me?" Anna protested. "I thought Russell would do that."

"I thought so, too," Father Garces answered. "I must tell you, however, that he doesn't appear in my dreams about it. There's just you and Jack and Malik."

"But, doesn't it take money to publish a book—like, lots of money?" Anna asked anxiously. "I don't have any idea how to get something published."

"The money will come," Father Garces assured her. "I'm not sure the source of it, but the money will come."

Russell Layne had gotten up during their conversation and turned away, looking out the window of the hospital room. Jack had told him the Jemez Pueblo woman's predictions that Jack and Malik would remain after the meeting in June but that Digger and the others would be gone. He wondered silently about his fate in this whole matter and made a mental note to revise his will just in case he wasn't around to help publish the book. He thought of his contacts in the publishing business, too, and made a mental list of who he would talk to about helping Anna if he didn't survive the meeting in June.

Anna looked at Father Garces, but he had closed his eyes and seemed to have drifted off to sleep again.

Russell observed what was happening and motioned for Anna to leave with him. The two of them left quietly, both glancing at the priest as they departed his room.

They walked down the corridor to the elevator without saying a word, both lost in their own thoughts. As they left the elevator and headed into the attached parking garage, Anna looked at Russell Layne.

He saw the worried look on her face and stopped and turned to her. "You know, Anna, illumination is an exciting and scary thing to go through. I wonder sometimes if we will recognize it when it comes our way."

"I'm not sure why I feel this, but I think we will," she answered, "and I feel myself getting more ready to understand it with each passing day. I can hardly wait for tomorrow to get here."

Chapter 11

Whispering Spirals

The next meeting day, Tuesday, was ripe with anticipation. Everyone gathered in Thomas's office even before they were asked to meet. Malik took notes as they talked. Xuan and Thomas shared their thoughts on the well-planted clue. Anna shared her ideas from the discussion in the hospital room with Russell and Father Garces. Digger talked about his rainy-day thoughts on the Hindu clue and the role of special teachers in the progress of humankind. It seemed to everyone that three of the clues were now well explored.

While waiting for Jack to arrive, everyone shared and explored the experience at Acoma the previous Thursday with Russell Layne, who had not been there. Jack's demonstration that day was, of course, a special insight into the fourth clue, and it was now partially understood, too.

"This idea of an ongoing and everlasting energy in all things past and present fascinates me," Russell Layne started. "It is not a new concept, really, but this is the most convincing demonstration of it I've ever heard. I've also got a new-found regard for Jack. Does anyone know if he's coming to the meeting later this morning?"

"I think he is," Digger answered.

"Good, because I'd like to discuss these clues and revelations even further. First," Layne said, "energy might be eternal. The scientists tell us that new matter is not created, it just changes form. Perhaps we should now add energy to their assertion. New energy is not created, either, it just changes in terms of the way in which it is revealed or demonstrated or perceived."

As he completed this thought and paused to let it sink in, Malik hurried to catch up his notes.

"Second ..." he hesitated as he searched for the right words, "there is seed energy present in all things, including human beings, and that energy is so well rooted, so deeply established, that its eventual flowering cannot be denied. No matter what has happened through the ages or what happens in the future, the fruition of that which is seeded cannot be stopped. Apparently, this is not just true in terms of acorns growing into oaks or dandelion seeds dispersed to become dandelion plants, it's true in terms of ideas and truths, and it is true in the eventual destiny of all humankind."

No one interrupted him, so he continued. "Third, the energy of illumination is available to all persons and, in fact, is part of the undeniable seeds that are planted in all human beings. It appears that this seed of understanding, this seed of illumination, is now more apparent at an individual level than ever before in the history of humankind. As a result, the passing of this age and the initiation of the next age presents us with an ever-increasing number of illumined beings."

Russell looked at Digger before he went on. "Lastly, Digger is wondering if there might have always been a common way of communicating—a language or a specially constructed set of sounds—that might provide a way for people all over the world to discover these seeds within themselves."

"Exactly!" Digger interrupted. "No matter their native language or cultural background, I think there may be a means of common communication that has been long forgotten. That's why there is a Tower of Babel story. If this means of common communication can be found again, this communication will allow people to understand that truths in every collective experience of humankind have all come from this common source. We seven planners may be starting to uncover this common energy for ourselves in our meetings."

"We may uncover even more energies on the way to the meeting in June," Russell finished. "There are three more clues, aren't there?"

"Yes, that's right," Thomas answered. "In addition to the four you've summarized, there are the ones we've come to call the Sufi clue, the science clue, and the teacher clue."

Malik was nodding his head to confirm what Thomas had said.

Anna spoke up, saying, "Those three clues have not been very thoroughly explored, yet. Russell and I have taken the science clue, and Malik has the teacher clue. Thomas has the Sufi clue."

Just then, Jack Eaglefeather entered the offices.

Thomas glanced at his watch; it was ten o'clock. He said, "Okay, we'll organize some more efforts on these clues after the morning meeting."

Everyone got up and went into the reception area, which now held, thanks to Xuan and Anna, the significant personal symbols of each one of the planners. Malik's dream catcher took up almost one whole wall. Xuan had brought in a simple Zen painting and a crystal prism, and both now sat on the one remaining table, alongside a book of Chinese sayings from her collection. Thomas had contributed a landscape painting of a snow-capped mountain at sunrise that he found at a garage sale. Anna had brought a dried flower arrangement that included a preserved dandelion, its seeds still intact. She also brought in a throw rug from the Middle East that featured patterns none of them had ever seen. Russell Layne brought in an aerial photograph of the Nile River Delta that reminded him how all waters eventually become one water—first in an ever-widening river and then in connected oceans that surround the globe. Digger's addition to the meeting room was a large photo of the Milky Way galaxy, a color-enhanced photo that depicted it as a spiraling infinity of stars. He had even Photoshopped a caption for it that read, "Mystery and Pattern in Motion."

As they all greeted Jack, he held up his addition to the meeting room. It was a framed picture of Acoma Pueblo at sunset, as viewed from the north. The photographer had managed to frame the shot so that the top of the Enchanted Mesa appeared to be present in the foreground, and Acoma Mesa seemed so close that the space between them shrank to nothing. They appeared to be linked. A space on the wall had been left for Jack's picture, as he had already let Anna know its dimensions. Digger and Jack got it hung in short order, and that completed their now-special room.

Xuan and Anna had decided to arrange the room so that the pictures were mounted rather low on the walls. There were no chairs, so everything could be easily seen while sitting on the floor. In addition to a coffee table placed against the wall, there were lots of pillows. Xuan imagined that they would each sit in a circle at every meeting, and Anna furthered decided that they would each sit in a different place every time they met. This would become more complicated after they had met seven times, but, for now, it would offer a new perspective for each of them at each meeting. She also told Xuan that she would track the seating positions in relation to each other person and keep a record of it. Over time, this would create a seating chart with forty-nine sitting arrangements—or seven times seven.

For this first meeting in the newly appointed room, Xuan asked that everyone sit directly across from the object he or she had brought in. She then asked them to begin the meeting by focusing on their object and concentrating on the special feelings it invoked in them. At her urging, all of them closed their eyes and began to recall and remember and remind themselves how their meeting room contribution had become so special to them. She asked them to imagine that they were in the place where they had first seen their special symbol or where they had first ascribed a unique feeling to it. One by one, they closed their eyes so that they could reminisce without distraction. Soon, a flood of wonderful feelings began to wash over each one of them, and the meeting space absorbed these energies and took on the highest aspirations of those who were there.

After a few moments, Xuan gently and slowly started whispering so that all of them could hear her soothing and melodic voice. "Imagine a warm, soft breeze as it caresses your face in that place where you have taken refuge."

All of them began to imagine the breeze on their heads and faces.

"Now feel it on your shoulders and across your arms and hands," she continued. "Feel it rustle through your hair and touch you on the back of your neck. Let it shiver your spine and remind you how alive you are." Her voice remained slow and soft.

"Let yourself imagine that you are an integral part of the beautiful scene you have conjured up—not a spectator or a passerby, but right in the middle of where you've come to be in your mind's eye. Even though it may have been created by others, imagine that you are creating it again yourself. Put in the colors, add in the smells, determine the textures, visualize the sights, and compose the sounds. Feel again the ever-present breeze that is flowing over every part of your body and touching all of you like a breath of rain-freshened air."

Xuan went further. "Soon, you feel lighter, and you can feel yourself being lifted up by this breeze. It is ever-so-slowly and ever-so-gently turning you around and around to enjoy this place you have created. You can see it from every point of view, and you are moved by its beauty. You continue to create it in your mind and add to it in more and more detail. Peace and serenity engulf you as you absorb your special place and let it fully surround you. You feel powerful and humble as this beautiful world continues to unfold, no matter where you look or smell or touch or listen."

She kept going. "Timeless moments go by, and soon your gentle turning slows to stillness, and the breeze lets you land again in the midst of your sacred place. You realize that you have created this place in which you find yourself and that it is the most wonderful place you have ever been. Ultimately, you know it is special because it came from inside of you—from your mind and from your heart. The external beginning was only a template upon which you could create. You also know you have touched a place inside yourself that can create these places and thoughts and feelings. You have found within yourself that which makes good, that which creates wonderful, that which inspires incredible, that which is without limit, that which sets you free, that which gives you peace, and that which places you in awe. You have found a breeze on which you can always ride. It is the ongoing, unseen wind of creation within you."

Xuan stopped talking right there. She wasn't sure where, exactly, but it felt like time to stop, so she did. No one stirred, and the silence continued for several minutes.

After a while, some of the Planners moved. Everyone turned in the direction of Russell Layne as they slowly returned to the room in which they had started. All of them felt uplifted, renewed, invigorated, and filled with purpose—a purpose born of feeling the good within themselves and of feeling the power within to create an expression of themselves that was pure and good and strong and right and connected.

~   ~   ~

Russell wasn't sure what to say or where to begin. Finally, he simply said, "Thank you, Xuan. I found myself in a rain cloud and became a drop of moisture as I fell into a mountain stream. I got caught up in flowing down the stream through the canyons and past the boulders along the way. I smelled the pine trees and enjoyed the bouncing, jostling ride through cool, cool waters until the stream slowed down as it reached the foothills and began to level out. Then I saw maple trees and cottonwoods and flowers on the hillsides as I joined other streams and became part of a larger flow. Soon I joined the river and meandered into a wider stretch of water that slowed down even more. As I neared an ocean, the river separated into dozens of shallow paths, like fingers on a hand, and then I heard the ocean waves and felt the sting of salt and knew I was part of something even larger, an expanse so huge I could not even perceive it. It was quite a journey, and yet I knew, somehow, that it was not over, yet. I got this sense that I was being drawn up into another rain cloud and that I would make another journey, through another stream, again."

"Hmm," Xuan responded. She smiled. "I noticed that when I was no longer a spectator in my scene, when I let myself be a part of the scene, it took on an entirely new aspect." She paused for a moment and then continued, choosing her words carefully. "What we all just did together was also really neat for me, because I've never been the whisperer before. I have no idea where those words and ideas came from or why I started whispering them aloud. They just came to me and were out of my mouth before I could think or evaluate or judge them. They seemed like the things to say, and I said them as I felt them myself. The words just came through me."

Digger said, "I thought maybe you planned it out ahead of time. Are you saying you didn't plan it?"

"I didn't," Xuan answered. "Maybe I just knew that each one of you was focused on your special place and that made me feel safe in my special place. Maybe the collective special feelings we generated together added up to something even larger and more special."

"Like, the whole is greater than the sum of the parts," Thomas conjectured.

"Yes, I think so," Xuan hesitated. "Or it's a like-attracts-like kind of thing."

Jack Eaglefeather listened to all of this and then said, "Until the words can come from you and through you, there can be no true understanding. They cannot be someone else's words or even words you try to write in advance; they can only come through you in the very moment you are moved to utter them."

Anna asked, "So the clue about teachers and doors is about finding the words that make sense to only us?"

"I suppose that's right," Jack answered, "but it may be a lot more. I've thought about that clue a little, because I was a teacher for thirty years. As a teacher, I talked about things through words—words that had to be eventually thrown away so that the student could fully experience the learning itself without the words. Without absorbing the learning, the words were just words. After the experience, the words were collected again in a way that made them unique to the student. In this way, they grew more accurate and became their own."

"But how do you know if you've collected the right words in the right order and drawn the right conclusion?" Thomas interrupted.

Jack looked at Thomas for a moment and then just shrugged his shoulders.

"It seems to me that most words we call true are just partial truths or opinions or traditions," Russell chimed in. "When your individual truth connects you with a larger truth, a truth beyond the published truths of mankind, truth with a capital 'T,' I think you know it somehow and you know intuitively how to express it. Then it is no longer partial for you."

"Or maybe you have to be somehow connected to that 'Truth' in the first place to even feel it as true," Jack added. "Perhaps you must be connected in an unbiased, pure, and unencumbered sort of way so that you can really experience a new truth and not just be someone who repeats an indirect and shallow understanding of an old but oft-repeated truth."

Malik listened and wrote down everything that was said. He and Anna were beginning to develop a routine whereby, after each staff meeting, she would read his notes aloud to him, and he would clarify for her anything that wasn't clear. Thomas had instructed them to collaborate after every meeting so that they could enter these notes into a Braille format. He hoped this would allow Malik to edit them himself, but Anna had confided to Thomas that progress on this front was slow because neither of them knew how to read Braille.

In addition, Malik still struggled with all the inconveniences of being blind and mute. It slowed him down and it frustrated him. At the same time, he knew his body was slowly replacing his lost visual perception with other perception abilities that made him unique—and gifted. Even two years after becoming blinded, he felt that his auditory capacity was still improving, just as he had once imagined it would. His transcription test had been his first proof of this expanded auditory ability. Now he relished this ability and was glad it was his. But he still hated being blind.

As Malik came back to the room from his moments of reverie, it was Digger who asked Jack, "Is there something wrong with reciting old truths or clichés even before there's a full understanding of them?"

The import of the question seemed to hang in the air. They all repeated it for themselves several times over and swished it around in their mind like wine from a newly opened bottle.

Finally, Jack attempted an answer. "I guess it is not wrong," he spoke slowly and deliberately, "but it is dangerous. Old truths and clichés point out the way, like teachers in a classroom, but the old truths are only a map. They tell of the journey. They highlight the important features of the landscape. They tell us how far we need to go or in what direction we need to travel or even which way to look, but maps are not the journey itself. Words are not the understanding. They are at best a picture."

"A picture with just two dimensions," Russell added. "Flat. Accurate as far as it goes, even pretty, perhaps, but incomplete in its flatness. It lacks vitality. It has no life to it. It is often just words and lines, and it represents a potential experience or maybe someone else's experience, but it is not the real experience at all."

Digger said, "I learned in anthropology courses that if the same words and understandings are repeated enough times by enough people, then they become a collective understanding, a culture—even a tradition. Then it has the weight of numbers behind it and, eventually, the weight of time to prop it up. Even in the face of new understandings, these old traditions continue to hold sway and become institutionalized."

"So they become religions for all the wrong reasons," Thomas concluded. "It makes a hero out of someone else, and people step back, applaud, and exclaim great things about someone else while the passage of time and the countless repetitions of the hero story obscure the importance of actually following the map and having the hero's experience for themselves."

"Yes," Xuan rejoined the discussion, "and even if the understandings and maps are mostly right, that which is wrong in them gains the weight of repetition, too, and the wrongs become perceived as truth right along with that which is right."

She paused to take a breath. "The untruths become embedded inside the truths, and soon it all becomes impossibly confused."

"Furthermore," Russell added, "the lack of vitality in the words and maps becomes another problem within the problem."

"But as long as the incessant feedback loop continues and the popular repetition continues," Digger said, "this flattened bunch of partial understandings grows and grows and grows over time. Soon, these understandings feed back on themselves and look to themselves for justification. And they repeat themselves so frequently and so incessantly that they become deeply ingrained in the cultural organism and become seemingly indisputable. Minds close around them."

"And just like Xuan said, the wrongs become ingrained, too." Russell was up and pacing the floor now. "These wrongs grow, too, and they grow right along with the clichés and the truths and the worded understandings, and they can be just as large—like some sort of tumor."

Xuan added, "So the truth, over time, carries the inherent flaws of the carrier: cultural bias, individual perspective, misinterpreted experiences, imperfect teachers, and inaccurate words."

"Yes and the carrier is never-ending, mindless repetition," Digger said, "and that is eventually regarded as tradition and undisputed truth."

"Yes, and the words carry as much wrong as right, as much truth as error, and as much insight as blindness," Russell summarized.

Digger said, "So the teacher opens the door with words, but there is no learning until the student walks through the words and actually experiences the understanding on the other side."

"And that understanding is devoid of words until the student puts his or her own words on this understanding," Xuan said.

"And no one else can do that for them," Thomas added.

"No. It has to be his or her own," Russell said.

"And it can't get stuck in time or it loses its vitality," Xuan said. "When that happens, it becomes rigid and codified. Truth, as a conclusion, is precarious and dangerous. All the words that are frozen in time or stagnant in a book are dead unless they come alive in the experiences of each and every student of life," she summarized.

"The real essence of the universe is the ongoing process. It is only the process that lives on," Russell said.

"And we are living that process right now," Thomas said. "We're just continuing the process that will culminate with this meeting in June. Until we get to the new understandings revealed in that meeting, we really won't know for sure what doors will be opened and what we will discover."

Chapter 12

Developments

Weeks passed. The June meeting was only two months away as the Planners started their workday on April 16, 2010. Russell Layne was late, as had become his habit, but everyone else was on time.

Xuan had reminded Thomas during breakfast at her apartment that the Web site was almost complete and needed his approval. It was a small site—not much more than an online brochure—but they had hired a search engine optimization service, and Thomas felt the site would have some positive impact. Most of the content was being developed by Anna and Xuan, but there were still a few questions to be resolved before it could be finally put online.

For one thing, the meeting at Acoma was scheduled to begin at sunrise on June 15, and the planners assumed it would end at sunset on the longest day of the year, the first day of summer, June 21. That would make the meeting seven full days. Thomas still wondered how they would fill seven days of meetings without an agenda, but he tried not to worry about it and figured the meeting would end up being exactly what it was meant to be.

Xuan, Anna, and Thomas met briefly around his desk.

"Should we mention the prisms on the Web site?" Xuan asked. "Where will people pick them up?"

"Our driving directions on the Web site list the north and west entrances, so we should have the people pick up the prisms as they walk into the Acoma Land," Thomas decided. "We also need someone to direct the traffic at each entrance— that is, if there is any traffic."

"Do you see the prisms just being handed out from boxes, placed on tables, or lying in the road?" Xuan asked as she winked at Thomas and waited for him to decide.

"I think we should just place them on tables beside the road. If someone wants a prism, they can pick one up, and if they don't, well, then they don't," he reasoned.

"Should we mention them on the Web site?" Xuan asked again.

"I think we should," Anna said, "and I'll get to work on finding someone to run the entrances, too."

"Okay," Thomas agreed.

"Should we ask people to RSVP?" Xuan asked.

"Do you think they will?" Anna asked. "I mean, I don't think we can compel them to do so, do you?"

"No, but it could prove useful in case we have to order more prisms," Xuan replied.

"How many are ordered?" Thomas asked.

"Twelve thousand," Anna answered.

"Oh, come on!" Thomas exclaimed. "Twelve thousand? We'll be lucky if there are five hundred people, and, besides, the pueblo will be overwhelmed if we get more than a thousand. It's the master teachers who matter the most at this meeting, and I don't really care if this Web site attracts anybody who isn't a master teacher."

"Speaking of masters, we still don't have a single one confirmed as coming to the meeting," Anna reminded them.

"I think we're getting closer," Xuan replied.

"Closer! Closer to what?" Thomas said. "My Sufi clue has been nothing but trouble since I started trying to figure it out. It doesn't feel like a clue at all, and I haven't even gotten past the opening line!"

Thomas was clearly frustrated; perhaps the uncertainty of their five-month mystery was starting to wear on him. Xuan looked at him, and he glared back at her and watched as she diverted her gaze. He wasn't of a mind to be consoled or ready to be anything but frustrated. He wished it was time for their regular morning meeting.

Though he had initially resisted them, the meetings that were supposed to be once a month and then once a week had become everyday occurrences that he now enjoyed. Thomas was surprised at this development, but they had turned into mini-events each day. They were almost always relaxing, and he often left them feeling refreshed and sometimes inspired. He and Xuan had discussed this development away from work and were of the opinion that these daily meetings were a benefit to both of them as well as the project.

Thomas also liked that Anna's seating chart idea had worked out well. Every day was a little different; not one meeting was like a previous meeting in terms of perspective, content, agenda, or the experience itself. In every meeting, Thomas noted, the person on one or both sides of him was likely different. That meant, of course, that the person directly across from him in the circle was usually different, too. In addition, the view from one's ever-changing position in the circle was typically altered. This not only kept perspectives from becoming stale or routine, it usually caused each person to be directly in front of another person's important symbol, helping them to enter the meeting through the mindset of that other person. Jack had even joked to Thomas that it felt like walking a mile in another man's shoes every time he came to their meetings. Thomas came to value this comment as accurate and eventually shared it with the whole group. When he did, Anna beamed.

While there was never an agenda, Thomas observed that Russell Layne would usually start the meetings with some spoken words, words pronounced in his resonant, soothing voice. Thomas willingly received these words, but it was actually Russell's intonation of the words, the sound of the words, that served to mesmerize him and calm him into silence. It seemed like Russell didn't just open the meeting, he opened the Planners up to the potential of their day as well as the possibilities of their endeavor. Thomas began to see Russell's uncanny ability to entice everyone, or at least him, to lay aside their worries and distractions. He was good at getting Thomas focused into the very current moment of their group experience.

When Russell was done with his unscripted openings, silence usually descended upon them. Their breathing would become rhythmic and measured. Their eyes would soon close. Their minds would become momentarily free of clutter, and they would all slip out of their personal egos. Eventually, someone would begin to hum or chant or whisper some set of words or collection of sounds—something that emanated from deep inside of them. The others would listen and dream and imagine and feel, and then enter some other space for minutes at a time. After a while, they would then mentally return to their meeting room and discuss that which needed to be discussed.

During March and early April of 2010, the participants informally reported their reactions in the meetings to Thomas. Malik wrote that he could see again when his eyes were closed and told Thomas how much he relished the return of his vision. Xuan told Thomas that she felt unrestrained by her rational perspective and unbounded by the walls of their meeting room. Digger relayed to him that he could travel anywhere in the world—to any time and any place. In his imagination, he could go back a thousand years, or more. He could live momentarily among the ruins he loved to explore even before they were ruins. Layne shared that he often found himself at Acoma, wandering aimlessly from the mesa that housed the church to the enchanted mesa and then back again. He wondered what this back-and-forth vision meant and even asked Thomas his opinion on it. Jack seemed more affected than the others by these meetings and spoke to Thomas about it one day in early April.

"Thomas, I never stop thinking about the future of Acoma when I am in these meetings," Jack started. "As the Iyatiku, the future of Acoma has been my biggest concern, my occupation, and my hobby these last eleven years. But I am worried about this daughter of mine. She presents a big dilemma."

"Do you have anyone who can advise you?" Thomas asked.

"In our meetings, I imagine myself in conversations with my father and grand-father as well as the keeper woman. I think it's making me crazy," Jack answered. "I would never argue with my father, but I argue a lot with the keeper woman."

"So, when you roll all those conversations and arguments together into one piece of understanding, what does it tell you to do?" Thomas asked.

"I should train my daughter to be the next Iyatiku," Jack answered. "The time is approaching, and there doesn't appear to be another way."

~ ~ ~

When this day's meeting finally began, Thomas put his worries aside in antici-pation of what this meeting would hold for him. Then, much to his surprise, he was the one who began to infuse the meeting with the hum of his own energy. It was his first time to venture into this role, and, at first, his voice was barely audible. As the others heard it and focused in on it, their collective energy gave it strength and power, and his hum began to fill the room. To Anna, it sounded like the mass at Easter, and to Xuan it sounded like the aum chant in a far-off Buddhist temple. Digger heard the hum of a hundred slaves in the midst of building a royal tomb in Egypt, and Russell imagined the distant, unheard whir of all the planets in the universe as they circled the suns and stars of the near and distant galaxies.

Soon, Thomas felt the sounds from within take him to another level of inten-sity, and he imagined himself rising from where he sat. He planted his feet solidly on the floor. He imagined taking a deep breath and seeing it as it exhaled from his body. He took in another one, a little deeper, and watched it leave, and the cleans-ing power he felt on the exhale made him straighten up like a ballerina and throw his chest out into the room like a soldier at attention. His arms rose up from his sides and extended out from his torso, and he looked down at his feet. He imag-ined a pattern on the floor. He watched as the pattern grew more visible on the carpet under his feet and then recognized it as the mathematical symbol for infin-ity. It looked to be about two meters in length overall: one meter in front of him and one meter behind, and his feet were straddling the point of intersection. Then he watched as the pattern began to move. It mesmerized him. First, he merely followed the movement with his eyes, but soon it overtook him to the point that he began to follow with his feet and then with his arms, too.

He was tentative at first, placing one foot forward and then turning slowly around. Then he took his other foot in another direction and turned his body into that. Then the first foot moved again and he turned, and then the other foot moved and his turn went another way. His arms maintained his balance without a thought from him, and he turned and turned some more.

Before long, he was twirling and twisting and humming even louder as he danced and whirled in his imagination, never leaving the template of infinity upon which he moved. Effortlessly, elegantly, he danced. Joy rushed through him, and wave after wave of peace seemed to ascend from the pattern on the floor into his dancing form. Spirals of energy seemed to be drawn up into the vortex of his whirling arms, and he moved even faster. Like the propeller on an airplane, he spun and spun and spun some more. The pattern of infinity took on another dimension as it expanded up from the floor and redrew itself around his dancing form. Soon, he was enveloped by it.

Now, he was like a double spiral, and he imagined himself in the parallel vortexes of a four-dimensioned form of energy—a pattern that he saw as a description, a formula, a template on which the universe was framed and hung and built. It was the model on which the heart and mind and spirit and intention of all humankind was constructed. It was impossible to distinguish now if Thomas was making this four-dimensioned infinity or if it was making him. Dancer and pattern were one. Symbol and dervish were the same. There could be no distinction between them, and it went on like that for several minutes.

Soon his humming grew quieter, and Thomas's imagined dance slowed down and then slowed down some more and, finally, slowed to nothing. Deliberately, Thomas sat down. All eyes in the room remained closed and the even, measured breathing continued. The humming stopped altogether as silence regained its hold on the room. The Planners basked in its peaceful embrace for several more contented moments.

Xuan, sitting to Thomas's left, reached out for him with her hand and opened her eyes. He instinctively reached for her as he opened his eyes, too. He had the satisfied smile of discovery on his face, and she returned a brief nod of recognition as their hands touched on the floor between them. No words were spoken. Soon, the rest of the Planners had returned to the room.

Everyone looked at Thomas as if expecting some comment, but he was still aglow from his dance of understanding. Finally, he spoke.

"The clue says, 'The mysteries of Mohammed are known by those who dance with him.' Just now, I imagined that I was dancing like a whirling dervish. I've never seen a dervish or even read a description of how they dance, but I have been so tormented by this clue that when I finally let go of my frustration about it, I was able to align myself with something inside of me that showed me, informed my body, instructed my spirit, and provided me with what I needed to know." Thomas looked around as he finished speaking and noticed that everyone was looking at him with knowing smiles on their faces.

"What?" he implored. "Did you see what happened? Were you tuned in to what I was imagining?" Thomas was awestruck and confused at the same time. He pondered for a moment what their knowing smiles were saying to him. "Could you see me dancing? Oh, my!" He answered his own question and searched each one of their faces for some sign of judgment or disapproval. There was none.

Then Digger spoke up and said, "It was actually incredible, Thomas. I've never seen anything like it."

Anna and Xuan and Russell concurred with murmurs of agreement. Even Malik nodded, for he had seen it, too, in his own way. This response emboldened Thomas to talk about it.

"One of the things about the dance was this vision I had of an infinity symbol that seemed to tell my feet where to go. Then, it was eventually mirrored—I don't know how to describe it—by a propeller-like shape or pattern that came out of the motion of my outstretched arms. Then I felt the two patterns merge with each other, and what I saw became even more complex—but I couldn't see it, because I was part of it, and it was part of me. We became the same, somehow. What I remember most was that all my actions and motions and whirling around seemed to follow the pattern of this spiraling vortex. It was like there was a template, with several dimensions, along which I was moving. I didn't know where the next move was coming from or where it was going or how I would do it or if I could do it. I just followed the template.

"There was no fear of doing it wrong," he continued, "and yet there was no sense that I had to conform to the pattern. I did. I mean, I did conform to the pattern. At least I think I did. When I chose to follow the pattern, I could move faster and more proficiently than in those moments when I slowed down to consider doing something else or when I became conscious of myself as separate from the pattern."

Digger spoke. "Yes, I saw the infinity pattern, too, but what you describe as a propeller around your arms looked like a second infinity pattern to me. In fact, when you were going the fastest, the two infinity patterns were connected to each other, and your body formed some sort of axis between them and around which they spun, or around which you spun or something. I don't know. It's hard to describe."

"Yes, that's it," Xuan added. "All his movements were centered on some invisible parallel axes that ran up through his spine." She turned to Digger and asked, "Did you notice how straight he was during that dance? Hi posture was perfect, but it didn't seem to require any effort on his part."

Malik joined in with a note of what he had seen. "It reminded me of a tornado," he wrote.

"I wonder if the whirling Sufis are a demonstration of some unseen energy," Xuan said. "Or maybe they know and understand something no one else has known or understood."

"Sure, they know something!" Digger declared. "Maybe it's all around us! The fact that we don't see it doesn't mean it's not there."

"What do you mean?" asked Thomas.

"Well, just think of all the great energies of the world that are created by turning, whirling, spinning things, Thomas. Things like tornadoes or hurricanes, like propellers churning through water at the back of a boat or spinning through air on an airplane. Imagine the wake that is left behind such obvious displays of energy."

Digger was searching for more examples when Russell Layne spoke up.

"And what about the wave energy of tsunamis or earthquakes or the energy that must be created while the earth is spinning on its axis, or the moon is spinning around the earth, or the planets are spinning around the sun, or even as solar systems are spinning around in galaxies?" Russell added as he adjusted his large frame amidst the pillows he was sitting on.

Xuan chimed in again. "Or what about the tides and the rhythms of the seasons and the cycles of migration and the energy of opposites like hot and cold or light and dark or life and death?"

"Or," Digger added pensively, "what about the unseen basis of a technology revolution based on a binary number system, just two numbers: zero and one. It's like either something is or it isn't, and the play between the two, the interaction between them, describes the message, the task, the reality."

"I think all these examples point to the model of existence as we now understand it," Russell said after a brief silence. "A few thousand years ago we discovered the wheel as a driving force, an explanation, a model of what we knew and what was possible or could be known. Now, we've developed an entire technology based on the wheel. Somewhere along the way, we took it further and came to recognize the propeller—a device that moves water and air and makes turbulence and wind. From this turbulence, things are put into motion, and through the collective force that is generated, we are moved or powered forward. Isn't it odd that the symbol for infinity is so much like a propeller that Thomas couldn't tell one from the other in his dream dance?"

"For crying out loud, Russell," Thomas interjected. "They're just symbols! They are not the reality! The cross of Christianity is just a symbol. The yin and yang is just a symbol. The Star of David is just a symbol, and the infinity symbol is just a symbol! Aren't we putting too much importance into all this talk of symbols?"

"Maybe we are, Thomas," Russell answered, "but how many people have died to defend those symbols? How many have been persecuted under the sign of those symbols? How many have used those symbols to define their lives, create their perspectives, and mold their view of the world? Symbols are a representation of a bigger truth."

"I think so, too," Digger joined in. "Too often, however, we have lost the truth behind the symbol. We just see some flat-line representation of it on a flag or a coin. Then the flag is displayed at the head of an army, or the coin is used to empower some empire or corporation or religion and is used to overpower others. Whatever vitality remains in that symbol is usurped or corrupted or distorted."

"Maybe that's the point of this whole discussion," Xuan said. "What if all the symbols of the last two thousand years are in need of an overhaul or revitalization? I mean, if all of them originally came from some basic understanding of the universe and how it works—you know, wheels and cycles and seasons and all that—then the symbols were all representations of the underlying totality as people understood it at that time. But now, our understanding is much greater. We understand more of the underlying totality, and, therefore, our symbols need to change in order to reflect that greater understanding and draw us up into a greater perspective."

"It's as if the symbol, the pattern driver, has now become the limiting factor," Digger continued. "It has become insufficient, and it no longer drives our understanding in a forward direction. It no longer pulls us to even greater insights or larger concepts. Instead, it may actually be holding us back."

"That may be it," Russell agreed. "We're stagnating under the glass ceiling. We're worn out from bumping our heads on it. Our symbols lack vitality and are no longer pulling us forward or inspiring our imagination."

"And too many symbols are serving a dead or dying past, a lifeless or limited understanding," Xuan added.

"I am reminded of all the visionaries who have said, 'it's as if you were dead,'" Russell concluded. "It is time to come alive again. The patterns, the symbols, the thinking, the focus, and the beliefs—everything needs to be raised again to a higher plane!"

"But wait," Anna said, "what about the fish symbol that the Christians use?"

It was Thomas who answered Anna without thinking, "I saw that symbol in my dance, but I saw it as just one half of the infinity symbol. It is incomplete, too. It's one side of the propeller but not the entire force-making symbol."

At that point, Malik saw his chance to interject a slip of paper that he had been holding for a few minutes. Xuan took it and started laughing. Instead of reading it out loud, she passed it along to Thomas.

Malik beamed as Thomas chuckled at his humor, too, and then said as he rose from the pillow on which he had been sitting, "Malik is right. It's time for lunch."

Chapter 13

Jemez Pueblo

Jack Eaglefeather and Malik left right after the meeting and headed for the Jemez Pueblo. Since he had found out about his daughter, Sha'wanna, Jack had thought repeatedly of contacting her to see if she was interested in becoming the Iyatiku at Acoma. He knew he must soon step down from that position; he knew it was the very indiscretion with Tuwabon to create this daughter that made him unable to continue much longer as the leader at Acoma.

At the last minute, he had arranged for Malik to accompany him, and they headed south out of Albuquerque, trying to get to Jemez Pueblo by early afternoon. He looked at Malik sitting quietly in the passenger's seat of his old pickup and watched with interest as Malik struggled to roll down the window.

Malik finally found the handle, began to crank it in the only direction it would turn, and rolled it down. He ran his hands along the sill to confirm it was all the way down and craned his neck outside the truck to feel the wind on his face as they entered the highway ramp. It was a cool, brisk day with the smells of early spring in the air.

Jack watched Malik, who seemed to be enjoying himself, as they reached highway speeds. Jack smiled and pulled the collar of his windbreaker up around his neck to stave off the chilly air as it swirled in through the window and around the cab. After a few minutes, he turned on the radio, and the two of them rode along in relative isolation through the highlands of New Mexico.

As he drove, Jack was reminded of the abandoned stone dwelling in the canyon south of Acoma, where he imagined he and Anna and Malik would gather after the big meeting in June. He had already weatherproofed it pretty well, repaired the doors and windows, and tapped into the water source, but the electrical generator needed fixing, and a new roof was required. He hoped he could get his cell phone to work there, just in case, but he knew there were land lines only twelve miles away at the Acoma Visitor Center. Usually, the cell phone signal was sporadic in among the canyons and mesas that ran south of the Pueblo, so a land line was a good backup plan.

Jack was glad when Malik soon rolled up the window, and he glanced over at him as he searched for his pad and pencil. He watched as Malik wrote a note and handed it over.

"Will the old keeper woman be at Jemez?"

Jack reflected a moment and then answered, "Who knows, Malik? She lives there, but she goes wherever she wants, whenever she wants. She doesn't know we are coming, so it will be just good luck if we see her."

"I want to meet her," Malik wrote.

"I tell you what, my boy, Digger and I were pretty amazed when she told us she knew about you. I think you ought to meet her." He looked at Malik and told him, "I'll ask if she's around when we check in there."

Malik nodded as if to say he had heard Jack's answer.

Jack saw that rain clouds were beginning to roll in from the west when they arrived after an hour of driving. He pulled up in front of the house where one of the Jemez council persons lived. She opened the door, looked past Jack, and saw Malik standing by the truck. She stepped out of her adobe home, and Jack introduced himself.

He asked permission to go to Tuwabon's residence, where he hoped to also find his daughter Sha'wanna. Permission granted, he and Malik got back in the truck and drove the few hundred yards to the east end of the Pueblo.

On the porch were three women. They were shaded by an old, corrugated metal roof held up by weathered gray cedar posts that leaned to one side. On a bench made of juniper and desert willow sat Tuwabon and Sha'wanna. The old keeper woman was the third person on the porch, sitting on her haunches near the rickety support post at the end of the flimsy-looking structure.

Jack glanced in Malik's direction as they drove up to the low, mud wall that divided the dirt in the yard from the dirt in the street. The dust they stirred up blew over the top of the truck and disappeared in a rush behind them. A clap of thunder boomed off in the distance, and a few drops of rain fell as Jack climbed out of his truck and walked through the ungated opening in the wall. Then he remembered Malik and looked back to find him closing the door of the pickup but unsure where to go. Jack went back to the passenger side of the truck and spoke softly to him. Malik stuck out his arm, and Jack took it and led him through the opening in the wall, across the tiny yard, and up to the single step that led onto the porch.

The three women sat there and did not speak as Jack and Malik approached. They waited for Jack to speak first. He gathered himself, removed his hat, and looked at each one of them in turn. Then, he spoke.

"Katzimo! I am Jack Eaglefeather, Iyatiku at Acoma Pueblo. This man with me is Malik Mohammed. He is a strong man who may live on the Acoma lands one day. We've come to discuss many things with you if you have time."

Tuwabon made eye contact with Jack and responded, "You are welcome here, Iyatiku." Then she added, "Your friend is also welcome. We have many important things to discuss with you. Is your friend our friend, too?"

Jack nodded slowly.

The old keeper woman looked more closely at Malik. "Is this the blind one who will be at the meeting in June?"

"Yes." Jack looked at Malik proudly. "He will transcribe the words from the meeting so there's a record of what takes place there."

Malik smiled and shuffled his feet as both of them waited for directions from their hosts.

"How does a blind man do that?" Jack's daughter Sha'wanna blurted out.

"Actually, he's gifted that way," Jack replied. "I don't know how he does it, but he does. I think his hearing is special."

Then the old Jemez keeper woman, who had drawn her vision in the dirt at Acoma for Jack and Digger, spoke up. "Iyatiku, I know why you came, and I will leave you to talk with Tuwabon and her daughter. Your matter with them doesn't concern me." She paused and looked at Malik. "Or him. Perhaps he will walk with me for a while."

"I think he wants to do that," Jack answered.

Malik nodded in the direction of her voice and smiled at the prospect of spending time with her.

Jack, speaking for the boy, said, "Yes, he will walk with you."

"Does he talk?" asked Sha'wanna.

Jack understood that she was curious and appreciated her directness. He didn't blame her for wanting to know more.

"No, he doesn't talk either, but he's quite a man in many, many ways," Jack answered. "In all my years, I've not met anyone like him."

The keeper woman rose from her place on the porch and shuffled over to Malik. She took his hand in hers and, without a word, turned him around and led him back out through the space in the wall and past the pickup, toward the main streets of the small pueblo.

Malik followed her lead, and she whispered something to him that made him let loose her hand and walk on his own by her side. Soon, they rounded a corner and were out of sight.

Jack sat down on the porch to reveal his thoughts. He started slowly by addressing both women. "Since I found out about you, Tuwabon, and you, Sha'wanna, I have been troubled. I have also felt many feelings for both of you—good feelings. What I have learned has been a blessing, and I am glad. But I also know that the very fact of your existence, Sha'wanna, means I must give up my one mission in life: Iyatiku at Acoma Pueblo. It is a position of honor and importance and a role that has been in my family for five generations or more. I always thought I would die in that position, as did my father and grandfather and many fathers before them. It would have been my highest honor, I'm sure."

His voice was beginning to crack so Jack paused to compose himself, collect his thoughts, and let his words sink in.

He continued. "But I have dishonored the position, too, and I must find and train a replacement. I am told that you have been well raised, Sha'wanna, and one day wish to be Iyatiku at Jemez Pueblo." Jack looked intently at her as he led up to the main objective of his trip. "Since your mother is in training to be Iyatiku here at Jemez, I was wondering ..." His voice trailed off and then, finding it again, he asked, "Would you consider training to become Iyatiku at Acoma?"

Jack could tell that Sha'wanna was surprised by the question. She didn't respond immediately, and Jack watched her closely as she glanced at her mother and then looked off just over Jack's head to the storm cloud in the distance. He turned and looked, too, and felt the wind die down to a breeze. He looked back at the daughter he did not know. She had a small child, too, and he wondered what it would be like to move them both to Acoma and away from Tuwabon. He watched as mother and daughter looked at each other.

He saw Tuwabon take her daughter's hands into her own and heard her say, "You should follow your heart, Sha'wanna, and all will be well."

Sha'wanna smiled, as did Tuwabon.

"Why are you asking me to become your apprentice?" Sha'wanna asked.

Jack shifted his weight and felt the wind pick up again. "Well, I am impressed by what I have seen in you so far and by what I have heard about you," he began, "but I also like the fact that you are part of the lineage."

Tuwabon turned in Jack's direction. "I warn you, Iyatiku, she is sometimes like a stubborn colt and not so easy to train." She laughed comfortably as she spoke of her daughter, and Jack could tell she was proud of her. "She aspires to be Iyatiku one day, Jack, and even though she is young, I think she will eventually become a wise and compassionate leader in the Pueblos." She turned and looked again at her daughter as if to prompt her decision.

Sha'wanna straightened up, and Jack saw her set herself as if to do battle. She was of medium build and kept her dark hair short, with a clip just above her left ear to keep it out of her face. She had a small scar in the cleft of her chin and another on the bridge of her nose. It gave her a rugged look, accentuated by her Levis and red flannel shirt. He looked into her intense, dark eyes, which seemed to reveal a certain resolve in her that Jack had not yet seen for himself. He liked it as he heard her say, "I'll need three days to decide, Father, but I am honored that you asked me."

Jack was surprised to hear her call him father but he was glad Tuwabon had told her. He knew there would be many hours of discussion over the next three days between her and her mother, but he also knew, somewhere deep inside, that the decision they came to would be good for everyone.

"Well, this I know," Tuwabon said. "No good comes of staying the same. Acoma should have a female Iyatiku. Maybe Sha'wanna will be the first, and that would be an honor for all three of us."

With Sha'wanna's answer to consider his proposal and the measured nature of her response, Jack felt a great sense of relief. Tuwabon's apparent support of the proposal also made Jack think that Sha'wanna would say yes. He relaxed and began to converse with them on other topics concerning Jemez Pueblo, the grand-daughter, and the meeting in June at Acoma, about which both women had a great deal of curiosity.

Chapter 14

Thunder Voice

A few hundred yards away, Malik and the keeper woman entered her small adobe home next to the building that housed the main kiva at Jemez Pueblo. As she began to talk to him, he felt the quiet power of this woman and was drawn further into that power as they spent time together. Finally, she said something that might have terrified him if it weren't for the fact that he trusted her already.

"Malik, we can make you talk," she said. "Your powers of listening have developed even more because you lost your sight. It is best if you remain without sight a while longer, but now it is best if you can talk."

Malik nodded knowingly and scribbled a one-word question for her: "How?"

The keeper woman stood up, went into another room, and came back with a rolled-up blanket. She let Malik feel of it as she explained its significance.

"The line of keepers at my Pueblo goes back many generations to the time when we lived in the cliffs beside the river. We have had this blanket since that early time, and it was handed down to me when I finished as an apprentice keeper and came to live here many years ago. It has a special energy for us and has helped heal many people of many things."

Malik clutched the blanket close to his chest and imagined the countless people who had felt its power and been changed by it. He thought back to his experience in the church at Acoma when Jack told them all of the ongoing power in trees and the ongoing energy transfer from the people buried beneath the church floor. He had felt that power and momentarily lived in that energy. He wondered if this blanket had a similar ability to collect and impart to him the timeless energy of thoughts and words and deeds of those who had touched it or been healed by it over hundreds of years.

Malik was in awe of the potential it must now hold and did not know what else to do but nod in the direction of the old woman, as if to say "okay."

She took the blanket from him, unrolled it, and laid it on the floor along an east-west axis. She then took his arm and led him to the west end. She placed herself at the east end. The horsehair blanket measured roughly four feet by seven feet, and what few markings remained visible were crude in design and faded by time. No one had ever dared to repair its frayed edges or repaint it, for fear of impacting its perceived powers.

She instructed Malik to lie on the blanket on his back, with his head to the east. He knelt down, turned over, and then tentatively stretched himself out in the direction of her voice. She helped him so that his body was completely centered on the blanket. She had him put his arms to his side and his heels together. She aligned his head so that he was facing straight up, and then she folded the blanket over the top of him so that only his head and face were showing.

Malik began to relax in the knowing touch of her hands, and then she got up and went a few feet away to a wooden hutch by the wall filled with her secret measures. She began to chant as she prepared a collection of herbs and plants and dirt and water and mixed them into a paste in a small, flat bowl.

She discontinued her murmuring chant long enough to ask Malik if he was doing okay.

He nodded. He was actually more than okay as he imagined himself cocooned within the energy of this blanket, completely and safely wrapped like an Indian child in a papoose. He smiled as these feelings grew stronger and stronger.

The old woman knelt down at his head and reached into her bowl with three fingers of each hand. She took her keeper's mud and ran her fingers over Malik's throat from his collarbone to the bottom of his jaw. These six lines were on the east-west axis on which Malik was aligned.

She then took four fingers of each hand and dipped them in the bowl. She proceeded to draw four lines from each of Malik's eyes downward to his ears. These eight lines were perpendicular to the other lines she had made and on a north-south axis.

Lastly, she dipped just one finger into the bowl and made a single line all the way from Malik's throat and chin, over his mouth and along the top of his nose, past the bridge, and up to the crown of his head. As she finished this line, her chanting stopped, and she slowly passed her hands over his head and chest.

Finally she spoke. "Please lie very still while I go outside to summon the voice of the wind and the power of the sky. Don't move at all," she instructed.

Whatever she had put on Malik's face and head was starting to itch, but he determined that he could stand it for however long it took her to summon the energy of sound.

As soon as he heard her step outside, there came a huge clap of thunder, and the wind picked up noticeably. Malik could hear it making a low, moaning sound as it wound itself around the small adobe structures of the village. A few loose boards made slapping noises nearby as they tried to extract themselves from the buildings that had long been their prison. The sound of rain began to drown out their complaints and mesmerized Malik as he lay there, trying his best to be still.

In a few minutes, he heard the keeper woman come back inside. Malik wondered if she might be wet from the rain, and when she knelt down and leaned over him, he felt water dripping from her onto him.

"The song of the thunder sky is good," she said, "and the voice of the wind is good, too, but the two of them together is a sign that holds much power." She touched Malik on the forehead and got up. "Can you stay still a while longer while I make a potion to bring life to your talking?"

Malik heard her shuffle a few feet away and then heard glass objects clinking against each other, ceramic items sliding on wood surfaces, metallic things being placed back into the single drawer of her hutch, the sound of stirring and whisking, the gurgling of liquids being poured from their bottles, and the sound of caps being removed and then put back in place. He wondered how she knew what to choose and mix. He wondered how she knew the right quantities and ratios and proportions. He wondered where and from whom had she learned what she knew. Finally, he wondered if she had ever cured a voice.

When she returned to him, she said, "I'm glad you have not moved." She knelt above his head again and unwrapped the blanket. She put her left hand under the back of his neck and helped him to sit up. The lines of mud were dried, the energy from them already imparted into his throat and jaw and face. She lightly brushed off the lines and took the small, simple cup in which she had mixed her keeper's remedy and placed it in his hands.

"Drink this slowly," she said.

He did as he was told. It was bitter to the taste but slid down his throat quite easily, and when he was done, she began to hum a single, even tone. After a moment or two, she commanded him to join her as she intoned a sound, and Malik tried to duplicate it. With his lips closed tight, he tried to match her tone. He let out a low, throaty sound at first and then listened as it filled his throat and resonated in his facial bones and, finally, tickled his sinus cavity. As if the sound could not be held back, his mouth opened up and emitted the weak but definite sound of aum.

The keeper woman now changed her tone to match his. From a quiet aum to an "ah" sound, they matched again. She then changed her tone to "oh," and he tried to match that tone. The she tried "eee," and he soon figured out how to match that. When she tried "uh," he struggled but eventually duplicated that one, too. And finally, she produced the "eh" sound, and he reproduced it, as well.

At this point, he had matched her tone in terms of its musical value and the sound of the vowel. Actually, it was an octave below her tone, but it was the same note in the scale. Whenever he finally learned the vowel she was emitting and reproduced it exactly, his extraordinary hearing allowed him to hear a third note that was higher in pitch than both of their notes. This extra tonal sound was quite pleasing to him.

She heard it, too, and when she knew he was hearing it, she softly spoke and told him its name.

"That is the spirit sound, Malik. It is always there whenever two voices are perfectly in tune on the same vowel sound one octave apart. All the music of my people is based on discovering this spirit sound—the sound of oneness. It can only be reached through perfect hearing, for one must hear the sound before one can duplicate the sound." She paused and then went on. "I am called a keeper or a seer. You have perfect hearing and are a listener or hearer. I have heard that you can hear two sets of words at one time and recall them for writing. I have known of this only once before, many years ago, but I never met the woman who could do this. She was a Hopi Indian from the Arizona Pueblos, and she was blind, too. She could not write—not even her name—so her power was used for hearing and singing chants that she made up herself. The older ones thought she was a miracle."

The keeper woman from Jemez Pueblo looked at Malik. "You can write the words on paper. Soon you will be able to talk the words, too, but it will take a while. I will come to one of your meetings in a week or two, and you must not try to speak any words, yet. When you are alone, you should hum the notes we just hummed together over and over again. There are only so many human vowel sounds, less than twenty I think, and they are the roots of all talking. You must first learn to reproduce those sounds, and then you can learn to talk the words."

Malik nodded to indicate he understood.

"When you have learned them all, you and I will meet, and we will take the next step. Then you will truly become the messenger."

As they stood up from the blanket and made ready to walk back to Tuwabon's house, the keeper woman said one more thing.

"You should tell no one of this. I will tell the Iyatiku what we have done, but only the three of us must know for now."

With that, she once again took his hand and led him out to the dirt path that led back to Jack and the pickup ride home.

Chapter 15

The Equals Sign

On a Saturday two weeks into May, Anna joined Russell Layne to help Father Garces move from the hospital to a nursing care facility in Albuquerque. He had regained some of his strength, and the doctors decided he would be better off outside a hospital setting. After seeing to the various details, the three of them went to the facility lunch room and sat down to eat.

"So, is everything going well with respect to the meeting plans?" Father Garces asked.

"It seems to be moving in the right direction," Russell answered, "but Anna and I are charged with figuring out the sixth clue on the remote chance that we can get a hold of the person in time for the meeting."

"That's the clue about science, isn't it?" asked Father Garces.

Anna answered, "Yes. 'Everyone who is seriously involved in the pursuit of scientific truth eventually becomes convinced that a spirit is manifest in the laws of the universe.'"

"That's Einstein, isn't it?" Father Garces asked.

"Yes, that's right," Russell answered.

"Well, if the smartest man of the last century has come to that conclusion, I find myself hard-pressed to argue with it." He smiled at Anna as he finished his sentence.

"But I think of spirit as more of a feeling thing—you know, a matter of the heart," Anna interjected. "It's not a matter of the mind, is it?"

"Good question," said the father. "Most of us in the world are in the habit of seeing heart and mind as two different things. When Einstein got out there to the outer reaches of our understanding, our human intelligence, maybe he saw something that merged the heart and the mind and left him the impression that they were really one—or at least he thought them so integrated as to be inseparable."

"That's a problem," Russell said, "because the world is pretty convinced that we live in a world of separation, a world of opposites. Your church is based on the continuation of this notion: good and evil, love and hate, saint and sinner, even life and death. How can one reconcile these polarities?"

"By adopting the same perspective as the smartest man in the world," Father Garces answered quickly. "By seeing all-inclusively, like from a mountaintop or from outer space or even some bigger perspective."

"Could you explain that further?" Anna asked as she retied her ponytail and watched the old priest.

"I can try." Father Garces sat up straighter and leaned toward Anna across the table. "Too often, our human view causes us to see one side of the equation but not the other side. In terms of energy, which is what Einstein spent his life studying, you can't properly describe any reality without both sides of the equation, hence the axiom: 'For every action there's an equal and opposite reaction.' For darkness to have meaning, it must have light. For truth there must be illusion, and so on. The key to this, I think, is that we must focus on the equal sign, not on the light or dark—not on the truth or the illusion. We must see both sides of the equation and focus on that which joins them together. In other words, the equal sign is the glue. It is the vitality. It is the transactional understanding itself. It's the energy of unification."

"Okay," Russell interrupted, "I think I see what you are saying, Father, but how is that accomplished if we're not as smart as Einstein?"

"It may not be easy, Russell." Father Garces turned to face him as he spoke. "Let me see if I can state it in a less confusing way." He took a sip of his iced tea as he collected his thoughts. "I think we must radically re-form our view of humankind in the context of this insight. If a pine cone seed creates a pine tree or an acorn creates an oak, the question becomes, what is the seed of mankind designed to create? Surely we were not made to create wars and hunger and slavery and greed and persecution?"

Anna said, "Many people believe what the Bible says, you know, that all men are sinners. It seems that we are stuck making wars, ignoring hunger, chasing wealth, and persecuting other people."

"If that's true, Father, maybe we are stuck in this perception of opposites," Russell said, "and have been stuck there for thousands of years."

"Yes, maybe we are, and I think we're stuck because we haven't figured it out yet—not totally, anyway," Father Garces answered. "When we think of an infinite force that created everything or knows everything, we generally think of that being as acting upon some indescribable void and then, in the act of creating within the void, becoming a separated entity called God or Allah or Yahweh or a thousand other names. The religions of the world then contend with each other as to what to call this entity and how to describe this entity and compete over whose descriptions are most correct or most powerful or most worthy."

"Isn't that the crux of it?" Anna asked. "Doesn't it matter who is right and what is true?"

"This may surprise you, Anna, but I don't think so," answered Father Garces. "Every tribe throughout the history of time—whether biblical or native American or African or Aboriginal or European—assigned a word or collection of sounds to label themselves. They came to call themselves 'the people,' and now our historians know of three or four thousand tribes or more, all of whom called themselves 'the people.' In a similar manner, they all assigned a name to the mysterious life force they felt helped them, protected them, fed them, created them, and kept them together. The label for this unknown or partially understood force, the 'great named one,' if you will, evolved into a couple thousand names, too. They couldn't explain this force or presence very well, and they all experienced it in different ways, but it was a presence they all felt in some way or another. It was, and is, the same force in every instance, but it ended up with a thousand names, a thousand descriptions, and a thousand man-made characteristics."

"So are you asserting that the names are unimportant?" asked Russell.

"Yes," answered Father Garces. "But there's more to what I'm saying." He thought about how to make his next point concise and easily understood.

Russell looked at Anna, and she returned his glance as they awaited Father Garces's next words. The aged priest still had the frail look of an old man, but there was vitality in him, especially in his eyes, that caused Anna and Russell to hang on every word he uttered.

"The point is that when this force is given a name, any name, it creates the illusion of being a separate force, a force outside of man himself, outside of life itself," Father Garces said. "This is a distinction that is wholly inconsistent with what I now see as true. Consequently, almost the entire world developed under the impression that there was and is 'the people' on one hand, and there is the 'great named one' on the other hand. Even when the people would see themselves or name themselves 'the people of the great named one' or the 'chosen ones,' there was, and is, still the separation. It is this separation that is the ultimate misconception, the essential falsehood. We somehow lost the equal sign altogether."

"Why did you say that almost the entire world developed this two-way view?" Anna inquired. "Didn't everyone see it this way?"

"Well, the major religions of the world came from this view and seem to be stuck in this view," Father Garces replied, "but the so-called pantheists didn't. Their so-called religion is life itself, and everything around them lives and breathes and is made within the one sphere of their existence. There are not two spheres. There is no heaven and earth or even good and evil. There is just life."

"So a life that lives within this single view and experiences this wholeness as their entire existence has no need for religion?" Russell asked.

"And no need for a 'great named one,'" Father Garces added. "They can live and feel and act and think right in the middle of their life, right on the equal sign between any two seemingly opposing forces, and right in the middle of their existence."

Russell picked up on this. "Because their worldview, their perspective, puts them within the sphere of life itself, they have no need to name it or fight over it or defend it or worship it or even discuss it."

"Right, they're no longer separated from it," said Father Garces. "They don't have to describe it. They just have to live within it and not let themselves become separated from it."

"It lives within them, and they live within it," Anna suggested. "It truly is just one, isn't it? It's just living on the equal sign of life."

"Yes, it is," Father Garces said, "for as long as we choose not to name it and thus make it separate or make one into two. In other words," he continued, "there is no God separate from me."

Russell finished the other side of the equal sign for Father Garces's thought. "And no me separated from God," he said.

Anna watched as a profound quiet descended on their table in the nursing home cafeteria. She sat in awe of what they had just realized, made real for each of them: the unnamed truth of oneness.

The silence was first broken by Russell. "I think this must be the meaning behind the Adam and Eve story, a story that is essentially the same in dozens of creation stories around the world, including the Torah and the Koran. Like many mythological stories, it is told in past tense. In other words, it speaks of the understandings after the separation event from the symbolic garden of life as one. As a result of this separation, man came to tell the story of separation and view himself as separate. To tell the story, man had to name himself and, as well, give a name to that from which he thought he had become separated."

"Then he felt the need to chastise himself and blame himself for the separation," Father Garces added. "Then he came to view himself as inferior or lesser, and then he came up with the concept of the great named ones, the so-called gods."

"So that's how we as human beings began to form religions, too," Anna chimed in.

"Yes. And it has developed that now the very existence of religion, all religions, reinforces this separated view," Russell said. "The churches put forth and promote this separated view, which they need to maintain in order to justify their existence. Could it be that our meeting at Acoma in June is intended to bring an end to this view?"

"I think that's it," Father Garces finished, "but there may be even more."

After a few moments, Father Garces continued. "Russell and Anna, let me ask both of you something. The so-called equal sign is a mathematical symbol, right? Maybe it's a symbol from the study of logic or philosophy, too. I'm not sure. Anyway, it seems like a two-dimensional symbol to me, at least as it is written on the page or as it is conceived in the mind."

"Okay, I see where you're going," Russell said. "There doesn't seem to be any active energy to it. It just sits there, an almost passive bridge between two dissimilar or opposite phenomena."

"Like you said earlier, 'every action has an equal and opposite reaction' sort of thing," Anna said.

"Okay, it's passive. Go on, Russell," said Father Garces as he turned to Russell and encouraged him to finish his thought.

"For that equal sign to gain an action status instead of a passive status, it needs another dimension that means equal but infers even more." Russell was not thinking so much as he was visualizing some simple but simultaneously complex matter. "Where do we find a more active and explanatory symbol that can function like an equal sign yet somehow links two identifiable and opposite strands of reality into the same single reality?"

"It's the helix," Anna whispered.

"Say again," implored Father Garces.

"The helix," Anna answered. "You know, the DNA thingy. Two strands of genetic code running parallel to each other like the equal sign and yet twisting and turning in three dimensions. It is a symbol of life, so it has vitality. It is a symbolic carrier of the seeds from a man and the seeds from a woman, so it is, really, an equal sign that also means new life."

Russell sat back in his chair and muttered, "That's it, Anna. You're right."

He looked over at Father Garces, who was smiling at the discovery Anna had made from their collective discussion.

"Yes, that's it!" Father Garces said. "Look at all the integration inherent in that symbol, the movement that is implied, and the future that is promised ..." His voice trailed off as he searched for more descriptions.

Russell stepped back into the conversation. "Yes, look at the possibilities; they are endless and infinite."

"But they are all rolled up in one," Anna added reflectively. "It is the equal sign, but it takes the two separated opposites and sends them off together like they are linked on some great, new adventure!"

"Right!" Russell added again. "It's no longer opposite and equal. It's together. Merged. The connection point is no longer flat and uninvolved like a two-dimensional equal sign but instead becomes the focus of the merger and leads the so-called opposites on a braided forward track into an unavoidable condition of oneness."

"I think that is the truth of it right there," said Father Garces. "If your helix symbol creates the action required to stop viewing the world as separated, and it creates the action required to see the world as unified, the need to name the great named one falls away in favor of a unified, single energy with no need to be named."

"So all energies are now explained and described as coming from within a single source?" Anna tried to clarify.

"Yes," Father Garces replied. "In a unified alignment, the opposites become one, and the true seeds of mankind become visible within the totality of Einstein's single spirit behind the laws of nature."

"Agreed," said Russell. "That means the forces at work inside of us and outside of us are singular and total at the same time. Even though we don't yet understand how sunspots affect us, we can be sure that they do have an impact and are on the helix with us. Whether or not we understand geomagnetic forces or tides or planetary rotations, we can be assured that they are within the laws of nature, within us, and that they are impacting us within the seeded reality of the universal helix on which we exist."

"Exactly, Russell," exclaimed Father Garces. "I have recently read that a black hole in outer space puts out a sound. It booms across the universe like the cry of a whale that used to carry across the basins of the ocean. They even assign it a musical note value that is currently unfathomable to most of us and certainly not heard by any of us. By their calculations, it is fifty-seven octaves below middle C. Even though we can't currently understand its impact on us, you can be sure that it is impacting us. We are part of it, and it is part of us. Maybe stars and planets make notes, too. Maybe there is an entire symphony in space. If there is, we can be sure it is affecting us. We haven't proved it or named it, but it is there anyway. Before Newton ever named gravity, it was there, impacting us every day. How many things like gravity do we not yet know about or haven't named but are impacting us anyway? It stirs the imagination, doesn't it? The possibilities are literally endless or infinite. All we have to know is that these possibilities are of this single source and are factored into the helix of unity on which we also travel and have our being."

"And we can know that it is good," Anna said.

"Yes, and I think the understanding behind the science clue is now uncovered and revealed to us," Russell said.

Now Anna understood a little more clearly what to expect at the meeting in June. She felt as though she was ready—ready to experience the meeting, ready to be at peace with whatever happened there, and ready to help Malik write his notes and create the book when the meeting was over. She was at peace as she realized that it wasn't the people in the clues that they had been looking for all this time; it was the energy within the clues and the new levels of understanding that each clue contained. Once the clues were all fully developed, she knew that her understanding and the understanding of her fellow planners was enough to attract to the meeting exactly what was needed.

They all got up to return to Father Garces's new room in the nursing home. For the second time that spring, Anna had a sixth sense that Father Garces might not be with them much longer. He had become a hero of sorts to her, and yet she knew she couldn't hold on to him. Or hold on to any hero. *Heroes are traps, too,* she thought to herself, *because they keep us on one side or the other of the equal sign. Either we believe in them or we don't, but with either choice, the ultimate outcome is the same: we stay in a state of separation.*

Anna felt as though she must no longer live anywhere but on the leading edge of the unified helix of life. Now, for Anna, the meeting could not get here fast enough.

Chapter 16

Kahwehstimah

Mt. Kahwehstimah rises to a height of 11,300 feet and sits mostly north of Acoma Pueblo. It remains snow-capped all year long, and what makes it sacred to the Pueblo Indians is simply the long-held tradition of viewing it as sacred. It is no different than sacred things in most worldviews. Somewhere in the distant past, a group of people could not explain the mountain. Perhaps they reasoned that something so singularly unique and so unlike the mesas among which they lived must be special or sacred. Its mysteries were unexplainable to them, and so it came to be regarded that way.

For a thousand years, this message of uniqueness was repeated and passed on. Generation after generation, the teachers and elders of the people were constant in their sacred regard for Kahwehstimah, and, over time, it attained a sacred place in their myths and their customs. It became an integral part of their culture and their ritual. Now, it was a part of who they were and a part of who they had become. They saw it every day; it was a constant companion. It led them like a guide and served them as a point of reference. From it, they set their direction or found their way. It was a beacon and a compass, always in their sight.

Jack and Malik met Sha'wanna at a reservation trading post near Interstate 40, and the three of them filled the bench-style seat of Jack's old pickup. The road to the base of the mountain was a washboard gravel road that wandered up to near the summit from the west. Jack worried whether his truck could make the ascent, but they purchased water and a few supplies, and he decided to try for the top despite his concerns.

After just a mile or so, Jack asked Sha'wanna her thoughts on becoming Iyatiku of Acoma Pueblo. Malik listened as they conversed.

"I am honored, but I feel like I need more training," she began. "I'm also worried that the people of Acoma may not accept a woman after so many years under the guidance of men."

Jack listened closely to what she said and thought long and hard how to answer her. Finally, he did. "I'm pleased to hear many of the things you say. I hear your humility and am glad for it. I know from it that you are open to the ways of the Iyatiku."

He looked quickly to the left as the rumbling of the truck on the rock-strewn road launched a bevy of mountain quail from under their nesting bush and up into the clear mountain sky.

"I will be able to show you many of the ways of an Iyatiku," Jack went on. "Others will also be your teachers; the keeper woman from Jemez Pueblo has many powers, and your mother and her mentors can show you things I can't."

"Yes, I know. All my teachers will be women except you. Do you think I will be accepted by the women of your Pueblo?" Sha'wanna asked.

"That's important, too," Jack answered, "and I think that once they know your heart is good, they will welcome you. They will have much to teach you, too."

"Will you tell them I come from your blood?"

"I don't know that yet," Jack answered. "Some may already know, but I do not know if they know. Women have their secrets. That is their way. I think those who know may be expecting me to tell them soon, even if they already know. But, I think they long to return to the old ways where women, not men, were the Iyatikus at Acoma." He looked out the window as he reflected further and then finished his thought. "They will prepare the people of the Pueblo for your coming. The Acoma woman's council is a wise one, and they will know the best way to do it."

"Why has a male been the Iyatiku at Acoma for so long?" Sha'wanna asked. "Was it a political decision?"

"I suppose it was political, at least to some extent, but mostly it was done in fear," Jack replied. "The female Iyatiku at Acoma committed suicide by throwing herself and her child off the nearby Enchanted Mesa a thousand years ago. When everyone heard what she did, it caused the men at Acoma Mesa to lose confidence in the leadership of women, and so they selected a young man to be Iyatiku in the hope that the women would eventually forget the tradition. He lived to a very old age, and by the time he died and selected the next Iyatiku—another male—the tradition of female leadership was gone from the collective memory of those who still lived at Acoma."

"So the women forgot."

"Yes, apparently they did, and the men helped them do it."

"When was it decided to change it back?"

"There has been pressure for many years—three or four generations, I think— but my grandfather and father resisted, and so have I, at least until now."

"What is Katzimo?" Sha'wanna asked.

"It's an agreed-upon declaration of unanimity among the men when making council decisions at Acoma. It's like a password or secret handshake, I suppose. It is seldom used around the women," Jack answered.

"I heard from the keeper woman at Jemez that Katzimo is the ancient name of Enchanted Mesa. Is that true?"

"Yes, but very few people know it," Jack answered, "That mesa has been called 'Enchanted' for many, many years. There is no reason to change it now."

"The keeper woman says it is time to change it," Sha'wanna said.

"I know what she thinks," Jack answered. "When she told me that you were among us again, I was confused and did not understand. She thinks you are the woman who leapt with child from Enchanted Mesa a thousand years ago, and she thinks you have returned to finish the work that you did not finish then."

"I know. She told me and my mother this story last night. She thinks I should accept your offer to enter training for Iyatiku at Acoma."

"That's good if it is what you want," Jack answered as he looked at his daughter. "Is it what you want?"

"Yes, but she also thinks my name here should be Katzimo and that I should change the name of Enchanted Mesa back to Katzimo, too. She thinks it will help win over the men."

"That would be crazy," Jack said, "and we should think very long about those suggestions she makes. She is always full of suggestions, especially when it comes to Acoma." He chuckled as he said it but then added, "You and your daughter would be welcome at Acoma, however. Of that I am sure."

"Do you think me too young to be Iyatiku?" Sha'wanna asked him as they neared the summit and the end of the dirt road.

"I worry about your age, but only a little," he said as he turned off the engine and set the brake. "All of the Pueblos need to keep their young people involved and living on the ancestral lands so the Pueblos can regain their vitality. Everyone thinks this is so. I think you and your daughter will help bring vitality back to Acoma."

Malik, who had been taking all of this in while he smelled the mountain air and breathed in the dust coming through the hole in the floorboard of the old truck, spoke for the first time.

"I will be living at Acoma, too. I'm still young."

It was barely audible, but Jack and Sha'wanna both heard it. Jack turned his head quickly in Malik's direction.

"So you are talking now?" he asked. "I should've known that old keeper woman was working on something with you." He smiled at Sha'wanna. "Whatever she tried, apparently, it worked." He leaned forward and looked around Sha'wanna at Malik. "Was it her doing?"

"Yes," Malik admitted, his voice sounding a little louder. "She said she would tell you."

"Well, she hasn't yet. That woman likes her secrets, too," Jack laughed.

"I'm not very good at talking yet," Malik admitted, "but I can speak most of the sounds now. I've been practicing for a few weeks but only when I'm alone."

He was not easily understood. His consonants were confused, and sometimes he got mixed up on certain words. But Jack understood him well enough and knew it would get better with practice.

"Our keeper woman healed him?" Sha'wanna asked as she turned to face Jack. "That shouldn't surprise me, I guess. I've seen her powers before."

"As I said, you can learn from her," Jack responded. "She has lots of power."

"It was easy," Malik stated calmly. "She used this really old blanket that she said had healing history from long ago and a nasty-tasting tea of some kind."

"I've seen that blanket and felt her power with it myself," said Sha'wanna. "When I was twelve, I fell off a large boulder near Jemez. That's where I got the scars on my chin and nose. My mother took me to her because I was having head-aches. She wrapped me in the blanket and mixed up some herbs and made me drink them. They tasted awful, but the headaches never came back. I thought she was crazy, but everyone else thought it was pretty normal."

"Many things look crazy when we don't understand how everything works," Jack offered. "We know so very little."

"How does she do it?" Malik asked.

"That is her power and is not mine to talk about," Jack replied as he opened the door and got out of the truck. "You'll soon learn, both of you, that everyone has a power." He paused and stretched his legs from the drive and then announced, "We must walk the rest of the way up the mountain. Let's go."

He went around to Malik's side of the truck and steadied him as he got out. Then he offered his hand to Sha'wanna as she scooted over to the door. He caught her eye and held her gaze for a moment. He smiled that this was his child, come home to Acoma.

Jack knew the mountain fairly well from several trips there as a boy and three summers there as a teen, but it had been more than ten years since his last visit. He remembered some ruins not too far up the trail and also recalled that it wasn't an easy path, especially for a blind one like Malik.

"The terrain is kind of rough, Malik. How do you want to do this?" Jack inquired.

"Just give me an arm," Malik answered without pause as he stuck out his arm to demonstrate, "and don't let me get too close to the edge."

"We've come too far to let that happen, young man." Jack laughed and stuck out his arm as instructed.

The three of them started up the rocky trail, which soon narrowed in front of them. Jack motioned for Sha'wanna to lead the way. Ahead of them was a drop of a thousand feet or more, and to their left, perched on a bluff about five feet above the path, were the ruins Jack remembered. Jack found the set of eroded steps that led up the bluff and helped Malik negotiate them with some difficulty.

Sha'wanna, just barely thirty years old, was in good shape and had been an athlete during her school years. She scampered up the bluff beside the steps and began looking through the ruins. They weren't much more than a few rubble stone walls, but Jack pointed to the inside of what had been a room of some kind. Sha'wanna noticed the old kiva pit right in the midst of it. Within this rubble, she found them a few flat spots, and they sat down looking south over the fallen walls toward Acoma.

Though the Pueblo was just twenty-five miles to the south, it was not easily visible even from their vantage point on the mountain. Jack had forgotten his binoculars, but he remembered he could see it with the naked eye when he was younger.

"Can you see Acoma?" he asked Sha'wanna as he pointed in the direction he thought it should be.

"No. Unless that's it in the valley right over there," she answered, moving his arm slightly west.

"Well, I don't see it, that's for sure. I must be getting old," Jack said.

"I just turned twenty, and I don't see it," Malik joked.

That made Jack and Sha'wanna laugh and, they all started to relax, but a sudden burst of wind caused them to remember they were near the top of a mountain.

Jack's demeanor changed as he focused his gaze out over the southern horizon toward home. He felt as though he was on top of the world. The mountain he looked up to every day was now the place from which he looked. From here, he didn't need to find his bearings, and there was no question about his place in the world. He saw things from here that he could not otherwise see. He viewed his world on a scale that was more grand than any scale and, yet, less clear than any scale, too. It lacked the detail that distracts, defines, and narrows the focus—and, he realized, it had been too long since he had come to the mountain to gain this other perspective.

"My father always told me to live in the valley but see as if from the mountain," Jack said. "I forget those words sometimes, but they are good words."

And even though he couldn't see Acoma from his place on the mountain, he felt it in his bones. The winds of recognition sent a chill over him as he sat between Malik and Sha'wanna. He knew that these two new people in his life were important to his future. They were in his life for him to teach, and yet, he knew they were in his life to teach him, too. He felt like all three of them carried a lesson for the other two. Though the teaching was not yet apparent to any of them, he knew it would appear when the time was right.

~   ~   ~

Like the gentle breeze that caressed them, Jack's voice tumbled out of him as he began to intone a chant he had learned at the knee of his father.

It was the first time Sha'wanna had ever heard one of Jack's chants, and it touched her immediately. She sat in rapt attention as she focused her eyes to the south. She realized right then that this man, her newly found father, had secrets and powers of which she had never dared to dream. Each word of his unfamiliar incantation struck a chord in her and sent waves of feelings through her body. But more than that, it touched her inside, and she found herself wanting it to go on and on. She was energized and yet motionless. She was fully aware of everything and thinking of nothing. She wanted to weep in reunion and laugh in joy. She felt compelled to cry out in recognition and was moved to silence. She was filled to the brim but with what, she wasn't sure. She stayed where she was but felt as though she were being transported into a whole new world impossible to describe but all-too-familiar nonetheless.

When Jack completed his chant and opened his eyes on the mountain, it was Malik who spoke first.

"I don't know how to write what you say," he said. "Do you know where it comes from? Is it a Pueblo language?" He turned to his left as he reached for Jack.

Jack took Malik's hand and placed it on his own knee and said, "I don't know, Malik. I've tried to figure it out for years. I've heard my elders speak the Keresan language of the Pueblos, but these sounds are not like it. My father taught me these chants when I was about thirty, and he said his father taught him when he was thirty. He had no explanation for them. It is a mystery."

"Can you teach them to me?" Sha'wanna asked.

"I must teach them to you," said Jack. "You are of age now, and you will be Iyatiku one day, but I don't know where to begin. I think there are seven different chants, but I've never seen them written down and can only recite them when I am moved to do so. Even more confusing for me, I don't know which one will come out when I feel the urge and first begin to speak."

"Is it some older language, then?" Malik guessed.

"No, I don't think so," said Jack. "Maybe it's a special set of sounds, an organized set of sounds, but not a language that I can tell. Each incantation starts out the same but then diverges and goes its own way. I am drawn into it so much that I don't remember any of it after it is over."

"There are some repeated patterns," said Malik, "at least that's what I hear. When I dream of the time I was the writer at the last meeting, I see the letters I write, but I don't recognize them. In my dream, I don't hear the sounds of what they are saying, either, I just see myself writing, so I don't know what my written words sound like. Maybe my words are the same as your words, Jack."

"Maybe they are, my boy, maybe they are. Perhaps it will be revealed at the meeting."

"What's the deal about this meeting?" Sha'wanna asked.

"It's only a few weeks away," Jack answered. "It will take place at the church on Acoma Mesa, and when it's over, Malik and Anna and I will move to a small house in the southern part of the reservation, where he will write his notes from the meeting. By then, you will likely be my apprentice, Sha'wanna, and I will be helping you become the next Iyatiku." Jack looked at her and smiled again. "You will be the best one they ever had. I am sure of that."

"I want to go to the very top of the mountain," Sha'wanna suddenly suggested. "Does this path go there?"

"Yes, it's not too far," Jack answered as he stood up and stretched. "Malik? Are you up for a little more climbing?"

"Let's go," he said. "I'm ready."

Section III:

Envisioning the Ecumensus

Chapter 1

June 2010

There comes a time in every life when intentions finally meet the moment in which they must become more than mere intentions. They collide with the inevitable discovery of their worth. They seek that instant when desire overcomes obstacle, when resolve defeats inertia and purpose finally evolves into its self-defined truth. For the Planners, that moment was upon them. The long-awaited meeting was to begin the next morning, and an afternoon of aspirations evolved into an evening of expectations. Nighttime turned to timeless anticipation. Anxiety turned to restlessness. Sleep knew no quarter. Dreams found no place. Morning came too soon and yet not soon enough.

Six of the Planners were already at Acoma Pueblo preparing for the meeting that would begin at sunrise. They had done what they could to prepare the place and to prepare themselves for seven days of meetings. They knew these meetings would not be conference tables and suits, laptops and doughnuts, charts and presentations, but they did not know exactly what they would be. So they gathered at dawn in front of the old church on Acoma Mesa to see what would become of their day and the six that would follow.

Thirty miles away, Russell Layne drove as fast as he could to get there but did so with a heavy heart. He had planned to join the others at Acoma the night before but had stayed in town overnight when he received word that Father Garces's condition had taken a turn for the worse. When he arrived at the hospital, he found that Garces had died just an hour before. Russell discovered that arrangements were already taken care of and did not see any way to be of further help. He decided the best way to honor his friend was to keep on going with the project the good father had helped to inspire. Russell went home to sleep but hadn't slept much and was running late—even for him.

He was still on the interstate when his attention was drawn to a person on the roadside ahead. He tapped his brakes and slowed to get a closer look. The hitchhiker turned to face him as the sound of his car broke the early-morning quiet of the empty road. The tires kicked up the gravel as they slowed even more and eased onto the shoulder. The two men's eyes met briefly. Russell decided to offer this person a ride.

He signaled the hiker to join him as he began clearing some space in the front seat. The hiker smiled and picked up his things—a backpack, a small cap, and a leather-wrapped bundle—and came over to the door.

Unlike Russell, he was slight of build, and he sported a well-trimmed beard, shoulder-length hair, and a ready smile. His brown eyes were calm and focused, and they met Russell's eyes with a steady, gentle gaze.

Russell reached into the backseat, where he always carried a supply of bottled water. He brought two bottles forward and offered one to the man before any words were exchanged. The man smiled in acceptance, opened the water, and took a long drink.

"Thank you," he finally said as he wiped his mouth with his sleeve. "I don't know my destination, well not exactly, but you seem like a good way to get there, somehow." He then offered his hand in introduction and said, "My name is Chris, and I am a traveling musician. That is my flute in that pouch."

Russell shook Chris's hand, glanced at the pouch, and said, "I'm Russell, and I'm only going about twenty more miles down this road before I reach my turn to Acoma Pueblo. You're welcome to go with me that far."

"What's at Acoma Pueblo?" Chris asked. "I've met some travelers the last few months who said they were going there, too."

He shouldn't have been surprised by the question or the comment that followed it, but at that very moment Russell Layne's intent came face to face with the reality of what he had started years before. He formulated his answer based on what he thought would soon begin at Acoma even as he drove to meet up with it.

"You may find this hard to believe, Chris, but today the world as we know it will start to die. At a seven-day meeting at Acoma, an essential world evolution will begin to take shape. The meeting will start at sunrise this morning."

Russell looked at Chris for a response.

Chris turned around in his seat to check the eastern horizon behind them. "Sunrise is not too far away," he said. "This crack between the worlds of light and dark is really my favorite time of day. It's a good time to start an important meeting. The dawn holds so much potential, and the promise at sunrise is so full. Would it be okay if I traveled with you all the way to Acoma, too?"

Russell, already missing his friend Father Garces, was glad to say yes. He smiled at the prospect of companionship and the change it might bring to his mood. Chris smiled, too, and for a while, at least, their two paths converged into one.

After a few miles of silence, Chris said, "Russell, I sense that you know more about this meeting than you are telling me, and, frankly, I know a little bit about it myself but didn't know the name of the place until now. Acoma, is it? I like the sound of it. I've known of this meeting for a couple of years. In fact, I have been hitchhiking west from India for several months already. Now that I'm so close and the time is so near, I must admit that I'm glad my travels are almost complete."

Russell was surprised at Chris's revelation, and yet he half expected it, too. The Planners had sensed from the outset that word of this meeting would get out somehow. They didn't know exactly how it would happen, just that it would. The conversation with Chris was really just another proof of their accurate premonitions.

Russell turned to face Chris. "Wait a minute," he said. "A couple of years? I mean, exactly how many years have you known about this meeting?"

"I don't know," he responded. "Maybe five or six. Maybe hundreds. Why?"

Startled at this answer, too, Russell began slowly. "Well, you're right. I do know a little more than I've told you, but I don't always understand what I know. It started in India when I got singled out for a message from a guru near New Delhi some years ago. For a few years I ignored it, but now it has almost consumed me. I've thought of little else for the last year or so. An old Catholic priest who died just last night inspired me to action in September, but I have to admit that the guru in India planted the first seed."

"I suspect it was planted long before that, Russell," Chris said. "Long before."

His words echoed in the silence as Russell reflected on them.

Chris looked at Russell for a minute. "Now I remember you," he said. "I saw you that day in New Delhi. A tall guy in India gets noticed. As I remember it, the guru called you out, and you stood near the back of the crowd while he told you of your mission. I think it was his assistant who delivered you a written message."

"That's right," Russell said. "You were at that meeting, too? Now that's a coincidence!"

"Yes, I was there, but it may not be as coincidental as it appears. I had wanted to meet you when I first saw you that day, but I got distracted, and when I looked for you later, you were gone."

Russell turned to him, still incredulous. "Did you know that I would be singled out by the guru that day?"

"Yes, he and I had spoken of it, but he only knew of a general location in the Western U.S., so it has taken me a while to figure it out and find it. I'm glad our paths crossed this morning."

"Me, too," Russell admitted. His voice was still tinged with incredulity.

"In fact," Chris continued, "I think I'm part of the meeting in some way or another as well. That's what the guru thought, too. The name 'Malik' keeps showing up in my meditations. I want to find him once I get there. I think he may be a blind boy, actually. Do you happen to know him?"

Russell let out a whoosh of air through pursed lips. He felt himself soften a little as he let down his guard and considered these unexpected revelations from the traveler named Chris. Softly he replied, "I do know him, indeed. He's part of the planning team that was assembled for this meeting. I'll introduce him when we arrive."

"Yes, that'll be good," Chris said, and he then seemed content to watch out the window for several miles. He spoke again as they neared the Acoma exit off Interstate 40. "We need some music, Russell."

"Sure," he agreed, and reached for the car radio.

Chris reached out his hand and gently stopped Russell's arm before he could turn it on. He untied the leather laces of his pouch and gingerly extracted a simple, brass flute. He moistened his lips, wiggled his fingers to loosen them up, and put the instrument to his mouth. He began to play a soothing melody line.

After a few moments, Russell felt his body begin to relax. He looked at the scenery as the car sped down the highway. Tears began to form in his eyes as he thought of Father Garces and the loss Anna would feel when he broke the news to her. He thought of the meeting and the years of effort that it represented for him. He thought of all the unexpected events of the past year that continued to make it seem like destiny itself.

The seeds they had been planting were now in bloom, and the fruits of their labors were not far behind. Russell knew one thing for sure: the fruit does not last long on the tree. The window of time in which the harvest must take place is short, hardly any time at all when compared to a season or an age. Seven days in the space of seven hundred thousand days is just the blink of an eye. In that window—seven days at Acoma—the fruit of two thousand years had to be harvested, preserved, and turned into nourishment that would propel the world forward for another two thousand years. One day too early or one day too late, and the harvest would be no good.

A wave of recognition coursed through Russell's body as he felt the urgency of this moment and he watched the new dawn move slowly toward the full light of day. He felt the calming embrace of the muted desert colors around him as the asphalt rose up to carry them forward. The music of the flute soothed his heart. He knew that it was time—and he was not late.

Chapter 2

It Begins

As the eastern sun crested the mesa tops at Acoma, Jack led the Planners up to the door of the church. Malik was just behind him and walked unassisted over the final fifty yards. Behind him was Thomas Walls, and behind him was Anna Izturias. Xuan Lee and, finally, Digger Lamar brought up the rear of the small procession. They all wondered what had happened to Russell Layne, but cell phones were turned off and there was no way to reach him.

Before they entered the church where the meetings would begin, Jack Eaglefeather turned and announced, "We are here, fellow Planners, to meet the seven Master Teachers of our time, and we are here for seven days. This is Acoma. The Great Spirit lives here with us, and we have no fear of what is to come."

Jack stood on the uppermost step leading to the church and was framed in the tall, arched doorway of the old adobe structure. The other Planners looked up at him and waited for him to say more. He felt their energy and inhaled deeply as he took it into his body. His spine tingled with their power. He focused his eyes on the sunrise and exhaled with a mighty rush of air. Then he slowly inhaled again and gathered his feet firmly below his slightly bent knees. He cupped his hands to the sides of his mouth, rose up onto the balls of his feet, and with all his might roared that one word of consent and agreement, "Katzimo!"

His voice echoed across the valley and pierced the early-morning reverie. No noise arose to compound it or drown it out, and it slowly disappeared in the distance. The silence that followed was magnificent. No more voice was required, and Jack seemed satisfied. He turned and entered the church.

The Planners followed him in, and when all of them were seated, Jack remained standing and spoke again. "In my dreams last night, I met a man. He told me his name, but I don't recall it now. I will know him when we meet again. We sat facing each other in my dream, and I began to whisper a chant I had never heard before. Soon, his voice replaced mine, and he was softly murmuring the same set of sounds. And then I said them again. And then he did the same. And we began chanting back and forth together. It went on for a long time in my dreams. That man will reach Acoma today and will soon be in our midst."

As they had walked up to the twelve-foot church doors a few moments before, the Planners could not know of a second group of people now gathering at Acoma. There were already a hundred or more who were setting up their camps in the flats between Acoma Mesa and Enchanted Mesa. From this place they could see both mesas at once.

Near a few scrubby trees and a collection of boulders, a woman in their midst raised both her hands above her head and spoke a single word, "Peace." There was something in the way she said it—like a command or a request or a suggestion, and yet it did not order them or ask them or leave any room for discussion. It was spoken with authority, but the woman who spoke it had no visible trappings of authority. Her name was Mirissa, and she seemed to have power: power in her voice, power in her manner, and power in her eyes.

These first arrivals at Acoma, strangers to each other and strangers to her, felt her power and placed themselves under her spell. They ceased all their talking and sat down in silence. They rustled about for a few more minutes, but then a hush fell over them. Many closed their eyes. Some began to hum or sing softly. For them, too, the meeting had begun.

Russell and Chris arrived at the western entry of the Acoma Valley. Jack's daughter Sha'wanna, now in training to become the next Iyatiku at Acoma Pueblo, was positioned at this entrance. She had never met Russell or Chris, so she treated both of them no differently than the rest who had already come through her post. She motioned to Russell to park alongside the cars already parked outside the fence line of the reservation, and Russell did as he was told. He and Chris grabbed their stuff. She showed them the table that held the crystal prisms, as if to invite them to take one. Neither of them did. They nodded in her direction as they began the two-mile walk to the church on the mesa, and she nodded back.

Malik's teacher, Susan, was positioned at the northern entrance some miles away. She had agreed at the last moment to take a week off from work to be a gatekeeper at this point of entry. She, too, had a portable table that held hundreds of crystal prisms, and there were some twenty cars already parked at her fence line. From there, her visitors walked across the cattle guard that stretched from one side of the two-lane road to the other. After that, it was just a mile or so to the gathering place between the two mesas.

None among the Planners would hazard a guess as to how many seekers might come to this meeting. Besides the Web site that had been published some six weeks earlier, there had been no publicity at all. The site had received some 80,000 hits, but no one had called to offer their help or e-mailed to announce their intention to come. No one asked about accommodations or where they could eat. No one asked for directions or a list of the rules. No one asked for an agenda. As a result, none of the Planners knew how many might come, but Susan thought to herself early that first day, *This is manageable, after all.*

Sha'wanna thought the same thing as they each awaited the next arrivals.

Susan did not have long to wait. A dilapidated VW van sputtered up, and she signaled for it to park with the other cars. The van had no tags or license plates, and it lurched and backfired as if it might not go another mile.

Out of this van emerged a tall and elegant woman. Her slender frame, coffee-colored skin, loose-fitting clothes, and sandaled feet gave her a cool and casual bearing. She stretched her arms above her head as soon as she was clear of the van, yawned, and surveyed the scene around her.

She looked at Susan and asked, "Where do I find a blind boy named Malik and an Indian called Iyatiku?"

The power in her voice was unmistakable, too, and yet she barely spoke above a whisper. Susan saw the wisdom in her soft, brown eyes and pointed south, past the fence line.

"They will both be down at the second mesa on the left in an old adobe church," Susan said. Before she could stop herself she added, "I love those sandals."

The woman gazed at Susan for a moment and then asked, "Is the blind one your son?"

"No. He's my student," answered Susan.

The woman nodded and smiled knowingly. "I have known him before and will go to where he is." Then she added, "So that you know, I am Amoria, and I thank you, teacher of Malik." With that, she reached out and touched Susan lightly on the forehead, turned to the south, crossed the old cattle guard, and began to walk the final mile to Acoma.

Susan knew that she had encountered a Master Teacher. She felt energized in her presence and was moved by her touch. She felt hopeful and thankful and could not contain her smile as she watched Amoria's long strides propel her toward her destination.

~   ~   ~

Up at the old adobe church, Jack and the Planners had arranged the twelve wooden benches in a circle on the packed dirt floor. They were sitting and talking while they waited for Russell Layne. Thomas was already on his third cup of coffee. Xuan sat next to him on a bench near the eastern wall. They did not know that Russell and Chris were more than an hour away.

Malik was sitting near Jack, and though he was not yet accustomed to using his newfound voice, he began to hum and then to form some words. His boyish intonations were tentative and in the tenor range.

Jack listened as Malik tried to repeat some sounds that he had heard from Jack and, soon, Jack joined him. The two of them voiced a simple incantation together.

The others sat in silence, eyes closed, and immersed themselves in the chant. Jack's powerful bass voice was louder than Malik's, but the young boy's voice gained power as his confidence rose. It wasn't long before their voices were locked together, an octave apart. As the sound of one mirrored and supported the sound of the other, a third tone began to emerge above the two of theirs. It was higher and lighter, distinct and clear. It was the spirit voice that the Jemez keeper woman had identified for Malik when she first helped him find his voice. This spirit voice added a third part to the already powerful effect of their chant. Reverberating all around the church, their chant soon bounced off the walls and echoed unto itself and grew in power like a fast-approaching train in the cavernous sanctuary.

Unable to resist, Digger, Xuan, Thomas, and Anna were soon drawn into this all-pervasive sound. They lent their voices, and their energy, to the chant. The impact of it intensified even more.

In the silence below the mesa, the people gathered there began to hear it, too. At first it was faint, but after a while it reverberated off the rocks and bluffs and mesa walls that formed the circular valley in which they chanted this simple spirit song. As old as time itself, the sound grew until it covered the sound of footsteps coming down the roads to Acoma.

Russell and Chris paused as the sound reached them walking in from the west. Amoria's long, gliding strides came to a halt as she walked in from the north. All of them stopped to hear the chant more clearly and to absorb it more completely into their bodies, minds, and hearts. It resonated inside of them and sank into the very core of their beings. The chant was unfamiliar to their ears, but the feelings were more familiar than breathing itself. They recognized it in some unknown place within themselves before they resumed their walking. As they felt the tug of the collective energy in the gathering they had set out to find, their pace quickened.

And they knew that they were near.

~   ~   ~

Poised on a bluff at the farthest southern point of the Pueblo lands some nine miles from the church, another one was near, as well. His imminent arrival was not known to any who were already there. As he closed in on Acoma, there was no road on which to walk. His feet were sore and tired. He had lost weight on his journey; food and water had sometimes been scarce. His name was Carlos Portales.

Under the cover of his full-brimmed hat, he, too, was feeling the rhythm of the chant—like the drumbeat of a powerful heart, at first, and then like an old-time melody. He had only heard it once before, somewhere near Santiago, but he recognized what it meant for him as soon as he stopped to listen. Like the others, he knew that he was near.

He had walked for almost a year toward Acoma because a voice in him had told him to do so. He experienced the hospitality of countless people in Chile and Brazil and Venezuela. He conversed with dozens of priests, bishops, and Mayan holy men as he came through Central America and Mexico. He spoke with those of the ancient traditions wherever he went and was quieted by the stars in the nighttime skies under which he slept. He was humbled by the magnificent mountains that loomed around him and the rain forests he traversed. He was lifted by the laughter of children he encountered and mesmerized by the murmur of waves along the shores he touched. He listened to the simple truths of simple people as he meandered through their lives.

To some of those he met, he spoke of his mission and what he knew about the meeting at Acoma. To others, he did not. Most of them tried their best to understand—and some of them did—but he knew the people might not be ready for such a new and lightly traveled road. New is discomforting for everyone, but it was the discomfort that pushed him to seek this new path for himself. As he walked, he embraced the discomfort of change. As he walked, he felt what the people would feel. As he walked, he faced his own fears—and, by facing them, overcame them one by one. His passion pulled him forward each morning and pushed him from behind each afternoon.

It was when he reached New Mexico that he ran out of road for the final time and was forced into the ultimate discomfort of following nothing but the compass of his heart. Over the final stretch of desert, the last mountain climb, and the steady trickle of a high-desert stream, he traveled. Past bluffs and mesas and hard-scrabble flatlands he walked. Dead-end thickets and impassable brambles opened up into arid, wind-blown valleys until his unmarked path brought him to rest on a cliff south of Acoma.

It was there that he heard the chant that started in the church and resounded throughout the valley, and it was only then that Carlos Portales knew that he was where he was going. He rejoiced that he would soon knock the dust off his sandals and drink from the fountain of understanding that he imagined Acoma to be.

~   ~   ~

When the Planners stopped their chant and opened their eyes, they were surprised to see two more people among them in the church. Sitting on a bench by himself was an Asian man in a crimson robe. His black, coarse hair was tied back in a small ponytail, and he smiled playfully as everyone noticed his presence.

He greeted them with a slight bow of his head and the words, "Aum. I am Min Tzu."

Xuan recognized the robes of this Tibetan monk. He was as broad as he was tall, but he seemed to fit on the small Acoma benches quite well. His cross-legged posture looked natural, relaxed, and well-grounded, and a smile lit up his broad, round face. Everyone in the room was drawn into that smile, and a growing sense of joy swept through them all.

Xuan went to sit next to him, and when she did, he looked at her, reached out, and touched her on the forehead. She felt the energy in his touch and could not quit smiling. Though her doubts about this project had long since subsided, a new wave of certainty coursed through her again; she now knew for sure that she was where she wanted, and needed, to be.

The second newcomer was standing quietly and unobtrusively by the large wooden doors to the church. From his attire—a multi-hued robe with a ragged hem and a cloth headpiece that covered most of his face—he appeared to be an Arab. His neatly trimmed beard, deep-set eyes, and clothing gave him the look of a Muslim. Only when he had the attention of everyone in the church did he step lightly into the circle formed by the twelve benches and bow from the waist in all the four cardinal directions: north, east, west, and south. Playfully and ceremoniously, he bent deep from his supple waist. In between bows, he stood tall and magnificent and surveyed the room through keenly focused eyes. His posture was perfection. His bowing was humble, his manner was confident and sure.

Everyone's attention shifted to this man. He slowly began to move about in a circular pattern. He paused ever so briefly in front of each of the Planners, and not so briefly in front of Malik. He seemed to mark Malik for a later encounter, and soon he was moving faster and faster in the circle. He stopped in a minute, and with a small flourish, he introduced himself.

"I am Tariqah. For many lives, I have studied and lived inside the mysteries of life. Now, finally, I understand many truths, and I will be a teacher to those who come here to learn."

Tariqah looked closely at the Tibetan monk and said with a smile, "You are a wise man, yes?"

The monk locked eyes with the Muslim, and they were frozen together for one long moment.

Finally, the monk replied, "There is one cup of wisdom in one man but there is true wisdom only when the cups of many men are poured together. We will pour our cups together at Acoma, and all the world will see what they are willing to see."

"And hear what they are willing to hear," Malik added without thinking. Of course, he was hearing these two teachers, but he was also feeling their energy as they spoke and moved about. He heard them clearly, and he started to write the first words of the meeting right then.

"Ah, the blind boy is among us," Tariqah said as he whirled around to address Malik directly. "You, my boy, will hear us well. You will help us understand anew the truths that all men seek. You are the perfect messenger, and many will want to call you prophet or teacher or a hundred other titles. You will not let them. The flattery of men will not make you a fool."

He reached out and touched Malik on the forehead and then sat down next to Thomas and looked him over for a moment.

"This one is full of questions," Tariqah said, "but he, too, will understand. His heart is open, and he has begun to know love."

Thomas squirmed on his bench and tried to keep his eyes on the Sufi. He could only look him in the eyes for a moment before the intensity of Tariqah's gaze drove his eyes to the ground. His palms began to sweat, and he tried unsuccessfully to dry them on his pants. He wished the moment would pass. It did, as Tariqah touched him on the forehead, and he relaxed.

Then the monk spoke up again and said, nodding in Xuan's direction, "This one is here in faith and is not constricted by beliefs. She will show us the faith that has no borders or colors or preconceptions. She is a truth on which the truth can be inscribed. She is here in openness, and so she has no limits. She knows hope, and hope produces the momentum from which all progress comes. She will show us these things again."

They then both looked at Jack and Digger. And they both smiled.

Of Digger, the monk said, "This one is knowledge—not knowledge born of experience, but knowledge born of books and contemplation. He sees the patterns of men and understands that there is a template behind the patterns. He sees the cause behind the effect, but soon he will help us see the cause within all effects. He will merge the two ways of understanding and help us see the one. He will see the whole panorama in the march of humankind and point us to a better view."

Of Jack, Tariqah made the following assessment: "He lives within the truth and knows no separation from it. He remembers the roots, and the roots are in him, but he does not know from whence they came. He will show us the way to find the source of who we are. He will lead us to that place where action and thought are joined together forever."

"And there are more to come," said the monk in a matter-of-fact tone.

Xuan looked around and was reminded that there were only two of the expected seven Master Teachers in the church with them.

The monk named Min Tzu cleared his throat, took a deep breath, and uttered a simple, repeated sound. "Aum ... Aum ... Aum ...," he chanted.

Without a word, all of them instinctively fell into a collective silence. The aum sound energized the church all over again in order to attract more teachers. In the moments that followed, they waited collectively for the morning to begin unfolding again.

Chapter 3

Two More

It wasn't long before there was a knock on the big church doors. Thomas went to open them. On the other side, still standing outside on the steps, was the tallest woman he had ever seen. He guessed her to be seven feet tall. Her coffee-colored skin glistened in the sunlight outside the church, and her brightly printed African robe caught his eye as she towered over him. He stepped back in surprise when she smiled down on him and extended her arms to embrace him. Awkwardly, he found himself returning her embrace, and he felt the intense warmth of her touch.

Amoria then walked into the church and the others watched her in silence. Finally, she asked Thomas, "Are you Malik?"

He turned and pointed to Malik on the far side of the circle. "Over there," he said.

"And what about the one they call Iyatiku?" she asked him.

Jack stood up and waved his hand in response to her inquiry.

"I have heard of you both and was inspired to find you on this day. I am glad my journey is over for now, and it is my honor to be in your presence and meet you heart to heart." With that, she bowed her head slightly to each of them and took a few moments to adjust her eyes to the dimly lit church. She then located an empty bench, walked over to it, and slowly sat down.

After achieving some degree of comfort on a bench made for someone two feet shorter than her, she proceeded to make eye contact with Xuan and Digger. She looked at Min Tzu, then Anna. She smiled and seemed to recognize Tariqah sitting quietly in the circle. She breathed a long, light breath as she settled in.

Almost immediately, Min Tzu began his simple chant again. "Aum … Aum … Aum …," he intoned. Once again, the others soon followed suit, and the thick-walled structure of the Acoma church began to reverberate again with the well-known sound. Except for that sound, there was no sound. Except for that energy, there was no energy. And in that one place in time, there was no other place. Or time.

Soon, there came another knock on the door. Before there was time to open it again, the door opened wide, and there stood Carlos Portales. Jack turned pale as he recognized the man from his dream the night before. Carlos held his hat in his hand, humble, gentle, and glad to be there. His crooked teeth shone bright, and his mouth formed a line of demarcation between his bushy mustache and his cleanly shaved chin. He flipped his gray, braided ponytail from the front to the back of his sky blue shirt, and his bright green eyes focused into the limited light as he tried to make out the people in the room. He let loose a hearty laugh as the energy from the church rushed past him like an unseen wind through the wide-open door.

"I am Carlos Portales," he boomed. "I bring you greetings from all the people of Argentina and Venezuela and Brazil and Chile and Mexico. My name means 'windows,' and I will help build windows to our meeting so we can see the truth ahead of us. These windows will be opened wide and tall. Through them, we will all see the door. I am Portales."

With that, he walked directly over to Jack and greeted him in Spanish. Jack laughed at his salutation as he stood up and stuck out his hand. Portales did not take it at first. Instead, he reached out and touched Jack on the forehead. Jack closed his eyes briefly as he was touched and then looked at Portales again. He did not speak, but then Portales took Jack's hand, and their greeting was complete.

When Jack sat back down, Portales sat down heavily on the same bench. Weary from his long walk, he exhaled a long, deep sigh. He took off his sandals and banged them together three times as he looked around the humble church and studied the pictures and hangings on the tall, plastered walls of the rectangular space. He saw the circle of hand-hewn benches. He smiled again and then declared, "It is a beautiful place! Simple and beautiful! When do we begin?"

"There are more to come," replied the red-robed monk, and he began his chant again, "Aum … Aum … Aum …"

Malik knew this sound and so did Jack. It was one of the many sounds contained in all of Jack's chants, but Malik had never heard it just by itself. He only knew it as part of a larger collection of sounds, like a single word in a compound sentence. He did not know the meaning of this sound by itself, but not knowing the precise, lexicographic meaning of the sounds did not seem to hinder him or, for that matter, anyone else. The meaning of this word did not matter.

On more than one occasion, Jack had theorized to Malik that maybe the words were meant to be unrecognizable. He suggested that maybe they weren't intended to be hemmed in by some static definition or limited by some narrow connotation. Jack thought it more important that the words not be known to the listener, so that the mind of the listener could be minimized in the listening process, and the heart of the listener could be optimized. In this way, like music, the essential soul of the listener would be touched without the clutter of the mind's attempt to process unfamiliar words or categorize these words into another group of endless feedback loops or prior and stagnant understandings.

Jack had also told Malik that sounds like "amen" or "aum" were just parts of phrases in his chants. He guessed them to be parts of a larger wisdom; a larger set of truth-laden sounds. Though these single sounds had somehow been venerated over time as whole words, he now understood them to be incomplete. Endless recitation and mindless repetition of these fragments over time did not make them any more complete. Like poorly remembered phone numbers with missing digits, these partial sets of sounds that had survived through history, only served to transmit incomplete knowledge. Jack had already explained this to Malik. The complex messages in the ancient chants and the soul-level communications possible within them had become lost or forgotten or obscured through the centuries. Jack had even had a discussion with Russell Layne regarding the Tower of Babel story. They concluded that maybe these partial sets of sounds were all that remained from the dissolution of the common language thousands of years before, as intimated in that fable. They both surmised that the group of people now arriving at Acoma might somehow remember these ancient sounds, too.

~   ~   ~

As Russell and his new friend Chris neared the mesa, Chris motioned for Russell to turn and look behind them. Stretched out along the two-mile road they had just traversed were a hundred more people. Bunched in groups of three or four and talking among themselves, they were coming to the meeting, too. Russell stopped and surveyed the scene for a moment, and then Chris pointed to the flatland area between the two mesas. For the first time, Russell noticed the crowds gathered there, as well.

"I wonder how many will come?" he said.

Chris shrugged his shoulders. "I don't know, Russell, but there is one in that gathering that I must stop and see. Do you want to come along?" Chris turned back to him as he spoke.

"No, I think I better go on up to the church first and check in with the rest of my team, I expect that is where Malik will be. You're welcome to join us later if you'd like, and I'll introduce him."

"Okay. Good," Chris replied. "I may have another with me as well. It is she that I expect to find, and her name is Mirissa. In previous lives as a man, she was known by some as Issa and by others as Yeshua or Jesus."

"Oh, that's incredible!" Russell said. "Have you been known by other names, too?"

"Yes, I have been called Krishnamurti, but it was several lifetimes ago. In fact, that's when I learned to play the flute. Now I prefer to just be called Chris. It's a little simpler for everyone, especially in the West." He smiled at Russell and continued. "Thanks for the ride, and thanks for listening with your heart when that guru spoke to you many years ago. I believe humankind will be elevated once more due to the widespread impact of this meeting." With that, Chris touched him lightly on the forehead and turned to go to the camps between the mesas.

Russell stood still and reflected for a moment on what Chris had said. He felt the effect of his parting touch as he then began his final steps up to the mesa top and the church that rested there.

Back at the two entrances to the valley, Susan and Sha'wanna were busy with a steady stream of new arrivals. Susan had sent roughly 150 people walking toward the meeting since daybreak. Sha'wanna had sent eighty-five or ninety. The people they ushered in were of every color and nationality, every size and bearing. Some of them took a crystal prism, but some did not. Susan and Sha'wanna did not know what made people choose the way they did, but it didn't really matter to them. They were busy with the next arrivals.

Some of the travelers reported to the women that many more were on the way. The incoming flights at the Albuquerque airport were sold out for the remainder of the week. Hotels in the city were already filled up as people made final preparations before their trek to Acoma. The interstate highways were sprinkled with hitchhikers from the north, east, west, and south, all of them looking for one more ride to carry them the final miles. The simple name "Acoma" was on every tongue. The excitement was palpable, and anticipation was building by the hour.

~ ~ ~

Following an afternoon of discussion and contemplation in the church and the arrival of Chris, Portales said, "Let's go speak to the people who are gathered between the mesas."

With that suggestion, all twelve persons in the church rose as one and as dusk drew down, Jack led them out into the crack between the worlds. The sun had already set to their left as they walked north from the church. They passed the natural water cistern and stopped at the edge of the northernmost point of the mesa top. Some 360 feet below them, the crowd of a hundred had grown and now looked to be approaching four hundred.

The Iyatiku of Acoma Pueblo stepped forward, and someone below saw the twelve of them. Word of their presence spread through the crowd, and silence soon fell upon them all. Like a teacher surveying his students, Jack cleared his throat and gathered his thoughts. He took a deep breath and let it out slowly. Peace descended on the moment, and he smiled.

He then began to softly speak one of the chants that he knew so well but did not know how he knew. After just a few moments, the others on the mesa top joined in, and their voices rose in unison. Those below the bluff heard it, too, and soon, they were chanting along, as well.

Jack's speculation was right. Everyone recognized and knew the chant. All the sounds of it were apparently hardwired into everyone's ancient self. As he chanted along with the hundreds of people below, he came to understand this clearly. The words and sounds emanated from each throat, each heart, and each voice together, perfectly intoned; there was no need for the people to be taught. The sounds were already known—like some genetic verbal code—and they encircled and enveloped and enchanted that valley, from the flats to the surrounding mesas and back.

Like an echo that had been silenced for too long by the passage of time, the sound was unleashed at Acoma, and the chant began to take on its own identity. It was no longer beholden to those who spoke it. The chanter became the listener. Action and reaction became one. Intent and purpose blended with outcome and impact. There was no one to make the sound, and there was no one to hear the sound, either.

After a while, Jack stopped the chant. It stopped instantaneously in the crowd, as well. Everyone seemed to know it a split second before it stopped, and, just that quickly, it was done.

Without missing a beat, Malik handed his note from the afternoon contemplation to Russell Layne. It read, "The mantra for today is 'Help me hear the thee in me.'"

Russell surveyed the others and then signaled to Portales, Min Tzu, and Digger. The three of them came over to him, and he looked them in the eye. He handed the paper to Min Tzu. Without a word between them, they knew what to do: they immediately took off to join the crowd below. When they reached the flats, they began to spread the first mantra to the people who had come to seek it out.

The nine who remained on the mesa top walked back to the church to uncover the first understanding. They walked in silence. For the Planners, the power of Jack's chant when voiced by hundreds had been incredible. The volume was thunderous. It had penetrated every part of the heart, every corner of the mind, and every aspect of the beings that were there. It had washed over them like an ocean wave. They were overwhelmed by its singularity and focus. They were awestruck by its totality. They were humbled by the fact that they couldn't explain it, and they now realized just how very little they understood. Their religion, whatever religion they thought they knew or believed, had not prepared them for the power of this evening. Their vision of "god" or "allah" or whatever name they had grown accustomed to using had never been this large or all-encompassing. They were awed.

As they filed into the candlelit church, Xuan and Amoria picked a bench and sat down. Russell and Anna did the same. Chris the hitchhiker and Thomas the skeptic joined Jack the Iyatiku and Tariqah the Muslim as they paused just inside the door and then found a place, as well. When Malik came in, Jack rose to help him and soon all nine of them were seated.

No one spoke at first, but then Malik began quietly. He repeated the mantra that Min Tzu, Portales, and Digger were sharing with the crowd below: "Help me hear the thee in me." He paused to take a deep breath and repeated the words again. "Help me hear the thee in me." Soon, a rhythm developed as his repetitions continued, and everyone began to intone the mantra with him. "Help me hear the thee in me." Each repetition, slowly spoken and deliberately paced, took seven counts; one count per syllable. "Help me hear the thee in me." The slow intake of breath in between took seven counts as well. Then the mantra repeated. "Help me hear the thee in me."

After several repetitions, Amoria changed the rhythm of her breath so that she breathed in while the mantra was repeated, and, while the others were taking their breath, she repeated the mantra alone on her exhale. Xuan picked up on this change and joined Amoria in the alternate breathing pattern. Then Russell did the same. Now the church was filled with an unbroken repetition of the mantra, continuing in this way until they had all centered themselves and come back down from the display of power they had been part of some moments before. The regulated breathing and the hopefulness of the mantra grounded them and energized them for a long night of discovery and contemplation.

~   ~   ~

Meanwhile, Min Tzu, Portales, and Digger weaved their way through the crowd between the mesas and shared the mantra with everyone they encountered. Those who heard it from one of them then passed it along to others, and in this way the mantra was soon known by all. They were instructed to keep this thought, this hope, at the forefront of their consciousness for the rest of the evening and in the morning when they awoke. "Help me hear the thee in me. Help me hear the thee in me."

Soon, the whole area between the two mesas was buzzing with this mantra. Whether spoken aloud or whispered under the breath, the mantra began to take hold of the crowd. It served to focus everyone on the simple desire to no longer view themselves as apart from that which they were seeking to find. It was not an easy viewpoint to implant, simply because the mantra still bespoke two entities—"the me" and "the thee." Despite these initial and obvious limits, the people responded in trust. They seemed to understand that it was only a beginning, so they embraced the mantra as a necessary step on the path to something more. In it, they perceived an experiential knowing that would eventually become a habit of perception.

The last person the three messengers came to in this dissemination was the woman named Mirissa, of whom Chris had spoken to Russell. Min Tzu, Portales, and Digger came to her at the edge of the crowd farthest from Acoma Mesa.

The sun had set some thirty minutes earlier, and dusk had turned to dark in the space between the mesas. Mirissa, however, drew the attention of the messengers up to the crest of Enchanted Mesa, where the mesa top was still bathed in light.

Digger quickly looked back at Acoma Mesa and saw that it was totally dark and then looked again at Enchanted Mesa and saw it still bathed in light. Even though he knew it to be some forty feet taller than Acoma Mesa, he didn't think its height adequately explained the presence of light after sunset. He didn't understand what was going on.

He looked at Mirissa, as if to ask her how and why this was happening. She only smiled and said to him, "Not all light is from the sun." She said it so simply and so confidently that Digger believed her without question.

Min Tzu and Portales saw it, too, but they had seen things like this before, and explanations were less important to them.

They looked at Mirissa, and then she said, "I am to join you in the church on the mesa tonight. Will you show me the way?"

Digger answered, "Yes. I think we're done here, and we need to return, as well."

"Are you Digger?" she asked as she stopped and faced him.

"Yes."

"I am known in this life as Mirissa, but I knew you when they called me Yeshua and I lived in Nazareth. You were my sister." She reached up and touched Digger on the forehead, and he smiled in recognition as she spoke again. "I've not been to church for a long, long time. Please lead me there, Digger," she said.

With that, they started back through the crowd and heard the mantra being repeated by groups of people as they went. Every group they passed was speaking it in earnest and seeking the experience that it promised.

Mirissa smiled as she walked, and people looked up from what they were doing to gaze on all four of them for just a moment or two. Portales was his usual effusive self and showed his large smile easily. Min Tzu was recognized as a holy person by his robe and his measured, easy movements as he wove in and out of the potpourri of people.

Digger watched and said nothing as these Master Teachers greeted, smiled, touched, and laughed with those they passed. His role of observer was well ingrained in him, and the power of this experience was not lost on him at all. Fascinated by this entire adventure, he only wanted to know more. He wanted to know more about these teachers, Tariqah and Amoria, Portales and Min Tzu. He wanted to know more about Chris and Mirissa, too. He speculated as to how each of them fit into the clues the Planners had worked on all spring. Finally, as he reflected on what had transpired so far on this, the first day, he was eager to know just where this week would lead and how it would impact his life.

Chapter 4

The Rest of the Teachers

As the four of them arrived at the door to the church, Mirissa stopped. Her dark, flowing hair shimmered in the coach-light candles on each side of the heavy wooden doors. She looked at the rusted iron hinges, metal joining straps, and planks of thick, rough-hewn wood. She saw the dents in the old, ringed handles and sliding steel bars. She ran her hands slowly over the aged wood with its holes and gaps and worn-out carvings that had been so meticulously inscribed with the crude tools of a bygone time. A shiver ran up her spine and through her arms as she remembered her experience with heavy wood in a life long ago.

"This church represents so much history," she said, "and so much progress, so much suffering, and so much that is not understood." The other three listened as she spoke. "It is right that we stay in the church a while longer but all things built by man will pass away one day. The model of church was conceived at a meeting like this one and has gotten lost in the men who tried to control it, the men who kept its secrets from the rest, and the men who distorted its truths to serve their own purposes. It has become that which was not intended."

With that, she reached for the doors, effortlessly opened them wide, and led the other three inside. The rest were engaged in conversation, and all of them looked up as Mirissa, Min Tzu, Portales, and Digger joined them.

Chris saw his age-old friend, Mirissa, and nodded in recognition. He got up and spoke briefly to her and Portales as Min Tzu and Digger found places to sit. After their conversation, Mirissa and Portales also found places to sit.

Chris cleared his throat to speak.

"The Master Teachers are now all assembled, and it is time for introductions," he started. "On my left, this is Mirissa. She has also been called 'Issa' and several other names through the ages. She is the master soul of the age that is ending as we meet, and many have known her as Jesus or Yeshua the Nazarene. In other lives, she has been a mother and a father. She has been a slave and a prince, a child and a patriarch. She has lived a hundred lives and traveled a thousand paths. At this meeting she is a Master Teacher who will help us better understand the purpose of these past two thousand years and will help us find the key to the door of the next two thousand years."

When Chris was finished, Mirissa smiled, got up, and went over to Anna. As she reached out both her hands, Anna took them and stood up with her. They looked into each other's eyes and stood silently together for a minute or longer in unspoken communication. Finally, Mirissa reached out and touched Anna on the forehead. As the two of them sat down together on Anna's bench, Chris turned his attention to Tariqah.

"This Muslim is known as Tariqah. He has traveled with Rumi and others. He was the head of the great library in Alexandria in the ninth century, and he has been a scholar, an astronomer, and a barrister. He was a son to Mohammed and a builder on the Great Wall of China. He helped train the soldiers in the army of Napoleon. He is now a Sufi, and he is one of the Master Teachers for whom you searched all spring." Chris smiled, and Tariqah sat down with a flourish befitting a whirling dervish.

Just then, Amoria gathered her lengthy frame and stood up slowly. "Is this really necessary, Chris?" she asked.

"Oh yes. It is." Chris replied. He continued, "Amoria is an African in this life but has lived in many cultures and many times. She was a Mayan chieftain, and she lived in the islands off the coast of Greece. She studied with Socrates and traveled many years with teachers whose names are lost to history. She was a Navajo shaman and a guru in Pakistan. She was a sculptor and a warrior and a farmer. She operated a ferry, an inn, and a school. She learned from countless thousands, and now she is a Master Teacher, too. She is also the answer to one of your clues."

She sat down as the one also called Krishna continued. "The Tibetan over there has been a Buddhist, an American slave, a Roman, and a Persian. He taught philosophy at Oxford and soldiered under Arjuna. He was a student of Confucius. He was a Sherpa and a Cossack. In this life he is a friend to the Dalai Lama, and for this meeting he is a sage who will help us find the focus for the next two thousand years. This monk is Min Tzu."

The Planners watched closely, rapt with attention, as they heard more details on the people, the seemingly infinite souls about whom they had speculated for months. They were astounded by everything they heard and the details Chris had provided so far. They were even more fascinated by the realization that they had surmised so little—that the cryptic clues were so unlimited and their thoughts about them so small. They were beginning to glimpse a larger understanding of the expanded truths all around them and the infinity of possibilities in each and every person they beheld.

Suddenly, Digger interrupted, "So, lives and people really do come again and again to this earthly life?"

Chris looked at him and smiled. "Yes. Once something is created in the mind and heart of what you may call the divine, that something, or someone, changes form a thousand times but never, ever dies. Death is like a tree that has been pruned for winter. There is a change in outward appearance, but the cycles of all the seasons go on and on forever. The rebirth of every life happens again and again and again."

"And who are you in this ongoing cycle of life?" Thomas asked.

"That is harder to answer than you might currently imagine," Chris replied. "You have heard of me when I was Krishna, and maybe as Babaji. I have been a teacher in a dozen lives. I was there when a young Babylonian stumbled onto what would eventually become the wheel. Before that, I helped others learn how to contain and utilize the fires of nature so that mankind could use it for many useful purposes. I have been a medicine man and a high priestess. I have been a shipbuilder and a bridge builder and a queen. I have been a pauper and a slave and a merchant. I have been wealthy, and I was a simple, poor attendant to Siddhartha when he transformed himself from prince to Buddha. I have learned that the seed of my soul is infinite. There is no limit to what I can do when I am not caught up in being a limited version of me."

The Planners were amazed and dumbfounded as they tried to grasp what Chris was telling them. It was far beyond what they had imagined. This discussion was taking the world as they knew it and expanding it in every conceivable direction. Their perception of it was growing larger by the minute. The potential was limited only by the restrictions they imposed on themselves. They all hungered to know more and thirsted to explore their own lives from a whole new point of view.

"Tell us more, Chris," Anna implored. "Please, tell us more."

"Well, there's Carlos Portales over there. He has been a window, a door, and a gate for many people and numerous untold events. He launched a thousand ships as the king of Portugal. He inspired Michelangelo and funded da Vinci. He wrote with Hume and Locke and brought to light the concepts of personal liberty and democracy. He walked with Mohammed and argued with Aristotle. He was one of the masters at the last meeting like this. If the blind one could see, he would recognize the sandals he wears; he has always worn them. Like all of us here, he is a teacher, a wise one, and a sage."

The Iyatiku of Acoma was completely absorbed in Chris and his introductions. If even half of what Chris said was true, Jack was astonished. If, and this was more likely, Chris had only scratched the surface of these stories, Jack knew that he couldn't grasp it all anyway—not in its entirety.

Finally, Jack spoke. "We have become convinced that there are seven teachers due to come to this meeting, and you've only told us of six. Where is the seventh?"

Chris pondered the question for a moment and then slowly responded, "The seventh is here, too. He has been among you for all this time, but he does not know it—and so you do not know it either. When he awakens to his true identity, it will be more apparent to some of you, but even then you may miss the significance of who he is. His awakening may take place in this lifetime, and perhaps even at this meeting."

Even more than what had already fascinated the Planners, this news absolutely took their breath away.

~   ~   ~

Xuan immediately leaned back on her bench. She was incredulous at what Chris had said. Could it really be one of them? She looked first at Russell Layne. Wasn't he the one who put this all together? Wasn't he the one who got the message in New Delhi and was singled out to be the driving force? Wasn't he the one the priest called aside and to whom the clues were given? Wasn't he the one who was so well read in these matters of religion and history and even referred to himself as a lecturer? *Yes*, she thought, *he must be a Teacher.*

Then her thoughts turned to Jack Eaglefeather. *Maybe it's him*, she thought to herself. Jack was a lifelong spiritual leader of sorts. He had the trust of his people and served them well. They came to him for guidance and council. His wisdom was obvious. He knew the ancient chants. He had the foresight to agree to use the sacred places of Acoma for this gathering. *Yes*, she thought, *it must be him.*

Then Xuan looked at Malik and began to feel that maybe it could even be someone as young and innocent as him. He had overcome so much. He was in touch with his dreams and knew that he had been at such a gathering before. He listened so well and remembered so much. Xuan thought he had insight uncommon for a boy so young. He was obviously special. *Yes*, Xuan thought, *it could be him.*

Then Anna asked Chris, "What do you mean by 'awakened to their true identity'?"

And Chris answered, "Only when someone has accumulated the understanding of several lives do they figure out who they really are. It took me dozens of lives before I could become a teacher. When I finally became a Teacher, I also realized how much more learning there was to do. I soon became humbled and began to see the wonder and infinity of this creation. Then I finally saw myself as part of the creation and not apart from the creation. When that shift finally took place, I no longer saw myself as separated. But the first step for me was humility. I had to take what I thought I knew for sure and realize that I knew very little. I had to admit that the creation, as I perceived it, was infinitely larger than I could conceive."

Then Min Tzu added as he shifted his position on the bench, "That indeed is the first step—knowing that you do not know."

"And dismissing what you think you know," said Amoria. "It's just letting go of the need for security so you can be free to see the incredible potential in the mystery of it all."

"What we think we know holds us back. It is like keeping the shades drawn in the windows of our house," Portales added. "Our beliefs in how things should be are what actually preclude us from seeing how they really are. We blind ourselves and cannot see the mystery and wonder of it all."

Mirissa then spoke softly to them all. "It's as if you are dead."

"The patchwork robes of the Sufis," Tariqah interjected, "and the humble life-style we embrace are what allow us to see the countless whirling energies around us. Eventually, we learn how to merge with the infinite energies and leave our imagined separateness behind."

After Tariqah verbalized this understanding, he stood and demonstrated it by whirling around in front of his bench. In an instant he was gone from there and appeared again by the doors at the back of the church—and then, just as suddenly, he was at the front of the church on the dais. All the Planners watched in amazement, but the Teachers merely smiled. In an instant, Tariqah was back on his bench and smiling, too.

"Humility, a belief in mystery, a sense of wonder and wide open perceptions—these are the critical first steps." It was Chris again who spoke in summary. "But it can only happen if we ignore what we think we know and if we eliminate the constant feedback loops of our previous understandings. When we truly take the initiative to explore the infinity of the creation, and when we refuse to operate from our extremely limited view of things, then and only then can we see with humility and awe."

Mirissa spoke next. "Just as the leaders of the Jewish religion could not see me when I was here as Jesus, so it has transpired that the followers of all religions can no longer see the infinity of the creation. They get distracted by rules or hero worship or a thousand other little things." She arose from her bench and went to stand behind Malik. She placed her hands on his shoulders and continued, "The biggest mistake of the last two thousand years was the mistake of making Jesus and Mohammed and Buddha into heroes. No Master Teacher wants to be a hero. It is a trap, and it traps us—sometimes for hundreds of years at a time. Worse yet, it traps and deceives the ones who would learn from us."

Then Min Tzu spoke again. "The infinity of it all is so very, very large that when a religion obscures that infinity and tries to control its followers and prevent them from seeing that infinity, the religion itself must be cast aside, and truer cognitions must be formulated."

"But they are not new cognitions," Amoria suggested. "They are just a return to the truth, which is as old as the creation itself."

"Yes," Tariqah affirmed. "They are re-learnings, re-cognitions, and re-understandings. It takes learning again what has been forgotten or remembering anew that which used to be known without words. Re-cognitions are like letting the wind of the ageless truths chase away the chaff of religious distortion in order to get at the real wheat that makes the bread of life."

"Malik," Chris spoke one more time, "let's write this down as the first new understanding of Acoma: Be humbled in the creation; assume a sense of mystery and wonder. Know that you know not." And that was what Malik wrote down.

Chapter 5

The Second Morning at Acoma

The Planners slept well that night, except for Malik. He was up most of the night in the church writing notes and recording what he remembered from the day. As usual with him, he recalled everything of which he was a part.

Though Malik could not see what was going on, he knew the Planners were sleeping in the old monks' quarters adjoining the church. Jack had gotten the long-abandoned quarters re-roofed. He and other members of the Acoma council had even excavated the dirt floor until they uncovered the three-hundred-year-old tiles hiding there. As Digger had surmised, a long-forgotten painting depicted this part of the church quarters and had guided the restoration. Now, the court-yard was functional again. Only Malik and the Teachers remained in the church proper, and he could tell from the occasional voices and other noises there that they weren't sleeping—at least not much. He sensed from time to time that some of them would leave and then return. This happened several times during the night, and he was unsure how many of them were taking part in these departures and returns.

Sometime around three a.m., on her return from being away, Mirissa sat down next to Malik and interrupted his writing by saying, "You probably don't remember, but we were together some two thousand years ago in Alexandria. I was the one they called Yeshua."

"I dream about it," Malik answered, "but my dreams do not have names or faces. All I see in my dreams are seven different kinds of sandals."

Mirissa looked at him closely and said, "Your writings were meant to be a record of that meeting, too, but after the meeting I returned to Jerusalem and did not know what became of the scrolls you wrote. It was logical for me to dem-onstrate the model called church that we devised in that meeting into the Jewish culture into which I had been birthed. We knew it would be dangerous so you and the others could not go where I went. I lost track of all of you. I was saddened when a messenger from Alexandria came to me a year or two later and told me that your writings had fallen into the hands of people who did not care for them. Eventually, they were lost when the cave in which they were stored was flooded."

Malik listened intently to what she was saying and waited for more.

Mirissa looked at him and reached out to touch him gently on the shoulder as she continued. "This time, your writings will not be lost. Instead, they will be published in several languages for the entire world to see. You will not be credited by name in that publication, because it is important that the readers of your accounts not be swayed by your identity or your Muslim name. Much of what is happening here and is being recorded by you will upset certain powerful people. They will fear losing what has been established. They will not want to endure the discomfort it will bring them, and, initially, they will regard your words as a threat. They will be tempted to see the understandings as pronouncements against religions. But that is not how it will always be. Our words, your writings, will eventually be seen as an inspired addition to what they think they know. As with all good and needed things, these additions will gain wider acceptance as time goes on."

Mirissa studied the face of this young boy and saw the innocence and sincerity he brought to this important task. "This time of rejection and doubting will be hard on you, but you should not lose your faith. Almost every significant tradition in the history of humankind has a story in which a young boy leads his people from the brink of trouble. You are such a boy, Malik, and your position as an outsider will help people trust and believe your accounts of this meeting. All of the Teachers here will visit you from time to time while you are writing your notes, and you will be well cared for. When you are done, there will be even more for you to do."

"What is my ultimate identity?" Malik asked her. "How do I awaken to it?"

"You'll awaken to it like everyone else," Mirissa began. "Like everyone else, you are an eternal being and have lived many times before."

"So my dreams of transcribing the events of the last meeting like this are dreams of a former life?" Malik inquired.

"Oh, yes!" she answered. "That is where we first met. Tariqah and Min Tzu were there, too, but they were known by other names and living other lives. Min Tzu was a Magi, and Tariqah was from India. You were just a young boy then, as you are now, and you didn't live very long once you returned to your home. You died in an epidemic the very next year."

"So I have had other lives?" Malik rephrased the thought as he tried to let the confirmation of it expand his image of his ultimate identity and who he really was.

"Yes, a dozen or more, but I think this life may be a special one for you. It may be the one in which you awaken to your true identity." Mirissa took both Malik's hands in hers and looked at him as if he were looking back at her. "It won't be long before you will be able to see again, Malik, but not until after your writings are published. At first, being able to see again will be a stumbling block for you, because you will not be able to hear as well as you do now. Then you will once again find yourself in the Middle East, where you have lived other lives, and you will be a teacher there. For many years, no one there will know of your connection to the book, but, eventually, you will become known as 'The Acomite,' and a few may figure it out. You will earn their respect from the teachings you bring them, and you will be known as a man of peace. You will also come to be seen as a man of wisdom, and during those years you will awaken to your true identity."

Mirissa let go Malik's hands as she finished speaking. He felt her power of understanding and compassion leave him, and he immediately wished she would take his hands again. Instead, she reached over, touched him in the center of his forehead, and said, "Thank you, Malik. Your trust in this meeting is a force that helps to move it along. It has taken you many lives to learn how to trust, and it is very important that you never travel without it again. Do not lose your faith in the inevitable progress of humankind."

With that, she left his side and was soon departed from the church again. Malik knew that she would return, and he finally fell asleep, thinking of what the rest of the morning would bring.

~ ~ ~

As the sun rose on the second day, the Planners prepared themselves for another day of conversation, meditation, and discovery.

Xuan and Thomas rose early and slipped out of the sleeping quarters to walk together in the dim light of dawn. They avoided the gathering crowds to the north and descended from the mesa to the south, where the level ground had produced the corn for ten centuries or more. The day was dry and brisk, like most summer mornings in the high country of New Mexico, and they walked arm in arm to stave off the chill of the light morning breeze.

"So, sweet man, what are you thinking this morning?" Xuan asked as she searched his eyes for some sign that he was awake enough to talk.

"Actually, I've been thinking of the closeness we've developed these past few months, the nights we spent together—especially the night before we came down here to Acoma." He took her in his arms, and she hugged him close. "I don't know what will happen when this is over, Xuan, but I'll cherish those days and nights for a long, long time."

"I will, too. I miss it already, and it's only been a few days." She turned to him, smiled, and stretched onto her tiptoes to kiss him on the cheek. He bent toward her and received her kiss as he looked into her eyes.

"I also think about the conclusion of all this," he added as he started walking again. "In fact, I'm consumed with those thoughts. What will happen to you and me? What will happen to the others, and what will happen to all these people who have come here for this meeting?"

"Once an organizer, always an organizer, huh?" she smiled. "Well, for starters, I think all the Teachers will fend for themselves just fine. Having found their true identities, they don't seem to worry much about anything."

"I know," Thomas replied. "What's that about, anyway? They seem so sure of themselves, and well, I don't know how to describe it, they all seem really free of worry."

"Well, I think they understand that they aren't really tied to this earthly drama. They seem connected to it but not caught up in it."

"Maybe that's it," Thomas said, "but I've also been thinking about the yellow column in the sand painting Digger and I saw months ago. I want to ask one of the Teachers about it, because I think it has something to do with what happens at the end of these seven days."

"Yeah, me too," Xuan started. "Digger told me yesterday that he'd been thinking about something the Jemez Pueblo woman told him. She said that the last day of the meeting would be like the dandelion seeds that are carried up into the wind so they can land again, grow into that which only they can become, and then begin their cycle all over."

She saw the worry in Thomas's face and eyes.

"No matter what happens, Thomas, I want to be right next to you on that last day, just in case it is the end of something more than this meeting. For all we know, it might be the end of the world."

"I don't think that's it," Thomas said. "It'll be the end of something, that's for sure, but maybe it's just the end of the world as we perceive it and not really the end of the whole world, per se. Maybe it will be the end of our limits or the end of our old and tired perceptions. I just don't know."

"That would really be something, wouldn't it?" Xuan said as she thought it through again. "I mean, if the blinders are taken off so we can see the whole panorama of reality as it truly is, that would be incredible!"

"I just hope I've had my coffee by then, or I'm liable to miss the whole thing."

"Coffee or no coffee, I still choose being with you some more. Do you think we'll get that choice?"

Xuan watched the sun sneak up over the mesas to the east and looked back to see if their meeting place was yet in the light. She turned Thomas around and pointed to the very top of the two adobe bell towers on the old church. They shimmered in the sunlight and, as they both looked on, the bells rang three times to announce the second day at Acoma. It seemed to call them back. Thomas stole a kiss as they turned to go and it affirmed Xuan's hope for their togetherness.

When they got back to the church, all the Planners were up and eating the breakfast their hosts had prepared. Jack made sure Xuan and Thomas got something to eat and drink, too, and they went to experience the second day, together.

Chapter 6

One or Two

As they all gathered on the benches in the church, it was Anna who posed the first question of the day. She was nervous and worried that her question was too simple, but she spoke it anyway.

"Where does the devil fit into all of this?" Her question was not directed at any particular teacher, and all of them gave it some thought before Amoria spoke first.

"From the limited perspective of just one life lived in one place at one time, there do seem to be opposing forces in the world. We have come to call them good and evil or right and wrong or gods and devils, but these things do not exist as two. They are just mental constructs that are left over from our past misunderstanding of how things really are."

"For example," Portales interjected, "the entire earth is always bathed in light, but from any given place on the earth, it appears to be half light and half dark. Night and day are somewhat evenly split, but absence of light is only tied to a stuck-in-one-place perspective. When our viewpoint is larger, we realize that there is no absence of light. The light, the sun, is always on, but this is not so apparent from a limited point of view."

"But what about good and evil, or birth and death?" Anna persisted. "Those have nothing to do with light and dark."

"Not directly, I suppose," Tariqah broke in, "but they do depend on a limited perspective in order to promulgate the myth of their existence. The obvious day/night perception has made us all into day/night thinkers. We have this deep-seated habit of thinking in pairs and contrasts. If the perspective is expanded, however, there is only life and nothing else. Even the cycles of death are a part of life."

"We humans used to sacrifice virgins in the midst of our fear during an eclipse, but now we understand eclipses better," Min Tzu continued. "We spent winters in fear, wondering if the life-giving forces of spring would ever return, and we developed dozens of rituals to induce the life force back into the places we lived. But those life forces were never really gone, and now we know that spring is coming again, despite our rituals and our sacrifices. The rituals are actions that were simply not on point. They had no appreciable impact on the eclipse or the return of spring. They may have had some impact on our short-term attitudes, but the main impact has been to color our viewpoints with inaccurate perceptions, faulty perspectives, and a collection of limited-use rituals. All of these so-called opposing forces exist in the minds of men but not in the real world."

Russell chimed in. "And our religions are chock full of this kind of paired thinking. They continue to limit our perspective so that we stay stuck in the various dualisms that we thought accurate at one time," he said. "Perhaps they were the best descriptions we could muster in more primitive times, but now we know more."

"Look at all of us now," Chris suggested. "Everyone in this room, including you Anna, has died a dozen times or more. Sometimes it appeared to be unjust or ill-timed or accidental or intentional. Sometimes, our death appeared to cause great hardship for those around us or for those who may have had a hand in our demise, but here we are again, living on the earth and learning more about our true identity as beings that are much larger than one earthly experience."

"And the problem is that we rely on a limited perspective to understand these appearances of life and death," Mirissa explained. "It is our perspective that is skewed, but not our lives. For example, my death as Jesus led to all sorts of misunderstandings. When I returned after just three days, I was trying to demonstrate the principle that life goes on, that there is no death from the perspective of the larger and infinite life force. Perhaps I came back too quickly. Perhaps humankind wasn't yet ready to understand that there is change within the life force—change of form, change of address, and change of venue—but there is no death of the ultimate identity. At the same time, and this is crucial, there is no change to the life force itself, and there is no leaving the life force. I am no more special than anyone else, except that I understand this and have awakened to my true identity."

"So as Jesus, you didn't die for my sins?" Anna asked.

"No, not yours or anyone else's," Mirissa answered. "Your so-called sins and misconceptions and off-target behavior will cause your own earthly deaths over and over again until you awaken to your true identity. No one is able to do anything about that except you. No one can awaken for you."

"That understanding took me several lifetimes," Portales admitted. "I really struggled with that one."

"Me, too," Tariqah said. "Now, I don't much worry about dying here on earth anymore, because I know and understand the whole process and I have come to accept that, even in death, I am alive again."

"For me, it's always a hard transition," Amoria rejoined. "It seems like I'm about to get comfortable with my earthly circumstances when my deaths occur. I always remember that there are other things in store for me, but I still have trouble letting go."

Chris spoke again. "The truth is that there is only the one life force: the creation, the infinite and multifaceted reality of a forward-moving process. Death is the transitory phenomenon, but life is permanent and cannot be stopped or defeated or truncated," he said. "Awakening to our true identity requires that we understand the unwavering existence of this life force and its inevitable intent to continue in each one of us."

While everyone was soaking that in, Chris looked around the room as if to invite another question. When none were forthcoming, he continued. "The best known example of this, despite the misunderstanding, may actually be the so-called death of Jesus. They tried to kill him, and here we are two thousand years later still talking about him and meeting with this version of him called Mirissa. Unfortunately, that being named Jesus or Issa or Yeshua lived on in the people's mythology not because he was any more special than anyone else, but because they missed the point of his life and his teachings."

"Isn't that ironic," Portales chimed in with his usual big grin as he looked at Mirissa, "we're talking to Jesus right now so I guess he, or she, didn't die after all."

Mirissa's smile grew into a chuckle, and she smiled back at Portales.

"Yes, I've been remembered because my life has been profoundly misunderstood," Mirissa said. "That's ironic, I suppose, but it is a good thing that any of us Teachers are remembered. This keeps our teachings and examples out where they can be discussed for years and years, and it eventually ensures that our teachings will one day be correctly understood."

Malik tried his best to keep up with and notate the essence of this discussion. "If the one life force or lack of dualism is today's re-cognition," he asked, "how should I phrase it in my notes?"

"That's not so easy," answered Tariqah. "I prefer the old Muslim phrase, 'There is no god but god.'"

"I like just 'Know that I am God,'" offered Amoria.

"I like 'the Great Spirit in all things,'" said Jack.

"Or simply 'the Tao,'" Xuan offered.

Min Tzu smiled at her when she mentioned the familiar Chinese word for the never-ending process of creation.

"How about 'the infinite and unnamed Is'?" Russell suggested.

"Or simply 'the ongoing river of life,'" Min Tzu said.

Then Portales spoke up. "To name it is to separate it from ourselves again. For thousands of years it has been given hundreds of names. If you ask me, it's been named enough. Eventually, the discussion of the names leads again to the idea that this force is something separate from us. Actually, we are in the middle of it, not separated from it."

"Yes, I think that's right," said Xuan. "We are of it and we are in it, but there is no 'it' apart from us."

"Then there really is no god," Thomas hypothesized. "There is just the life force that runs through us and runs around us and is in us no matter what."

"But we can't talk about it unless we name it. Can we?" Russell asked rhetorically. "What about the continuous, spontaneous re-creation of each and every moment?"

"I'm going to refer to it as the ongoing and infinite force of life in all that is," Malik said decisively. "If someone wants to discuss it further or change it later, please let me know. Perhaps when I am finalizing my notes something better will appear."

"I like it," said Mirissa as she repeated it to herself and then aloud. "The ongoing and infinite force of life in all that is."

Digger objected quietly, "But the problem with that is it's too conceptual and doesn't sound very personal. I think most people have come to personalize their gods and goddesses so they can relate more easily," he continued.

"In the coming centuries, that is exactly what must be changed," answered Tariqah. "The habit of reducing the infinite into little personal finite perceptions is the first step in getting it messed up again. This time, we must let the spirit of the concept retrain us to live within it, to elevate us into it, and learn how to wrap it around ourselves."

"It's very subtle," Portales admitted. "Seeing the world from a solely personal perspective is like seeing the earth as the center of the universe. We all used to think that everything rotated around the earth, but now we know it is not accurate. Nor is it the case that a personal view is required. Humankind is ready to move beyond that egocentric view. We must now see ourselves as part of the universal creation process, because our egocentric view is no longer viable."

"Yes," added Mirissa, "we are in the creation process and not the objects of the creation process. It is not here for us. We are here in it and are part of it, and we are expressions of it."

"Then there really is no God, no Allah, no Yahweh, etcetera?" asked Thomas again.

"That's right, Thomas," Amoria answered quietly. "There is no God separate from us. There is no Allah separate from us. There is no force separate from us. All things have life, spirit, and infinity."

"And there is no thing, no man, no woman, no child, no beast that is separate from God or Allah or the creation process, either," Chris added. "There is only the one, the unified, the infinitely connected and interwoven reality of the ongoing creation."

Malik wrote it all down, and they broke for lunch.

~   ~   ~

Later that afternoon, Malik spoke and said, "Based on what we've heard so far, I think the mantra for this evening should be 'Help me see the thee in me.'"

"Okay," said Russell as he stood up and stretched his legs. "The mantras seem to be developing in such a way as to bridge the conceptual gap between the separated perception and the unified understanding. Does anyone else sense that, too?"

"I agree," Chris responded. "By the end of the week, everyone who is here and repeats the daily mantras each day will have no doubt of the unified concept the mantras impart. The unified understanding will gradually replace the perception of separation and two-way thinking."

"Yes, repetition is the way to change a mind over time," Russell reiterated. "It is also the way to teach a heart to hear. A new understanding requires both."

"Why can't we just call this whole thing love?" Anna asked. "Isn't that the best description of the creation?"

"Yes and no," Chris responded. "The word 'love' has come to mean too many things to too many people for too long. It has been well used and it is good, but the new understandings require mindfulness and an intent that the word love confuses rather than inspires. The life force is made of love and so many other processes that it is no longer wise to restrict it. It is my experience that understanding opens the door to love, and it will do so at Acoma. There must first be understanding."

There was silence for many moments; the discussions for the day had reached their end. Then Jack began to murmur a chant, and the church was quiet except for his voice. Soon, all of them were chanting with him, and a unification of their spirits soon ensued.

This chanting went on for twenty minutes or more. Malik lost track of time, but when it was over, he wrote the second re-cognition: "There is no god but God. There is no life force except the life force. There is no thing or being separate from the Great Is of all."

When Malik rested his pencil, the chanting ceased, and once again, silence descended upon them.

When evening came, they all followed Jack out to the northern edge of the mesa top and lined up to communicate to those between the mesas. The crowds below had been growing all day long and now numbered a thousand or more. As the thirteen stood in silence, the crowd soon came to know of their presence, and silence came over them, too. Jack cleared his throat to speak, and another chant soon passed over his lips and went out like a bell into this silence. Again, the genetically recognized chant soon reached all who were there. Its repetition soon resounded through the valley, even more powerful than the day before.

When it ended, Malik handed his note to Russell, as he had the evening before, and Russell read it. The note said, "Help me see the thee in me."

Once again, Russell motioned to Digger and Min Tzu and Tariqah, who knew what to do. When darkness fell, the second mantra was reverberating throughout the valley.

Chapter 7

Before the Dawn

All through the night, a steady stream of people continued to descend onto the sacred land of Acoma Pueblo. Like a river whose tributaries are too numerous to name, the seekers kept coming from every direction and from every possible place on earth. They came all through the day and through the night, as well. The river of seekers widened and deepened with each passing hour.

Though Susan and Sha'wanna were tending the gates, they could not stay awake all night long. When they dozed off, they were awakened by an improperly tuned engine that backfired before it came to rest or by the sound of gravel against the undercarriage of a car leaving the roadway. The makeshift parking lots at the two fence lines were overflowing.

Sometimes, the good-byes of hitchhikers as they were dropped off by their rides disturbed the generally subdued proceedings at the entrances, but the arrivals of the new ones proceeded without a problem. These pilgrims needed no direction from the gatekeepers. On a night when the three-quarter moon was softened by thin, wispy clouds streaming across the dark blue skies, the newcomers merely followed those already ahead of them on the trek to the gathering grounds.

As they walked by the mysterious Enchanted Mesa, they knew not what lay ahead. The massive rock offered no answer and greeted them in silence. None of them knew the stories of fear that this mesa could tell. None of them knew its future. All they knew was that it did not invite them any closer.

But as soon as they passed it by, their attention was drawn to those gathered between the two mesas. The second mantra from the evening before was being repeated again and again. It beckoned them to join in. Sometimes it was a murmur, but sometimes it grew in volume like the crescendo of a choir. The sound of it rose and fell, breathing its rhythm like drumming in the night. It created a field of energy that could be heard by all and seen by most. The new ones were pulled into this energy. It permeated them until they could not resist. Room was made, and they took their place wherever they could find it.

Under the light of this same moon, the Planners found themselves together in the courtyard adjoining the church. The candles were snuffed, and the new roof blocked the view of the moon. Each of them was lying on the makeshift beds. It reminded Anna of summer camps and Thomas of sleep-outs with boyhood friends. He and Xuan lay next to each other and snuggled up against the chill atop the plateau.

It was Digger who first broached the subject that one of them might be the seventh Master Teacher destined to help design the message for the upcoming two thousand years. Though he had considered every one of the Planners, all of whom measured up in one way or another, he was no closer to figuring it out.

"What did Chris mean when he said that the seventh teacher was already among us?" Digger asked the group. "I suppose it could be any of us, but I can't decide who he is talking about." Then he added as an afterthought, "By the way, I don't think it's me."

"I've narrowed it down to Jack or Russell," Xuan responded as she raised herself up on one elbow to engage in conversation. She spoke through the darkness in Digger's direction. "I don't think it's me, and I don't think it is Thomas, either, but I guess it could be. He certainly has some of the qualities a teacher should have."

Thomas smiled as Xuan was talking and then poked her playfully in the ribs. His looks of affection were swallowed up by the darkness as he realized that excluding him from consideration might have been an awkward thing for her to do. "It's not me. I'm sure of that, too," he said. "I think it's Jack."

"I think so, too," said Anna, "or maybe Malik."

To this Malik quickly replied, "It's not me. I've not yet found my ultimate identity."

"Well, none of us has found our ultimate identity," Russell noted. "Every once in a while over the years I've thought I knew my purpose and who I really was, but I have no real perception of my ultimate identity, yet."

Then Jack spoke up. "I think it might be all of us. It seems as though we each have some of the qualities a Master Teacher needs, and yet there are voids in each one of us that preclude the designation, as well. Maybe it is all of us, somehow. Is that possible?"

"Maybe," Anna started in. "I think anything is possible at this point. Everything I thought I knew has been expanded to such new heights. I've now come to believe that anything is possible."

"I agree," Thomas added. "When we started this whole thing, Russell said we would likely be changed forever. Being with these Master Teachers has opened my eyes like I never imagined. There are no longer any limits on what I can believe for myself or the world. After this kind of experience, I can't imagine myself doing anything but sharing with others what I have learned. That doesn't make me a teacher, and I'm certainly no teacher yet, but I can envision teaching what we learn when this meeting is over."

"I feel the same way," said Digger. "How could one stay quiet about the things we've seen and experienced? It really has given me a whole new perspective."

"Does anyone remember when Min Tzu and Tariqah were going around our circle and describing each of us?" asked Xuan. She found herself looking in the dark for the faces that went with the voices she was hearing.

All of them were quietly affirming what she said with an unseen nod of their heads or an almost inaudible mumble. Then Russell spoke again.

"I guess I missed that bit of revelation from those two, but when I was alone with Chris on the ride to Acoma, I got a sense of myself from him—that I was purposeful and able to help put people together for a common cause."

"I agree totally," Xuan said. "I've not met anyone in my whole life as purposeful as you, Russell. No one," she said sincerely. "You set your purpose for this meeting and have guided this little band of Planners with a deft touch and a gentle, kind spirit. More than that, you have opened every one of us to this experience. It's been incredible already, and we're only two days into it."

"So you think Jack may be right?" Russell responded. "Does each of us possess that which, when all put together, makes us a teacher? Is that it? If so, I don't quite understand how they will make us into one Master Teacher instead of the seven people that we are right now," he finished.

"I don't think they will," Anna answered. "I think that whenever one of us meets a person who is open to learning what we have learned, the teacher in us will appear and the student in them will appear, as well. Each of us is ready to blossom into a teacher when the time is right or when a teacher is needed."

Xuan heard Anna's thoughtful comments with a newfound regard. All she could think to say in response was, "You are so right, Anna. You are so right! We've seen how to become teachers, and all any teacher needs, all that each of us needs, is the willing mind of the seeker."

"And these Master Teachers will show us even more over the next five days," Russell said. "We'll all have to learn what they are teaching, because I think we will be teaching soon, too. Our role in the company of all these Master Teachers is not to discern the direction of the next two thousand years. Our place in that task is small. But our role in disseminating and demonstrating this new direction will be much larger. We'll be teaching those who will, in turn, be the teachers for the next two or three generations. That will get the new direction established."

"Will we be like the twelve disciples in Jesus's time?" asked Anna.

"I suppose so," answered Russell, "but I think we will be many more than twelve, and we will have Malik's notes to help us keep the message pure and simple."

"More than that," Digger offered, "we will be teaching a way of understanding rather than the message of one man or one dogma. It won't be about heroes or beliefs. It will be much bigger than that."

His words seemed to reverberate in the silence and echo around the room again and again as all the Planners fell quiet. The phrase, 'It will be much bigger than that' became the thought to which they all went to sleep. It was past midnight now, and they had been up since dawn. Sleep was essential, because the next day would be bigger than this one, too.

~   ~   ~

Meanwhile, the six Master Teachers were gathered in the church next door. Only two mantras had been taught so far. The first, 'Help me hear the thee in me,' and the second, 'Help me see the thee in me' were becoming well absorbed by the people below.

"I like these mantras we are teaching," said Amoria. "I think they will create the new habits of thinking that the next evolution requires."

"I like them, too," said Chris. "They fit the unseen pattern perfectly."

"And the mantras teach the unifying pattern of thinking that eliminates the separation," Min Tzu added.

"The key is to demonstrate and to remind the new teachers that there is one life force," said Tariqah. "There is only the unnamed and infinite Is, and there can be no separation, no me or thee, no us and them, no here and there, no then and now."

"As for the first mantra about hearing," MinTzu began, "it's when we are quiet that we begin to really hear and the silence can be so loud. Sound and silence are braided together like the endless spiral of creation." He playfully flipped his ponytail as he spoke. Then he laughed at the image.

"Yes, I think so, too," Carlos Portales offered. "Whether we are listening or not, the sounds of the infinite are coursing through us. Even if we don't hear them consciously or don't have a description of them or don't know what they are or what they mean, they are in us, and they are reaching us and teaching us in very subtle ways."

"I agree," Chris quickly answered, "but what we hear is as important as what we don't hear. The two of them, together, are the essential teaching in these mantras. The 'me' thinks he hears from the outside, while the 'thee' knows the hearing is from within. Hearing from both directions at once elevates our hearing."

"Yes," said Mirissa, "the silence defines the sound, and the sound describes the silence. They are not two. When all of us know how to hear them as one, the separation will end." She paused for a moment as if mulling it over again. "Help me hear the thee in me. I like it, too."

With that, the teachers agreed on the import and the role of the first mantra.

Then Tariqah, the Muslim, put forth his thoughts on the second mantra already circulating among the people below the mesa. "Help me see the thee in me." He shifted on his bench and said matter-of-factly, "There is only one changed word in this mantra. It changes from hearing to seeing. It seems almost the same as the other one to me."

Chris responded quickly, "Sure, in a way it is," he started, "but all our senses can lead us, and all of our senses can mislead us, too, because we are so accustomed to perceiving in a certain way."

"Chris is right," said Amoria. "We're used to seeing with our eyes open. We are accustomed to seeing in varying degrees of light and with varying degrees of attentiveness."

"But seeing with open eyes is only one way of seeing," Portales interjected. "Seeing everything in that one way doesn't bring us understanding."

"No. In fact, it brings us misunderstanding, because it is only half of what can be seen," Min Tzu said. "I sometimes see better when my eyes are closed. When I am quiet and have closed my eyes, I am not constrained by sensory input from outside myself. Instead, I am receiving input from an interior source."

"That's how it feels to me, as well," added Portales. "It's like I have to close down the windows, the obvious perspectives in my view, in order to see through a different window that only comes into view when I remove the exterior input. I call them my spiritual eyes."

"The Westerners have a saying that at first 'We see dimly and then face to face.'" Tariqah said. "Our external view is dim and incomplete, but inside ourselves is the rest of what we need to see, and even more." He paused before completing his thought. "That is, I suppose, 'the thee in me,' the Allah in me, the God in me, the infinite in me."

"That's true. It's all inside of us," answered Mirissa. "We all have the wiring, the coding, and the seeded design. It is always inside of us so that we can hear it and so that we can see it."

"But those of us in this room already know all this," Chris reminded them. "Our task now is to impart our knowing to those who do not fully know. Our purpose is to reset the pattern for the next two thousand years. We are riding a wave of expansion. Like a pebble thrown into the glassy pond, this is the next ripple in the spiritual growth of mankind. It is bigger than the ripple that produced the pattern called 'church.' And it will take more people to teach the pattern. That is why we are here at Acoma."

"To uncover and teach the next pattern for all of humankind?" asked Amoria.

"Yes," said Tariqah, "but it is more than that. We are here to teach the teachers. Our numbers are too small. To make it easily understood to as many as possible, we must teach a larger group of teachers and send them out to teach."

"And send them out to show others how to teach the pattern, demonstrate the pattern, and symbolize the pattern." Min Tzu then finished with this: "And that's what we will do."

Chapter 8

Symbols

When the other Planners had finally fallen asleep, Malik had quietly made his way into the old church. He got there in time to record the discussion among the Teachers. He was fascinated to hear such clear and purposeful thinking and the level of agreement between these sages and wise ones. Because of their vastly different backgrounds, there was no attempt to put forth a certain religious understanding. There was, however, an intent to uncover and reposition truths and patterns that had no man-made boundaries and no preconceived systems of thinking. They were open to unlimited possibilities. For Malik, it felt like a glimpse of infinity. The entire world of possibility opened up before him, and he was comforted by the knowledge that there might be a new and larger direction for all humankind that could be demonstrated and taught to everyone. He knew there was a new pattern emerging that could serve to expand the conceptual processes of everyone who saw it and understood it.

As Min Tzu finished his comments regarding the mantras and unifying patterns, Malik quietly asked the question, "What does this new pattern look like? I mean, how would you describe it?"

The Teachers knew, of course, that Malik was among them, and all of them turned to see this boy who could not see them. He was sitting apart from them near the door that led to the sleeping quarters at the front of the church. His papers and pens were on his left, and he appeared to have already completed several pages of notes.

Mirissa spoke first. "All patterns eventually become symbols," she started. "The symbol is the shorthand for the pattern, and there have been many patterns and symbols through the ages. First, there was the line, and from it came the club and the arrow and the spear and, eventually, the new concepts of direction and linear thinking."

Malik began writing as fast as he could.

Mirissa continued. "Next, there was the circle, and mankind's recognition of it caused a notable shift. By embracing the symbol pattern of the circle, humankind made certain progress in terms of mechanical discoveries, like the wheel and, later, the pulley and, eventually, the half-circle or the arch. As those discoveries blossomed into even more sophisticated spin-offs, humankind began to understand the conceptual import of the circle. It came to fuel, inspire, and symbolize new ideas, like wholeness and completion and totality."

Then Chris picked up the storyline for Malik. "Another significant pattern discovery was two lines crossed. As an 'X' or 'T,' two lines crossed came to symbolize the basic building-block principle of structure and the use of opposing forces to provide support. From the two lines crossed came all manner of discovery in terms of architecture, transportation, and more weaponry. It eventually led to triangulation and math and geometry. It moved mankind forward even further. Unfortunately, perhaps, it also became a device for torture and death. Almost everyone used it for that, but the Romans made it famous, and two lines crossed came to be known simply as 'the cross.'"

"I didn't like that one," Mirissa laughed.

"You know, I never quite understood why the Western religions made that their symbol," Tariqah interjected. "Why would anyone want to use a symbol of death and barbarism as their calling card?"

"Oh, come on, Tariqah. It was a rallying point," Amoria answered. "It was brilliant marketing in a way, and it was necessary for a while, especially in a political sense. It was simple and easy to demonstrate or reproduce. People could rally around it and easily express their dislike for the heavy-handed authority figures that used the cross to torture and kill."

"But unlike so many symbols, it became frozen in time," Mirissa said pensively. "The symbol of the fish would have been so much truer to the next progression. It would have been better if the cross had died."

"I liked the fish, too," offered Min Tzu. "But it was only half of the next pattern."

"That's right, but it was a necessary step in pattern recognition," Carlos Portales said. "The sign of the fish is exactly one half of the infinity pattern. That's the pattern completion that intrigues me the most."

"Well, after several generations, the infinity symbol has expanded the thinking of humankind," Tariqah agreed. "The idea of unlimited scale and unlimited potential has served to increase the vision for most people." Then Tariqah placed his favorite into the conversation. "I'm partial to the spiral. Like a dervish or a tornado or a typhoon, the spiral is a very active pattern. It feels powerful to me, and it feels infinite, too."

"The spiral," Chris continued "is based on the circle, but it is so much more. Like the sunflower or the movement of water down a drain, the spiral has vertical dimension to it, too. It braids its way to its end result. That results in circular action plus vertical action—two actions simultaneously. I think the spiral is a symbol that is starting to advance the thinking, too"

"Right, the fish symbol is half of the symbol for infinity and the spiral symbol is a more advanced characterization of the circle. The two of them, when they are combined, are the root symbols of the next pattern," Mirissa said.

"My sense of it," Amoria tried to explain to Malik, "is that all the opposites disappear into this larger pattern. No matter what the opposites may be—productive and nonproductive, good and bad, light and dark, fear and love, even life and death—they are all merged together in a single flowing dynamic that is braided together like Min Tzu's ponytail."

"That's what I sense, too," Min Tzu confirmed. "The infinite spiral pattern includes all those historic phenomena, from line to cross to circle to spiral and on to infinity. Even so, it's not the parts that are important but the combined progression through time of those parts in motion. Motion creates a totality, and that's all that ultimately matters: the totality."

Chris added, "When the parts are no longer the focus and the mind is focused on the larger pattern instead, the spiral energy can be seen in its entirety. But there is, I think, one more concept to include in this discussion for Malik." He sat silently for a moment in order to gather his thoughts and, more importantly, devise a simple way to express them. "This spiraling infinity has at its core what some have called the elementary dynamic of progress. First, there is what is. Then there is a natural tendency to discern and promulgate its opposite, or what isn't. Finally, when these two have merged together, there is a new and improved *what is*."

"So this is a description of progress?" Malik asked.

"Yes, or better said, the force pattern behind progress," Amoria responded. "It is as inevitable as the sunrise. There will always be what is, and there will always be what could be, and then there will always be a new creation that results from the merger of the two." She thought for just a moment and added, "It's a pretty simple and ongoing dynamic, really. It never changes direction. It is always forward and can never work any other way."

"The best way I've seen to demonstrate all of these patterns and symbols together is the helix," said Portales, trying to provide a window of understanding through which the blind boy could see. "It's like the human DNA models some of us have seen. The male and female energies join together in a new creation; the old creation meets the new creation, and the outcome moves forward and changes the world forever."

Then Chris spoke what seemed to be the third understanding. "So the end result is a world, a universe, that is ever moving forward, and it is a forward dynamic that cannot be stopped or reversed. It cannot wait, and it cannot pause. All life, all actions, all thoughts, all of everything is driven by and carried on this ever-forward pattern."

"You are right," Min Tzu said. "In this double-helix pattern of possibilities is the integrated, harmonic, and expanding energy of the creation. In this pattern is contained all the patterns. In this revelation is all revelation uncovered and explained and understood and seen."

"This pattern contains all of the accumulated symbols that have helped mankind progress this far," Mirissa agreed. "It has the line, the cross, the circle, the fish, the spiral and the infinity symbols, and, finally, the braided double helix. This symbol is the imprint upon which all people will think and imagine and conceptualize. This, in turn, will lead us forward to even greater awareness and more expanded concepts. These new and larger truths will become known by utilizing the helix pattern as the model for our thoughts and dreams and visions for the next two thousand years."

With that, Amoria, Tariqah, and Mirissa rose up and stretched. Chris and Portales did the same. Min Tzu got up and walked over to Malik. He asked him to stand and took his hand. The seven of them turned and walked toward the door of the church and went out into the moonlight. The Teachers all knew where to go.

"Are we going to see those who have gathered between the mesas?" asked Malik as he searched for confirmation of what he already knew.

Min Tzu just squeezed his hand ever so slightly as he led him north.

"Yes," said Mirissa. "Let's go see who has come to be taught and who is ready to learn."

~　　~　　~

The path off the mesa going north descended almost 360 feet through the boulders and traversed over the crude, man-made steps chiseled into the rock years before. It was a well-worn path a thousand years in the making for just such an occasion as this. It took Malik and the Teachers nearly thirty minutes to descend it. Many of the people between the mesas were asleep in their makeshift bedding, but some were awake even at three in the morning. The soft and persistent humming of the mantra was murmuring its message around the camps like the constant babbling of a rock-strewn stream. Some campfires still glowed in the bright moonlight. People looked at the seven of them as they approached each camp, and thousands of quiet greetings were exchanged as they traveled around.

If Malik could have seen what was going on as they walked through the crowds, he would have understood why most of the greetings were unrecognizable to him. More than that, he would have seen to whom a given greeting was directed. Most of the names were foreign to him. He heard several greetings before he knew one: "Teacher." Then he heard a dozen more before he heard "Wayshower" and "Master," then many more before he recognized "Imam," then "Shaman," then "Wise One." Soon he noticed "Guru," and soon enough thereafter he heard "Light Bearer" and "Mother" and "Rabbi."

Now the greetings were going too fast for Malik to keep up, and more people were being awakened. As the newly awakened added their greetings to the mix, the clamor grew louder and the greetings grew more numerous and went faster still: "Babaji, Krishna, Buddha," then "Rumi, Jesus, Mohammed, and Holy One." Soon, Malik also heard "Abraham, Confucius, Sainted One, and Avatar." And the greetings kept coming as these seven walked through the crowd. Into Malik's ears and heart and mind came every imaginable name for teacher, master, and enlightened one.

Malik's head was spinning, his senses overloaded. He held tightly to Min Tzu's hand. He had no way to write everything down and worried that he couldn't write it anyway, as the hundreds of sacred names and revered designations for these master souls came at him like a torrent of insight and revelation. All the greetings were spoken with respect and joy and adulation. They bespoke the varied cultural and religious backgrounds of the ever-growing crowd. It all became quite a jumble for Malik's ears to hear and his mind to sort.

The Teachers had a reason for showing this to Malik. They were demonstrating that the names were essentially the same. The name chosen by each greeter for these Teachers was not tied to the teacher but was tied, instead, to the greeter. The collective effect on Malik was to show him that the name did not matter. The chosen words and descriptions did not matter half as much as the feelings of respect and humility and openness and reverence they contained. Only the heart in the greeting mattered at all.

The teacher of any truth must have the learner—the open mind that wants more truth. The learner must seek the teacher. He or she must revere and respect the teacher and be open to learning the message of the teacher. Ultimately the two are intertwined into one process, the forward dynamic of knowledge. Ultimately, like all forward progress, it changes, too, and the final progression includes the inevitability that the student will move past the teacher to another process.

The seeming chaos of this experience somehow produced a state of relaxation in Malik. He became aware that the experience of walking through the crowd and hearing all the names was the teaching he was meant to have that night. The common thread in all of this commotion was the realization that there had been thousands of teachers, thousands of enlightened ones, thousands of saints and gurus and sages. He recalled what Jack had observed when they went to the top of Mt. Kahwehstimah. The commotion of the names, the plethora of titles and designations and salutations were like being in the valley with its details, limited sightlines, and narrowed focus. When Malik let go of trying to discern each of these thousand names, they blended into one name, one huge sound. They built for him one tall mountain from which the details were out of focus and unimportant. This mountain let him see it all and gave him the perspective he needed to see it all as one.

Malik now understood that through their many lives, each of the Teachers had taught and written and counseled inside specific and limited frameworks, but he also understood that the drive inside of them to teach and write and counsel was from a single and unlimited frame of reference. This experience also showed him that the drive to learn, expand, and discover was from the same innate dynamic—the inevitable forward progression of humankind. This demonstration for Malik among the people in the crowd brought the point home to him in unmistakable terms. He could now accurately record the third understanding.

When he returned to the mesa top and found his papers and pens, he wrote what he understood; to wit, the teaching and learning of humankind was a constantly forward movement. Stagnated and codified truths from the past were no more than building blocks that no longer moved forward. The truths from previous understandings would continue to be relearned, but they must also be expanded and, like the rings of a tree, they would grow and build into something larger and more useful with each passage of time—a day, a year, a century, or an age.

Malik recorded the third understanding like this: "In that way, all truths are moving forward. If it is not moving forward, it cannot be true."

Chapter 9

The Fourth Morning at Acoma

As the Planners began to stir the following morning, the number of people between the mesas had grown to three or four thousand. Digger was up before sunrise and walked around the entire perimeter of the mesa top in the predawn light. Over the mountains out of Old Mexico, a summer breeze brought clouds from the Pacific Ocean. The clouds were high and flat and scattered. They held no promise of rain, but a little extra humidity felt good on Digger's dry skin.

He stopped just past the natural cistern atop the main mesa and looked down at the ever-gathering collection of people below. Trained to appreciate the differences in peoples from around the world, Digger was impressed by the diversity of this group. He sat on a boulder and pulled out his binoculars. Though the light was not yet full, he could see pretty clearly. As one would expect, there were hundreds of people who appeared to be from the host country; their casual, Western dress made him think they were North American.

But there were people from all over the rest of the world whose dress or skin color or facial characteristics marked them, too. There were Asians of every possible description—from the islands and the plains, from the coasts and the hills. There were Africans from the deserts and Africans from the jungles and from the forests and savannas, too. There were South Americans from the cape and from the isthmus and the highlands in between. There were Muslims from Indonesia and Saudi Arabia, Hindus from the deltas and the foothills of the great mountains. There were Tibetans from the steppe and Mongols from the flats. There were Canadians and Brits, Iraqis and Aussies, Brazilians and French, Malaysians and Swiss. There were Sudanese and Vietnamese and Japanese. There were Italians and Slavs. And there were dozens and dozens of others, as well. Digger likened them to the soups he loved so much and saw that Acoma had become, for this one week, a melting pot of the entire world.

Then he put down the binoculars and looked over the crowd with a wider, less focused eye. From this perspective, the view was wholly different. All he saw was one people in one place seeking one mind. From this place, he could not focus on the details of their differences, for their differences blended together. All Digger saw through this lens was their oneness.

This was even more remarkable to Digger when he remembered that they came here in response to some unexplained stirring inside themselves—a stirring that could not be readily expressed or easily understood. They came to an event that was barely publicized. They interrupted their lives and put down what they were doing for this trip. They created a singular focus that drove them to organize this week in their lives in this way. They demonstrated their dedication—and that impressed Digger the most. It put each one of them into a category of seeking that he could appreciate. Their very presence at Acoma gave him a perspective on them that revealed to him the essence of who they really were.

As he watched, he wondered how many of them had quit jobs or temporarily left their families. He wondered how many of them spent all their savings or borrowed from a relative or sold some property in order to finance the trip. He wondered who had traveled the farthest or had taken the longest time to get to Acoma. He knew there must be rich and poor and those in between. He wondered who had come on foot or bus or car or plane.

Digger wondered how many had fasted as they traveled or fasted after they arrived, and if they did it because they were out of money or because they thought fasting would clear their mind or cleanse their body. He wondered if they were solitary pilgrims, seekers, or initiates. He wondered if they sought the company of sages or the companionship of others on the way. He wondered if they were just searching for spiritual nourishment or for something more.

From atop the mesa, he knew he could not answer these questions, but he supposed that this group was unlike any collection of people ever gathered together before. In the history of the world, as far as Digger knew, anyway, a gathering like this had never taken place. Yes, there had been meetings at the beginning of other ages, but none on this scale. The presence of this many varied and different people gave it power. It gave the gathering promise and it gave it magic.

As he turned to leave his lookout, he glanced beyond the throng to Enchanted Mesa. He thought he knew the story of this mesa from his research and from what Jack had told him, but this morning he saw something he did not expect. As he watched, there appeared a bright shaft of light on the mesa top. As the wind picked up around him, Digger saw a small whirlwind dancing in the beam of light on the top of the empty mesa. The dust particles in the whirlwind were illumined by the light to create a shining, whirling column like nothing Digger had ever witnessed. He stood mesmerized by the scene. He recalled the sand painting from months before and remembered the clouds that had encircled the mesa in that picture. He remembered the yellow column that stretched up to the clouds and beyond. Now as he looked from a mile away, he could also see the wind and light and clouds. Was this the event that had been foretold? Was it just a trial run or a warm-up to that event? Would there be more events like this?

His attention was then drawn to the sounds of the newest mantra from the flats below. He wondered if one of Jack's chants was in progress back at the church, and in a flash, he wondered how a thing becomes enchanted. Does it receive the energy from a chant? Does it somehow become opened up to take in the power of a chant? Perhaps, he speculated, this rock was alive, too, just like the rocks on sacred mountain in the fifth clue. He wondered if the collective recitation of mantras and the chants every day, all day, was producing an effect at this abandoned and fear-filled mesa. Was the old story being transformed? Was it being rewritten? Perhaps he didn't yet know the whole story after all. Maybe the complete story had yet to take place.

When the wind calmed down and the light disappeared as the clouds returned overhead, Digger looked away and then back again. The light and the whirlwind were gone from view. He stayed at the cistern's edge, lost in thought for several minutes. The sun was now rising above the rim of the valley but was still somewhat hidden by the clouds. Digger headed back to the church.

When he got there, preparation for the day was already underway. Jack's early-morning chant was done. The Planners and the Teachers were in discussions regarding the mantra that had been inspired in them during Jack's chant. Min Tzu was speaking as Digger found a bench on which to sit.

"'Help me feel the thee in me' is perfect," Min Tzu began. "First one hears and then one sees and then one feels. I think that is as it should be."

"So do I," echoed Portales. "It's a natural progression."

"Yes, it is," added Chris. "It's a definite forward movement that continues to erase the line of distinction between the 'me' and the 'thee.' Our feelings lead us further into what we hear and see and on to the next natural step in the process."

Amoria added what she knew. "And it will solidify the step for everyone. We remember more intensely when we feel something than when we read it in someone else's writing or when we hear it spoken in someone else's words," she said. "Feeling the connection—I mean really feeling it—is crucial to the eventual understanding."

"Well, that was pretty easy, huh?" Tariqah summed up. "Help me feel the thee in me. Is it too early in the day to take this third mantra to the people down below?" he asked, looking first at Chris and then at Russell Layne.

Chris looked at Russell, too, as if searching for a sign. Russell spread his arms out wide with upturned palms and said nothing. Portales got up and opened the tall, heavy church doors as if to head down to the place between the mesas.

Before he could leave, however, Mirissa said, "Let's try it among ourselves for a while and see if the feeling gets transmitted down to the people without any of us speaking it to them directly."

And so they did. Mirissa started the recitation of the mantra in a soft and measured voice. Again, there were seven syllables, and the recitation each time took seven beats during the measured outflow of air. "Help me feel the thee in me," they all said together as they exhaled. The inhale, without words, took the same seven beats in time. Eventually, some of the Planners and some of the Teachers changed their breathing pattern so that the words were flowing continuously from their collective voice.

The walls of the church began to reverberate with the rhythm of the mantra. The wisdom of it hung in the air. The power of it seemed to flow out the doors, and the truth of it was collected by the breeze and carried over and through the buildings around them on the mesa. It spread as it went, and, soon enough, someone sitting in silence heard it come wafting over the bluff and down to where she was in the crowd below. Like a small, still voice in the early-morning sun, the mantra merged into her meditation, and soon she found herself repeating it over and over again.

Others nearby heard it, too. Perhaps they heard it from this woman, or perhaps they heard it from atop the mesa, or maybe they heard it from within. It did not matter; soon, the mantra for this day was reaching the people. In less than an hour, the thousands between the mesas were lending their voice to those voices in the church.

Mirissa smiled as the mantra now echoed off the walls of the valley around them. Had they been able to hear it, they would have also known that the mantra had gone out from Acoma Valley and into the world as well.

Chapter 10

Teaching the Teachers

After an hour or more, Mirissa and the others stopped, and the church grew silent.

It was Xuan who broke the silence with a question for Min Tzu. "How will we know if we are to be teachers of the expanded vision?" she asked. "None of us are teachers now, except for Jack."

Min Tzu looked at Xuan gently. His compassionate eyes saw her confusion as well as her willingness to understand. "Teachers of the truths that come from this meeting will be different," he said, "because they will not teach a fixed or dogmatic truth. That kind of teacher, unfortunately, tries to teach from his or her own experience to someone who has not yet had the experience. The message is often lost in the translation of misheard words, faulty phrasing, or selective understanding."

"No. No. No!" Amoria interrupted. "I don't think humankind will survive another two thousand years with that kind of teaching. Dogmas that have developed around the world for thousands of years are turning against us right now in one way or another and must be eliminated as quickly as possible."

"That's right," Min Tzu continued, unfazed by the interruption. "The teachers for the next two thousand years must teach understandings and practices not learnings or conclusions that are frozen in time. The understandings and mantras can be done without a teacher. If the insights and practices are done every day, the truth will come to the practitioner without any more from the teacher."

"Exactly!" Portales said. "The understandings and practices are the door. We only need to show them the door and get out of the way."

Tariqah said, "Once the seeker absorbs the understandings and practices the mantras every day, they can merge with the one. No preacher, teacher, shaman, mullah, priest, imam, or guru can take them to that place, anyway." He went on. "When the people realize that there is only one reality and only one creation in which all things happen, there can be a sharing of understanding—a teaching of the mysteries. Until then, teachers are more likely to get in the way of that process."

"Teachers must become more like guides," Chris offered. "The truth is different for all people, but it can only become real in each person by unifying their seeing, their hearing, their feeling, and their knowing from the understanding that is already within them. A teacher is outside of them and can only point the way."

"And the teacher cannot become the message for that one person," Tariqah added. "Each person is a different enactment along the path of the one path and must ultimately teach themselves from their own true heart. They must become the teacher and the student in their own life."

"Each person is in the reality themselves and is not apart from it." This time it was Mirissa speaking, and she went on to say, "Using the practices will lead them to their ultimate identity. The practices and the understandings will be their constant reminder, and, eventually, they will reach the final goal: their ultimate identity."

Mirissa's words always seemed accurate and defining. They often summarized the discussion and sometimes served to end it at the same time. There was often nothing left to add. Aside from her life as the master soul at the last meeting, she had lived and learned a great deal from many other teachings in the years after her experience as Jesus of Nazareth.

Although she was the most recognized master soul in the recorded history of mankind, all the Teachers knew that she had not been the first, and all of them were aware that she was not to be the last. They knew that the memories of the previous Teachers were just missing, not recorded, and so not part of the record. The Teachers realized that the myths and stories and partial truths regarding her and others had led to confusion and misunderstanding. They viewed this meeting as the opportunity to set the record straight again, to wipe the slate clean once more and to simplify it for the next two thousand years.

Chris had been most well known as Krishna. He sat forward on his bench and began to speak. "There is a story of a tower called Babel that tries to explain the thousands of languages now being spoken around the world. It may be a Western story, but its origin does not matter at all; most people have heard it in other traditions, as well."

He looked around the church and saw that everyone was nodding their head in recognition, so he continued. "It has come down in history as some sort of threshold event that changed the world forever, but it was not as it seemed at all. First, it is a story of the one common language that was known by all people at some bygone time. Jack Eaglefeather's chants are spoken in this language, and that is why Jack and his Pueblo were chosen to host this meeting. But it is more than that. The language is a root set of sounds that first require the listener to be in the right frame of mind and heart in order to hear and understand. Though they are not words as we've come to know them, every soul who hears them can understand their message only when they are listening at some very essential place in their being."

"And the words mean nothing?" Xuan asked.

"They mean nothing in terms of words," Chris answered. "They are sounds, sure, but they have rhythm and pattern, too. They can be learned through repetition, but unless they are heard and felt in the right place in each person, they are just so much babble."

"Why do they have power in us?" Thomas inquired.

"Because their message, their power, reaches us at a subconscious level, a level that is beyond words," Chris said.

"So how does this help us as teachers?" Digger inquired.

"It is the perfect teaching, really," Tariqah the Sufi interjected. "It's like the power of gravity, because it doesn't have to be understood as a word or even a concept in order to have a powerful and daily effect on our lives."

"It is like the sunlight," Min Tzu chimed in. "It's always there without having to be explained or understood."

"And it's like water," added Amoria. "Water is essential to who we are and to our ultimate survival, but we don't have to understand it in order to seek it or require it. Every time we hear the common sounds, we are reminded of our common ties to the universe, our common place in the creation, our common link to the rhythms of the world and to all people. The common sounds tie us again to each other. All distinction and difference are stripped away and rendered nonessential."

"And that is the ultimate teaching," Mirissa continued, "teaching without words. There's no language barrier, no misunderstanding, no confusion over definitions or connotations or cultural distinctions."

"Without even knowing it," Portales said, "the listener is taken to that place within himself or herself that hears and sees and feels the essential experience of all things. It doesn't come from a teacher or from some mental construct or some understanding of dogma or rules or a so-called written truth; it is simply a soul-level knowing without words."

Always the archaeologist, Digger then asked, "So why wasn't the Tower of Babel ever completed?"

"Well, it is an allegory or a teaching story first and foremost," Chris answered, "but it is also a story that tells of the future, not just the past. I think it is finally about to be rebuilt here at Acoma." Chris looked out the open church doors to Enchanted Mesa, a mile away. "That mesa to the north of here is a tower, too, and it's been abandoned for centuries, just like the Tower of Babel was abandoned. I've been looking at it every day since I've been here, and there's something about it that draws me to it."

Thomas spoke for the first time. "I think we've all been watching it," he said. "It figures prominently in two things Digger and I saw several months ago. The first was a sand painting done here in a sacred kiva at Acoma. The second was a dirt drawing scratched in the sandstone dust here on the mesa top. I think Enchanted Mesa figures into this meeting somehow."

"I saw it bathed in light this morning before the sun had risen fully," Digger revealed. He said it as though he still didn't believe what he had seen.

"Thomas and I saw it bathed in light the other morning, too," Xuan said.

"I've seen a light around it once this week, too," Jack admitted. "I've never noticed any unexplainable light on that mesa before, and I've lived here most of my life."

"It lights up every time you do one of your chants, Jack," Portales whispered.

"Really?" Jack asked.

"Yes, every single time. I don't know what to make of it yet, either."

"You guys may think I'm crazy," Malik interrupted, "but I've also been hearing and feeling some sort of low, rumbling sound from that direction ever since we arrived, and I don't know what to make of it, either."

"The mesa is a magnet," Mirissa said. "That is why the people know where to go when they arrive. It is drawing them to that area. It is imbued with power. I don't know if they hear it consciously, like Malik, or if they have seen the light, too, but at some level they are drawn to it, that's for sure."

"I noticed this morning that the people between the mesas are spreading out in the direction of that mesa," Digger observed. "I never thought we would have so many people here or that we'd get so close to it."

"I think they will continue to spread that way, Digger," Amoria said.

"So do I," Tariqah added.

"When the area between the mesas is filled up with people," Chris spoke to them again, "and when the mantras are spoken as one voice by all the people, I think there will be an event at Enchanted Mesa like none have ever seen before."

"What kind of event?" Xuan asked, first looking at Chris and then at Mirissa.

"I don't yet know," Mirissa answered.

"Neither do I," Chris said.

"It will be powerful," Tariqah said.

"And spectacular," added Min Tzu.

"And it will be transforming, too," Amoria said with a smile.

"For me," Portales began, "it is always about windows or doors, and I imagine that mesa is a door." Portales looked at Jack before he continued his thought. "Yes, it will be a door of some kind. I don't yet know where this door will lead, but it is my experience that when the mind is unified over one thing and the heart is in agreement, the door can only lead to a good place for all who walk through it."

"Katzimo," Jack muttered under his breath.

"Will it be scary?" Anna asked.

Amoria looked at Anna and said, "It can be scary, Anna, because every door that opens in front of us means that there is a door that is quickly closing behind us. There's no turning back, so it's scary."

Anna smiled sheepishly at Amoria's attempt to alleviate her fears. "I just wish someone else could go through the door before we do and then lead us through." She stammered as she finished, "And they can tell us what they see and hear and feel."

Amoria looked compassionately at Anna and then answered, "No, they can't Anna. For you, or any of us, to uncover our ultimate identity, we must have the direct experience of going through the door ourselves."

"That's right," Chris said, "the only true knowledge is that which we find for ourselves and experience ourselves."

Anna felt her fear subside a little as Mirissa gently spoke to her, too.

"As a part of the forward progression of humankind," Mirissa said, "the forward progress of each individual is the most important aspect. As each one of us moves along the inevitable progression, the whole of humankind moves a little further forward, too."

"If we become satisfied that someone else has done it, we block our innate drive to do it ourselves." Tariqah was speaking now. "The first time I let go of that fear that you are feeling, I felt more liberated and freer than I had ever felt. It was hard to do, but it was at that point that I found my ultimate identity, and that has led me to this point in my evolution."

"I guess I'm still stuck on needing a teacher or an imam or a guru or a priest," Thomas countered. "Why is that?"

Min Tzu offered simply, "Because you think you can avoid doing it yourself."

"Or because you fear it," Chris added. "The truth is that you don't need the teacher anymore, Thomas. You don't need the hero or the saint or the savior, either. At some point they become obstacles in your spiritual path, rather than helpers."

"They become walls instead of doors," Portales said. "None of us can walk through or see through or hear through a wall."

"The mantras and the understandings will give you everything you need," Mirissa reminded them with an assuring tone. "And there will come a time when all who desire to move forward will have mastered the daily use of these tools as the essential first step."

Malik had been writing copious notes all morning and was growing tired when he blurted out, "So is that the understanding for today?"

"I would say the way forward must include experiential knowing," Portales offered.

"I would call it the imperative to pursue experience directly," added Min Tzu.

Russell Layne spoke. "What I hear is that only direct knowing has value in the quest for our ultimate identity."

Jack Eaglefeather nodded in agreement.

"I like all of those," said Mirissa. "Experience is the only knowing we truly remember, anyway. The experience never leaves us once we have known it for ourselves."

Malik wrote all these comments down and promised that he would craft the exact phasing later. Thus, the imperative of experiential knowing was made part of the understandings being developed at Acoma.

Chapter 11

On Top of the World

Early in the morning of the fourth day, Digger and Malik left the church without a word to anyone. After a morning of meditation and contemplation with the Teachers, the rest of the Planners descended the main mesa and went out into the crowd—a crowd that now numbered close to ten thousand.

After milling around with the people in the flats, the Planners were drawn to a part of the crowd near the base of Enchanted Mesa. They edged closer to see what was going on, and as they looked at the rock bluff face of the mesa, they were surprised to see several figures climbing toward the summit. Several hundred people were watching these men and women. There were about twenty climbers in all, making progress in their quest for the top of this long-abandoned tower of rock.

As the Planners neared the launching point for this expedition, they saw Digger and Malik. On the ground near these two, they saw a pile of crystal prisms in the reddish dirt. Xuan recognized them as the ones that were picked up at the entry points to the reservation. As she and the other Planners looked on, they saw Digger loading some of the prisms into the backpack of a dark-skinned man, who then moved toward the boulders at the base of the rock and disappeared from their sight. Some minutes later, he could be seen making his way up the rock.

Then a stout but athletic-looking Asian woman positioned herself in front of Digger, and he began loading her backpack, too. Malik was counting the prisms one by one and placing them where Digger could reach them. After he had loaded twenty prisms into this woman's pack, Digger let her know that it was time and she began her climb, too.

The Planners watched this for several minutes. Then, a woman who looked to be Mediterranean lined up behind a burly-looking man dressed in overalls and the footwear of a farmer. Behind him came a thin man with the wild hair of a Caribbean and then a swarthy man with a turban who was wearing tennis shoes. Lined up behind these four were several more. In that line were the people of the world, and there was no limit to their differences, no question as to their common quest. They all got loaded up with twenty prisms and headed up the rock.

Russell looked at Jack. This was his rock, and it had not been climbed in a thousand years, because he, the Iyatiku at Acoma, and all his predecessors, had deemed it off limits. Russell was conscious of the gift of this meeting place and worried that this impromptu and unauthorized quest might offend Jack or upset the people of the Pueblo. Instead, he was surprised to see a smile on Jack's face.

Jack leaned toward him and whispered, "They've found the trail."

Russell looked at him in disbelief and whispered back, "I thought the trail was wiped out a thousand years ago by the thunderstorm. You mean it is still there?"

"Well, I don't know for sure," Jack answered quietly. "I've never tried to find it. I respected the tradition."

"Will your people be offended by this intrusion?" Russell asked.

"I don't think so, but no Iyatiku I know of has dared to climb it all these years. My father never tried and neither did my grandfather. They both told me the trail could still be found if one knew where to look. They thought it was on the other side of the mesa, not on this side, so I guess they never really knew for sure, themselves. After they showed it to me, I kept the information to myself because the fear of death on this rock still haunts our people."

"So, the Iyatikus have always kept this secret from everyone?" Russell asked.

Before he could answer, Jack's daughter appeared from behind a group of people and saw her father. She approached him cautiously and admitted, "The keeper woman from Jemez Pueblo told me the trail was here, so when Digger and Malik asked if I knew a way to the top, I told them I thought I could find it. Malik is certain that all of the prisms should be gathered together and carried up to the top of the mesa. We've been working on it all morning long. I hope it's okay with you, Father."

It was at that point that Jack realized Sha'wanna was ready to assume the mantel of Iyatiku. She had decided that holding the mesa in fear was no longer necessary or important. To Jack, that seemed like a big first step. He looked at her and decided she was right.

"I think it is time. Yes, it is okay." He then looked up at the almost sheer walls and said, "Is it a difficult climb?"

"I don't know yet," Sha'wanna said. "I'm going up later with a load of prisms, too, and then I'll let you know."

Russell said, "Wait a minute, are you planning to take all of the prisms up there?"

"That's what Malik wants us to do, but I'm not sure why," Sha'wanna answered. "Digger thought it was a good idea, too."

As they talked, Jack surveyed the four-hundred-foot-high mesa from a new perspective—the perspective of possibility, not fear. He had seen the long view of Acoma Pueblo from Kahwehstimah, but the idea of seeing the view from atop this nearby mesa was even more intriguing to him. At the same time, however, it was still foreboding. It flew in the face of everything he had always known and believed. It was like looking into the sun. Though he always wanted to, he feared what might happen.

He looked at Sha'wanna and asked, "When are you going up there?"

"As soon as Digger loads my pack," she answered.

Jack felt the conflict rise inside of him to a level he had never known. He reminded himself that this was forbidden. He wondered what the council would say. He wondered what his father would do. He was tempted to go up there himself, to see for himself. He did not want to hear about it from others.

Sha'wanna was watching him, and he looked at her for a moment, then away from her determined gaze. He shifted nervously from one foot to the other as he hurriedly debated the options in his head. He thought about what had been revealed to him the past few days and wanted to have this experience that only he could have. He realized that his experience would be markedly different from everyone else's—that it would be uniquely his and his alone.

Finally, he declared, "I'm going up there, too. Is there a backpack I can use?"

He looked over at Digger, who produced a backpack and handed it to him. Jack slipped it over his shoulders and turned around so Digger could load it. Sha'wanna put on her backpack and got in line behind her father. Soon, they were loaded and began the climb.

After winding their way through some boulders as big as a car, they came to an impasse, where their way was blocked by a collection of even larger boulders.

"This is where it gets difficult," Sha'wanna said. She bent over and moved some smaller stones on the ground in front of them. This revealed a narrow passageway under the boulders. "We have to remove these packs and crawl through the opening below where these two boulders come together." She immediately removed her load and dropped to her knees. Pushing the pack out in front of her, she crawled through the opening. Jack followed her example, and soon they were on the other side.

They found themselves in a small box canyon with no exit except back from where they had come. Sha'wanna pointed straight up a thirty-foot wall on their right. On top of this wall was a scraggly piñon tree and a rope that dangled down the bluff. Jack recognized the rope as just like ones from his childhood—ropes made by hand at the Pueblo for a thousand years or more. It appeared to be quite old, and he grabbed it with skepticism and gave it a tug. It was still solidly attached. Nevertheless, he looked at Sha'wanna for encouragement.

"Well, Father, we won't get to the top by staying where we are." She reached over and took the rope and looked for the first toehold she could find. She hauled herself up a few feet and then found another toehold to her left. Then she found another, and soon she was up the thirty feet to the base of the tree above. She threw the rope back down to Jack. He repositioned his backpack, grabbed the rope, and followed her route up the bluff.

They then headed west for fifteen or twenty steps on relatively flat ground and began to wend their way through some rocky debris up a slope that wound below a rock overhang. Then they turned up a crease in the bluff and used a tree to hoist themselves onto a ledge. Finally, they were up some one hundred feet above the floor of the valley, and they paused to catch their breath.

Jack looked back to see the view, but the boulders were still blocking their line of sight, and Jack could only see blue sky above them as they crouched on a ledge against the rock wall to rest.

After a few minutes, Sha'wanna rose to her feet and pressed on. After about fifty feet around a slight bend, the narrow ledge ran out, and she angled up and back to the east again. The way wasn't clearly marked, and she went slowly. She searched for signs or footprints of some kind—indicators of where the others had already gone, but in the rocky terrain, evidence was scant. She looked up toward the top of the pinnacle, but the other climbers were obscured from her view. She looked back at Jack as he paused to get his bearings, too.

He moved closer and hesitantly placed his hand on her shoulder. Their eyes met. For the first time, Jack felt a rush of connection, a feeling of fatherhood for Sha'wanna. As they looked up the bluff together, he smiled and softly said to her, "Let me take the lead for a while. After all, an old Indian ought to be able to find the way on his home rock."

Sha'wanna laughed. "Yes, an old Indian should be able to do that."

Jack took off to the west between two boulders and then up a steep incline back to the east. He then had to switch back to the west as they gained altitude. They came across some crudely fashioned steps in the rock, just twelve of them, which formed a hairpin turn around another boulder and back in the other direction. This section of trail then passed between two rock walls for some thirty paces. It was much cooler in these shadows. When they emerged from the shadows, they were climbing again. They were now some two hundred feet above the valley floor. Jack paused to rest again at a wide spot in the trail. He removed his backpack full of prisms.

"Why do you think Malik wants these prisms up to the top?" Sha'wanna asked as she leaned against the bluff.

"I've no idea," he answered, "but he seems to have good instincts." Jack spoke in short, choppy bursts as he tried to catch his breath. "I think we ought to follow them. You must have thought it a good idea, too, or we wouldn't be halfway up this rock."

"Yes, I did. What's the significance of the prisms, anyway?" she asked him.

"Well, one of the clues for this meeting involves another old Indian, a yogi from the subcontinent of India, who was known as Yogananda. He wrote poems and started a kind of religion in California. He used prisms to make his point about the hundreds of religions in the world," Jack recounted. "He said that religions were like the rainbow colors from a prism: all manner of colors on one side but all of them emanating from just a single source on the other side."

Jack withdrew a prism from his backpack and held it up as he examined it. The crystal material felt cool and smooth to his touch. He turned it toward the noonday sun to see what colors it would produce for them. Predictably, the prism produced a wide array of colors that fascinated him and his daughter for a moment or two.

"What does this have to do with this meeting you are in? I mean, what does it mean here at Acoma?" Sha'wanna asked.

"I've come to believe that the rainbow may be beautiful, but it is not the real story. It's like an illusion or a secondhand story. The real story is the light that makes the rainbow in the first place," Jack answered.

"Yes, but the real light will blind you, won't it?" Sha'wanna challenged.

"Perhaps it will," Jack responded pensively, "but the colors of the rainbow have blinded us in a different way for too long now. I think the Teachers are teaching us new ways to see the light directly, so the indirect and misleading lights of the rainbow religions don't confuse us anymore."

Sha'wanna heard these words but looked at her father in disbelief. "You think that can be taught?" she asked.

"Yes, I do," he said quietly. "These Teachers, they have a way about them. It is clear to all of us that they are true masters indeed." Jack put the prism back in the pack, tied off the flap, and looked again up to the top of the mesa. "Right now, though, we better keep going. I hear more carriers coming up behind us."

They started out again—west under an overhanging rock shelf, then east, then a switchback to the west again. They moved up a crevice in the bluff, where they found one stunted and solitary pine. After working their way along another ledge, they neared the top. They heard the people already on the top talking among themselves. After they changed directions two more times and ascended the final rise, they, too, scrambled to the top.

Jack stopped and looked in awe at what he saw. He dropped his pack as he looked to the north and then to the south. The panorama across the valley of his life was unending. He didn't know where to look first. There was Kahwehstimah, the guidepost of his life to the north. There was Acoma Mesa, the shelter of his existence to the south. There were the canyons and mesas that formed the perimeter of the valley and the farmlands in between that provided his food. He looked east and then west. His view was not obstructed, and he could see clearly as he slowly turned in a circle to his right. The high noon sun rained its bright light upon him, and there was nothing between it and him. There was no shade to be found, no cloud under which to take refuge, no wind to distract him from the sun's summer heat, and nothing to diffuse the light. Never had Jack seen it so clear. He smiled. A feeling of magnificence and awe overwhelmed him. He wanted to laugh out loud, but the moment seemed too sacred for laughter.

"Katzimo! Katzimo!" he whispered under his breath. His slow, circular turning continued, but now he felt an urge from within to do even more. He took a few tentative steps and then whirled around to look behind him and then whirled again to look to his left. Soon, his whirling turned into spinning like a top and dancing like a dervish. He hollered "Katzimo!" at the top of his lungs and then did it again and again. Like a frisky young colt, Jack ran and jumped and played on this rock.

He felt like a conqueror. He was atop the largest symbol of fear that his people had ever conceived, one they had always known. Here he was, the Iyatiku of Acoma, the keeper of the secret, the promoter of fear, the leader of superstition, the protector of the misunderstood and the guardian of limits. Here he was atop Enchanted Mesa.

By his presence on the mesa, he tossed aside the very things that underpinned those roles: the traditions and the unfounded fears. By being on this rock, he threw away that which he hadn't dared throw away before. He repudiated the history of all he thought he knew. He suddenly understood the mysteries that he thought were beyond his understanding. He no longer accepted a man-made limit for himself or his people.

More than that, he had not been instructed in these changes. He hadn't been told or taught that he ought to make them. He hadn't thought of them or verbalized them. He was simply living these new understandings. He climbed the mesa. He was poised on the precipice. He looked in every direction. His blinders had been ripped from him like a pair of useless glasses. He became one with everything he could see and feel and hear and smell. He was, for the first time in his life, larger than Iyatiku. He was free of his title. He was unleashed from his small view of the world. He had transcended his beliefs—beliefs that had become more limiting and less comforting with every passing day of the last year. Like an enslaved man loosed of his shackles for the very first time, he felt light and free. It made him want to dance and jump and celebrate some more.

So he did.

Chapter 12

A New Mesa

The top of Enchanted Mesa was largely flat and level, but the ground was uneven. It was about fifteen hundred feet long from east to west and not much more than four hundred feet wide from north to south. Like the Acoma Mesa, with which Jack was so familiar, this mesa also had a depression in the undulating rock surface that held rain water for most of the year. This natural cistern was almost full from rain that had fallen the week before, and Jack was drawn to it as his celebration of newfound freedom wound to a close.

Sha'wanna and the others had unloaded their prisms in a couple of random piles around the mesa. Some of the carriers were starting back down to get more prisms, and the ones who had come up behind Jack and Sha'wanna were now arriving and unloading.

Others down below had taken over for Digger and Malik so they could follow Jack and Sha'wanna. Malik's blindness made the going slower than for the rest, but Digger stayed with him, and with only an hour left in the day, the two of them arrived at the top. Like everyone else, Digger was taken by the unlimited view. Jack went over to Malik and quietly spoke to him as he was getting his bearings.

"Bringing these prisms up here was your idea, huh?" Jack whispered. "Do you have any idea what should be done with them now?"

Malik answered quietly. "I think so, but first I must feel this place out a little. Which way is the easternmost edge, Jack?"

"It's straight ahead," Jack answered as he turned Malik to the east.

Malik extended his arm. "Will you help me over there?" he requested.

Jack led him to the edge of the mesa top. Malik lifted his head and stretched his arms out to the sides. When he did, a sudden burst of wind rose up, and they were both blown back away from the edge a couple of feet. Malik wasn't fazed by this gust, and Jack watched as he regained his balance, took a deep breath, and absorbed all the energy this wind brought his way. After a moment, the wind died back down. Malik smiled and seemed satisfied.

"Now can you take me to the northern edge?" he asked and extended his arm again. Jack took it, and after they were turned around, he led him to the northernmost edge, near the center of the rock.

Again, when they arrived, the wind kicked up. Malik seemed to measure it and absorb it unto himself as he had done on the eastern edge. His nostrils flared as he breathed it in and smelled it a couple of times. He felt its impact on his outstretched arms and felt it as it blew his unkempt hair around his face. Jack watched with curiosity but did not find Malik's behavior unusual. When Malik was satisfied, he asked to be taken west, where he once again measured a new burst of wind and repeated his previous actions. He remembered what his father had taught him about reading the wind, and now he was doing it on his own.

Finally, Jack knew to lead him south, to the edge where they had all first attained the summit. Here, Malik took in of another burst of wind and lingered a moment, as if to process what he learned.

"I smell water," he said. He then turned to Jack and asked, "Where is the center point on this mesa, can you tell?"

Jack surveyed the entire top and quickly realized that the natural water cistern looked as close to the center of the mesa as could be determined without measurements and equipment.

"There's a depression in the rock where water has collected. That looks to be the center, or pretty close, anyway," Jack answered.

"How big is the water?"

"About forty feet across both ways and pretty much a circular shape."

"That will be the center point of the prism layout," said Malik. "There must be two circles of prisms stretching east and west that use the water circle as their point of intersection, like the figure eight."

Digger came over and overheard Malik's instructions. "How big should the two prism circles be, Malik?" he interjected.

"As big as you can make them," Malik answered decisively. "And it will take every prism we have to complete it properly."

"We ordered twelve thousand prisms, and all of them were picked up as people were entering the reservation. How many were re-collected down below before we left?" Digger asked.

"We had most of them, I think. There may be some that are still uncollected," Malik answered. "Complete the two circles as best you can. We could have it completed by morning if we find enough carriers to get them all up here tonight."

He thought for a moment and then added, "Leave the gap for the missing prisms on the south side nearest the trail."

With that directive, Digger and Jack looked at each other, and then Jack turned to find Sha'wanna. He saw her near the trail that led back down to the bottom and began walking toward her and picked up his empty pack. Digger stayed behind with Malik, but soon everyone else had begun the descent back to the flats below.

The mesa top was now empty except for the two of them, and Digger tried to envision the prism layout as dusk came upon them. An almost-full moon began its ascent in the east to light the way for the night of work ahead.

When Jack and Sha'wanna started back down and stopped for the bird's-eye view of the crowd between the mesas, they guessed the crowd to number about fifteen thousand, maybe more. After a few minutes of descent, Sha'wanna posed a question to Jack.

"Why is it always harder going downhill? I mean, you'd think it would be easier."

Jack reflected for a moment as he caught his breath and then offered his response.

"I think it is more deceptive than one would think. First, there are the physical explanations—different muscles being used and more speed being generated. Then there's the impact of each step; each descending landing has more speed and more weight. That means more opportunity to lose one's balance and fall. The fall then adds a lot of speed, and control is completely lost. That's one explanation," Jack said.

The teacher in him was so easily called forth, and he was beginning to feel as though he had more to teach with each passing day of this meeting. He was beginning to see new truths about his world, and he also knew he was partly responsible for teaching Sha'wanna all he could about becoming the Iyatiku at Acoma.

"There may be an even larger understanding in this. If going up is actually easier, what if going up teaches that we are designed to always travel up or forward or higher? The measured, deliberate, careful ascent is perfect. It strains and tires us, but it feels right. The chance of falling out of control is almost eliminated. One is facing the ascent, almost embracing the rock on the way up, so it feels connected and right. On the way down, one is facing the other way. One's back is to the mountain, and a disconnection takes place. There is no longer any embrace."

"Yeah, I guess that's true," Sha'wanna replied, "but you can't go uphill without also having to go downhill. It seems like at the end of one's life, the uphills and the downhills would be just about even, wouldn't they?"

"Good observation," Jack laughed. "I think what I'm saying is on a different level. I don't know for sure, but what if part of our genetic code includes the imprint, the seed, to always be compelled in a forward direction? No, wait—an upward direction, perhaps. Or maybe outward is a better word. Yeah, outward," he repeated as if to give it emphasis. "Outside ourselves to discover more than what we know, and upward to our vision, maybe that's it—all of them."

"As opposed to what?"

"Well, downward or inward or stuck. Reduced and not expanded. You know, reduced by fears and secrets and limits that we've imposed on ourselves or had imposed on us by others."

"But these limits provide us comforts, too."

"Yes, and satisfaction, complacency, habits, and traps," Jack replied.

"So you're saying that our genetic imprint includes a drive to expand? Is that it?" Sha'wanna asked.

"Yes, and a drive to not be comfortable or habit driven," Jack answered. "The idea that going up is surprisingly easier than going down demonstrates that imprint," he concluded. "Maybe it's a clue. It reinforces a continual need to know more, see more, hear more, and feel more of the infinity around us and within us. We must be moving forward and upward in order to find it and know it within ourselves. Maybe our natural affinity is to keep searching for the mountaintop."

When they finally reached the flats, the rest of the Planners were loading backpacks for another group of carriers. All of them, including Xuan and Thomas, decided they also wanted to experience the Enchanted Mesa, and, along with Russell and Anna, they prepared to strap on a pack and go to the top with the fifty who were already loaded up.

The moon had ascended higher in the sky. Its red and magnified orb had given way to its more familiar yellow self.

Xuan asked, "Do we have enough light to make this climb?"

"We'll have this moonlight until about four in the morning," Jack answered, "and I think it is enough."

The next group was about to depart when Portales stepped up and declared himself ready to lead the way. "I am a window," he reminded the Planners. "I will know the way in this much light." With that, he grabbed a load of prisms, turned toward the rock, and took off slowly for the top.

Jack and Sha'wanna watched them leave and then turned to go back through the crowd to the church. Before they could go very far, Jack spotted and acknowledged the rest of the Teachers nearby.

Sha'wanna did not know who they were and glanced at Jack. Before he could introduce her to them, she touched his arm and whispered, "I've got to go back to the other mesa for a while."

"Yes, that's fine," he said.

She excused herself as Tariqah sat down at the base of a boulder. Soon, Mirissa, Chris, Min Tzu, and Amoria also found seats on rocks or on the ground, while Jack remained standing. As the crowds inched in around them, the late evening meditation and discussion began.

Jack started, "My daughter and I found ourselves talking about genetic imprints on our way down the mountain. Can you Teachers explain the importance of imprints to me?" He sat down in the circle of teachers.

Tariqah was the first to address the question. "It's no real secret anywhere in the world that mustard seeds become mustard plants, and dandelion puffs become dandelions, and acorns become oaks, and so on and so on." He paused for moment and looked around the moonlit circle. "So, it's not too big a leap to presume that human beings must also have genetic destinies, too."

He was about to continue when Min Tzu laughed. "So I should have been an oak tree?"

"No, you look more like a dandelion," laughed Chris.

Tariqah chuckled lightly and then went on. "We all know the obvious human genetic imprints, like size, shape, skin color, eye color, and all that. Less obvious are the thousands of genetic imprints about which we do not know. Some of these unknown imprints probably include things like motive, direction, drive, and who knows what else. Maybe things like purpose or fairness or generosity are in there somewhere, as well." He paused and seemed to have reached the end of his initial answer, so Min Tzu offered his insights.

"The investigations of genetic phenomena by the scientific community are just beginning, and the likely discoveries over the next hundred years will be as expansive as the knowledge explosion of the past hundred years," Min Tzu started. "What we're talking about here may not be physical genetics but some other kind of imprinting. The best way I can explain it for myself is that I'm on an upward spiral of understanding, and there's some kind of imperative in me to continue. When I recognize a new understanding, it spurs me on to find another one, or the next one, and then another one, and then another one."

Chris interjected, "So it's not so much about the understandings we come to discover but that we continue chasing the understandings and discoveries that result. Is that it?"

"Yes. I think so," Amoria agreed. "Our seeded imprint is to continually reach for the infinite. It is our highest innate motivation, and it means we must imagine what each next understanding looks like so we can recognize it when it presents itself."

"And we have to know how to seek it and where to look for it," Chris added.

Mirissa spoke. "I think this meeting at Acoma is meant to uncover the secret of seeking and, further, to uncover how to teach the secret of seeking," she said. "If everyone knows the mantras that set the mind and heart into proper relation, then they will know how to seek. If properly positioned and understood, the questions of where to seek and how to seek become self-revealing."

"Have we gotten to that part of the learning in this meeting yet?" asked Tariqah.

"I think we've started," Chris answered slowly. "The expansions and new mental constructs are the mental or mindful part of the process, and …"

Amoria finished the sentence for him, "… the mantras are the heart portion of the process."

"And the merger of the two, the braiding of heart and mind, becomes the gateway through which unlimited understanding can take place and the ultimate identity of each person can be uncovered," Mirissa added.

"And finding this gateway every day is the ultimate imprint for every human being," Tariqah concluded. "We are designed to live in the wholeness of understanding that the gateway reveals every day."

"Truths will come from this seeking," Jack surmised.

"Yes, they will," Amoria answered, "but the truths and facts and discoveries will no longer get turned into beliefs and conclusions around which people will build religions or be encouraged to form limiting mindsets. Our teachings are just the tools and how to use them. They are the daily bread or morning meditation. If not revitalized each day, the discoveries become stagnated. Paying homage to stagnant and non-vital discoveries is not life sustaining."

"That is so right," said Chris. "Once enough people can accept that the infinite is where they live, and can learn how to consciously live there, too, the tools will just be tools—and they will be made available to everyone, with no strings attached."

"No strings," Amoria repeated.

"No strings at all," Tariqah and Chris answered together.

"None!" Mirissa echoed. "Everyone is designed to unfold their imprint, and their seeded design will unfold for each of them within the understandings. Our only job as teachers will be to show them the tools and point them to the infinite."

Jack looked around and remembered that Malik wasn't here to write this all down. It was now past midnight, and the meetings officially entered the fifth day.

Usually, Malik also provided the wording for the mantra each day. Jack was not sure what to do in this regard as he posed the next question. "What is the mantra for the fifth day?"

Min Tzu answered quickly, for he had been wondering about it, too. "The next progression is 'Help me be the thee in me.'"

"Perfect!" exclaimed Amoria. "Find your seeded design within the infinite—and strive to be all of it you can be."

"Yes, it is perfect," Mirissa stated quietly. She turned to the part of the crowd seated directly behind her and repeated the mantra to them, using her arms to signal that it should be spread around. "Help me be the thee in me. Help me be the thee in me," she said.

She turned around to again face the other Teachers encircling her. "It's time to go back to the church for one or two more conversations."

Chapter 13

Laying Out the Prisms

When the teachers went back to the church, Jack stayed behind to help with the now-urgent task of getting the rest of the prisms to the top of Enchanted Mesa. The newest mantra resounded through the Acoma Valley as some fifteen thousand seekers repeated it in quiet and steady unison. Jack helped load the prisms for the next group of fifty as others collected the prisms that were being turned in from those who had picked them up at the entrances.

The moonlit ascents went well enough. A pattern developed so that when one group of fifty was on its way back down, they spread themselves out along the trail to provide guidance for the next ones coming up, and soon the next string of carriers came along. When that group unloaded and came back down, they positioned themselves where the others had been and released them to finish the descent and reload for another trip. This pattern would repeat all night long.

When all the others were gone back down, the mesa was empty except for the Planners. Of them, only Jack was absent. About two thousand prisms were now on top of the mesa.

Thomas looked at the piles and then at Xuan. Malik and the others were at the other end of the mesa top. She seemed to be in a trance of sorts as she surveyed the scene.

"I wonder what Malik's prism layout will look like after all twelve thousand are in place," he said.

"It will look incredible!" she whispered. Still entranced, she stared in awe and imagined it completed in her mind's eye. Her soft voice held so much wonder that she didn't need to speak very loudly; the intonation conveyed all that she felt and all that she saw. "I can imagine it even before it is all put together." She leaned closer to him and whispered again, "Thomas, can you imagine it?"

"No, not really," he said.

"Oh, darling, look at the piles of prisms. Look at the glow that is coming off just these first two thousand or so!" Xuan's whisper grew louder and more insistent. "It's like two thousand candles or two thousand stars in the sky. Do you see it yet?"

Thomas couldn't see much more than a few piles of crystal prisms. He looked at Xuan and saw the amazement in her eyes as she gazed upon them. He tried to imagine what she was describing but he couldn't see it yet.

"Once you can see the glow of these first two thousand or so—and they are not even in alignment with Malik's pattern yet—then it's just as matter of seeing that same thing multiplied six times and enhanced to its fullest by being properly positioned," she explained.

Digger left the others and approached the two of them. He was drawn into Xuan's gaze. He looked at Thomas and then at the piles of prisms and then back at Xuan.

"Malik told us to line these up around the water," Digger said. "I'm not seeing what he wants. Do you two have any idea, because we've only got a few hours to get it done?" He kept looking at the prisms and back at Xuan, who appeared to be in a trance. Then he said, "You do have an idea of what he wants, don't you, Xuan?" She didn't answer him at first. "Xuan?"

She shook herself back into the moment and looked at Digger with a surprised sort of smile. She spoke in a quiet, awestruck voice again. "Yes, Digger, I see exactly what it looks like. It's going to be incredible!"

Now Russell Layne joined the three of them and said, "Then lead the way, Xuan. Tell us what we need to do."

With that, she took charge and pointed to the east, saying, "Let's start over there past the water and work back this way."

She looked again at the pattern so clearly impressed in her imagiception, laid it out in her mind's eye on the mesa, and spotted a pebble on the far side of the water that she used to mark the exact place where the pattern would begin. She walked over to one of the piles, took a prism in each hand, and headed toward the pebble. She strode purposefully east, past the water, and stopped about two hundred feet away while the others stood and watched. She turned and faced the water, crouched, and placed one prism on the ground where the pebble had been undisturbed for a thousand years. Xuan placed the other prism next to the first and looked up at Anna. She beckoned to her with her eyes, and Anna grabbed two prisms, too, and headed toward the place where Xuan was still fussing with the placement of the initial two.

Anna couldn't yet see the pattern, so she handed her prisms to Xuan, who took them and began to find their place. Soon, Thomas walked up with two more prisms, and Russell came right behind him with four. Anna followed with two more. Digger picked up two and gave them to Malik, then grabbed two more and got Malik started in the right direction. Not a word was spoken.

Xuan concentrated intently as she imagined the pattern again and again, then duplicated it on the ground at her feet. The rest of the Planners went back and forth from the piles to where Xuan had begun to lay out the pattern. Except for Russell, they all carried two prisms at a time. He carried four; his hands were large anyway, and two prisms in each hand felt natural to him. Even Malik continued to help, though it was not easy for him. Once, he almost walked into the water, but Digger saw it before it happened, hollered as he ran over to grab him, and averted a mishap.

While this was taking place, Portales appeared over the last rise. He was on the Enchanted Mesa for the very first time. The moonlight afforded enough light for a muted view of the valley, but he only paused a moment to enjoy it.

Right behind him, the rest of his group of fifty carriers arrived, and Digger showed them where to pile the next thousand prisms. Portales unloaded his prisms and uttered his first words since arriving at the top.

"This is a door like I have never seen before, but it is a door—that's for sure!" He turned around and surveyed the scene. "That water there, that is the keyhole to the door," he said. "Xuan must be working on the key."

He walked over to her and saw the emerging pattern of the prism layout. He could easily see the whole pattern, and even more. He knelt down next to Xuan and looked at the water, now just a hundred feet away.

Xuan stopped what she was doing for a moment, lifted her head, and brushed back the hair from her face. The vision she had seen was still there to guide her.

Portales whispered, "Do you see where the final seven prisms will go?"

Xuan looked at the pattern in her mind's eye and saw the exact spot into which the remaining prisms would fit. She nodded in response to Portales's question.

"Good," he said. "Sometimes, what is not there is just as visible as what is there. Do you see the hole into which the key will fit?"

"Yes," she answered.

"Great! The key has no place without the hole. The hole has no purpose without the key."

Xuan looked at Portales and smiled. "You confirm what I am imagining," she said. "You really are a window for all of us."

"When you begin your teaching, you will become a window, too," Portales replied.

"I believe that," Xuan responded. "I really do."

"Actually," he said, "you are a window already." He touched her on the fore-head, smiled as he stood up, and began to walk toward the trailhead. He turned back, looked at Xuan as she resumed placing prisms, and looked at the keyhole again. As he approached the edge, the other carriers who had come up with him began to gather around him for the descent. The moon was high, and all of them were soon on their way back down.

At the base of the mesa, Jack was preparing to ascend with the next group of carriers when Chris joined them, too. He was quickly fitted with a pack and loaded up with prisms as Jack reached the crawling space below the first two boulders. Chris fell into place at the back of the line, and up they went.

Chris could readily see the pattern of the ascent as he traversed it himself and saw how it corresponded to the expansions they were uncovering. Crawling through the gap between the rocks required humility. The ongoing line of carriers became the one force. Moving slowly up the sides of the mesa was an undeniable forward progression. Taking the steps to the top was the only manner in which the top could be attained. Following the trail was like following the illumined imprint. In the simple act of ascending this mesa, they were all living the five understandings revealed so far. Later that day, the sixth expansion would also be known. Chris saw it all unfolding as he came up to the hundred-foot resting place, and he knew that it was right.

At the top, Xuan and the rest of the Planners were now finished placing the first three thousand prisms. Initially, the rest of the Planners could only hand more prisms to Xuan, because they could not yet see the pattern. When she had placed enough prisms that the pattern became apparent to all of them, too, they all began to work in pairs. Thomas worked with Xuan and knelt down beside her to help as she started on the fourth thousand. Jack's group was en route with the fifth thousand as they talked quietly together.

"The last day is getting awfully close," Thomas began. "I still have no idea what will happen to us."

"Me neither, but I'm not afraid of it any more," Xuan admitted as she looked up from her work. "I'm actually looking forward to being a teacher, because I feel like we are being prepared so well for it. I'm just not sure where the teaching will take place for you and me."

"So you don't think it will be the end of the world, then?" Thomas asked.

"Yes, it will be the end of the world in some ways," she answered, "and it will be the beginning of a new world, too."

"What about you and me?" Thomas implored as their eyes locked together.

"I hope we end up teaching together somewhere," she confessed, "but I don't yet have any idea what that will mean. You and I as lovers may come to end, I suppose." She looked away for a moment and then looked back at Thomas. "If that happens, though, I will always know that without you, none of this would have been possible for me."

"Or me," Thomas said. "I wouldn't have been open to my own awakening." He handed her a prism and watched as she began to move it into position.

"And I wouldn't have uncovered my willingness to go forward or expand my life," Xuan replied as she fumbled with the prism and moved it around in the dirt. "We may have already served our purpose with each other, and now we will simply move on." Even as she said those words Xuan regretted them, but the words also served as a reminder to keep moving forward and freed her up to consider a larger future than she could have previously imagined. Regret or not, it was too late to stop imagining.

The prism was in place, and she reached toward Thomas for another.

"So you don't have any doubts?" he asked as he gave her the last one he had brought to her.

"No, that's not it. I just think I've come too far down this road to turn back. I am totally focused on what lies ahead, not what lies behind. I am free from so many things in my past. I can't go back."

"I'm still split," Thomas said. "I see a future as a teacher, but I can't quit thinking of the past that includes being a father to my boys. Those boys are a future, too." He stood up to go get some more prisms. "Maybe it's easier for you, Xuan."

"Well, I've always thought we were in this together. That's the future, isn't it?" She looked at him again and saw the signs of struggle in his face. "Oh, Thomas, I know it's harder for you but it's easy for me." She smiled at him wistfully and lightly touched his arm.

He offered a thin smile, took a deep breath as if to reset his resolve, and then looked around for more prisms.

Xuan watched as he headed for the nearest pile and then saw Jack's arriving group of carriers. Soon, the new loads of prisms were unpacked, and he and Xuan were busy again.

~   ~   ~

With Jack's arrival up top, all the Planners were on Enchanted Mesa. The sixth day arrived as midnight came and went, and the moon moved into the western half of the sky. More carriers loaded up more prisms down below. The mantra resounded again and again through the valley like a drumming in the night. Thousands more people streamed onto the reservation and joined the crowds below. Everything was happening right on schedule, but no one knew what the schedule was. The Planners were accustomed to surrendering to their uncertainty; they had learned to simply follow the flow of one moment into the next. There was no reason to think that it should be any other way.

When the rest of Jack's group had unloaded and headed back down off the mesa, Jack stayed behind. Malik asked Digger whether only the Planners remained and, if so, if he would gather them together for a meeting. Digger answered yes, and they all joined together near Xuan and Thomas. After a few moments, quiet came upon them.

In Jack, as it had happened many times before, the urge to begin one of his ancient chants welled up inside of him again. It was not an urge that he ever denied, but the urge only seemed to come upon him when denying it was not an option. He always seemed to be at a place where he could respond to the urge, and he could not remember a time when he hadn't responded.

He slowly felt the words tumble out of him, sounds that he knew and yet did not know. The sounds began soft and low and slow. He soon knew that it was a chant he had never uttered before. It had some of the usual sounds, but they were connected in an altogether unfamiliar pattern. After a while, the Planners quietly chanted alongside him.

Malik had not heard this chant before, either, and yearned to write it down, but a visual sense of the words did not come to him. He soon fell into the rhythm and pace of it and was mesmerized by the soothing sound of Jack's voice.

After a while, without stopping the chant, Jack stood up and picked up a prism. He walked over a couple of steps and placed it in the pattern. Russell watched and then did the same. Then Anna followed their examples. The chant continued as Xuan and Thomas and Digger picked up prisms from the newest pile on the mesa and placed them in the pattern as well.

Malik heard them shuffling around and surmised what was going on. He wondered if the mesa would awaken with its rumbling sound while this chant was unfolding; he quit chanting so he could listen. He sat motionless for a while. He did not hear the rumbling that he had heard before, so he went back to chanting and imagined the prisms all laid out as he had prescribed. He knew what the pattern would look like—like the infinity symbol—and he was sure that it was right. The breeze blew across the mesa, the moon was high in the sky, and Malik reveled in the process as it was being created around him.

The new chant continued, and the prism pattern filled out, one prism at a time. Anna and Russell worked together, as did Digger and Jack. Everyone followed Xuan's lead, and the work went quickly.

After a while, footsteps interrupted their reverie. Over the crest of the mesa came the Teachers. There was Mirissa, who had once been known as Jesus. There was Min Tzu, who had once walked with Buddha. Behind him was Chris, and in his right hand he carried the flute of Krishna. Amoria followed, graceful and elegant and dressed like a Navajo chieftain. Tariqah, the Sufi, came winding up slowly behind her, and Portales walked up last and looked down the trail to confirm there was no one else. All of them were drawn to the water, which Portales had identified as the keyhole waiting for the key. Malik sat near the cistern full of water.

Chris walked up slowly to Malik, knelt down, and from his shirt withdrew a prism. He gave it to the blind boy. To the rest, it looked like all the other prisms, but Chris whispered something to Malik, and Malik held it tight to his chest as he smiled and tried to look in Chris's direction. Chris patted him on the back and stood back up to full height as the Teachers gathered around them.

Speaking to them all, Chris said, "It is not yet time for these last few prisms, but Malik now has his for when the time is right."

As the Teachers looked over the mesa top, they heard the Planners chanting softly and working in pairs to lay out the prisms. They soon joined the chant, a chant they had all heard before, and all of them smiled as it resonated within them and touched their hearts. Soon, each of them picked up prisms, too, and began to help.

Eventually, more carriers came to the top with the next load of prisms to be placed around the water. In a short time, they were in place. The pattern was halfway completed.

~   ~   ~

For a moment, there were no more prisms to position, and the Planners and Teachers waited for the next group of carriers as they watched the last group depart. They completely encircled the cistern, spaced themselves along the water's edge, and continued to softly chant the unknown sounds as they sat down.

From his place in the circle, it was Malik who finally broke the murmuring reverie.

"I'm still frustrated that I cannot write these chants," he said. "I've tried several times, but no letters come to mind. I know no words to fit these sounds."

It was Tariqah who attempted an answer. "I think it is okay that you cannot write them. I do not think they are meant to be written."

"Now that you bring it up, I've never seen them written. I have only heard them," Chris confirmed. "There are seven of them, I think, but I've never seen them written or titled or listed, anywhere."

"How will we teach them if we can't write them down for reference?" Xuan asked.

"We can't hope to memorize all of them, can we?" Thomas added.

"I suppose you could," Amoria said, "but that might be missing the point. Once they are written, they lose some of their energy. Reading them does not bring them to life. Saying them aloud from the heart is the only way to keep them vital, the only way to give them life and impart them to another."

"I think so, too," added Min Tzu, "but even then, they cannot be imparted as a teacher to a student or a priest to a congregation or an imam to his followers. They must be shared at some level where the heart and mind are already prepared to receive the sounds and not the words."

"There is another way to learn them," said Portales. He was looking at the water that lay in front of them all and, yet, between them all as well.

Anna looked at him and then fixed her gaze on the same point at which he seemed to be focused.

She was inspired to speak. "You know, this pool of water has been collecting here for a thousand years," she said. "No one has touched it or felt it or drunk of it in that time. It is so pure. It has not known anything but rain and sky and sun and moon. It reminds me of the holy water at my childhood church. I can imagine the millions of raindrops that made it, the thousands of storms that caused it to be right here now for us. I can feel the power of its purity and innocence."

"It is simple," Xuan added, "and there is a connection between it and us."

As Xuan finished, she watched Anna lean over the water and cup her hands together. She dipped them into glassy, clear surface as ripples ran away from her hands. She took in the water and drew it to her mouth and drank. When she swallowed this purest of waters, a look of refreshed satisfaction appeared on her child-like face. She looked up again at the faces around her. No one said a word.

Amoria cupped her hands together and drank of the water, too. Russell did the same. And then, Digger followed suit.

Thomas watched all of this. From his vantage point in the circle, he saw the moonlight reflected in the water. It seemed to call to him, so he cupped his hands together, leaned forward, dipped them into the reflected moonbeam in front of him, and drank from the shiny, golden water as well.

"There it is!" Portales exclaimed. "The water will give you the power to learn all that you must learn. The water is the keyhole to the door."

"Yes," said Xuan. Her barely audible expression was heard by all. "We don't need to memorize the chants or see them in writing. They are like water from the skies above, like the water that courses through us all. It is already in our bodies and minds and hearts. The chants are in us, too, just like water. All we must do is uncover them and drink them in like a long, cool drink of truth."

"That's right," said Chris.

"And the sounds can never be written down," added Tariqah. "In fact, they will never be written down!" he repeated emphatically. "Like a flowing stream whose very essence cannot be caught in a bucket, or a wild horse whose true spirit cannot be corralled, or a butterfly whose darting beauty cannot be preserved in a jar, these chants cannot be written down. To do so would take the life out of them, and they would just be dead words on a page."

"Or they would be a map that is mistaken for the experience of the path," Digger reflected.

"Or they would tell of an infinite being that cannot be confined in a finite book," Russell offered.

"Or a wind that cannot be put in a bottle," Malik added. "I can't write these words for a very good reason. To write them is to kill everything about them that is powerful and vibrant and vital."

"You're so right," Amoria confirmed. "Trouble yourself no longer about this, Malik. The sacred chants have survived since the beginning of humankind but have never been written down. They will continue to survive to the end of all human life, as well."

"But there is more," said Min Tzu. With that, he carefully took a drink of the ancient waters, too. As though it was a wine that had been stored for a thousand years just to be opened in this moment, he drank it slowly. He savored it. He cherished it with a reverence born of waiting a dozen lifetimes for this one drink. Now his wait was over, and this wine was finally his. He swished it around his mouth and swallowed it little by little. He felt a power that he had never felt before. It wasn't power in terms of strength or insight, but power in terms of calm and certainty. He cleared his throat to speak some more.

"I am not who you think I am," he declared, "and I am not who I think I am, either."

He paused as everyone watched him closely. "The 'I' of me is alive no more," he continued. "I am much bigger than that. I am one with the infinite. I am every man. I am every woman. I am not separate. There is no I or me or any of that. I am not Tibetan, because I am larger than that. I am not Asian, either. I am greater than that, as well. And I am not Buddhist. I am even bigger than that," he continued slowly. "I am in the creation, and the creation is imprinted in me."

Tariqah heard all this quietly and then leaned forward, cupped his hands, and dipped into the pool of a thousand summers. He raised his hands quickly, and some of the water splashed on his face and hair as he hurriedly drank it down.

When he finished, he wiped his mouth with the sleeve of his dervish robe. He looked at Min Tzu and said, "You are being drawn into your ultimate identity."

"More with each passing moment," Min Tzu responded, "but first I must give up my old identity and the beliefs I hold about myself."

"The belief of who you are must be cast aside to create room in you for something even grander than who you thought you were before," Mirissa confirmed. "The imprint in your genetic code has nothing to do with nationality or religion or place of birth. Those superficial designations and labels are just limits to be transcended."

"The certainty of the imprint is a promise whose time has finally come," Amoria said. "We need nothing more."

"And it can't be ignored any more," Digger broke in. "I've studied dozens of cultures and histories, and all of them have ignored the imprint. Now they are gone from the face of the earth. Surrendering to the imprint inside of us must become a priority for millions and millions of people."

"And that is why we're here at Acoma," said Chris. "For it to happen for millions, it must only begin to happen one person at a time. The scale of this teaching must increase rapidly. Just the seven Planners and the Master Teachers is not enough to get out the teachings. To expand beyond one pattern, the pattern of beliefs, and into the next pattern of expanded and infinite understandings, the teaching must be carried to the world by a larger number of teachers."

"Agreed," Russell chimed in. "But there can be no imperative, no force, because an imperative just serves to set up another duality."

"That's right," Mirissa agreed. "The new teachers can only demonstrate the process. They can only teach the tools and will have no answers to impart. The imprints will be unfolded in each person just as their imprint requires. The teacher will know it is right for that person as it is unfolded and not before."

"How will a teacher know that?" Thomas asked.

"In much the same way that Xuan saw the pattern of prisms even before they were laid out on the mesa," answered Chris. "If they have taken the mantras to heart and have understood the expansions in their mind, then and only then can they hear the chants that contain the imprint for them. Simply put, that is illumination."

"When you know the ultimate self," Tariqah broke in, "you see through the eyes and mind and heart of the infinite. When you hold fast to that expanded viewpoint, you know what it looks like and feels like and sounds like, and all the rest. Your vision changes. Your understanding changes. Your heart changes."

"The mantras and the expansions and the unwritten words of the chants will bring that change to those who embrace them," Mirissa explained.

"And when there are twelve thousand teachers to speak of just those things," Chris continued, "the changes will happen more quickly and on a larger scale. When one person changes—just one person at a time—eventually, the entire world changes."

"That's the next expansion, isn't it?" asked Malik. "It's the assumption of confidence and certainty that the tools we teach will open the eyes of the world." He paused. "Is that it?"

"Exactly!" exclaimed Amoria and Min Tzu in unison.

Amoria finished the thought. "The new teachers will have confidence in the tools and teach them well. They will embody peace, and the rest will take care of itself."

"If it doesn't work," Portales laughed, "I guess we'll be looking for another meeting like this one in about two thousand years. I promise you, however, that I will help swing the doors so wide this time that we can survive until then."

"Survival won't be good enough. We will have to thrive this time." It was Min Tzu again. "The next twenty centuries will see unimaginable and amazing changes in humankind. There will be more people, and there will be fewer resources. Of that, we can be sure. I am certain of it."

With that, Portales leaned forward and took a drink of the water and sat back satisfied.

Malik and Mirissa were sitting directly across the circle of water from each other. Mirissa gazed upon this boy for a long moment and seemed to be talking to him with her eyes—eyes he could not see. Then she leaned forward to drink, and so did he.

He cupped his hands with confidence, and even though he could not see the water, he knew it was in front of him. She cupped her hands at the same instant, and they dipped their hands into the water. Her eyes never left him, and they drank from their cupped hand at the same instant in time. Then they sat back, too, and relished the moment, together.

After all of them sat silent for a while, they rose up as one. The next group of carriers arrived and began unloading their packs. There was work to be completed, and soon they were placing the prisms again.

After another thousand were placed into the pattern, this time on the west side of the keyhole, Chris and Tariqah came over to Malik and asked him to come with them. The Teachers then began the descent to the flats and back up to the church. While the Planners continued making the pattern of prisms, the Teachers prepared for the sixth day and got some sleep.

Chapter 14

The Sixth Day

The last load of prisms arrived on the mesa as the moonlight diminished in the western skies of Acoma. From atop the four-hundred-foot pinnacle, the Planners and carriers paused to watch it set. Except for the glow now emanating from the prisms already in position, there was little light, and the dawn was still a few hours away. Even so, the Planners could see well enough to complete the work, and they placed the last load of prisms as Malik had envisioned.

The six thousand prisms on the east side and the six thousand more on the west intersected through the natural water cistern that contained the pure water of transformation. This layout followed the form recognized over the world as the symbol of infinity—the symbol that had pulled and inspired the thinking of humankind for the last two thousand years. Early in those years, only one half of the infinity symbol was seen. The fish perspective fostered certain elements of progress, but late in the age, the rest of the symbol was finally uncovered to reveal the entirety of the symbol. Its never-ending continuity elevated the perspective of humankind once more and foretold a destiny of unlimited progress and understanding not previously perceived.

As the blinders and self-imposed limits were gradually removed from the perspectives of humankind, the linear understandings gave way to three-dimensioned visualizations. The beginnings of science and the discoveries that would change the world were initialized. What Malik and the Teachers envisioned now was the next logical step in that process: a four-dimensioned understanding that utilized the infinity symbol as its basic building block and forecast the expanded use of the spiral helix symbol to inform and create the next progression of humanity.

Though he was back at the church with the Teachers and could not confirm it for himself, Malik had been right about the few missing prisms and the gap in the pattern near the trailhead. The final descent for the Planners went well, and soon,

Enchanted Mesa was empty again. This time, however, there was no fear in its emptiness. The promise in the prisms and the power of hope had replaced the fear.

The Planners wearily returned to the church. After a long night of work, sleep was foremost on their minds. The sunrise was just thirty minutes away as they reached the doors of the church and filed in to find Malik and the Teachers. The church was immersed in silence.

The Planners took in the scene, wordlessly found places to sit, and joined the others in the quiet.

Then Malik spoke. "Now I hear the thee in me." The words hung in the air as the silence resumed.

"Now I see the thee in me," Amoria said. These words echoed through the old church, and then silence returned once more.

In a few moments, Chris intoned these words, "Now I feel the thee in me."

Quiet descended again.

After what seemed an even longer pause, Mirissa spoke. "Now I know the thee in me."

Only their breathing was audible. Like the rhythmic pulse of the ocean waves or the sound of pine trees whispering in a morning breeze, the mantras sank into the Planners' subconscious minds. Like the roots of a tree, these recitations became well planted, and their roots reached deeper and deeper with every repetition.

Then Portales broke in. "Now I show the thee in me."

The Planners heard the subtle changes in all these mantras from when they had first been introduced and knew the changes to be the logical progression of what had been started just six days before. The mantras had changed from hope to reality—from desire to fact—and the Planners listened for more as the silence descended again.

Finally, the revised sixth mantra was delivered. Min Tzu announced, "Now there is no me or thee," and these words were absorbed and fell softly onto those who heard them. With no words to replace them, they resounded again and again through the hearts and minds of all who were there.

Tariqah then suggested the wording for the seventh mantra so quietly that it cut through the air like a whistle. "I can be the thee in me." It settled comfortably upon them like an autumn leaf that fell through the air to the very ground of their beings.

Mirissa whispered, "I will be the thee in me," and the assumption of completion fell upon them like a mist.

And finally, Chris declared it in a voice that ran through each of them like a freight train in the night, "I am now the thee in me."

This was the seventh mantra. Malik wrote it down and then held the paper out to his right to be passed around. It was taken from him and went from one hand to the next.

Amoria nodded. Min Tzu smiled. Tariqah blessed it silently. Chris affirmed it with his eyes. Portales just exhaled and passed it on. Mirissa wrapped her hands around it and embraced its wisdom. The mantras were now completed.

The Planners silently watched all of this, and the feeling of completion reached them, too. Thomas felt the truth of this mantra. Xuan understood its significance. Anna embraced its certainty. Jack was humbled by its wisdom, and Digger felt it in his bones. Russell affirmed its logic.

The mantras had done what they were intended to do. Two became one. The perception of separation was ended. Neither me nor thee could retain its identity any longer. No me. No thee. There was now only what there had always been—a single creation, a single life force whole and integrated and beautiful and perfect and full and timeless and interconnected unto itself.

~   ~   ~

Xuan asked, "I think I know the mantras well enough, but I don't really understand how they connect to the understandings or expansions or to the unwritten chants. Can anyone explain it to me?"

It was Min Tzu who answered. "The first expansion is the expansion of humility—to know that we know not. This also requires the understanding that we are a part of something much larger than has previously been understood—larger than our nationalities, larger than our religions, larger than our concepts and belief systems."

"I get that," Thomas said, "but what about the second expansion?"

"It follows easily," Tariqah replied. "The second expansion affirms that there is only one force, one dynamic, one process. Naming it only serves to separate it from all of us who are really just another part of it. The expanded view that must now be understood is that there is no name. It is without a name. By not naming it, we can see our true relationship to it. All of us are in it, and it is in all of us."

Russell spoke, seeming to ask and to state simultaneously, "So discussions and disagreements and arguments about it become pointless?"

"Yes," Tariqah responded. "How can there be a war over which force is right or better or more powerful when there is only one force?"

"Besides," Chris added, "it is like arguing over who owns the sun. It is the wrong question and can only produce a misleading answer. It's a nonsensical argument and a question that needs no answer."

"So explain to me again the import of the third expansion," Digger asked.

"This meeting is a perfect example of it," Portales offered. "It is simply the knowledge that the one force is a forward-moving force, a growing force that continues to reach for the utmost and ultimate expression of itself."

"Men and women are part of this reaching for ultimate expression, too," Chris said. "As part of the creation, all people help to move it forward with ideas and understandings, actions of kindness and helpfulness, expressions of science and discovery, improvements in healing and teaching. All of us are movers in the infinite and ongoing creation that is always moving forward."

"There is no going backwards, either," said Amoria. "Going forward is an imperative that cannot be altered. Once a new level of understanding is uncovered, old understandings become secondary and incidental."

"Right," said Tariqah. "Being satisfied with the old view is inconsistent with the forward movement of all humankind. Like the old crops plowed under each year after harvest, the old views are only compost for the new nourishment. The old views must be laid to rest."

"It's like pruning the tree of understanding," Mirissa concluded. "Failure to prune will stunt the growth and eventually kill the tree. Satisfaction with and adherence to the old becomes an increasingly heavy weight—a weight that serves no purpose but to slow down the infinite forward movement of creation. Not going forward is the same as going backwards."

"Okay. I think I see that, too," Russell broke in. "What of the fourth expansion? How do the new teachers position that one?"

"Simply stated," Mirissa started, "the fourth expansion requires direct experience. It replaces teaching through words. The model that Jesus and Mohammed and Buddha all helped to teach used words to expand the focus of people around the world. Now that their focus has been sufficiently expanded, it is apparent that teachings are not enough. Teachings without experiential knowing are misleading. Now it is time for an expansion of knowing through experience."

Anna said, "But the new teachers will be teaching through words, too."

"Yes they will, Anna," Chris agreed. "But there is a significant difference. The mantras and the expansions are meant to open the minds and hearts of the listeners so that the ancient chants can be heard. When they are heard, the person will know exactly what to do and will require no words from the teacher. It's experiential teaching."

"So the mantras open the heart?" she asked.

"And the expansions open the mind," Chris answered.

"Only then can the true imprint of each person be discovered," Amoria said. "It cannot be taught to them or determined by anyone else but them. The ancient chants will allow them to have a soul-level communication that will change them in a way never experienced before."

"That change," Min Tzu said, "will only be expressed in action. When that change takes place in any person, they will be unable to ignore the inner drive to experiential knowing. It will become their mission to take action within the mandates of the other expansions."

"So, the new teachings will be process, not substance?" Malik asked.

"Yes," Chris responded. "The substance will come from the seeded imprint of the person who allows himself or herself to understand the expansions and recognize that they are a part of the One."

"And there is the fifth expansion," Portales reminded them. "It is the doorway that no one can ignore. Everyone must walk through it. Each human seed cannot become anything but the elevated human being that was intended all along."

"But, how does one know they have found their true imprint?" Xuan inquired.

Mirissa explained it again. "Those who do not feel the mantras or do not truly know the expansions will not be able to make sense of the chants. They will derive no lasting or significant plan of action for themselves."

"Those who are enveloped by the mantras," Amoria reminded them, "will train their hearts to recognize when they are inside the One, and they will always act from their heart. Then, and only then, will the expansions make sense, and their mind will embrace them, too."

"And then the ancient chants will be heard at the deepest conceivable level, and all things will be possible for those who hear them in that way," Mirissa said.

"That is how all of us have come to understand it," Chris said.

"And that is how we can do what we do," Min Tzu added.

"Yes, that is how," Portales said.

"From our imprint within the one life force," Amoria confirmed.

"So, we can have confidence in that?" Xuan asked.

"Yes, you can be certain," Tariqah assured her.

"The path to ultimate identity requires no words, no religion, no guru or shaman or imam or savior," Mirissa said quietly. "All those figures can talk about the path to ultimate identity, but your certainty comes in the process of finding it for yourself, walking it for yourself, and understanding it for yourself."

"And it is there to be found—one person at a time," Amoria reiterated.

"There have been hundreds of examples," Chris reminded them. "Each one of us has been an example in one way or another for many lifetimes. But our examples, when written and understood from the limited perspective of those who did not yet understand, have only resulted in limited understandings. The processes developed here at Acoma will be spread to the world in a whole new way. Never before have so many been trained in the processes. Never before have so many been trained to not be concerned with answers. Therein lies the key to expansion for all of humankind."

"And it comes none too soon," Portales said.

"But what about the seventh expansion?" Thomas asked.

No one answered. The old church grew silent once more. Thomas looked at Tariqah. The whirling dervish knew the answer but chose to say nothing. Xuan glanced at Amoria, and the elegant African woman knowingly smiled back at her. Russell shifted nervously in his pew and looked to Chris for an answer, but he, too, remained steadfast in his silence. Anna looked at Mirissa. Surely this former Jesus would know. She did, but no words came from her, either. Jack then looked at Portales. Wouldn't the man who claimed to be the keeper of the door be able to answer the question or point the way? Portales just grinned and shrugged his shoulders.

Finally, Digger looked at Min Tzu, the Buddhist. He sat cross-legged, smiling, and offered nothing in response.

Malik, of course, did not see all the glances and looks and smiles and shrugs among the Teachers and the Planners. Finally, he was inspired to answer the question himself.

"The seventh expansion requires a different descriptor, a new word, so that it is not clouded with any history," Malik said. "The seventh expansion is the understanding that will be called 'Ecumensus,' and we will experience it together, tomorrow."

That ended the exchange. Soon, Jack got up and excused himself to go get some sleep. The rest of the Planners followed him, except for Malik. He had not been up all night like the others, so he remained with the Teachers. There was more for him to do.

Before the Planners settled in for a nap, Jack conferred with Russell. "It seems like we ought to get the seventh mantra down to the people below."

"I think you're right," Russell agreed, "but I think it can wait a few hours."

Jack looked at Russell's tired eyes. "Yes, it can," he said.

With that, Jack found his bedroll and went to lie down. Russell did the same. Xuan, Thomas, Digger, and Anna were already falling asleep.

Chapter 15

The Sixth Evening

Around noon, Jack and Russell got up and led the Planners around through the people to spread the seventh mantra, "I am now the thee in me." With some thirty thousand people now present, this took all afternoon, but around seven that evening, everyone was back in the church. As they arrived, the hum of the mantra could be heard between the two mesas and beyond. More were still streaming in to Acoma Pueblo.

As these six returned to the church, the rest were about to leave for the usual evening pronouncements. Tariqah escorted Malik. The Planners joined them, and they all proceeded to the edge of the bluff. Once again, they stood in a line where everyone down below could see them. The crowd hushed as Russell spoke.

"Tomorrow, this meeting will end, and all of you will know its final message and what it means for you. We have been honored to use these sacred lands for this historic purpose, and we are indebted to those who have helped accommodate all of us as well as all of you. Tomorrow evening we will disperse. We thank all of you for coming. Your hopeful and positive seeking has energized this entire process, and we are certain that it will not be in vain. Thank you very much."

With that, Russell stepped back and rejoined the Planners. The Teachers came forward in a single line and faced the crowd as one. Malik remained on Tariqah's arm, and, as had been the case a few evenings before, the crowd greeted them with a hundred discernible greetings of teacher, father, rabbi, imam, guru, master, priest, shaman, reverend, sage, holy one, and other salutations that indicated their recognition of these Master Teachers for who and what they were.

Malik could not know that some of these salutes were also meant for him. A few in the crowd recognized him from previous lives as a teacher, too. Tariqah looked at Malik and smiled to himself. He recognized those titles that had once been his as well, and he knew many of the greetings were for Buddha and Krishna and Issa or Jesus. He recognized Asian greetings and knew they must be for Min

Tzu. He finally heard the Farsi word that was translated as "Sufi" and smiled at this, too.

Amoria heard titles and words of respect and adoration that could only have come from the Mediterranean rim or the African continent and was pleased that these people had made it to the meeting.

Portales heard dozens of words for his many lives in and around the Catholic Church and was surprised to hear the name "Portales" among those now being shouted. He raised his fist high in the air in recognition, and it was shouted again.

Soon, Russell stepped forward once more and raised his hands to quiet the festive crowd.

"It has been incredible to meet and talk with these Teachers, these Masters, for these past six days. They have shown us the next step in the spiritual evolution of humankind and have charged many of us to be the new teachers of this step. We are honored. Now, it is time for these Teachers to speak directly to you."

Russell stepped back again, and Chris was the first to step forward. More salutations of adoration were shouted from the crowd, who soon hushed as he spoke.

"I am honored to receive your greetings and respect, but nothing I have ever done is more important than what you will do from this day forward. You come here from dozens of belief systems, all of which are only partially true. They are the many-faceted rainbow colors of the one true light. You will soon be teaching something that is larger than those beliefs and closer to the light. I invite you to let go of your adoration for these wonderful teachers, and for me, so that you can open yourself up to your own full potential."

With that, he stepped back into line, and a thoughtful hush fell over the crowd.

Next to speak was Min Tzu, who began immediately. "Asians, Buddhists, Confucianists, and Taoists: What you know after centuries of wisdom has been filtered through the finite minds of men. What you know has taken on the limits borne of words. It is now time to step past those limits and release them all for evermore. It is time to discern your highest, truest path from within your own true self. It is time to leave your previous teachings behind and to live from a place that is far beyond what you have been taught before."

Amoria then stepped forward. She merely stood there smiling until the crowd got quiet again. Her presence was commanding, and she stood tall and still. Finally, she spoke. "All our writings before this have not envisioned enough. We have been caught up in laws and rules and taboos and codes. All of us up here, and all of you down there, are so much more than rules and laws. From this day forward, you will embrace the vision of who you really are, and you can then teach and impart the processes for finding that vision to all who seek it for themselves."

As she stepped back, Portales came to the fore, but first he stopped and embraced Amoria, and both of them smiled at each other. He then straightened his shirt and fiddled with his moustache. He thought to remove his wide-brimmed hat and patted down his long, gray hair. He surveyed the crowd from east to west and then boomed out his words.

"All of us have been taught many things in our lives. Some of them are right, but many have been misunderstood. Soon, the door through which we will go will be opened wide. There will be no one between you and your vision. When you have learned how to live your vision, how to become your vision, there will no longer be a wall into which a door need be cut. You will all be doors and windows through which the vision of unified humankind can be seen and embraced." Portales bowed and stepped back into line.

A murmur of understanding in the crowd began near the front, and soon it grew until it overtook the entire throng. While it did not grow in volume, it increased in intensity, and into this groundswell of understanding stepped Tariqah. He let the buzz continue for a little while and then raised his hands and let it be known he was about to speak.

"There is no longer a need," he began earnestly, "to separate ourselves into tribes or nations or religions. I do not need to be seen as Sufi or Muslim or Christian or Jew or Hindu or Pantheist or any of the others to know who I truly am."

The crowd began to murmur again, and he let the sound rise up and then settle back down as he stood resolute before them.

"The only association we now need is that connection to the vision that will allow you to be heard as you teach. Now, all of us are people of the expanded vision, and now we must include all people in that vision. When they see us and hear us, they will not find objection. They will let go their man-made limits in favor of a personal envisioning process that has no limits at all. You will teach that process. It will be right and good."

As Tariqah was finishing, Mirissa stepped up next to him, as did Chris and Amoria and Min Tzu and Portales. Mirissa signaled for Tariqah to bring Malik to join them, and Tariqah went back a few steps, touched Malik's arm, and offered his own. When they returned and all of them were in a united front, Mirissa spoke.

"Much of what you know has been taught before. Most everything that you regard as sacred has been learned from within some culture or tradition or tribe. But these teachings have become bogged down in these cultures or traditions or tribes and have been distorted beyond recognition. The sacred truths must be released from the shackles of these distortions. Humankind does not need these origins or the shackles they impose. Humankind does not need a savior or a prophet or a shrine. Humankind does not need a temple or a synagogue or a sacred collection of walls or stones or buildings. These are all prisons. These are shackles from which all persons must eventually escape and from which all persons must finally be freed. It does not matter who did it once before or who said it long ago or whose insight uncovered a truth. None of that matters anymore."

Now Malik spoke. "For the times ahead," he said, "there will be no hero or leader or wayshower or saint. Now, the only thing that will matter is for all people to embrace a process of discovery—heartfelt and humble discovery. There are no answers to be given, no teachers to hide behind, and no writings about which to debate. This time, there will only be the process. And the key to this process will rest entirely on the infinite truth inside each person, and no other thing will matter."

With that, the evening pronouncements ended. The recitation of the seventh mantra resumed and the sixth day was done. Only the seventh day lay ahead of them and the anticipation of it was great.

Chapter 16

The Seventh Day

It was just before dawn on the longest day of the year when the Planners arose. Jack woke them early. They quietly gathered together outside the church near the cistern. From here, they overlooked the crowds below and saw the Enchanted Mesa to the north. Malik was with them, as were Jack's daughter, Sha'wanna, and Malik's teacher, Susan.

Jack asked Sha'wanna if all the preparations had been made concerning the old stone house where he, Malik, and Anna would gather to begin the process of publishing Malik's notes.

She nodded. "It's ready."

Then, Russell spoke to Anna. "The money and the arrangements for publication of Malik's notes are all completed, too," he said, and he handed her a slip of paper on which were written a name and a phone number. "When you have gotten settled, Jack will help you call this man and arrange a meeting here at Acoma. He has been briefed regarding some of the details and I trust him to provide you and Malik exactly what you need, but, Anna, you will be in charge of getting Malik's transcriptions published."

Anna started to protest, but Russell cut her off before she could get very far. He looked her squarely in the eyes and laid his hand on her shoulder.

"Just follow your common sense and listen to your heart," Russell told her. "It will all fall into place. Hire anyone you need to get it done. As in these past seven or eight months, you will have all the money you need." Then he smiled at her. "Even better, you won't have to ask me to approve it." He looked at the Enchanted Mesa. "I'm going up there to see what happens."

"Won't I be up there, too?" Anna asked.

Jack answered quickly. "Yes. You and Malik and I will be up there, but we will come down from the mesa at the end of the evening, and the three of us will depart for the old stone house right away. It's about an hour's walk from here. Hopefully, no one will notice us."

"What about the rest of us?" Digger asked.

Russell responded, "Everyone will have a choice, though I don't think anyone will choose to stay behind."

Xuan took Thomas's hand and declared, "I'm definitely going wherever this day leads me."

With that, she looked at Thomas. He looked away and didn't say anything.

"Oh, I'm going for sure," Digger said. "I wouldn't miss this for the world! It'll be huge!"

"I have no choice but to play out the string," Russell admitted, "and no reason to stay behind, either. I think I'm as ready as anyone can be."

"Ready for what?" Thomas interjected. "That's what I can't figure out."

Just then, the Planners were joined by another person. Jack spun around to see who it was. She had a walking stick now and looked more frail than Digger remembered, but he recognized her anyway. It was the Jemez Pueblo keeper woman who had drawn in the dirt for him and Jack—the same keeper woman who had helped Malik find his voice and helped Jack find his daughter. She carried with her a single dandelion.

She looked first at Jack and said, "Your daughter will soon be the Iyatiku at Acoma. It is as it should be." She then looked at Sha'wanna standing to her right and she reached over and tapped her on the foot with her stick. "When today is done, Enchanted Mesa will be held in fear no more. You will change its name to Katzimo, again. As the Iyatiku, you will teach the new story to those who come to ask of it. It is right again."

She then looked at Malik across the circle from her. His head followed her voice, but he could not know she was looking at him until she spoke his name. "Malik," she said, "Your writing will go quickly, and, when you are done, you will be led to me. We will find your eyes again."

With that, she made a small hand signal to Sha'wanna, and Susan and the three of them turned to leave. Then the she paused and looked back at the Planners. "Do not be afraid. The wind will be at your back, and you will be like the dandelion I hold in my hand."

With that, she held the seed ball like a candle in front of her age-lined face. She took a deep breath, and with a whoosh she blew the seeds of her dandelion up into the bright blue sky. Looking directly at Thomas Walls, she said to him, "I wish I could go, too." Then she turned again, and the three women departed.

Everyone watched for a moment as the three of them started back through the dirt street houses on Acoma Mesa. Malik listened as the sound of the keeper woman's shuffling sandals was accompanied by the clicking of her cane in the rocky dust. Suddenly, he heard something else—the rumbling sound that came from the other mesa. Now, it was loud enough that the others could hear it, too.

Jack looked in Malik's direction and asked, "Is that the sound you've heard before, Malik?"

"Yes," he answered. "That's it."

Just then, the ground swayed underneath them, and Xuan reached out and grabbed Thomas's arm to steady herself. Jack reached for Malik, but the swaying stopped as quickly as it had begun, and Malik did not seem affected. He immediately spoke of another matter.

"I think I have figured out the key to Jack's chants," he announced. "I still can't write them or see them in my mind, but when the Teachers are among the people, the people shower them with many words and greetings and titles. I do not recognize most of those words either, but the sounds are familiar to me. They are the same sounds as in Jack's chants. They sound sacred and mysterious. They are full of awe and respect and wonder."

"But aren't Jack's chants all different?" Xuan asked.

"Yes," Malik answered, "but all of them contain the same sounds. They're just arranged in a different order in each of the seven chants. It's like they are a collage of sacred sounds that resonate with everyone who hears them."

"That's fascinating," Russell commented to no one in particular. "Perhaps Enchanted Mesa is really somehow connected through time to the Tower of Babel. Perhaps the common language is returning, and the people are coming back together. I think it is the beginning of the final return."

"You're right, I think," Digger said. "Somehow, the people know the common language already."

"And so do we," Xuan said. "It mesmerizes me and affects me in ways no spoken words ever have."

"It's like music for me," Digger added, "but when it's happening in me, there are pictures, too."

"It's like in my dreams," Malik said. "I can see again, but what I see is a vision. It seems to be a picture of things yet to come."

"Or yet to be imagined," Russell said.

"And some of those things will be here sooner than we think," Xuan said.

"I think that is why we are here at Acoma: to help bring the pictures of the future into focus so that they can be imagined, envisioned, and brought to life," said Russell.

"What you envision will one day come to pass," Malik declared. He said these words with such conviction, such a sense of knowing, that everyone paused and let it sink into who they had become. They knew that he was right. What they had envisioned was coming to pass.

Xuan spoke again. "The vision that comes to me during one of Jack's chants is almost always one of harmony, cooperation, and helpfulness," she said. "I mean, there's no conflict in my vision. There's no competition for things like food or water. There's no strife among the people over purpose or direction or right or wrong."

"I think that is because the vision is so singular," Russell theorized. "In a world of burgeoning population and dwindling resources, there is no room for competition. There can't be haves and have-nots. There can't be rich and poor. There can't be fat and hungry. Our vision for our individual selves must be allowed to blossom into an expanded vision for everyone."

"Yes," Jack summed up. "The vision must include everyone. It must be a vision that expands in an ever-outward direction and includes all people everywhere."

"Everyone," said Digger. "It is humankind's dualistic insanity that leads them to struggle and compete instead of managing and cooperating. I don't think the insanity of competition is a path we can follow any longer."

"But humankind can't be forced into this vision," Xuan cautioned.

"No," Anna said, "it can't be forced on them from the outside. It can only come from the inside of their ultimate identity. That's what I get from all of this. Our new job will be to teach and inspire the discovery of each person's ultimate identity, and when that succeeds, the changes, the expansions, the understandings will bring the vision to fruition."

"You're right, Anna," Malik confirmed again. "We won't give the answers as we see them. We will only help them find the way to hear Jack's chants. When they do, they will see the vision of the Ever One, and they will find their seeded imprint for themselves."

"That's how I see it, too," Jack said.

"And that is how it will be," Malik declared.

The seven of them stood in silence, as they had many times before. Their months of being together would end today. What they had planned was nearly complete. None of them knew for sure what lay ahead, but all of them knew, each in their own way, what these past eight months had meant. It was about discovery and insight. It was new and yet it was consistent with what they already knew. They were now expanded into realms of thought and feeling and experience that none of them ever imagined. They had come together under the influence of dreams. They had thrown out their preconceived notions and replaced them with expanded understandings. They had opened themselves to the new and questioned the veracity of the old. Finally, they had pictured something larger, something without limits, and something with no man-made ceilings.

Xuan felt the morning breeze as it played with her hair. She looked at Russell. "Thank you, Russell Layne."

He looked back at her and nodded.

Digger looked at Jack and said, "Thank you, Jack Eaglefeather."

Thomas put his arm around Anna's shoulders and smiled at her. All of them looked at Malik and saw someone even more special than they knew he was when he was hired. It was a moment in time that would not soon be repeated, if ever.

Anna instinctively extended her hands to both sides, and Thomas took the one nearest him and extended his hand out in the other direction to Xuan. She took his hand and extended her other hand out to Russell. His large hands engulfed hers as he reached for Malik's hand on his other side. Malik sensed what was happening as he reached his other hand out, where it was taken by Jack. Digger reached out in both directions and completed the circle of hands with Jack and Anna.

Their circle drew closer until they were shoulder to shoulder. The sun peeked up over the horizon, and a gust of cool morning wind caressed them. They stood in silence and absorbed these energies into themselves. Finally, Russell spoke.

"Frankly, I had no idea it would come out like this." he said quietly.

"Incredible," Anna offered.

"Amazing," Digger said.

"Enlightening," Xuan added.

"And scary, too," said Thomas.

"Katzimo!" Jack declared.

"Ecumensus!" Malik announced.

All of them gripped their hands harder for one last time, then broke up and turned back for the church. The sun rose fully over the horizon and cast its light on the seventh day at Acoma and on all of them again.

When they arrived at the church and opened the door, the Teachers were waiting for them. Mirissa came up and spoke briefly with Malik. She led him over to stand with them as the Teachers faced the Planners. Mirissa spoke first.

"We did not mean for it to be this way, but in our lives as Masters and Teachers, we have been walls, not doors. Humankind has put us on pedestals, and they thought it was right to make us untouchable—no longer human. Now that must change, and, today, it will change."

With that, she went through the old wooden doors one last time and left the church she had begun two thousand years before.

"None of us meant to be worshipped or adored," Min Tzu spoke next. "Perhaps it has served some good, but it will be no more." He turned and went out through the doors of the church as well.

"This time," Tariqah continued, "there will be no claims of divinity. There will no parallels to kings or popes or high priests. Each person will find his or her ultimate identity and it will not rest on the belief in another." He looked once more at the Planners. He touched Malik lightly on the forehead with his index finger and went through the old door, too.

"My path is easy now," Amoria started. "I need no rules except the teachings in my heart. I am not limited by someone else's thinking or policies. I am not required to trust their insights or their finite understandings. I am one with my ultimate identity. There is no me to be adored or ignored." She, too, touched Malik on the forehead between his eyes and smiled. Her long legs carried her up to the big double doors. She looked back at all of them and then turned and left the church behind.

"It has actually been easier in my lives to be adored and revered and admired," Chris smiled, "but I have also enjoyed many lives in obscurity. Either way, people will now be free of the Teachers so that they can choose to rid themselves of the last obstacle to knowing their true identity. And they will choose to do that." Chris touched Malik's forehead, too, and then smiled at Russell as he left them and walked through the doors himself.

Now, only Portales remained with the Planners. "We have begun to make the new door," he said. "It will be quite a door. Many, many people will go through it today, and for the next two thousand years it will only get wider and higher and larger. Our destiny is through that door." He looked around at all the Planners.

With that, he took Malik's arm and began to lead him out of the church. As he did, he gestured for the others to follow. When they were all outside, Digger and Jack closed the doors on the church one last time. They put in place the wooden plank that bound the two doors together and kept them closed. Jack gently ran his hands along the face of one door and then turned around and whispered quietly, "Katzimo. Ecumensus."

Portales smiled and said, "Let's go."

Chapter 17

Ecumensus

As Portales led Malik by the arm, they passed through the old houses on the mesa. Jack looked at Mt. Kahwehstimah in the distance to the north. The energy of this lifelong companion coursed through him again. He had seen it every day of his life. He had climbed all over it and fished its lake. His people had harvested its trees. He had never been so far away that he could not see it somewhere on the horizons of his life. The morning sun was still in the eastern sky and glistened on the sacred, snow-capped peak.

"You know," Xuan commented as they all walked together, "today is the summer solstice, the longest day of the year. There is more light today than any other day."

"Yes, and there is less darkness than any other day, as well," Digger added as they passed by the cistern at the northern edge of the mesa.

They wound down through the boulders and were soon off the mesa and among the people again. The buzzing from the seventh mantra served as a backdrop while they wound their way in and around those gathered between the mesas. After a while, they arrived at the base of the Enchanted Mesa. In among the forty thousand, they found the Teachers and the twelve thousand who would go to the top. They joined them near the start of the trail.

It was Portales who jumped atop a boulder and announced the instructions for the twelve thousand who would scale the rock again and become the new generation of teachers.

"When you begin this climb to the top, you will now travel with a sense of wonder in what the one life force has created in you, with you, and for you. As you travel higher, each step will draw you further into your illumined imprint with certainty and confidence. When you arrive at the top, the unbounded wholeness of the creation will embrace you, and you will envision who you really are. At that point, you will become a teacher of the Ecumensus."

With that, he jumped off the boulder, turned, and spoke to Malik, who reached out in the direction of his voice. They headed up the trail together, slowly. They crawled through the opening below the boulders. They climbed up the single rope to the small piñon tree. They kept moving forward. It was difficult for Malik, but an occasional gust of wind reminded him of his father and spurred him on. Though he had been over this difficult terrain before, he was not discouraged by the difficulty. His eyes could not see, but his vision was strong, and Portales would help him find the door.

Down below, Jack had begun to intone the seventh mantra with renewed energy, and soon it was reverberating around the Acoma Valley once more. More than forty thousand intoned it as one voice. Twelve thousand of them, those who had picked up a prism when they entered Acoma and then turned it back in to be carried to the top, readied themselves for the final trip. They would go first and would be followed by the Planners and then the Teachers, who would come last. A carrier from the night before waited for Jack's signal, and after Jack was sure Portales and Malik were far enough along, the carrier led the journey to the top.

The trail to the top of the Enchanted Mesa could only be traveled single file. No one was sure how long this would take, probably all day, but no one seemed concerned about it, either. It was a journey that required full attention and awareness. There were no shortcuts. There were places to pause and catch a breath and places where it was easier than others, but there was only one way to the top and every person who chose to go to the top knew this to be the case.

By noon, there were more than three thousand at the top. After all of them went near the edges to take in the views, some gathered in small groups and talked or returned to their mantras. Others napped or meditated quietly. The wind skipped across the mesa top from time to time, and a few clouds rolled through the New Mexico sky to offer momentary respites from the sun.

The prisms were laid out in the infinity pattern Malik and Xuan had envisioned. With the natural water cistern in the center, the prisms formed the symbol that took up almost half the area of the mesa top. The glow from the prisms was not easily visible in the full light of day, but as the sun moved across the sky during the afternoon, the rainbows from the prisms moved with it and would do so until evening.

Finally, around seven in the evening, the Teachers, Planners, and remaining one hundred readied to make the trip up the once-hidden trail. Xuan and Thomas stepped away from the crowd to talk.

"Well, the time has come," she said.

"I'm really nervous," Thomas admitted. "I'm not sure I can go up there again." He rubbed his hands together as he looked at her and waited for her to say something.

"I'm nervous, too," she responded, "but it's that good kind of nervousness, you know what I mean? I'm a little scared, too, because I don't know if I'll ever be coming down from that mesa again."

"Yeah, I know." Thomas answered. "If I don't come down, who will be the father for my boys? It feels like I would be abandoning them."

Xuan understood his dilemma and searched for the right words. She took Thomas's hands in hers and pulled him close. She saw the tears forming in his eyes, and she wrapped her arms around him and hugged him tight.

"You have to do what is right for you," she reminded him. "Some of you has always doubted parts of this endeavor, and you can honor that if you want to. No one will blame you," she added.

"But what about you, Xuan? Will you blame me?" he asked as he looked into her eyes.

"No. Never. Not at all," she assured him. "There is no time for that. Besides, who can say that going up there together today will assure that we will be together tomorrow? I don't think there are any guarantees."

"Yeah, I know that, too," he answered.

"You also know, Thomas," her face brightened as she spoke, "that what you've learned here and what you've learned in these past eight months and what we've experienced together can never be forgotten. It can never leave you, and you can't leave it, either. You are now a teacher of the Ecumensus, whether you go up there today or not." Xuan searched for the right way to say it and then said, "Maybe you are supposed to teach what you've learned in the same town as where your kids now live. We don't know any different, do we?"

"No, I guess not," he answered quietly.

They saw that the crowd was now down to just a few and that it was time for them to head up the trail with the rest of the Planners and Teachers. Xuan looked up at him with tears in her eyes and said, "Thank you, Thomas. I will never forget you, and I will always love you. I've got to go."

She gave him a kiss on the cheek and hugged him one more time. Tears were streaming down his face as he kissed her on the forehead. She turned and walked away to join the others.

As she approached the two large boulders that marked the beginning of the trail, Xuan looked back once more. Thomas had sunk to his knees at the base of the mesa, but his eyes were trained on her. She signaled to him one more time to come with her and looked at him imploringly. He saw her invitation but could not move. Finally, she bent down to crawl through the first doorway, and they were gone from each other's view. Halfway up the trail she looked again and saw him walking back toward the church. She shed another tear, then wiped it away on her sleeve and turned back up the trail.

~ ~ ~

The longest day of the year produces the longest sunset of the year. The sky at Acoma was clear and soon it would be full of stars. When they were finally all on top, Malik asked everyone to find a prism and to stand beside it. The sun was down, the rainbows were gone, and the glow from the prisms was more easily seen as the sky slowly darkened in the crack between the worlds. The view from four hundred feet above the valley afforded an ideal vantage from which to see the last light of day as it lingered in the west for another hour or so.

When the twelve thousand people were in place around the prisms of the infinity symbol, Tariqah the Sufi dervish went to the place that had been left open near the trailhead and spoke as he began to slowly dance his whirling dance.

"A dervish does not make his own dance," he said. "He dances in the pattern that makes up the building block of the creation."

With that, he reached into his garments and produced a missing prism. He dropped to his knees and placed it in the space that had been left for it. He then stood up and walked to the edge of the water. He cupped his hands to drink. When he had drunk his fill, he threw back his head, stretched out his arms, crossed his feet, and began to whirl around and around so quickly that he became elevated above the water and right over the center of the symbol that the prisms formed. The light of the prisms rose up with him and seemed to propel him higher and higher as he whirled.

A wind arose, and soon there was a shaft of golden light, too. The wind braided itself around the light and together they ascended hundreds of feet into the air. Tariqah disappeared from sight. The wind settled down, and the light returned to the prisms.

Portales smiled. "He found the door," he whispered to Malik. "We will find it again and again tonight."

Then Chris stepped up with his simple, brass flute in hand. "Music is not of man; it is from the infinite, and a musician does not make his own music. He hears and plays within the pattern that seeds the whole of creation with music." He reached into his trouser pocket and pulled out the next missing prism. He placed it adjacent to the one Tariqah had placed. He went to the water, too, and holding his fingers on the holes of his flute, he dipped it in the cistern, filled the flute like a long, tall glass of water, and drank it all down.

Then he lifted the flute to his lips and began to play. The nighttime air was immediately filled with more music than had ever been heard. The mesa rumbled as if to accompany the flute, and he kept playing as once again the lights from the prisms rose to form the double spiral symbol of creation. The wind and the light danced in unison with the music. As they braided themselves together, Chris let himself be taken into the vortex of this phenomenon, and he, too, was lifted higher and higher until he was gone from view. The music died down slowly as the light and wind subsided. The mesa continued to rumble below their feet, and there was no fear.

Malik heard all of what happened and could imagine the rest. He heard the music and felt the wind rise and then die down again. He heard and felt the rumbling rock beneath his feet as it responded to the music of the empowered flute, and he knew that Chris was gone. The sheer power of the event made him smile.

Jack was standing next to Digger and observed, "That looks just like the vision of the sand painting, doesn't it?"

"I think that's it exactly," he whispered back. "It's just like what the Jemez keeper woman drew in the dirt, too. I wonder how they knew."

He finished speaking just as Amoria stepped up and withdrew a prism from her shirt and placed it in the prism pattern—another missing piece to the puzzle.

Then, she spoke. "The pantheist knows no dance and plays no instrument, and yet she moves to the rhythm of the earth and sings from her heart to the stars. Our lives are lived in the pattern of the One, and there is nothing for us if we get lost from it."

She stepped to the edge of the water. She knelt beside it, cupped her hands in it, and then drank the water slowly. She closed her eyes and said, "I am now the thee in me."

Others around the symbol of infinity took up the last mantra again. "I am now the thee in me. I am now the me in thee." It did not matter which word came first, me or thee. Or which word came last, thee or me. It sounded just the same either way, and the mantra got louder as everyone joined in.

Amoria looked up to see the spiraling helix forming above her outstretched arms. When the mantra reached a certain volume, she was lifted up into the shaft of wind and light and was carried along on the certainty of her understanding. With her eyes focused upward, she climbed higher and higher into the braided configuration, the backbone of creation. Soon, she was just a speck, and then she was gone from view.

The sound of the mantra diminished, and the mesa grew quiet again. By now, Malik and Portales were smiling ear to ear. The jovial keeper of the door, the portal of all seeing, removed his large-brimmed hat, tossed it off the mesa like a Frisbee, and stepped forward. He carefully placed his prism into the pattern. Unlike the others before him, Portales drew from the water first, drank of it, and then spoke.

"Ah!" he said. "There are doors to the infinite all around us. First they must be envisioned with the heart of our ultimate identity, and then these doors can be truly seen." Gracefully, he laid his body next to the water. Eyes wide open but without a sound, his heart imagined the vortex again. He began to float ever so slowly off the ground as the light began to increase. As he stayed still, the wind picked up again. The lights from the prisms reached upward until they crossed and blended with each other. Woven together and spinning like a propeller, the entire formation began to turn 'round and 'round, and soon Portales was a part of it. It rose higher and higher until he, too, had spiraled up the helix and out of their view.

This time, however, the winds did not subside, and the light did not return to the ground around the prisms. Now, the infinity symbol had taken on a vertical dimension that was easily visible to everyone on the mesa. Like parallel spiral staircases, the light intertwined with the wind to produce a helix that reached into the sky as far as could be seen. True to his ultimate identity and the promise he had made all week long, Portales opened wide the door.

Though it was nearing ten o'clock, the whole of Enchanted Mesa was now bathed in light. The prisms pulsed with a light so clear and pure that to look at even one of them was difficult. To look at all of them was impossible. The swirling wind increased in intensity as it rose from atop the mesa but right on the surface, it was calm. Min Tzu stepped forward to speak and placed another missing prism into place. Like Portales, he first drank of the water and then faced the center of the spiral.

"We who have been with you these days in Acoma have been known as keepers of the unlimited vision, but that has never been so. All persons are keepers of the vision. First, however, each and every one of you must find the vision. It has always been inside of you, and you have our blessing to seek it for yourself. You will not need us any longer. Now you can find it on your own. Find it you must, and find it you will."

With that, Min Tzu looked from one side of the spiral helix to the other. He looked into the eyes of each of the twelve thousand in just an instant. He then closed his eyes. Instinctively, everyone else did the same. When their eyes were fully opened again, he was gone.

Only the light and wind remained.

Mirissa was almost the last to come forward. "In my life as Jesus the Nazarene, I said that what I did, and even more, could also be done by you. It has not been taught. Because of you, it will now be taught and understood. The potential of every person will now be properly envisioned, and that is how it was meant to be all along."

She bent down and drank of the water. She looked up into the vortex and then looked back to Malik Mohammed one last time. "Do not let them worship you or put you on a pedestal," she told him. "Point them to the vision of the infinite inside themselves. Stay away from crosses."

Malik nodded in the direction of her voice and smiled. Mirissa threw her arms to her side, tossed back her hair, and she was gone into the spiral helix of infinity.

Malik paused for a moment, reached into his shirt, and withdrew the seventh and final missing prism. Xuan saw this and went to where he was standing and took his arm. He recognized her touch but gently pulled away and said, "I know I can find it myself. Just point me in the right direction and tell me how many steps."

She turned him to the left and said, "There are seven."

He confidently went forward seven steps, knelt down, and felt around on the ground until he found the last gap in the pattern. He touched each adjoining prism to assess its alignment. He turned his prism to match what he perceived and slipped it into place. In an instant, the vortex shifted. The light intensified. The wind whipped itself into the frenzy of a tornado.

Malik backed up, unsure what to do. Russell looked at him and did not hesitate. All six and one-half feet of his body walked toward the center of the light and was soon lifted up out of sight. Xuan and Digger watched for a moment, clasped hands instinctively, and, together, they followed him into the spiraling helix. Wide-eyed, Anna watched the three Planners depart and then went to stand by Malik. Jack did the same.

Almost immediately, one of the twelve thousand grabbed the willing hand of the person next to him and walked into the wind and light, too. The mesa rumbled again, and the water flew up into the mix. More people grabbed the hand of the person behind them in line and stepped into the unknown. Soon, they all held hands and eagerly pushed forward until their turn came. Though it remained orderly, the speed picked up with each passing moment. People ascended into the vortex at a rate of one every second. There was no time to rethink the decision to go, as the pace picked up again; people ascended at two, then three per second. Like the seeds of the dandelion, they were carried up and away to become the teachers of what had been envisioned at Acoma. They would now be spread around the world and the process in their hearts would inform the next two thousand years. In just under an hour, all twelve thousand were gone.

The wind died down. The rumbling in the mesa subsided. The prisms lost their light. Jack gingerly picked one up, looked at it as if he had never seen anything like it before, and then quickly put it in his pocket. He looked up to see if the vortex of light and wind was still there. His knees were shaking from the experience, but he did not go down. He wiped his brow, exhaled a long, deep breath, and began to collect himself.

Anna wept quietly, and tears streamed down her smiling face. Never had she seen such power or heard such music or experienced emotions of this magnitude. She looked at Jack with eyes still wide open in wonder.

Malik grinned from ear to ear and whispered, "Wow!"

Never one to waste time, Jack checked the view in all directions as the still-full moon reached the midpoint of the nighttime sky. He knew he might not see from this perspective again. Then he looked at Anna and Malik. The three of them were the only ones left on the mesa. He put his arm around Anna.

"Anna, you look like you've seen a ghost," Jack said.

"That was amazing!" she said as she wiped away more tears and leaned on Jack for a moment. Then she smiled up at him and said, "This doesn't happen in El Paso."

"It's the first time for me, too," Jack chuckled, "and I'm from around here."

Malik could tell by their voices that Jack was on his left. He stuck out his arm, and Jack took it as if he had been his guide for years.

"We've got a book to write, Jack. You better help me off this mesa so we can get started."

Jack looked at the blind boy and smiled with admiration. Then, he remembered Mirissa's last words and said, "That old stone house has a few comforts, and I'm sure we'll be all right there, but, come to think of it, there sure isn't a pedestal anywhere in sight. Is that gonna be okay, Malik?"

"Perfect, Jack. Just perfect."

THE END

Epilogue

Twelve thousand teachers ascended from Enchanted Mesa on the summer solstice in 2010. Like dandelion seeds cast far and wide on a windy afternoon, these new teachers were dispersed to every corner of the world. They are now teaching the mantras and the understandings. When there is an open heart and an open mind in their presence, the ancient chants emanate from them, and those who truly hear the chants find their ultimate identity.

It is still the case that the chants cannot be written down.

Thomas eventually moved back to Mississippi to raise his boys. Jack, Anna, and Malik completed the notes from the Project 4000 experience in just six months, and they were published in time for the first anniversary celebration of the Ecumensus at Acoma in late June, 2011. Sha'wanna became Iyatiku at Acoma Pueblo in 2012.

Seven Mantras	*Seven Understandings*
Now I hear the thee in me.	Be humbled in the creation; assume a sense of mystery and wonder. Know that you know not.
Now I see the thee in me.	Within us is the infinite, and we are part of the ongoing life in all that is. Ever one is all, and all is ever one.
Now I feel the thee in me.	The truth of humankind is forward movement. If it does not move forward, it is not true.
Now I know the thee in me.	The human destiny is to uncover the seeded design of illumination and find our ultimate identity.
Now I show the thee in me.	We only truly remember direct experience. To know directly is to know forever.
Now there is no thee or me.	Certainty of our place within the one pulls us forward to find ourselves within the one.
Now I am the thee in me.	Uncover, hold to, and act on the vision of the ever One in everyone. Ecumensus.

Printed in the United States
215633BV00001B/77/P